"You're beautiful, Ambrosia . . ."

he whispered as his mouth trailed downward. "You're everything a man could desire . . ."

She was breathing hard and shaking, caught between the strange, sweet warmth she felt whenever she met his eyes and an instinctive need to defend her modesty. She was totally unprepared for what was happening to her, and the queer little shivers that raced everywhere in her body made her feel weak and filled her with confusion. Yet Ambrosia did feel pleasure and reassurance, along with fear—a terrible fear—of the power he held over her . . .

Other Avon Books by
Rosanne Kohake

FOR HONOR'S LADY
CHASTITY MORROW

Ambrosia

Rosanne Kohake

AVON
PUBLISHERS OF BARD, CAMELOT, DISCUS AND FLARE BOOKS

AMBROSIA is an original publication of Avon Books. This work has never before appeared in book form. This work is a novel. Any similarity to actual persons or events is purely coincidental.

AVON BOOKS
A division of
The Hearst Corporation
1790 Broadway
New York, New York 10019

First Avon Printing, October 1985

Dedicated fondly to

Nellie Sabin, the editor who believed in *Ambrosia* when it was three wonderful chapters and a terrible outline.

Susan Elizabeth Phillips, mentor and dear friend, who listened and gave advice only another writer could give.

Kathryn Falk, who gave me and every aspiring romance writer the hope, help, and courage to believe in happy endings.

With special thanks to

The Cincinnati Public Library, especially the librarians of the Groesbeck Branch, who were always courteous and helpful.

The readers of *For Honor's Lady* and *Chastity Morrow*, for their letters and support that mean so much to me.

Rosanne Kohake
P.O. 399127
Cincinnati, OH 45239

Prologue
Manhattan
Autumn 1859

Aaron Rambert stared at the house, at the single, dim light that glowed from within on the moonless night. The wind howled through the barren trees, whisking leaves about in eerie circles in the darkness. The house seemed out of place in the darkness, its light warm and beckoning, a reminder to any who passed by that the man who lived here was a doctor, accustomed to visitors late at night, accustomed to being roused from sleep to tend to another's needs. Aaron had watched that house for over an hour now, had waited until all but that single light was extinguished.

His lip curled in disdain. Hatred had brought him here, the hatred and jealousy of a lifetime. He took a flask from his shirt pocket and drew a long swallow. Now the solution seemed so simple, so easy. And so perfect a revenge. A fire, a terrible fire would sweep through Drayton's house. No one would get out alive.

Aaron took one last swig of whiskey and tethered his horse to a tree a few hundred yards from the house. He made his way stealthily toward it, remembering the fires he had set as a child. He had been very good at setting them. They had burned strong and bright, and no one ever suspected that anyone had set them at all. A lamp fallen from a table, they said, when he set a fire in his stepfather's study. A cigar tossed thoughtlessly into a stack of hay, they said, when he'd set fire to the stable to kill his stepfather's favorite stallion. It had all been so very simple. And this could be simple too. No one would ever suspect anything, if he was very careful.

He circled the house slowly, checking the doors, then each window, finally locating an unlocked one and quickly slipping inside. The room he entered was small, with shelved walls holding dozens of books and a huge desk stacked high with papers. He paused, allowing his eyes to adjust to the darkness of the room, staring at the shadows until the various shapes became familiar to him. He recognized a desk lamp and moved to lift it, thoughtfully gauging the amount of kerosene in its globe. It would be enough. But this room would be the last. He replaced the lamp on the desk and felt his way to the door. He opened it slowly, his eyes darting about the hall, catching sight of the lamp that burned low near the front door. He made his way slowly to the opposite side of the house, avoiding the light, entering the parlor. There he lifted a table lamp and found it nearly full.

He smiled as he spilled the lamp's contents about the floor with a swift, sweeping motion, saturating the carpet, the upholstered furniture, dripping a trail to the yellow draperies which skimmed the floor. He set the lamp aside and drew a match from his pocket, his eyes gleaming with anticipation as he struck the match to his heel and touched it to the kerosene-drenched fabric. A fascination flared in his eyes as the small, flickering flame grew brighter, hotter, leaping upward with a sudden whooshing sound. A childish smile of wonder curved his mouth. Slowly he backed away, the light glowing warm and orange on his face. He watched from the threshold of the parlor, entranced. But then he remembered where he was, what he was doing. He spun about on a heel and made to hurry down the hall.

"Drayton?"

The voice, soft and feminine, stopped him short. His

feet were riveted to the floor as his eyes fixed on the woman who blocked his exit. In her hands she held the small lamp that had been left to burn near the door. She gasped in fear and shock, her hand flying to her breast.

Aaron stared at her face, at the green eyes that seemed huge in the lamplight, at the long, dark hair that fell below her waist, at her white, flowing gown. His panic at being discovered and the strong whiskey he'd drunk all night kept him from thinking clearly. It never even occurred to him that Drayton would not be here, that Drayton's wife might be in the house alone.

"Who are you? What do you want?"

Aaron could hardly even breathe for fear that she might scream and awaken Drayton. The thought ran again and again through his mind. She'd seen him! He was caught! His entire body began to shake with the terrible anticipation of facing his stepbrother. Drayton would kill him.

The woman took a step toward him, confused as well as frightened now by his silence. "I asked who you are," she repeated.

She had scarcely uttered the words when a noise from the parlor made her gasp. Her eyes darted to the eerie orange light that flickered on the wall opposite the parlor.

Aaron saw his only chance for escape and quickly slammed his fist into the woman's face. She flew backward, her head striking the floor at the same moment the lamp did. Glass seemed to shatter everywhere and a hungry tongue of red leapt about her. It was only then, when Aaron saw her lying sprawled on the floor, that he realized she was far along with child. An icy sweat broke over his brow and ran down his neck as he stared in horror at her motionless form. The flames were licking at her long, dark hair, at the flowing white gown. . . . She moaned softly and stirred, but Aaron turned away from the sight of her and ran for the door. He could not save her; to do so would be to hang himself. And Drayton—he could never face Drayton.

Aaron's heart was pounding furiously in his ears, his lungs aching as he ran, never once looking back. In the moonless night he mounted his horse and galloped swiftly away.

Part One
Bamberg County, South Carolina
February 1865

Chapter 1

Dusky shadows lifted quickly from the winter-brown hills of South Carolina as the brightness of the eastern sky triumphed over night. Squirrels and rabbits and deer lifted drowsy eyes to meet the sun's light, and the noisy chatter of newly wakened birds broke the solemn quiet. Ambrosia Lanford drew a deep breath of sweet morning air and smiled. Spring would arrive early at Heritage this year, she thought. On the first morning of February, the sky was bright and cloudless; the air moist and heavy with dew; the ground, a fertile brown-black, awaiting the turn of the plow.

How she loved the land that lay before her! Land that was her birthright; land that she'd held on to with her own sweat and labor. Ambrosia knew the hills of this land as well as she knew her name. She knew the tallest tree, the deepest pond, the most treacherous patches of marshland, the lushest thickets of wild blackberries. Each of the fields that stretched long and flat beneath the sun was as much a part of her as her green-gray eyes or coal-black hair. Her own hands, once soft and tender, had broken ground for spring planting for the past two years. She had seen to the tending, the watering, the harvesting, the preserving of the simple food crops which were now Heritage's lifeblood.

It had not always been so. If Ambrosia closed her eyes for a moment, she could easily imagine that she was a child again, that this morning which hinted at spring was a morning of long ago. She could picture Mr. Partkin, the overseer, in a crumpled white shirt and mud-stained breeches, could hear his gruff voice barking orders to the field-slaves as they shuffled in a haphazard procession toward their day's toil. From a distance would drift the comforting drone of their deep, resonant voices singing the rhythmic, mournful melodies Mammy called work songs; from the veranda would come the murmur of unimportant conversation and the pleasant tinkling of iced glasses on a heavy silver tray. . . .

Ambrosia forced open her eyes and scanned the world that lay before her this morning, so quiet, so peaceful, so very changed from the world she had once known. These days Ambrosia did not allow herself much time for remembering, for there was far too much work to be done. It had been over a year since she'd been able to buy a pair of shoes, and the slaves had gone barefoot even longer than that, except in the coldest winter months. A great deal of ingenuity had gone into finding a workable substitute for shoe leather, which was simply not to be had. She tossed a rueful glance at the odd-looking, coarse-fabric shoes she had made with her own hands, recalling the countless pairs of satin slippers she had once taken for granted. Still, prunella shoes served their purpose, while there were some things for which there were no substitutes. Salt, an absolute necessity for preserving foods, particularly ham and bacon, had become a precious commodity everywhere in the South. Just a few weeks before Ambrosia had heard of a family so desperate they tore up the floorboards of their smokehouse and boiled them just to retrieve the salt. She stared for a moment at the nearby smokehouse, knowing it was nearly empty now, wondering how long it would be before she would be doing the same.

She would do anything to hold on to this place, her

home. Heritage was everything to her now, her past, her present, her future, her life. The only dream to which she still held fast.

Heritage was a young plantation by Charleston standards, though the land, which lay northeast of the Bamberg County seat, had been in the Lanford family for generations. Charles Henry Lanford had set foot on Carolina soil in the late 1600s, and his two sons, William and John, had served admirably under General Sumter in the Revolutionary War. Both were members of the Jacksonboro Assembly, which drew up the state constitution.

Jackson Lanford, Ambrosia's father, had built Heritage with an eye toward future generations, certain that he would raise many sons to carry on the proud Lanford name. Rising loftily from the crest of a gently sloping hill, the sprawling, two-story structure of light-colored brick crowned with a windowed dome cast an imposing shadow on the rich, fertile land. Broad piazzas, reminiscent of Charleston, stretched across the front of the house, offering a view of the long avenue that wound past an impressive row of huge, shady oaks. Though less than a quarter of a century old, Heritage was considered one of Carolina's great plantations.

Just a score of years before, tall, handsome Jackson Lanford had been the most sought-after bachelor in Bamberg County. But Jackson was a man's man who took no interest in simpering belles and, in fact, did not enjoy the company of females at all. When he finally did wed Lucille Grayson, a delicate, blond beauty, no one, least of all his bride, ever guessed that Jackson had married strictly to beget a suitable heir.

During the first years of their marriage, he labored with such love and enthusiasm at Heritage, overseeing every detail of the running of their home, that Lucille was totally convinced of his devotion. She became pregnant almost too quickly to be proper, and nine months to the day after the grandest wedding in the history of South Carolina, Melissa Anne Lanford was born.

Jackson hid his disappointment well. He had a daughter who was the picture of her lovely mother and he was certain there would be many more babies and many sons. But during the next two years, Lucille suffered four miscarriages, each of which Jackson accepted with less patience. Finally, after a long, difficult pregnancy, Lucille gave birth to a second daughter, Ambrosia, and gratefully accepted the news that there would be no more children.

For Lucille, it seemed the reprieve came too late. She was thin and pale, robbed of her health and radiant youth by this sharp-featured, dark-haired baby, so unlike her first lovely daughter. And after years of being the center of attention, Lucille suddenly was confronted with a disinterested husband who took no interest in the child she had given him, who never once even asked to hold her. Worst of all, he announced that he had hired an overseer for the plantation and that he was leaving for Charleston the very day of Ambrosia's christening.

Jackson plunged himself into other matters, embarked on several business ventures, and cultivated influential friendships throughout the state. For a man who had always achieved his purpose in any endeavor he pursued, the plantation was but an unpleasant reminder of his one failure.

Ambrosia was only four years old when her father announced his plans to represent his district in the South Carolina legislature, but she never forgot the uproar when her father came home to campaign for the election. The whole house was scrubbed and polished; every corner was inspected.

There was nothing more exciting in Ambrosia's life than her father's visits to Heritage. During those wonderful, short days, she would be on her best behavior as she followed him about. She would listen with rapt attention when his valet, Josiah, told tales about places her father had been and the wonderful, important things he had done. His dark eyes glowing, his broad chest swelling

with pride, Josiah would call Jackson Lanford a great
man, a man of history. Greatness, Ambrosia learned, had
little to do with being tall or lean or handsome, or with
wearing fine clothing. It had more to do with what was
inside, with honesty and courage and conviction. Father
was not fawned upon for his beauty and tolerated for his
behavior like Mother, or Melissa. And because beauty
was something that seemed to have passed Ambrosia by,
she instinctively aspired to be more like him. She could
not change her angular face and prominent cheekbones
into Melissa's perfectly rounded, rosy cheeks; she could
not exchange her large, almond-shaped eyes which fluc-
tuated between a deep green and a dark, somber gray, for
Melissa's wide blue ones; she could not change the sorry
fact that she was shorter than every other child her age,
and would probably never be willowy and graceful like
her mother. But she could be courageous and strong if
she tried hard enough. And so she began to try very, very
hard.

While her sister was becoming the belle of the county,
Ambrosia was becoming the terror of the plantation, performing acts of bravery as were never before witnessed in
Heritage's history. On a dare she rode her father's tem-
peramental stallion without a saddle and even managed to
keep her seat when the horse decided to jump the stone
wall by the south pasture. She climbed to the top of every
tree within a mile of the house. Twice she left the manor
house at midnight when there was a full moon and spent
the night in the burying ground, just to prove she wasn't
afraid of anything. She even learned to play a mean game
of cutthroat poker. Not the harshest punishments, nor the
sternest threats, nor the soundest reasoning ever managed
to subdue her. She bore all discipline without a single
word, maintaining a stiff, haughty posture and a cold
look of total conviction in her green-gray eyes.

The turning point of Ambrosia's life came when her
father paid an unannounced visit to Heritage and arrived
just in time to see his daughter plunge from the top of a

dangerously high pile of cotton bales to the ground below. Jackson galloped at full speed to her side, swinging down from his horse before it had even come to a full stop. To his absolute astonishment, Ambrosia respectfully declined his assistance and struggled shakily, but unaided, to her feet. He stared at her face for what seemed like a long time, noting the determined gleam in her eyes and the defiant lift of her chin. For a moment he thought she had miraculously escaped without any injury at all. But then he noticed the strange, unnatural bend in the arm she held so protectively against her body, and he knew at once that it was broken. Yet she stood there in silence, not uttering a single word, not shedding a single tear. A deep sense of pride welled up inside him as he continued to meet her gaze. Her eyes showed no trace of the excruciating pain she must be feeling, only a fiery kind of courage he'd seen in few men and had never thought to see in an eleven-year-old child. Then a thought struck him like a bolt of lightning—Ambrosia was his daughter, his own flesh and blood. She was not like other little girls, diligently learning to pour tea and sew samplers, swooning and giggling uncontrollably, or doing any other of a hundred things he could not tolerate. Ambrosia was his daughter. *His*, not Lucille's. And he decided then and there that he would see to the remainder of her upbringing.

The break was a clean one, but it still took weeks to mend. Ambrosia would have willingly broken every bone in her body, however, for the attention her father suddenly heaped upon her. She could not begin to understand why it had happened, and she was as surprised as anyone else when he announced that she would be accompanying him to Columbia when he returned for a legislative session the third of October. She watched as Melissa played every kind of petty trick in the hopes of coming along. But Melissa, who always got her way, didn't get what she wanted this time. Jackson refused to take her, even when Lucille pleaded and begged in her behalf. And Ambrosia could not have been happier.

Though Charlestonians liked to call it "a town aspiring to be a city," Ambrosia's first glimpse of Columbia in October of 1858 was of imposing state buildings; a main street of closely packed, wooden and brick stores and businesses, with planked sidewalks; hundreds of frame houses with high, cool basements; and several beautiful mansions on wide, shady, gaslit streets.

Ambrosia took up residence in her father's house, a modest structure within walking distance of the statehouse, and was introduced to scores of Jackson's friends. One woman in particular, whose husband was one of Jackson Lanford's closest political allies, took an immediate liking to his daughter.

Elisabeth Woodard was a pleasant, intelligent woman nearing forty. She was childless but not really regretful of the fact, and she possessed a clever, calculating mind to which her husband Daniel owed a great deal of his success. Ambrosia offered Elisabeth both a challenge and an excuse to associate more closely with Jackson Lanford, whom she found most attractive. Elisabeth took Ambrosia under her wing and set about teaching the child everything she'd refused to learn from Lucille. Ambrosia became a diligent reader and learned to mimic the polished prose of a lady whenever she was forced into conversation.

But her happiest moments were those spent in the comfortable parlor in her father's small house near the capital, listening to him rehash the most significant issues of the day with his closest friends. For hours she would sit quietly in a corner chair, pretending to be deeply engrossed in sketching a picture or diligently at work on a piece of needlework, when she was actually devouring every word of overheard conversation and relishing the marvelous authority and strength she heard in her father's voice. She was enthralled, caught up in the contagious fever of politics, feeling the same self-righteous indignation as her father over the ''Beecher's Bibles,'' rifles sent by New England abolitionists to antislavery settlers in Missouri. She learned to hate the words *Yankee* and *Republican,* and to despise those political extremists who would destroy the South by abolishing slavery. She treasured every moment she spent with her father, though there was nothing of real intimacy in their relationship, and she remained little more than an admiring observer. Still, for the child who had always been ignored whenever she was not being chastised, a few words, a nod of recognition, a smile of approval were quite enough. Her father had taken her from a world where she had never fit in and allowed her to feel that somehow, someday, she would finally find a place in life just as she was.

It came as a crushing blow to her newfound pride when her father enrolled her at the South Carolina Female Collegiate Institute, Barhamville Academy, a school for young ladies from the best Southern families. There Ambrosia was grouped with girls her age who were constantly chattering and whispering about secret adolescent passions she considered utter nonsense. Once again she felt terribly out of place and alone.

She managed to receive excellent marks and remained docile during the first quarter, but she was bored quickly with books and studies and found the regimentation increasingly tedious. Even walks on the academy grounds were permitted only when Dr. Marks, the founder, offered a personal escort, for though the place was entirely enclosed against unannounced visitors, the school was an irresistible lure to daring youths attending nearby South Carolina College; and locked gates were no real deterrent to eager young men with ribald intentions. Whenever an intruder was noticed on the grounds, the girls were immediately ordered to their rooms, where they were to remain with all blinds tightly drawn until that intruder was evicted. The more curious and brave young ladies usually managed to catch a glimpse of the interloper escaping, or being apprehended and escorted off the grounds, and excitedly reported bits and pieces of information to the other girls at dinner that evening.

". . . and it was the same one as last week!" Sheila Strother whispered with wide, adoring eyes. "The tall, blond one who rides that incredible bay—I actually saw him jump the fence! But he waited until they were almost upon him before he did . . ."

A chorus of thrilled sighs echoed around the table, and Sheila grinned her satisfaction. Only Ambrosia sat in utter silence, indifferent to the conversation.

"He's just about the most handsome man I've ever seen," Sheila went on, "and he's *so* brave! Can you imagine? Jumping that fence every Saturday for a month! Why, he's—he's practically a hero!" She closed her eyes and smiled as a deep sigh of longing escaped her. "If only I knew his name! I'd do just about anything to find out who he is. . . ."

"Then why don't you ask him?"

Every eye flew instantly to Ambrosia's face in utter astonishment. Not one of the girls could believe that she had suggested such a thing, and most of them had trouble believing that she had spoken at all.

"I suppose that's what you would do," Sheila countered smugly.

Ambrosia added a bit of cream to her tea and took a dainty sip. "It certainly is."

Sheila snorted and rolled her eyes.

"If you'd like, I'll ask him for you," Ambrosia taunted flippantly.

Sheila ground her teeth in silent frustration. Not only had Ambrosia stolen her audience of captive admirers, but she was threatening to perform an act of courage far beyond anything Sheila would ever have considered. If she was caught, it would mean instant dismissal. On the other hand, if she succeeded, Sheila would learn the name of the dashing trespasser, and then, somehow, she could arrange an introduction.

"All right, Miss Lanford. We'll be waiting to see if you've got the backbone to go through with this."

For the next six days, Ambrosia went about business as usual, ignoring the taunting smirks and curious stares that plagued her all week long. Exactly according to plan, she managed to slip away from the other girls just after breakfast, and as soon as she made her way down the back stairs to the garden, she secured herself in a hiding place where she was certain she would not be found—twenty feet above the ground. When Dr. Marks and three other instructors made their daily inspection of the gardens just before noon, the girls, all painfully aware of Ambrosia's absence, held their breaths in terrible anticipation. But the midday repast was announced promptly at 12:00, and the student body was left to whisper and wonder over their plates about their comrade's temporary reprieve.

Ambrosia, perched on a hefty bough of the largest tree in the garden, patiently awaited the arrival of the celebrated intruder. Her eyes widened when she finally did see him, his blond hair blowing in careless disarray around his totally beautiful face as an incredible red-brown stallion flew over the fence and gracefully landed in the middle of the garden. Ambrosia hesitated, feeling a rush of unfamiliar feelings as she watched him, but when she saw him turn his mount in the opposite direction toward the school, she remembered her intentions and quickly made her descent—too quickly. Somehow, all her natural agility failed her on her very last foothold, and she fell with a "Whoof!" directly into a carefully tended patch of trailing arbutus. She struggled to her feet, thanking her lucky stars that nothing seemed to be broken, but before she could catch her breath and return herself to a semblance of dignity, the visitor had done an about-face and brought his horse to a halt directly beside her.

Slowly, with excruciating embarrassment, she raised her eyes to meet those of the mounted stranger. They

were blue eyes, pale and clear as a spring morning sky,
but they were full of mischief and warm, boyish charm
too, just like his dazzling smile. He was older than she'd
thought at first—at least eighteen, which seemed ancient
compared to her twelve years. But there was something
about him that captivated Ambrosia—a reckless confidence in his lightly raised brow, a challenge of some sort
which she recognized at once. For some reason, his smile
made her heart beat even faster. She felt her cheeks growing hot and red as she stood there, her back stiff and her
head held high, silently returning his stare. And only
when he dismounted did she recall her real mission.

"Good day, sir." She nodded tersely, her manner all
business. "I need to know your name."

He raised a bemused brow and took a step toward her.

"One of the girls—Sheila Strother—wants to know
your name," she repeated bluntly, holding her ground as
he circled around her without the slightest regard to the
ruined flowerbed.

"Does she now . . ." He sounded skeptical, but Ambrosia merely nodded. He was standing much closer than
he ought to stand, and she was beginning to think that
meeting him might not have been such a wonderful idea.
"And why isn't Sheila here to ask me my name herself?"

"Because it's strictly forbidden," she told him with a
lift of her chin. "She's afraid she'll be expelled."

"Oh. I see. And aren't you afraid of being expelled?"

She straightened to her full height, her proudly raised
head barely meeting his shoulder. "I don't intend to be
caught," she told him matter-of-factly.

"That's why you were up in that tree," he concluded.
Again she gave a nod. For a moment his smile faded and
he narrowed his eyes, as if considering the story, glancing up at the tree and then again at Ambrosia. Though she
was small and slender, and had not the slightest curve to
her bodice, there was still something about her that was
not quite girlish, some hint of maturity which struck his
fancy. "If I tell you who I am, then I will insist that you

return the favor,'' he said slowly, measuring her all the while.

"Fair enough," she returned promptly.

He smiled again, that same wonderful smile that sent shivers down her spine. "John Rutledge Bowman," he said with a low, exaggerated bow. "Ledger to my friends. Miss—?"

"Lanford. Ambrosia Lanford."

"Miss Lanford," he repeated, testing the sound of it. He glanced about the flowerbed for a moment, searching for a perfect flower from among the trampled ones, when a small splash of a different color caught his eye. He swooped down to retrieve a single tiny violet which had somehow taken root at the base of the tree. He offered it to her, and she accepted the tiny flower with trembling fingers and a somewhat awestruck expression. Then before Ambrosia knew what he was doing, he seized her hand and kissed it gallantly, and more than just gallantly, drawing her closer than she had ever been to a man before. "You are a very brave woman, Ambrosia," he whispered, pressing another kiss to her palm, and making her stomach feel jumbled and achy. A woman, he had called her. A woman! And that was exactly what she felt like when he said her name, or touched her. He was about to say more, but at that very moment, the sounds of furious voices and barking dogs and the heavy patter of footsteps on the path gave him no chance. He swung onto his horse and left the grounds in what seemed to Ambrosia to be one fluid motion, though she was more concerned with concealing herself than with John Rutledge Bowman's escape. Incredibly, Dr. Marks and his companions were so intent on apprehending the habitual trespasser that Ambrosia was completely unnoticed in the shuffle and managed to conceal herself in a remote corner of the garden until things settled down. She was even able to return to her room before dinner, where the name of the intruder spread like wildfire from table to table.

For a week or more, Ambrosia remained the center of

attention, repeating the story at least a hundred times
over before refusing to say another word about it. Yet she
thought of it, time and again, vividly recalling the bits
and pieces of the story she had not revealed to anyone,
the kiss he had pressed to her palm, the magic words he
had whispered, the tiny, wilted violet he had pressed to
her fingers. And in the next several weeks, the sighs and
whispers and giggles of the other girls began to make
sense to her, though something kept her from joining in.
Perhaps it was the uncertainty, the disappointment she
felt whenever she gazed at her reflection in the looking
glass and saw no change at all, in spite of all the changes
that were taking place inside. She was still not a beauty,
with her square jawline; her huge, gray-green eyes; her
thin and shapeless child's body. But she happily remembered that Ledger had spoken of bravery when he kissed
her, not beauty. He had recognized the very quality she
took most pride in, the only part of herself she truly felt
had value, the part she had struggled so to fashion after
her father. In doing so, Ledger had touched the deepest,
most vulnerable part of Ambrosia, a heart that had waited
a lifetime to be touched . . . and loved. After twelve
years of trying to be exactly like her father, Ambrosia
suddenly knew that she was meant to be something else.
She longed to be a woman . . . and all because John Rutledge Bowman was a man.

To Ambrosia's delight, she saw Ledger again soon after that first meeting. Since Ledger's mother was a close
friend of Elisabeth Woodard, he was a frequent guest at
their home, as was Ambrosia. After being thrown together several times during the following year, a very
special kind of bond evolved between the two of them.
Ledger was amused by Ambrosia's brief, candid comments and totally forthright manner, so unlike the
frivolous, scatterbrained girls he courted who talked for
hours on end and rarely said anything that made any
sense. He found Ambrosia refreshing company and often
exchanged winks or knowing glances with her whenever

a particularly flighty female tried to get his attention. But he was totally blind to the feelings he stirred in her. He thought her only a child and hardly noticed that she wore special gowns and arranged her thick, dark hair just to please him. He didn't see that Ambrosia was becoming a woman, and though her body was slow to reflect the inner changes, her heart was falling hopelessly in love with him.

Then one chilly February morning, Ambrosia's father paid an unexpected visit to Barhamville Academy to inform her that Melissa would be coming to Columbia for a "brief visit." Melissa, all of seventeen by this time, announced to Ambrosia on her arrival that she intended to stay much longer. It wasn't fair, she declared, that Ambrosia should have all the advantages, that she should meet so many exciting young men while Melissa was left with boring country swains who expected her to be content with a life like the one she'd left at Heritage. She would never be satisfied with a life like that, no matter what Mama said.

Within a month of her arrival Melissa became the most celebrated beauty in Columbia, gracing every one of the parties and galas and balls which bloomed with the decade's first spring. It seemed only natural that her name was linked with that of every handsome bachelor in town, including Ledger Bowman. But when the talk about Ledger and Melissa continued into summer, Ambrosia grew troubled. She was relieved when he went home to Charleston in July and certain that he would forget Melissa long before he returned for fall term at the University.

"I do miss him dreadfully," Melissa pouted to Ambrosia just after he departed for home. "He's truly the most divine man I ever imagined meeting! I just don't know how I'll manage to survive until he proposes." She tossed her head playfully, knowing full well that Ambrosia was taken with Ledger, as was every other woman in Columbia. It made him that much more irresistible.

''What makes you think he'll propose?'' Ambrosia returned calmly, her voice reflecting none of the panic she was feeling at the thought.

Melissa gave a short, condescending laugh. ''They *all* propose, if I want them to. And I do so want Ledger Bowman. I'd have to be a fool to let him slip through my fingers now.'' She lifted her chin and toyed with a soft, golden curl. ''He'll propose . . . you wait and see.'' She paused and her mouth curved into a confident smile. ''And I'll make him wait for an answer . . . at least a week or two. . . .''

Ambrosia said nothing to that, though her heart screamed that Melissa had to be wrong. Ledger could never fall victim to her silly tricks! He would turn his mind to important things, like the upcoming election, which might ''force'' South Carolina to leave the Union. Surely the possibilities of war would divert his attention to matters more urgent than a flighty, plotting female!

But when Ledger returned to Columbia for the fall term at the university, Ambrosia saw that she was wrong. There were no secret winks for Ambrosia, no knowing glances. There was only Melissa laughing and pouting and smiling and Ledger responding like a puppet on a string. And though Ambrosia gave no sign of her feelings, a part of her was dying.

Less than a month later Ambrosia was informed of the upcoming nuptials. She accepted the news without a word, keeping her hurt hidden from everyone, she thought, and in doing so, retaining some part of her pride. But at a party given by Elisabeth and Daniel Woodard to formally announce the engagement, even that was lost to the man she so desperately loved.

It was late in the evening and all but a very few of the guests had departed for their homes. Lucille, who had come to town the day before, had long since retired with a headache. Ambrosia sat in the parlor next to her father, sipping at a cup of punch, only half listening as the others talked and laughed and assured one another what a truly great event was at hand. Lanford and Bowman, two of the most prestigious families in all South Carolina, would be joined by a bond of marriage.

"I had a feeling this would happen when you first brought Melissa to Columbia, Jackson," Elisabeth told him with a coquettish smile.

At her comment Ledger's smile warmed and Melissa held his gaze. Ambrosia looked the other way.

"It was obvious to me from the very first," Elisabeth went on, doing her best to hold Jackson's attention. "Why, the moment I saw them together, I knew."

"Oh, come, Elisabeth," Daniel said stiffly, perturbed at the way she was looking at Jackson. "You know perfectly well that you were surprised by the news. Why, just this past winter I heard you tell the ladies at tea you were certain Ledger Bowman would wed Ambrosia someday."

Ledger gave a short laugh. "Ambrosia—why she's just a child!" he blurted out.

Ambrosia felt the color draining from her cheeks as all eyes momentarily fell on her. She straightened her back and raised her chin in an almost defiant gesture as she set her cup on the table and excused herself. But in the single moment when her eyes met Ledger's, he had seen. He knew.

In October, Ambrosia went with Melissa to Charleston, to the Bowman plantation on the Ashley River, where she gracefully fulfilled her role as sister of the bride. But it was a simple matter of going through the motions. She no longer cared for gowns or parties; they were painful reminders of broken dreams.

Eager to leave the happy newlyweds behind, Ambrosia returned to Columbia with her father. She had hardly resumed her classes at Barhamville when the results of the election reached South Carolina: Abraham Lincoln was to be president. Six weeks later, on the evening of December 20, 1860, Jackson Lanford was one of 169 men who signed a document in Charleston that dissolved the Union between South Carolina and the United States of America. South Carolina became the first state ever to secede from the Union, and war was imminent.

It seemed to Ambrosia that suddenly every man over sixteen and under sixty wore a uniform and talked of Yankee blood. Her heart filled with patriotic pride when she learned that her father was resigning his post in the legislature to outfit a regiment of his own from Bamberg County and that Ledger had already joined up with a group from Charleston. How could the Union ever hope to defeat an army of such men as these? She only wished that she were more than a schoolgirl, that she too could fight for what she believed in. But there was little any woman could do besides watch and cheer . . . and wait.

War was a distant thing for Ambrosia that first year, with life continuing much as it had in the past, except that so many of the men were gone. At school, Ambrosia fought hard against remembering her feelings for Ledger. She took on the most difficult courses of study and occupied herself every moment with something—writing countless letters, sewing, learning to sketch portraits—leaving herself little time to think, or to feel, or even to notice the changes that were finally occurring in her body. Her slim figure was finally developing firm, womanly curves. But it was happening too late. It simply didn't matter anymore.

Ambrosia rejoiced with the entire city of Columbia at the exciting news of the victory at Bull Run. The gallantry and courage of the Confederate troops was proven, once and for all. Yet as winter came upon the South, the news became less encouraging. Little by little the Union army chipped away at the Confederate border, and by spring of 1862, Lincoln's soldiers held Memphis and most of Missouri, and were very close to opening up the Mississippi River.

During that same spring a group of women from church and lay organizations in Columbia undertook to transform a resting room for soldiers at the train depot into a hospital. Ambrosia immediately volunteered her services, but because she was young and unmarried, it was several months before she was allowed to do more than scrape and roll bandages and launder linens. Only after the second Bull Run did the matrons allow her to share in the hours of dirty, backbreaking labor, assisting surgeons in their often futile attempts to patch together mutilated bodies; cleaning up human refuse and vomit; and offering what small comfort one could to men who had seen their last battle. For Ambrosia, the new challenge proved a godsend.

She was stronger of will and more capable than most gently reared women, accustomed to driving herself and to keeping her emotions under tight rein. When others collapsed in utter exhaustion or fled to empty their stomachs in revulsion, Ambrosia clenched her teeth and stood her ground. Her carefully guarded eyes; her smooth, level voice; her calm, steady hand masked the terrible anguish she felt day after day, as she tended the broken men who tearfully thanked her for her kindness. So many times a patient with a shock of unruly blond curls or a pair of dancing blue eyes reminded her of Ledger. And she had to steel herself against remembering the hopes in her heart that had been shattered so many months before. She was beginning to realize that she would always love him, that she would never, ever forget what she had felt for him, that concealing the pain of that love in her heart would probably be the most difficult thing in her life. She thought often of her father too whenever one of the men spoke in a low, authoritative tone, or eagerly engaged in political debate with one of the other patients. She could not help but wonder if one of the men she loved would someday . . . But she refused to allow herself to speculate. There was more than enough reality to be reckoned with at Wayside Hospital.

In May of 1863 Ambrosia received an urgent letter from the mistress of a plantation bordering on Heritage informing her that her mother was gravely ill; that Mr.

Partkin, the overseer, had been killed in an accident; and that the remaining slaves were left completely without proper supervision. Ambrosia arrived home less than a week later, totally unprepared for what awaited her. No one had tended to the flowers, the shrubs, or the lawn for months; and the house had been picked clean of curios and keepsakes, even easily transportable pieces of furniture. She listened quietly as Sheba, the head cook, and Andrew, her mother's favorite house-slave, told all that had happened in her absence.

"Massuh Jackson ain' been heah since way 'for las' spring, Miz Ambrosia," Andrew told her solemnly. "An' Mr. Partkin, he die two months back, aftah he fall from dat wil' horse he liked t' ride so much. Miz Elly, she try t' take ovah de runin' o' de place. She move herself right into de big house, since Miz Lucille been feelin' so poorly. But she don' know how t' gib de ordahs like a lady," he added with a wary glance over his shoulder and a noticeable lowering of his voice.

Ambrosia closed her eyes for a moment, fully aware of what Andrew meant by that. Everyone knew why Elly, the pretty, fifteen-year-old daughter of a poor tenant farmer had married the physically unattractive, fifty-year-old overseer of Heritage. There had always been talk about Elly and the airs she'd put on the moment she'd taken Mr. Partkin's name. For all her attempts to dress and act like a lady, Ambrosia vividly recalled the few times she'd seen Elly deal with slaves, screaming and slapping at them with a smile on her face, as if it gave her some feeling of triumph. "I'm home now, Andrew," Ambrosia told him quietly. "Elly won't be giving any more orders around here."

"Ain' many ordahs lef' t' give, Miz Ambrosia," Sheba told her sadly. "Aftah Elly take ovah, de people run off a dozen at a time. Only me, Andrew an' Sally lef' now," eyeing the young black girl who stood nodding in silent agreement. "I try t' tell dem t' stay on fo' while, but ain' nobody an' nothin' but me t' keep 'em heah, so dey run off.'' She snorted derisively. ''Dey say Pres'dent Lincoln make dem free. Dey don' hab no massuh t' gib dem clothes an' a house an' food, but dey's free.''

''Ain' nothin' been done 'bout spring plantin', Missy,'' she went on apologetically. ''An' Massuh Jackson, he write an' say he ain' comin' home for long while yet. De supplies is runnin' real low too. We been livin' on eggs an' de las' o' de flour. Don' know what we do when dey runs out. Maybe we have t' leave heah too.''

''Leave here?'' Ambrosia repeated in disbelief. She squared her shoulders and lifted her chin. ''No, Sheba. We'll never leave here. Heritage is our home.'' This place and its way of life were her birthright, and they were the reason why so many good men had already spilled their lifeblood. She did not intend to let this plantation, or the dream that had inspired it, die. ''Heritage is our home,'' she repeated softly.

Survival became a private war for the women whose husbands' and brothers' and fathers' bodies littered faraway battlefields like Gettysburg, Spotsylvania Court House, and Cold Harbor. There were too many places like those to remember the names after a while. Long lists of the dead, wounded, and missing were distributed almost daily at the depots of major cities and, from there, passed on from plantation to plantation. Ambrosia always braced herself for the worst whenever such a list found its way to Heritage but had thus far been spared the horror of finding her father's or Ledger's name. With a half-sigh of relief, she would return to working with the blacks on the vegetable garden, which now offered their principal source of food, or to directing the making of soap, or molding of candles, or hand-lapping of threads for cloth, or knitting, or any one of a score of tasks that she now performed as a matter of course. She found a strange sort of comfort in forcing herself to work so hard, in allowing herself so little time to think about what life might have been like had there not been a war, or what might have happened had Ledger returned her love. She simply concentrated on holding on to Heritage, on proving herself worthy of the task which lay before her.

Only once did she feel a pang of regret for the turn her life had taken, and that was just after her mother's death, when Melissa came to Heritage. She arrived from Charleston on the verge of hysteria, sobbing about the terrible shelling that had gone on for weeks and assuring Ambrosia that General Sherman was coming to burn the city just as he had burned Atlanta and Savannah. But it was only a matter of minutes before Melissa noticed the changes at Heritage. Ambrosia's weekly letters had prepared her for her mother's death, but not for what she found here. She walked slowly about the house, staring in disbelief at the worn draperies, the threadbare carpets, the empty shelves which had once held Mama's favorite procelain figurines. Some of the furniture was even missing from the parlor!

"Lord! Your hands look like a field-slave's, Ambrosia," Melissa told her with a horrified gasp when she found her making candles. "You work like a slave here! You even eat at Mama's table with that Elly Partkin, like she was acceptable folk. And how do you think you'll ever catch a decent husband dressed in stained homespun and those awful prunella shoes!"

Ambrosia turned away from the cauldron of hot wax for a moment and stared at her hands, remembering, in spite of herself, the way Ledger had kissed her palm so long ago. "There aren't any men to come courting these days," she said bluntly as she wiped her soiled hands on a worn apron and pushed aside any frivolous regrets about her appearance. She lifted her chin. "Elly's a hard worker and I'm glad of her help. And I really don't have a choice of whether or not to work, Melissa," she went on, her eyes sparking indignantly as her sister gave a grimace of distaste. "There isn't anyone else to do it."

"If you had any pride at all, you'd leave here," Melissa snapped back. "What in God's name are you holding on to? I'd rather starve than live like you do. I'd rather face General Sherman's army!''

"Then maybe you'd better go back to Charleston," Ambrosia returned evenly. "If you stay here at Heritage, you're going to have to do your share."

With a gasp of outrage, Melissa turned her back. She started for Charleston the following morning.

What in God's name are you holding on to? The question echoed in Ambrosia's mind as she stood alone in silence, watching the bright yellow rays of the sun dancing across the sleeping fields of Heritage, gently nudging seeds and roots and bulbs to waken to a newborn spring. In the distance, the windows of the house reflected the glory of the dawn like polished gems set to catch the light. This was her pride, her hope, her future. Wars might rage and cities might burn, but there would always be this: the beauty of a sunrise, the miracle of spring at Heritage. This was what she was holding on to, what gave her the strength to go on.

She drew deeply of the sweet, dew-kissed air and let her eyes roam lovingly over all the land that stretched before her. And then she bravely turned away to face the day.

Chapter 2

"The army will forage liberally on the country during the march . . ."

That simple phrase, part of the lengthy orders General William Tecumseh Sherman gave his troops after leaving Atlanta, transformed his army into an instrument of terror. Union forces had penetrated the South during earlier campaigns, but never like this. The rural lands of Georgia and the Carolinas lay largely undefended, prone before the attacking Union forces who eagerly sought to destroy what little strength remained.

General Sherman's primary objective was to end the war by destroying the South's railway system, but he also believed that the South deserved to be driven to her knees, that every man, woman, and child bore responsibility for secession, and that the civilians as well as the soldiers must be conquered. His foraging parties effectively accomplished that task as they trampled and burned an eighty-mile-wide swath through Georgia and on to Carolina. Though Sherman's original orders forbade the entering of homes along the route and encouraged the parties to proceed under the direction of a trustworthy officer, there was little or no disciplinary action taken against men who looted and burned at will. Indeed, these men found subtle encouragement for their actions in the lax control of their superiors. Many a homesick soldier, bitter after the long, hard years of war, mindlessly vented his frustrations on all that lay in his path. During the second week of February 1865, the results of the ''foraging'' had left deep scars on the lands of Bamberg County, South Carolina.

Major Drayton Rambert drew back on his reins with the skill of a natural-born equestrian and slowed his mount to a halt at the crest of a hill. He was a striking man, tall, broad shouldered, and hard muscled, his jet black hair and bronze skin contrasting sharply with his piercing ice-blue eyes. He frowned thoughtfully at the dark, clouded sky and, for a moment, gave in to his fatigue. He was weary of this endless traveling through swollen streams and swamps and wet, marshy ground. And he was weary of the lingering smell of smoke, the stench of rotting farm animals slaughtered for no reason at all, and the stark, blackened chimneys rising ghostlike from still-smoldering ruins. He took no pleasure in the burning, the smashing, and the destruction of what once must have been a quiet, gracious way of life. It sickened him. Nevertheless his broad back was straight and his posture erect as he paused on the hilltop and scanned the scarred landscape. Only his eyes mirrored his disgust with the scene that lay before him, a scene which had grown all too familiar in past weeks. He sighed and turned his gaze northward, wondering how far out of his way he would have to go to find food for his regiment. He had taken the assignment to prevent a less scrupulous officer from taking it, and it was certainly not a task he enjoyed. The first wave of ''foragers'' always rushed madly forward, stripping the land to the bone, leaving the legitimate parties who followed to travel miles out of their way just to find an unbutchered cow or chicken. The senseless destruction had made foraging dangerous business too, for the outnumbered Confederates often chose to ambush smaller parties such as this one and were constantly on the lookout for Yankee stragglers. There were countless stories of Yankees being tortured and murdered in retaliation, and most of them were true.

The gray swirls of smoke, some from fires set days before, rose in every direction to meet the angry gray sky. Drayton considered for a moment, then with a slight movement of his hand, directed his men north, toward a patch of untouched land on the horizon. A dozen men took up the determined pace, sensing that their mission would soon be accomplished.

The men who rode behind Major Drayton Rambert had been selected by him specifically, and each would have followed him into hell without ever questioning his sense of direction. A few of them were "old-timers" who had been with Drayton since the first Battle of Bull Run and had seen the stuff of which he was made in countless battles since. Corporal Laird, the only member of the troop who was over forty, liked to tell how the major had taken two bullets at Gettysburg and still managed to bayonet a Reb as the corporal tried to drag him off the field. And that was not the only time Corporal Laird had saved the major's life. Like most of the others, Laird was proud to serve under "Die-hard Drayt," as they affectionately called him behind his back, but the corporal wondered every now and again if Rambert really cared whether he made it home or not.

Men shared a lot when they lived together for months at a time, and Laird knew something personal about just about every man in the company, except Rambert. Jim Crawford, for example, a man almost as old as Laird, who claimed to be a ladies' man and the father of eighteen children . . . only six of them by his wife. Andy Essex was the freckle-faced clown of the group, always ready with a witty comeback, usually managing to keep the men in high spirits in spite of the homesickness and hardships they shared. Privates William and Kelly Riley were brothers as different as night and day, yet close to one another as two brothers could be. Kelly was quiet and even-tempered—he managed to keep hotheaded William in line most of the time. Jamie Clark was the skinny, blond boy fresh from Pennsylvania farm country, the youngest man in the company, just turned sixteen. Privates Jake, Cristoff, Jameson, Hunt, and Swenson were all simple family men brought into the war by a sense of duty or the Enrollment Act of 1863. They were a close-knit group of soldiers, all good fighters, loyal to their country and to each other. "Salt of the earth," Laird liked to think. Men who would gladly leave this god-awful war behind them and take up the lives they'd left behind them.

But Rambert was a different kind of man, a loner. He never spoke of home, or a wife or family, and was pointedly silent whenever the other men spoke of theirs. It was clear from his speech that he'd been well-educated, that he wasn't from rural Pennsylvania, like the others, though he'd enlisted there at the beginning of the war. The few clues Laird had to Rambert's past had come from a single incident just a few months before. The major had received a letter from New York saying that his father had died, that he should resign his commission and return home. That night Rambert had gotten himself very drunk and mumbled things Laird was sure he hadn't meant to share. He talked again and again about a woman named Kathryn, calling her name, breaking down as he cried out for her.

Drayton had ignored the request that he return to New York, but there had been a change in him after the arrival of that letter, an anger seething just beneath his surface, threatening to explode at the slightest provocation. He had always seemed to thrive on combat, on walking that thin, dangerous line between life and death, as if existing on the edge and proving himself gave him his only peace. But it was as if the reminder of home had triggered something inside him, a frustration, a bitterness that made him lash out at life itself.

In Atlanta, after the fighting for that city was finished, Drayton had even gotten himself into a barroom brawl with a newspaper reporter over a loose woman the major hadn't really wanted at all. Of course, the reporter had been one of those flashy, conceited types taken with his own importance, the kind who collected fees from soldiers for mentioning their names and exploits in print. But this man had done nothing to Major Rambert personally, and Laird had been surprised when Drayton challenged his claim to a garish blonde whose eyes said she would willingly accommodate every soldier in the place if each would wait his turn. The major fought for her in that same passionate way he always fought, making an enemy of the newspaperman and three other soldiers who foolishly assumed there was safety in numbers. Drayton had beaten them all, then calmly paid for the damage to the place and turned his back on the woman he'd fought for, walking away from her without a second glance. Laird hadn't really been surprised to see the major walk away, since he'd never seen Drayton take anything but a brief interest in any woman. He was a strange man in that respect, hard and distant, a mystery to everyone. But he was the best man Laird had ever ridden under, a man who possessed a natural ability to lead, a man who always saw to his men's needs before seeing to his own. For that Laird and the others respected and revered him.

Rambert led his men over another rise of land without pausing, but from the hilltop he noted what seemed to be a small outbuilding across a stream and just a few miles to the east. He instinctively checked his direction and proceeded toward it. The air was becoming cool and uncomfortably humid, and Rambert frowned darkly as the first rumbles of distant thunder shook the sky. He prodded his mount to take the first few hesitant steps into the swollen creek, then dug his heels lightly into the horse's stomach until they had nearly crossed the remainder. The horse snorted and tossed his head as he drew closer to dry ground, jerking insistently against the firm hands which held him back until all the others had crossed the stream. The major scowled as he turned his

head to check the progress of his men, feeling a strong
sensation of impending doom. He saw and heard nothing
beyond the splashing hooves and rushing water. Everything was quiet . . . too quiet.

As he reached the clearing on the bank of the stream,
Rambert reached instinctively for his Remington pistol,
and a few of the more observant men did the same. He
had just removed it from its holster when the eerie silence
became a mad cacophony of rapid gunfire, spur-crazed
horses, and Rebel war whoops. Scores of bullets rained
on Rambert's group before most of his men even had a
chance to draw. Almost immediately the major felt a
piercing sting in his left arm. He had drawn his pistol in
time to make an accurate target of one of the Rebs, but
then his horse reared repeatedly in panic, and he was sent
tumbling to the ground in the deadly hailstorm of lead. In
an instant he was on his feet again, assessing the attack-
ers and getting off four quick shots before aiming his last
bullet at a tall, gray-haired soldier who seemed to be the
leader of the group. The old man gasped and clutched
wildly at his chest as a large splotch of dark red spilled
out over his hand. Then his body teetered precariously in
the saddle and dropped with a heavy thud to the ground.

With ammunition all but spent on both sides the forces
engaged each other hand-to-hand, with most of the men
raising sabers; a few others, bowie knives. Drayton
hefted his saber and staved off a blow from a cavalryman
who could not have been more than fifteen years old. The
youth turned and drew his mount closer to the major,
smiling with confidence as he delivered a series of blows,
each of which met the major's gleaming blade with a resounding clank. For several moments Drayton anticipated the younger man's quick, sure movements, and
lifted his saber to negate every one. The boy had been
taught well, but his moves were predictable. Still, Drayton was beginning to tire. Every two-handed lift of his saber sent white hot pain through his wounded arm. He was
bleeding heavily and his muscles were starting to ache

and quiver. He was gasping harder with every breath, and his woolen tunic was soaked with sweat. The ruthless determination that had brought him through a hundred tight corners in the past was flagging, and he knew he could not continue to fend off the heavy-handed attack much longer. He had to take the offensive. But he could not summon the energy to do it.

He let out a weary groan as the cavalryman's horse reared and gave him a moment's rest. For a split second he felt himself succumbing to a strange, peaceful darkness which clouded and blurred his vision. But then he heard it. A terrible shriek of pain from Corporal Laird as he fell from his horse. Laird, the man who had fought beside the major for four long years and saved his life more times than he could remember. In that instant Drayton felt new strength pouring into his weakened muscles. His eyes blazed with fury as his sword evenly met his attacker's, then drew back with lightning swiftness and thrust to lay open the cavalryman's midsection.

The major was pivoting to face Laird's attacker even before he withdrew his bloody blade. After a few parries to feel out his new opponent, Drayton thrust with all his might, sending the saber deeply, deeply into the man's heart. A flood of scarlet splashed on Drayton's hand as the Confederate soldier slumped forward against his horse's neck. Their faces only inches apart, Drayton met his enemy's shocked expression, then stepped aside to allow his lifeless body to drop to the blood-soaked ground. A dangerous, feral brightness still shone in the major's eyes as he whirled, crouched and ready, to survey the scene. But his victim had been the last of the Confederates still mounted, and only one other remained on his feet. That man was wounded, and he swiftly raised his hands over his head when he realized that he was alone.

Drayton stared for a moment at the man, then slowly staggered toward the stream, his saber dropping heavily from a bloodstained hand which had long since gone numb and cold. He swallowed hard and drew a deep

breath as he splashed icy water over his face in an attempt
to clear his vision. Then he stood and turned back to face
the terrible aftermath of the battle. The ground was littered with blue- and gray-clad corpses, and only three
men besides himself were left on their feet: Essex, Hunt,
and Will Riley. Still swaying heavily, the major stumbled toward the body nearest him and began checking for
signs of life. The other men followed his lead but found
all but six of the fallen beyond help. William Riley stared
dazedly at his dead brother's face for a long moment before he dropped to his knees and buried his head in the
lifeless chest, sobbing like a child.

Drayton gave orders to Hunt and Essex to round up the
stray horses while he stripped the clothing from the dead
and made temporary bandages for the badly wounded.
Corporal Laird was still breathing, but just barely. He
had taken a cut in the abdomen and was losing a great
deal of blood. It was doubtful he would make it unless
that bleeding was stopped. Drayton took his time tearing
apart a ragged gray shirt and tunic and wrapping the
strips securely around Laird's wound. It was in doing so
that he noticed that Laird had also been shot twice in the
leg.

Private Cristoff had been hit by a bullet in the chest,
and his breathing was shallow and irregular. Knowing
that his chances were none too good, Drayton bound the
wound hastily and went on to the next. Jim Crawford had
fallen early, grazed by a bullet in the temple. The wound
had rendered him senseless, but once he regained consciousness, the injury probably would not have serious
ramifications. Jamie Clark had been wounded twice in
the shoulder and had also taken a bullet in the chest. His
young, boyish face was ashen from loss of blood, but his
pulse was strong and regular. He had a chance. Two
Rebel prisoners, though wounded, looked able to ride, at
least until they could reach adequate medical help.

By the time all the men had been patched together well
enough to ride and the dead had been buried, daylight

was waning. The rain was beginning to fall in a cold, monotonous drizzle. If the weather had been the slightest bit better, the major would have left Laird and Clark in the care of one or two of his men and gone for the regiment's surgeon. But there was no shelter here, only winter-bare trees and wet ground, and a cavalryman's tent offered no real protection from the elements. They had little choice but to seek out the nearest warmth and shelter and to hope it was not too far off.

Major Rambert let his stallion lead the way up a rise at a brisk walk, working his way toward the outbuilding he had seen from a distance. He was shivering now and could feel his flesh prickling beneath his rain-soaked clothing, but still he proceeded carefully. The ground was far too slick to take chances with the wounded. He reached the outbuilding, a small, abandoned shed of some sort with a gaping hole in the roof. He dismounted to have a look around. A door hung askew on a single rusty hinge, leaving the better part of the interior open to view. It was empty. He looked carefully about the building, until he found what he was looking for. A path of sorts, difficult to discern without the sun's light but there, nonetheless. He remounted and cautiously picked his way along the trail.

Drayton was astonished when he finally saw it. Shadowed by rain and dusk and gloom and tangled by winter-brown ivy, the house was virtually untouched—an awesome, beautiful sight to his tired eyes. The gentle flickering of firelight, reflected now and then on one of the windowpanes, was very different from the roaring flames he had seen this past week. He sighed with momentary relief, then reminded himself that it was not a welcoming fire he saw. This house was someone's home, and he was an invader, an enemy. There would probably be a struggle before the occupants of the house took in his wounded men. Most of the plantation houses which lay in the army's path had been deserted, but the rest were "guarded" by women and an assortment of loyal blacks. There was very little any of them could do—besides beg—to ward off an attack, even by a mere handful of Union soldiers. Still, Drayton was not looking forward to the confrontation.

The path had left them but a short distance from the house. Drayton paused to draw his revolver, then led his men quietly up the remainder of the long, tree-lined drive. The night was silent except for the muffled sound of horses' hooves on the already wet ground. The major brought his horse to a halt and prepared to dismount. At that moment the heavy door was flung open and a small dark figure appeared, silhouetted against a sudden flow of lamplight. The major squinted against the brightness, and just managed to make out the barrel of a shotgun which must have weighed almost as much as the woman who held it. It was aimed directly at his chest. He did not move to dismount and said nothing as his eyes adjusted more fully to the light. Then he noticed that the slender arms which held that gun did not tremble in the least, and he sensed more than saw that the eyes fixed on him did not waver.

"You're trespassing on private property." Ambrosia's voice was smooth and controlled and bore not the slightest trace of fear. "You have the count of ten to take your leave."

The major studied the silhouette for a moment longer, trying to distinguish his opponent's features. The voice was youthful in spite of its cool authority, and he could sense the slightest trace of impatience when it came again. "To the count of ten, I said. One . . . two . . . ."

"We don't intend to leave." The major's deep, resonant voice interrupted her and sent a cold shiver down her spine. "And if you intend to fire that thing at me when you're finished with your counting, I'd like to point out that I also have a weapon. Even if you are the better shot, there will be my men to contend with."

Ambrosia frowned and let her breath out slowly, considering. But the shotgun remained pointed steadfastly at

its target. The acrid smell of smoke had filled the air for
days now, and the tales of horror from nearby plantations
had filtered to Heritage. She had been expecting this,
waiting for it. "What do you want?"

He gave a slight nod of his head as if in a belated, or
perhaps sarcastic, attempt to appear polite. "I'm Major
Rambert, Seventh Pennsylvania Cavalry. My men and I
are in need of food and lodging for the night."

"You can take what food we have. It isn't much. But
you'll have to take it and leave." Her voice shook with
determination. "I won't have Yankees sleeping under
this roof."

"Some of my men are wounded; two of them need immediate attention."

"Then take them elsewhere, Major. They won't get it
here."

"You don't seem to understand, Mrs.—?"

"Miss," she corrected tersely.

He gave a short, stiff smile. "You don't seem to understand, *miss,*" he amended emphatically. "The men
are seriously wounded. They won't last the night in this
rain and cold." His tone was suddenly as hard as tem-
pered steel. "And I don't intend to take them anywhere
else."

The sudden tightening of his sun-etched features
frightened Ambrosia as she had not been frightened in a
long time. She swallowed hard. "Andrew."

A bent old black man whose entire body shook in fear
appeared swiftly at her side. "Get the lamp and bring it
here," she ordered without once taking her eyes off the
major or lowering her gun. "I want to see the major's
wounded for myself."

The old man shuffled back into the house to do her bidding, returning a moment later with an oil lamp, which
blinked and flickered in his trembling hands. He gulped
visibly as he took a step out onto the porch and gingerly
proceeded on toward the major, who waited none too patiently now in the slow, drizzling rain. As the lamp

passed Ambrosia, Drayton took a good look at the woman. She was small of stature, but her features were dramatic rather than delicate: coal-black Indian hair; a firm, square jawline with well-defined chin; a generous mouth; a straight, well-formed nose; a high forehead; and a pair of piercing, catlike eyes which easily dominated all else. There was much of a wild, gypsy maiden in that face, a pronounced, exotic kind of magnetism which mingled favorably with the courageous lift of her chin and the determined gleam in her eyes. She was much younger and much prettier than the major had expected.

As the light drew closer to the soldiers, illuminating the major's face, Ambrosia felt herself tensing, felt her arms rebelling against the weight of the heavy weapon she had supported for so long. She did not perceive the attractiveness in his face at first, only the overwhelmingly cold steadfastness of his features and the confident, almost arrogant lift of his brow. Eyes of a startling, icy blue contrasted sharply with swarthy, weathered skin and jet-black hair, and drew attention away from broad, muscled shoulders and a huge expanse of chest. Those eyes were lit with anger now as the cold rain dripped monotonously from the brim of his hat. Ambrosia swallowed against a growing tightness in her throat and clenched her teeth as she made a brief appraisal of the man, desperately seeking some flaw, some weakness in the eyes which did not leave hers. She could find none.

''Do my wounded meet with your approval, miss?'' he inquired with a hint of sarcasm. She had given no notice to the other soldiers, now well in range of the lamp's light, but she hastily proceeded to survey them now and was just as quickly convinced of their urgent need. She gasped involuntarily when her eyes fell upon one who appeared to be nothing more than a boy with a head of curly yellow hair, a head hanging lifelessly forward on his chest. Then she saw two who wore ragged gray tunics. She frowned and let out a lengthy breath, reluctantly lowering her shotgun. ''Bring them in.''

As she turned and made her way into the house, the major was aware of a shower of protests from another woman inside, who had not yet shown her face. "You can't mean to let Yankees here! In this house! Lord have mercy, Ambrosia, you've gone completely daft!"

"Here's the shotgun, Elly," he heard her reply in the same cool, collected voice she'd used when speaking to him. "You're welcome to keep them out if you're so inclined."

Drayton gave a short smile in spite of himself as he noticed a figure fleeing up the stairs, then let his mind return to the task of moving his wounded men into the room which was being prepared.

"Sheba, gather all the clean linens you can find and bring them into the parlor," Ambrosia ordered as she herself scurried about. "Andrew, light a fire in the parlor and start a kettle of water to boiling in the kitchen. Sally, I'll need Mammy's old healing box and candles, all that you can find. We'll need light . . . lots of it . . . and blankets. . . ."

By the time the last of the wounded had been carried into the parlor, a fire crackled begrudgingly about a stack of damp wood and several candles flickered in the large room. Drayton's first concern was for Corporal Laird, who had regained consciousness and was attempting a smile as the major knelt beside him to check his wounds. He removed Laird's boots and rain-soaked shirt, then wrapped a blanket about his shoulders and stripped him of his trousers. The gash in his abdomen had bled heavily at first, but the bandage seemed to have checked that, at least temporarily. The wound would have to be cleaned and rebandaged, but what worried Drayton more than anything else were the bullet wounds in Laird's upper leg. They had bled very little, but from appearances, both bullets were still lodged deep in the flesh of his thigh or, worse, in the bone. They would have to come out tonight if he was to live. Or the leg would have to come off. Amputation was the safer, easier solution and surely the one the regiment surgeon would prefer. But Drayton could not afford to wait for a doctor to arrive and make that decision. A day, even a few hours' delay could cost a man's life. He closed his eyes tightly for a moment, wrestling with the thought of what had to be done. Then he pulled a second blanket over Laird and moved on to the youngster, Jamie Clark.

Jamie had two clean flesh wounds in the shoulder and a third bullet in the chest. The shoulder wounds had reopened and were dripping bright red through the major's hastily applied bandage. He would have to be first.

Drayton knelt beside Private Cristoff for a moment, then drew a blanket over his face. Without a word he moved on to one of the Confederate soldiers.

The Rebel soldier was wounded in the leg and would have to have that bullet removed. Attention for the others was not as crucial. There were gashes and bruises and a few flesh wounds, but those could easily be tended later.

Again Drayton closed his eyes and his face reflected the turmoil within. When he opened them a moment later, Ambrosia was kneeling at his side, a small wooden box in her lap. He glanced briefly at the contents of the box, at the totally inadequate collection of salves and tools with which he was expected to save three lives. He took the box from her hands and gave a brief smile, shaking his head. But Ambrosia noticed that his expression altered instantly when the young blond soldier stirred and moaned. For a moment she saw something in those cold, blue eyes which spoke of vulnerability, pain, or fear or . . . but it was gone before she could name it. He abruptly returned the box to her and moved to the young man's side. She watched him guardedly for several moments then, wondering if he had dismissed her with the action. He looked cold and forbidding as he checked over the wounded soldier again, but Ambrosia saw that he did not deal roughly with the man's wounds. He rose to his feet, met her gaze, and motioned her to one side of the parlor.

"Three of the men have bullets that will have to come out," he told her quietly. "I will need a table and some rope, a needle and thread, a brazier or a pan of hot coals . . ." He paused. "Some whiskey, if you have it."

Ambrosia gave a small nod, took up the lamp, and led him into the dining room. It was a great room with many large windows and a huge oak table in the room's center designed to seat thirty guests. "I'll have Andrew fetch some rope and I'll get the whiskey and the rest." She made to turn away, then stopped and met his eyes evenly. "I'm willing to help, Major."

His stare was icy. She was young and unmarried and would probably faint at the first sight of a man's naked body. "You can help by staying out of the way." He turned abruptly from her and marched back to the parlor to get Jamie Clark.

Ambrosia stiffened, her temper flaring for a moment. But then she recalled her first days at Wayside Hospital and knew that the major had good reason to doubt her usefulness. She herself had seen dozens of well-meaning females swooning at the sight of blood or running to empty their stomachs as soon as a surgeon touched a knife to a man's flesh. Even she had found it difficult at first to observe some proceedings without feeling nauseous and light-headed. But then, as now, action meant life or death, and that knowledge had overcome any weakness that might have interfered with her abilities. She went after the major and gathered up a stack of clean linens, then followed him and a second soldier as they carried the young blond boy into the dining room. She placed the linens near the table, then hurried to get an almost full bottle of whiskey hidden in her father's study, calling to Andrew to bring a length of rope. Without being told, she brought in a large pan of boiling water and arranged everything she had in the way of tools on a serving cart.

Andrew's wizened face was drawn up like a prune as he shakily handed the major the rope and watched him tie the soldier's unconscious body to the table. He gulped and backed out of the room in horror, white showing all around his dark brown eyes as a thin, sharpened knife was withdrawn from the pan of hot coals and poised above the boy's chest. Private Riley, who had helped carry the patient to the table and was supposed to assist, went white as a sheet and followed behind Andrew, who was stumbling hurriedly out of sight. Ambrosia, who stood near the door, knew then that like it or not, the major would need her help. She slipped silently to take a place near his left elbow. For a moment, she watched him stare at the smooth, shiny blade of the knife—or perhaps he was staring at his hands, she thought, and wondering if he could carry through with what had to be done. Her eyes lifted to study his face, which was covered now with a sheen of sweat. His mouth was quivering slightly, his breathing labored, his eyes ablaze with some emotion closely akin to fear. Ambrosia waited in silence, a part of her reluctantly softening at what she saw in his eyes. At last, he angled the knife and made a precise cut into the boy's flesh.

It was several moments before the boy began to stir and moan, and she saw Drayton wince and swallow hard as he continued. Ambrosia was amazed at the speed with which he probed for the lead, retrieved it, and closed and cauterized the wound. And for all the cold ruthlessness in his face, Rambert's lean, calloused fingers were agile and gentle, and there was a skill to his movements that spoke of medical knowledge and experience. Ambrosia had seen dozens of surgeons that had not had his sureness or speed. She frowned thoughtfully and stole a glance at his face once again. The man was a doctor, she was certain of it. Yet his uniform was that of a cavalryman, and he had no tools of his own.

It was while he was bandaging the second wound that he reached for a damp cloth, only to find it thrust into his searching hand. His eyes lifted in surprise, which quickly changed to annoyance when they met Ambrosia's, but he accepted the cloth without comment and quickly returned to the task at hand. He did not look at her again, nor did he protest when she moved to aid him with cleaning tools or tearing strips of linen. It took less than half an hour to treat all the boy's wounds, and, mercifully, he remained unconscious the entire time. Ambrosia knew full well that his chances for recovery were slim, but it was to the major's credit that he was still alive when they moved him back into the parlor.

"You ain't takin' care o' the Reb before you take care o' Laird, are you?" The words came from Riley, who had paced the parlor while Drayton worked on Jamie Clark.

"Laird's resting," Ambrosia heard the major tell him. "The Reb goes first." Drayton nodded toward the gray-clad soldier and made to draw one of the man's arms about his own shoulder. He waited for Riley to do the same.

"I ain't helpin' t' save no Reb. Not after what they did t' us back there. Jake and Cristoff and—and Kelly . . ." His voice faltered as he thought of his brother, lying in a shallow grave not five miles from where they now stood.

"I won't order you, Riley," Drayton said quietly as Private Essex came to his aid. "Get some rest. I'll need you and Hunt to ride out in the morning."

The Rebel soldier leaned heavily on the major's shoulder as he half limped and was half dragged into the dining room. His eyes were full of fear as Drayton handed him the bottle of whiskey and told him to drink. He said nothing and did as he was told. Ambrosia prayed that the liquor would make him pass out and quickly, since it was the last bottle in the house. The soldier had drunk about half the bottle when his head began to loll, and Drayton took the remainder of the whiskey and told him to lie down. Ambrosia watched as he was bound to the table, then moved nearer to offer her assistance. The bullet had struck the bone of the lower leg. Drayton sliced through his trouser leg and tossed the blood-soaked material aside. He ground his teeth and took a deep breath, almost as if he knew what was going to happen. The moment he put the knife to the man's flesh, shrieks of terror and pain echoed piercingly throughout the house. The man's violent movements made searching for the tiny ball of lead nearly impossible. Ambrosia saw the powerful muscles in the major's arms flexing as he struggled to hold him still. A sudden frantic jerk against the knife sent a stream of dark red blood spurting like a fountain from the man's leg, and she clutched blindly at the spot, trying to keep him from bleeding to death. After what seemed like a lengthy struggle, the soldier finally went limp and silent. Ambrosia helped Drayton clean up the damage, sponging up the blood so that he could proceed, and within minutes the severed vein was expertly ligated with a piece of silk thread. The bullet was retrieved in seconds, and the wound closed and bandaged. When the soldier was lifted from the table, he was deathly pale from loss of blood, but he was still alive and his breathing was regular. Now his recovery was left up to God.

Ambrosia sensed a difference in Major Rambert when the last man, the one they called Laird, was brought into the dining room. "How bad is it?" she heard him ask as Drayton offered him a generous swig of whiskey.

"Bad. Drink as much as you can. You're going to need it." The major's manner was so abrupt that Ambrosia flinched as she busied herself with rinsing off the knife and pincers.

"You—you won't take my leg off, Drayton. Promise me you won't take off my leg."

The major said nothing, forcing a few more ounces of whiskey down the corporal's throat.

"You owe me a favor, Drayton," he gasped out, turning his head to avoid swallowing any more. "I want to collect on it now." He clutched insistently at Drayton's tunic and refused to drink any more. "Promise me!"

Drayton reluctantly met his eyes and gave a nod.

"You—you'll write Grace for me. Tell her I—I . . ."

"I'll write her. Drink." Drayton pushed the bottle toward his mouth. Laird took several gulps this time, then pushed the bottle away, breathing hard. "No. No more. I'll be all right."

Drayton took firm hold of his shoulders and pressed his back against the table. "I'm going to have to tie you down, John. It's for your own good." He wrapped the rope securely about his shoulders and torso, then secured his legs and knotted the rope repeatedly against the table.

"I—It was real good fightin' under you, Die-hard," Laird whispered hoarsely, the whiskey making his words weak and slurred.

"Damn you, Corporal," he muttered as he forced yet another swallow of bourbon down the wounded man's throat. Laird drank until he began to choke, then slowly gave a timorous smile. "Real g-good . . ." His voice trailed off and his chin fell abruptly to his chest.

Drayton took the knife from Ambrosia and placed it in the brazier until the metal gleamed red and hot, wishing all the while he had not made that promise to Laird. Ambrosia frowned at him curiously. She had never seen a doctor so particular about his scalpel before. Most of them simply wiped the filthy blade on their coat and went on to the next patient. He glanced up at her as he slowly withdrew the blade from the coals. "An old Indian medicine man's trick," he said to himself as much as to her. "Let's hope the evil spirits are appeased with the ritual."

She stared at him in shock. He was talking utter nonsense. But there was no time for hesitation as he moved the knife to open the flesh of Laird's thigh. The corporal's limbs jerked rigid in response to the sudden, intense pain, then dropped lifelessly on the table. Drayton breathed a sigh of relief as he probed the wound, easily locating the first bullet in a matter of seconds. It was the other bullet which gave him trouble. For what seemed an eternity he probed the wound, then cut and probed again.

The tiny ball of lead seemed to have vanished into the bone and muscle of the thigh.

Drayton swore under his breath as Ambrosia mopped at the blood from the wound so that he might make yet another probe. Sweat was pouring from his brow, his face was set with tension, and his eyes were a frightening blaze of blue. She saw him hesitate and wince with total concentration as he drove deeper than ever before. Then slowly, cautiously, he inserted the pincers, twisting them until the tiny bullet, clutched tightly in its jaws, was lifted from the wound. Ambrosia heaved an audible sigh of relief and she saw the major let out his breath too. The worst was over now. He handed Ambrosia the pincers and continued, closing and sewing the severed flesh, then bandaging.

It was after midnight when Laird was finally settled on a makeshift pallet near the fire, and well past one before the other men's injuries had been properly tended. Ambrosia followed the major about the parlor, tearing bandages and applying ointments after he had cleaned and checked the wounds. He said little to her beyond terse instructions now and again, which she promptly obeyed.

When they had finished he made a final check of Laird, then rose and left the parlor, his shoulders sagging with weariness for the first time since his arrival. Ambrosia paused as she gathered up her tools to watch him walk away. Then she frowned thoughtfully and hurried after him.

He had settled himself in a dining room chair and had almost finished what little was left of the whiskey. The bottle was yet in his hand, but his eyes were closed, his head bent.

"Major?"

His eyes flew open and Ambrosia knew a sudden fear. There was something about the way he looked at her that made her feel small and vulnerable, as she had seldom felt before. "Your—your arm needs tending," she said in a shaky voice which was totally foreign to her. "Before I put these things away . . ."

He glanced briefly at the tear in his sleeve, a gash which had long since dried. He lifted the bottle to his mouth and muttered, "It's only a flesh wound. I'll see to it later myself."

Ambrosia straightened her back. "Suit yourself, Doctor."

She turned her back on him, only to be whirled about to face him again by an iron-clad grasp on her arm. The strength of his fingers and the look in his eyes caused her to go pale for an instant, and she felt a strange weakness in her knees. "The name is Rambert," he said sharply. *"Major* Rambert."

"Suit yourself, Major Rambert," she repeated with noticeably less bravado, but managing to square her shoulders and keep her head high. Their eyes locked for a moment, each refusing to yield any ground. Finally he loosened his hold on her and gave a slight smile. "You're right, Mrs.—" He frowned, trying to remember. *"Miss,"* he amended. "What did that slave call you? Ambrosia? Yes, that was it. Ambrosia."

"The name is Lanford," she told him curtly.

His smile taunted her and he did not repeat her proper name. "Ambrosia suits you, you know. Though it is a bit long. Is that what your beaux call you? Ambrosia? Or do they shorten it to Amy?" He cocked his head thoughtfully and let his eyes roam familiarly over the length of her. "Amy . . . yes, it's much more appropriate."

She glared at him, feeling outraged at his presumptuousness and furious with herself for having offered to help him at all. He was her enemy; he had forced his way into her home. She ought to feel triumph at the thought of his going through life with an empty sleeve. "Do you want me to tend your arm or not?" she said through gritted teeth, her green eyes glowing with open hostility.

He held those eyes for a moment, almost as if he sensed that her anger was not entirely directed toward him, almost as if he enjoyed her discomfort. Then he gave a slight shrug. "You seem a capable nurse."

Ambrosia said nothing as she knelt beside the chair and placed the healing box on the floor near her knees. She lifted a scissors to the sleeve of his tunic, only to have him stop her. "No. I don't want it cut. It can be mended." Ambrosia held her breath until he released her hand, the mere touch of those long, lean fingers sending a current of warm awareness up the length of her arm.

He stood and unbuttoned the coat slowly. His eyes held hers, lighting with amusement when she blushed and turned away. She had seen two men stark naked in the last few hours and had tended them without the least show of embarrassment. But her face now reflected total innocence, and he felt a sudden admiration for this young woman who had put her inhibitions aside for the sake of another's life. He grimaced as he pulled the cloth free of the wound, then tossed his clothing aside and sat down again, clearing his throat loudly as he did so.

Ambrosia drew a deep breath to bolster her courage, then timidly raised her eyes only as far as the wound. But what she saw was enough to make her gasp. His shoulders and chest were riddled with tiny scars and large ones, and the strength in the muscles of his bare arms and torso was frighteningly apparent. His flesh was lean, and there was a hardness to it that made her know he could easily force her to do his bidding, in spite of his weariness. She swallowed hard and went about her work, making sure not to meet his eyes again. Cautiously applying a dampened cloth until the tiny bits of cloth and caked blood fell away from the wound, she applied an ointment and folded a square of linen to cover it lightly. She tore at a long strip of clean cloth and rose to her feet to bind it tightly around his arm, painfully aware all the while of his eyes upon her. She could not understand why her cheeks felt so hot, why his eyes caused her such anxiety. She knotted the bandage with an abrupt jerk that made the major wince, then quickly stooped to gather her things and take her leave. The major had other ideas. She had scarcely taken a step before he rose to block her path. Ambrosia's fingers tightened about the healing box, and her eyes hesitantly rose from the crisp black hair which covered his chest to meet Drayton's insistent stare.

"There—there's food in the kitchen," she told him in a small, breathless voice. "Sheba's seen to feeding your men . . . the ones that can eat, that is—"

"You're afraid of me, aren't you?" he interrupted her, narrowing his eyes.

Ambrosia squared her shoulders and stuck out her chin, which was barely as high as his chest. "Me? Afraid of a Yankee?" She gave a short laugh which was none too convincing before she tried to sidestep him. But again he blocked her escape.

"No," he agreed slowly. "You're not afraid of me because I'm a Yankee. But there's something about me that frightens you—"

"I am not afraid of you," she snapped hotly, her anger finally adding strength to her voice. "But that doesn't mean I feel comfortable about having you in my home, either. I would have to be a fool to trust a Yankee while the smell of your destruction still hangs so heavy in the air." Her eyes flashed with fury as she faced her enemy.

"You're quite a woman, Ambrosia," he said quietly, to her astonishment. He smiled at her again, a smooth, easy smile that made her tense again. "I never would have guessed that a woman so young and beautiful could—" He frowned suddenly, as if the thought of the wounded in the next room troubled him a great deal. "I thank you for the men," he finished a moment later. "As well as for myself."

He stepped aside then to let her pass, which she hurriedly did. The hour was late and she was bone tired and anxious to have her rest. She spoke briefly with Sheba and Andrew about keeping watch over the wounded and more importantly, over the major, giving specific instructions that she should be summoned immediately in the event of any emergency. She placed the healing box in plain view on a table in the parlor, then hurried up the stairs to her room, closing the door behind her and letting out a long sigh of relief.

"Ambrosia? Are you all right? Did they—?"

Ambrosia opened her eyes with a start to see Elly's terrified face. "No. They didn't hurt me. I'm well enough. Just very tired." She let out another sigh and began unbuttoning her dress, grimacing at the bloodstains which covered the bodice and skirt. It would need to be washed out first thing in the morning.

"What were you doing down there all this time? I heard that man screaming. It was terrible! Were they torturing him? Did you see what they were doing to him?"

Ambrosia poured fresh water into the washbowl and splashed her face and arms. "The man had a bullet in his leg. Major Rambert took it out."

Elly raised a brow. "Major Rambert, is it?" A moment later, realization dawned and her eyes widened in horror. "You watched him do it?" she whispered.

"I helped him do it."

"Lord have mercy! You actually helped save a Yankee's life!" she said incredulously.

"Two of the men are Confederates," Ambrosia told her quietly, not allowing her uneasiness to show.

Elly sank helplessly into the nearest chair. "If your papa ever finds out about this, he'll probably disown you!"

Ambrosia bit her lip and wondered briefly if indeed her father would ever be able to forgive her, or if she would ever forgive herself. "I'm tired, Elly. I'm going to bed."

"With Yankees in his house? You'd sleep with Yankees in this house?" She watched aghast as Ambrosia slipped out of her petticoat and walked toward her bed, clothed only in a worn chemise.

"Andrew and Sheba are keeping watch," she said absently, suddenly remembering the way the major had looked at her and feeling uneasy about sleeping with him in the same house. She shook off the thought as she settled her head comfortably on her pillow. Almost at once she felt her muscles go limp. For a few minutes she listened to Elly rant about the terrible things that were sure to happen if she dared to go to sleep, then she yawned, pulled the pillow over her head and heard nothing more.

Chapter 3

Ambrosia woke at her usual hour just before daybreak to the noisy chirping of birds. As the layers of a deep sleep slipped gradually away, she turned her head and noticed that the sky had cleared. She reluctantly forced her feet to the floor. She tensed as her eyes caught sight of movement across the room, then let out her breath when she recognized Elly, who stirred uncomfortably in her sleep in a worn upholstered chair. She was still fully clothed.

Quietly Ambrosia began gathering up her soiled clothing and went to splash her face with water. She stifled a yawn as she lifted the pitcher, then frowned and bit her lip thoughtfully, the pitcher still poised in the air. It was still very early, and there was a good chance that everyone in the house still slept. If that were so, then it might be possible to slip away for a few moments of privacy without being missed. Ambrosia eyed Elly and vented a weary sigh, feeling the need for some time alone. And the brief ablutions of the night before had hardly begun to free her skin of the sticky residue of blood. With a burst of decision, she threw on a clean dress, made a bundle of fresh undergarments, tied on her prunella shoes, and left the room. She stopped at the foot of the stairs just long enough to see Andrew's gray head nodding sleepily in the chair which blocked the parlor door. Several men were snoring loudly, but no one stirred.

Tiptoeing gingerly to the dining room, Ambrosia let out a tiny sigh of relief to see Major Rambert dozing in a chair, his long legs extended to full length in front of him. All was quiet.

With great care Ambrosia opened the door and slowly slipped out of the house, feeling the cool freshness of the crisp morning air on her face. She paused and smiled, savoring the moment and the morning, the precious time of peace and solitude, of escape from all that would trouble her for the remainder of the day. She eagerly ran down the front drive toward a private place she used on occasion these days, when there were so few slaves to work at all, much less haul water for a hot bath. The pond was not too far from the house, but it was well down a winding path through the woods and offered complete seclusion.

Ambrosia lost no time in removing her clothing and slipping with a gasp into the frigid water. Her skin tingled with the cold as she vigorously scrubbed with the tiny chip of soap she had hoarded from the bars she had made herself the years before. Then there had been an ample supply of lard. It seemed like centuries since she had enjoyed the luxuries of hot water and scented bath potions, and as the memory of such comforts whisked through her mind, she thought of how much she had changed in the past two years. Gone were the slight curves of adolescence, and in their place, finally, the firm contours of maturity. Her breasts had blossomed to a round perfection and her hips curved in a definitely feminine line from a trim waist. Her limbs were still thin, yet shaped and firmed by hard work. If only maturity had come earlier, she thought as her fingers drifted over the body she so seldom considered, then perhaps Ledger might have noticed that she was more than "just a child." She scowled and pushed the thought from her mind. It would have made no difference, since Melissa was still more attractive and appealing than Ambrosia could ever hope to be. She lathered her hair with unwarranted vigor to banish any memories that remained behind, then hurriedly rinsed the last of the soap from her hair.

Ambrosia was shivering when she left the water and she hurriedly sought the warmth of her clothing. Her teeth chattered as she pulled on her chemise, the worn cotton clinging stubbornly to her still-wet skin. She drew on her pantalets and a single petticoat, which she tied about her waist, then rubbed briskly at the flesh on her arms, which was still raised with the chill. She tossed her plain homespun gown over her head and bent down to pull on her much-mended stockings and tie the lacings which held together her prunella shoes. She had knotted the second when something made her start. Her head jerked up and she jumped to her feet, panting with fear and anger. Not three feet from where she stood was the Yankee major, one broad shoulder propped casually against the trunk of a large tree, his cool blue eyes meeting her panicked expression with a calm that made her furious. A hot vibration of utter rage shot through her. He took a step toward her, his mouth opening to say something as if he were totally unaware of her anger. Before he could utter a sound, her hand drew back with the swiftness of a cobra and met the flesh of his cheek with a resounding smack. Far from easing her hostility, the shock which registered on his face merely added fuel to an already raging fire. ''Filthy Yankee!'' She drew back without a pause to strike him again, and again and—

Ambrosia drew a sharp breath as Drayton seized her wrist tightly and prevented her hand from meeting its target. In one abrupt movement she was drawn flush against his broad chest. Her mind rang with a hundred words of violence and hatred she'd heard men use when they'd thought her out of earshot, but none of them seemed vile enough to express her humiliation at this moment. ''Bastard! Union dirt!''

Her eyes spit sparks of fury as she jerked violently against his hold, stamping her foot hard on his instep and lunging forward to bite whatever part of his flesh her teeth happened to make contact with. The major had fully expected her to be angry, but he was stunned by the savagery in her reaction. There was extraordinary strength in her slender limbs, fueled by a fierce determination he had seen in few men. His admiration for her raised a notch, but he was none too happy about the healthy condition of her teeth.

"Yankee filth!" she gasped out as he drew her arms sharply behind her back and twisted to avoid being bitten again. He moved his foot just in time to miss another assault on his instep, only to have her lift her knee in a vicious attack on his groin. Pure instinct made him deflect the leg not an instant too soon, but she had scored a direct hit on his temper with the attempted maneuver, and he let her know immediately that he had had enough. In a single motion he pressed her back onto the damp ground, knocking the breath from her lungs. His hands grasped her wrists high above her head, and his legs held hers fast beneath his own. With considerable pain, she drew a deep, sharp breath and let it out in a low, throaty groan, straining with all her might, flexing every muscle in her body with every ounce of her strength. But her efforts gained her nothing. He yielded not the slightest measure.

She gasped another breath and tried again, her face tightening and growing deep red with the effort as she snarled and twisted with all that was in her. She felt the frustration exploding inside her, fueling her with a surge of energy to lurch against his hold. She fully expected to be free. Yet his flesh did not budge. His fingers remained about her wrists like iron manacles, and the weight of his chest pressing against her breasts was almost unbearable. With a half-sob of defeat, she gave up struggling and closed her eyes, bracing herself for what was to come.

"Ambrosia." The voice was low now and soft, and the smoothness of it touched her ears like velvet. She

squeezed her eyes even more tightly shut and tried to ignore the odd, almost pleasant quivering she felt in her
stomach.

"*Miss* Ambrosia," he amended.

Her green eyes flew open, snapping with indignation.
"Do what you will and be done with it, you filthy Yankee pig!"

She saw a frown flit across his brow, then a spark of
amusement as his eyes wandered from her face to the
gaping bodice of her dress, where little of her anatomy
was left to the imagination. She instinctively pitched
against him again with renewed resolve to be free. His
hold tightened fiercely as she did so, until she could no
longer even breathe, until the sudden hunger in the blue
eyes made terror clutch at her heart. Some of her fear
must have been apparent to him, for he freed her a moment later and rose to his feet, offering her a hand to help
her do the same. She ignored the hand and stood shakily,
turning her back to him as much to hide her confusion as
to right her disheveled clothing and fasten the front of her
dress. He moved to pull a twig from her tangled hair. She
hurriedly jerked away.

He shrugged indifferently and lowered his hand. "I
did not come here to have my way with you," he said
with a touch of amusement, "though I admit that the
prospect is most tempting. . . ."

Ambrosia reached down to grab the last of her things
and spun about to leave, hoping that he hadn't noticed the
flush in her cheeks.

He took hold of her arm and prevented her from leaving. "Hear me out," he said firmly, in a different voice
which expected no argument.

She raised her chin and ground her teeth, offering no
resistance but letting a murderous fire leap from her narrowed eyes. Drayton drew a deep breath and scowled,
unused to such obvious mutiny. "I followed you here
this morning," he said coldly, carefully articulating each

word, "because I thought you just might be leaving the house to meet a friend."

She gave a skeptical snort and tossed her head. The major's brow darkened dangerously. "Like it or not, I'm acutely aware that you are the enemy. It would be most foolish of me to trust a Rebel."

"After you followed me here," she flung back indignantly, "it must have been obvious even to one of your dull wit, Major, that I intended to meet no one. There is no excuse for—for—"

"For taking pleasure at the sight of a beautiful woman?"

She was stunned speechless for a moment, even more so when she felt his fingers loosen and lightly caress her arm. "None," he answered low and husky, "except that I am a man." The eyes which met hers left no doubt as to his meaning.

Ambrosia swallowed hard, suddenly aware of her vulnerability. "Let me go."

"I'm not finished yet." His eyes hardened and his voice was once again cold, demanding. Ambrosia was relieved. "I do not trust you, Miss Lanford. I cannot afford to trust you. I do not want you or any of your people to leave the house without my permission. Not until after my men and I have safely left the premises."

She gave him a stiff smile. "I'll keep the suggestion in mind, Major."

Before he could catch himself, his brows arched in surprise and his fingers tightened painfully around her arm. "That's an order, Miss Lanford."

Ambrosia said nothing, but the arrogant lift of a single brow made Drayton's temper soar. For a long moment he considered slapping her. Had she been a man, he wouldn't have thought twice about thrashing her to within an inch of her life. But Ambrosia Lanford was a woman—very much a woman. And something in those hard green eyes told him that she would never be broken with a beating. Her vulnerability lay elsewhere, if she were vulnerable at all.

"It is unfortunate," he said slowly, letting a single finger drift over her cheek and noticing that she flinched visibly at his touch, "that we were cast as enemies in this war."

"Is there anything else, Major?" she snapped frigidly, not understanding why his touch made her shake inside. She forced herself to remain steadfast and tried not to show her relief when he heaved a long sigh and dismissed her.

"That's all."

Without another word, Ambrosia whirled and hurried toward the house, her fingers combing at the moist dirt and leaves that clung to her long, damp hair, her palms brushing at the mud on her skirt. The house was still quiet when she returned to hurry up the stairs and change into her very last gown. Elly was still sleeping peacefully when she slowly closed the door of the bedroom and tiptoed back downstairs toward the parlor. Andrew was yet dozing in his chair, and the first of the men were just beginning to stir uncomfortably beneath the brightness of the eastern sky. Ambrosia placed a light hand on Andrew's shoulder and whispered his name. The old man sprang to his feet in a flash, fumbling furiously to cock the shotgun. Ambrosia ducked as the barrel of the gun bounced dangerously about in her direction, then covered her ears and winced, waiting for the explosion. A moment later, when it did not come, she cautiously peaked out at Andrew and met a pair of embarrassed brown eyes. "Ain' nobody caused no trouble heah, Miz Ambrosia," he vowed contritely. He lowered the shotgun slowly, and Ambrosia let out the breath she had been holding. "Ah maked sure dos Yankees stayed put. Ah sho' did." He gave a weary smile and Ambrosia could not bring herself to scold him for allowing Major Rambert to slip past.

"Thank you, Andrew. Go along now and get some sleep."

Andrew stifled a yawn and scratched his shoulder wearily. "Sheba done been up half de night too. She be needin' some help wi' feedin' all des extra mouths. An' ah don' think ah'd sleep a wink anyways, wi' Yankees in Massah Jackson's house." He shook his head and rolled his eyes heavenward. "Lawd! If Massah Jackson evah—"

Andrew was cut short when the front door opened, drawing his attention. He blinked, his eyes like saucers as they moved from Major Rambert to the dining room and back again. He would have sworn no one left the house all night! He gulped and tossed a glance at Ambrosia, whose eyes were momentarily locked with the major's cold blue ones. Andrew frowned, belatedly noting Ambrosia's damp hair and the pink color that rose in her cheeks. He didn't like it, not one bit.

"My men will be wanting breakfast," Drayton said finally, breaking an uncomfortable silence.

"Yes, *sir*," Ambrosia responded sarcastically. The shakiness she had felt when he touched her had gone now, and she was angry with herself for ever having felt it. He was just a filthy Yankee, after all, while she was a Lanford. She would not allow herself to forget that again, no matter what he did.

The last of the ham was retrieved from the smokehouse and every egg that had been collected from that and the two previous mornings was set to sizzling in Sheba's skillet. Ambrosia and Sally saw to the gruesome task of scrubbing the dining room clean of any signs of the night before, and soon the major, his men, and the one conscious Confederate prisoner settled around one end of the table to breakfast.

Ambrosia tried not to think about the vast quantities of food being used up on a single meal, though that was nearly impossible after so many months of careful rationing. She clenched her teeth as the soldiers ate their fill, finding herself without an appetite but grateful for the sack of meal which had been wrapped in oilcloth and buried with a crock of sorghum just last week. With a reluctant nod to Andrew, she gave approval to Private Riley's demand for a fourth slice of ham, remembering the way Andrew had once given a nod to his boys to refill her mother's fine crystal water goblets or to clear a cluttered table. Not so very long ago her father had sat at the head of this table, and the chairs had been occupied by gentlemen in starched and proper attire, by ladies whose skirts had fallen in bright rainbows about the floor.

Ambrosia's eyes grew distant and wistful for a moment, until they met the major's and flared with renewed defiance. She was uncomfortable when he stared at her that way, as if he were trying to see something beneath her expression, some part of her that she had no intention of revealing to anyone. She felt relieved when his gaze finally wavered, caught by a movement in the hall. In the next moment all eyes lifted to take in the new arrival, and Ambrosia noticed that a tiny gleam of satisfaction lit in Elly's eyes at the attention.

Elly wore her best dress, a simple, light, printed muslin with tiny blue and yellow flowers. She had taken care to comb her hair, which fell in saucy brown curls over one shoulder, though her expression was anything but inviting. The smell of ham and eggs frying must have finally given her the courage to face the Yankees, Ambrosia thought wryly, and true to her nature, Elly could not help but flaunt herself in front of anything in trousers.

With a noticeable lift of her nose, Elly strode haughtily past the men and on toward the kitchen. Private Riley seemed to suddenly loose interest in his fourth slice of ham. He rose to his feet and moved to block her path. "Well, well. What have we here?" He let his eyes dip familiarly to Elly's generous bosom before rising to meet her disdainful glare.

"Out o' my way, you filthy Yankee," she spat.

Ambrosia's eyes widened a bit at that. She had never

known Elly to be anything but flirtatious with a man, any man.

"Let her alone, Riley." Rambert's words were low and calm, but the authority in them rang crystal clear.

With barely a hesitation, Riley settled abruptly back in his chair and watched Elly take her leave. Ambrosia cocked her head in curiosity, waiting for Riley to voice some objection, for his eyes sparkled with mutiny. "Didn't mean no harm, Major," he said at length, after he had taken his time cleaning his plate. "Jus' meant t' make the lady's acquaintance is all." His mouth curved into a smile which did not reach his eyes. ". . . Since you don't seem too eager t' share the other one with the rest of us." His eyes flicked suggestively over Ambrosia and she straightened indignantly at the insinuation. The major said nothing, but Ambrosia could see that he was not amused. Apparently something in his eyes conveyed that same impression to Riley, for the private thought the better of saying any more.

Ambrosia and Sally cleared the dining room table as soon as the men had finished with their meal. Ambrosia watched guardedly as the three Yankee soldiers, Riley, Hunt, and Essex, packed their gear and prepared to take their leave. Both the major and Private Crawford accompanied the men to the stable while the three saddled their horses. It was the opening Ambrosia had been waiting for. As quietly as possible she slipped into the parlor, hoping for a word with the one conscious Confederate prisoner while the Yankees were otherwise occupied.

The prisoner had been bound hand and foot, but was seated comfortably in the only remaining parlor chair, staring distantly out the window. Ambrosia watched Corporal Laird stir restlessly for a moment. She tossed a nervous glance over her shoulder, but neither Crawford nor the major was anywhere in sight. She moved nearer to the captive.

"Three of the Yankees are leaving now, Captain Rand," she told him in a low voice after a perfunctory introduction. "That means we stand a much better chance of taking them."

The soldier could hardly conceal his surprise. "And what exactly are we to do with them, ma'am, once we take them?"

"We hold them prisoner," she returned firmly. "We use them to keep any more Yankees from coming here, and burning—" She stopped short. The man was actually smiling at her.

"They're only the first, Miss Lanford," he said with a weary sigh. "There's no way to stop them."

Ambrosia opened her mouth to protest, but he cut her off before she began. "Do you have any idea how many Yankees are camped between here and Savannah? Thousands! Tens and hundreds of thousands and more . . . all of them armed and fed and well trained. Do you think for a moment we could hold them off with four Yankee hostages? Two of them half-dead?" He gave a short laugh. "And that's if we managed to catch that Yankee major off guard, which wouldn't be as simple as you seem to think."

"I'm not afraid of him," she said slowly, a bright gleam of accusation in her eyes.

The captain drew a long breath and spoke without guilt. "You ought to be afraid. You didn't see him fight, ma'am, but I did. Saw him kill a boy not old enough to shave without blinking an eye. Saw him drive his saber so deep in the colonel's heart that it came clear through the other side."

Ambrosia gulped at that and the soldier knew that his point had been made. "Beggin' your pardon, Miss Lanford, but as I was saying, I saw enough to make me wary of crossing a man like that. Even if I were a woman, I'd watch my steps real close-like." The defiant courage in Ambrosia's green-gray eyes died slowly away, and at length the soldier let out a sigh. "It ain't easy to admit it's over," he said softly, sadly. "But the way I see it, it just ain't worth dying for something that's already dead.''

Her eyes sparked with renewed rebellion as she rose to her full height and shook her head. "It's not over, Captain Rand. It will never be over. Not while a single loyal Confederate lives and breathes."

The soldier met her hard green eyes for a moment, then slowly looked away. Too many people felt as she did, and they would only make the inevitable take that much longer. He watched her as she turned from him and stiffly exited the parlor, hoping that she would at least have the good sense not to try the major's patience. She just couldn't know how dangerous a man he was.

Chapter 4

The remainder of the morning passed without incident. Sheba and Andrew were ordered to catch up on lost sleep, while Sally helped Ambrosia tend to the watering and setting out of the seedlings in the warmth of the early spring sun. Then there were soiled blankets and bandages from the evening before to be laundered and hung out to dry. Now and again as she went about her work, Ambrosia was aware of being under close surveillance, an awareness that filled her with anger and frustration. The Yankees had almost made her feel like a prisoner on her own land, Lanford land, and her only satisfaction came from knowing that she had conveniently forgotten to ask the major's permission to leave the house.

It was nearing sunset when she and Sally took down the laundry, folding clothing and blankets and rolling long strips of linen, some of them still badly stained in spite of their best efforts to clean them. Ambrosia returned to the house heavily laden and began sorting and putting away the laundry, while Sally went to cover the plants against the sudden, sharp chill of dusk. Ambrosia had just begun to set the table when Sally flew breathlessly into the dining room, her large brown eyes wide with excitement. Ambrosia dropped the silverware on the table and went to place both hands on the girl's shoulders. "Sally, what is it? Calm down now and tell me."

Sally waved both her hands about in the air, then bit her lip and shook her head as she tossed a long, cautious glance over her shoulder. "It Josiah!" she whispered breathlessly. "It Josiah!"

"Josiah? Where?"

"Out deah, Miz Ambrosia." She pointed toward the stables and Ambrosia instinctively took a step in that direction. "I told him 'bout de Yankees," Sally whispered. "An' he say he ain' comin' no closah. He say he seed 'nough warrin' an' Yankees fo' his life."

Ambrosia's eyes remained calm, but her brow pulled deeply with worry. Josiah had never before come home without her father. Yet Sally had said nothing about Jackson Lanford, only that Josiah was home. And if he had come home alone, then it must mean that her father was badly wounded, or . . .

"I'll be back in a few minutes, Sally. Before the Yankees have a chance to notice. You finish setting the table."

Ambrosia all but ran toward the stable, which was several hundred feet from the house. She threw open the door and raced inside, blinded momentarily by the cool darkness of the interior. She stopped short, whirling about as she heard the creak of a wooden floorboard.

"Miz Ambrosia?" The voice was low and cautious, but it made a smile of recognition break across her face. And as he stepped toward her and her eyes adjusted to the light, she saw all the memories of her childhood in those few brief moments.

"Josiah! Oh, is it really you? I can hardly believe my eyes!" Her green eyes brightened with tears as she let them feast on the familiar broad shoulders and huge brown eyes. He had always been a big man, with a wonderful, vibrant voice and a gentle, proud way about him. He had felt privileged to accompany Jackson off to war, and like many blacks who accompanied prestigious Confederate officers, he had been outfitted with a fancy uniform of his very own. Now that uniform was in utter rags upon his back. And the hint of secret inner pride that had always lit his large brown eyes was gone too. Ambrosia stared up at him, her smile fading as she breathlessly searched his face. "Papa?"

The dark eyes brimmed with grief, and the hope in hers faded. Ambrosia's stance wavered for a moment, though she was hardly aware of it. Josiah gripped her forearms to steady her. "He spoke of you at the last," Josiah told her. "He said I was t' come home t' you, t' be help t' you here . . . at Heritage."

Ambrosia drew a deep breath and straightened. "I shall need your help, Josiah. I shall need God's help." She swallowed hard and raised her eyes, prepared for the worst. "Ledger?"

"I ain't seen Massah Ledgah for a long time now. But he was just fine last summer. Just fine. He—"

Josiah's head jerked up at the ominous sound of a gun being cocked. Instinctively he made a move for his weapon, but he stopped at the sound of the low, cool voice threaded with steel. "I wouldn't if I were you."

Wary brown eyes locked then with the major's blue ones. The major gave a slight nod of his head and Josiah obligingly stepped away from Ambrosia. "Now the gun. Toss it out here, slow and easy. And don't make any quick moves."

The blue eyes never wavered all the while Josiah considered whether or not to surrender his weapon.

"Do as he says, Josiah," Ambrosia ordered quietly.

He dropped the weapon immediately at her order, and Rambert's predatory stance relaxed the slightest bit. "Who are you? What are you doing here?"

Josiah opened his mouth to respond, but before he had a chance, Ambrosia stepped forward. "His name is Josiah. And he is here because Heritage is his home." Her green eyes glittered rebelliously as she ground out the words.

Josiah felt himself shiver as the major drew a lengthy breath and exhaled very slowly. He could feel the tension heavy and dangerous in the air and wondered just what the major would do if Ambrosia pushed him too far.

"Can you talk, Josiah?" His eyes slipped from Ambrosia's to the black's.

"Yessuh."

"You are wearing a Confederate uniform."

Josiah lifted his chin and squared his shoulders. "Yessuh."

"And you were armed." The black man trembled visibly as he forced a nod. "Now, I'm asking you again, what are you doing here?"

"He is here because—" The retort died on Ambrosia's lips as the major flashed her a single, silencing glare. He would not hesitate to use his gun if she pushed him any further. She was suddenly sure of it.

"Josiah will answer for himself."

Josiah looked uncomfortably from one to the other, wondering why Ambrosia was playing such a dangerous game with this man. "Well, suh, Massah Jackson, he—"

"You have no master, Josiah. President Lincoln signed a paper that made you a free man."

Ambrosia stiffened at that, and Josiah gulped and shifted his weight. "Yessuh," he mumbled.

"Go on, Josiah. What about this Jackson fellow?"

Fire leapt in Ambrosia's eyes at the casual reference to her father, and Josiah could have sworn that the Yankee felt some satisfaction at her reaction.

"Well, suh," he began again. "I—I came back home t' tell Miz Ambrosia that—that Massah—that is, that her father—that he—he passed on." Josiah swallowed hard and met the major's cold blue eyes with a proud kind of sorrow in his large brown eyes.

"You will be considered a prisoner of war, Josiah,"

the major informed him curtly. "And you will be shot if you try to escape."

He moved to scoop up the gun Josiah had tossed to the ground, then straightened, and with a jerk of his head, ordered the black man to proceed in front of him to the house.

Few words were spoken as the two Yankees and their prisoners ate dinner that evening, but time and again Drayton's eyes sought Ambrosia's and found them elsewhere. He observed her performing her duties with total detachment, even while the other girl, Elly, made a show of sobbing endlessly over the news of Jackson Lanford's death. There were tears in Sally's eyes as well, and the old man Andrew used the back of his hand to wipe at his eyes when he thought no one was watching. But Drayton saw no tears in Ambrosia's eyes; something inside her would allow no such weakness. And it was that same something that made her unafraid of challenging him, even when it was reckless and foolhardy to do so.

"Crawford," the major said suddenly.

Private Crawford, who was the only one interested in his dinner that evening, paused to glance at the major as he took a bite of crusty bread. "Yes, sir?"

"There's a cupola on the roof. From it you can see for miles around." Drayton paused thoughtfully. "It's the best place for standing watch."

Crawford returned a conversational nod, then took another bite of bread. Drayton lifted a heavy silver spoon and examined it carefully as he spoke. "The men could be here as soon as tomorrow morning, or it could be another three or four days. And there's always the possibility that they won't return at all, or that we'll have other guests before they come back." He paused and laid the spoon to the side of his untouched plate. "From here on out, one of us stands watch while the other stays with the wounded."

Crawford sighed contentedly as he leaned back in his

chair and pushed his plate away. "I'm ready as I'll ever be, Major."

"Good. I'll relieve you in a few hours, Crawford."

The major left the table then and returned the prisoners to the parlor. Crawford followed a few moments later, going upstairs to take the first watch.

Ambrosia's eyes lifted briefly when Major Rambert returned to the dining room alone, just minutes after he had left with the others. Ambrosia returned her full attention to clearing the table, trying to ignore his presence, hoping that she had misread the belligerent expression in his eyes. She dreaded a second confrontation with him after what had happened this afternoon. But she knew that she had challenged the order he had given her, and that he was not the type of man who allowed anyone to challenge his authority.

"I would have a word with you, Miss Lanford."

Ambrosia paused for a moment, her worst fears confirmed by his brittle tone of voice. Without meeting his eyes, she reached for another plate and separated it from the soiled cutlery. "Yes?"

"Alone."

Ambrosia felt herself tensing, but she willed away her anxiety. "In a moment, Major."

"Now."

Her eyes lifted abruptly at the sharpness of the command. The cold blue eyes held hers, and she slowly laid aside the dish in her hand and wiped her hands on her apron. "Finish with the dishes, Sally. I'll be back to sweep the floor."

Ambrosia held her breath as she strode stiffly past him, pausing to take up a lighted candle, then leading the way to her father's study. But as soon as she set foot in the room, she realized her mistake. Her eyes were drawn at once to the huge, gilt-framed portrait of a young Jackson Lanford, his face vibrant and alight with confidence, his large, green-gray eyes filled with calm pride and assurance. Ambrosia stood in silence, staring up at the portrait, feeling the grief cut through the deepest part of her like a knife, feeling a helpless anger in the realization that he would never be coming home again.

For a moment Drayton was also silent as he watched the emotions play upon her face, watched the brightness finally touch her eyes. It was obvious that this had been her father's room. There was no woman's touch in the heavy dark-stained paneling, the massive oak desk, or the neatly arranged leather-bound volumes. Jackson Lanford must have been an educated, wealthy man, a man bred to enjoy the finer things of life. Yet he had died in vain like so many others, on some distant field of battle, leaving behind only sadness and broken dreams. It was easy to imagine the magnitude of his daughter's loss, hidden until now beneath those catlike eyes. Yet Drayton could not afford to feel compassion or any kind of softness where Ambrosia was concerned. His position was far too vulnerable. He and Crawford and even the wounded could be too easily slaughtered by two or three renegade Confederates if their vulnerability were known. And Ambrosia would not hesitate to turn them all over to any soldiers in gray who happened by, even if the Rebs meant to slaughter them outright. Particularly now, with the news of her father's death so fresh and painful in her mind. Drayton would have liked to allow her to grieve in peace, to look past her breach of conduct this afternoon and take a chance that it would not happen again. But his instincts for survival refused him that luxury.

"You were told not to leave the house without permission. And you deliberately disobeyed."

At the sound of his voice a defiant hatred overtook the sorrow in Ambrosia's eyes. But still she stood silent, staring at the painting, remembering the man she had idolized, the man she had believed invincible.

Drayton's fingers caught at her arm and she was whirled about to face him. "I said—"

"I heard what you said," she hissed through clenched

teeth, shocking him somewhat as she shook free of his hold and defiantly turned her back on him again.

He allowed her to step away from him, but his voice came again, smooth, silken and edged in steel. "When I give an order, I expect it to be obeyed."

There was a tense, dangerous space of silence.

"Miss Lanford."

She could hear his impatience, but she deliberately made no move to respond. How dare he—a Yankee—give orders here? In Jackson Lanford's home?

"Ambrosia." His voice had hardened even more.

She straightened and lifted her chin, fighting the tears of anger and heartbreak that clutched painfully at her throat. She would never let a Yankee see her cry. She would never give into them—Never!

Her breath caught sharply as Drayton gripped her roughly and jerked her hard against his broad chest, his fingers biting deep in the flesh of her arms. The green eyes which met his were bright with tears but narrowed and uncompromising.

"I've a good mind to bind you hand and foot like the others," he muttered furiously. His grip on her arms tightened until he knew full well that he was hurting her. Yet her eyes held no trace of pain or fear, nothing but hatred and defiance. He saw clearly then that his threats had no power to penetrate such resistance. But he intended to see it shattered, regardless. If not in one way . . .

He let out his breath slowly and his fingers loosened their ironclad grasp and began to knead gently at the bruised flesh of her upper arms. He was aware of the sudden look of uncertainty which shadowed her eyes as he did so, and he knew instantly that the maneuver had been well chosen. His blue eyes moved to dwell for long moments on her full mouth, and he noticed the tremor that passed through her as he once again met her eyes. No man had ever looked at her that way, making her feel totally naked, completely exposed. His eyes dropped to her lips again and she swallowed hard. Slowly, deliberately, he began to lower his mouth.

Ambrosia gasped and twisted violently to avoid his kiss. "What do you want?" she choked out as she struggled with all her might to be free.

He drew back the slightest bit and met her panicked expression with an air of confident authority. The room was so silent that the hammering of Ambrosia's heart made her head ache, and she knew that he must be aware of her deep, unsteady breathing. "When I give an order," he said softly, "I expect it to be obeyed."

He released her then and she quickly took a step backward, then another. For a long moment she stared at him, her breast still heaving painfully, her knees still unsteady and weak. "I will have your word that you will obey my orders for as long as I am here."

Ambrosia stared at him dumbly as she tried to gather some semblance of composure, as she tried in vain to reason away her fear. She felt her breath catch when he took a single step toward her, and it took all of her bravado to stand her ground.

"Your word," he growled more forcefully.

She lowered her eyes and drew a difficult breath. "Y—you have my word," she said in a quivering whisper. Her shoulders slumped as she said it, and he was fully aware of the effort it took for her to lift her chin and square them again. "Is that all, Major?" Her voice was still soft and trembling.

"That's all, Miss Lanford."

He watched her turn and leave the room, relieved that he had managed a truce without destroying her pride or breaking her spirit. He frowned slightly as the door closed behind her, remembering the way she had stood beside him the night before, cool, calm, without a trace of emotion, and the way she had fought him at the pond that morning. Drayton thought most women as transparent as glass these days, but Ambrosia intrigued him and attracted him more than any woman had since . . .

The memory of another woman of years past, a woman he had loved and lost, sharpened in his mind. Her eyes had been a brighter green, her hair dark and fine. It had been a long time since he had remembered the way that woman had smiled, or the way she had felt in his arms. A long time since the hurt had come to the fore. He vented a sigh and shook off the memories, suddenly aware of the dangers of playing this game of cat-and-mouse with a woman like Ambrosia. She had the power to make him remember far too many things he wanted desperately to forget.

Chapter 5

The soft golden rays of morning sun poured insistently through the bedroom windowpanes, stirring Ambrosia reluctantly from a troubled sleep. She forced her eyes to open, sighing at the day's bright yellow light, drawing comfort from the sight that she had not found in slumber. Wearily she rose from the bed and shuddered as her feet touched the floor, rekindling the dreams that had haunted her all through the night. She'd been running and running, trying to warn her father of the terrible danger at Heritage. She had stood at a window, watching him ride proud and erect in his splendid gray uniform up the long, curving drive, his mouth lifting slightly as the slaves gathered about him, cheering and welcoming him home. And then, suddenly, came a terrible explosion. A hundred guns firing at once until the wonderful, proud vision burst into thousands of charred, bloody pieces of flesh. Ambrosia did not know whether or not she had screamed aloud in terror, but twice she bolted upright from a deep sleep, an icy sweat covering her skin. For long moments the explosion had echoed in her head. And with it the agonizing sight of her father's body, horribly mutilated beyond recognition.

Ambrosia clenched her teeth against a wave of nausea that filled her stomach. She could not allow herself to dwell on the nightmare now, no matter how very real it had seemed. It was too important to concentrate on the here and now. Jackson Lanford would not be coming home, but his daughter would never let sorrow or fear interfere with what had to be done. She lifted her eyes proudly to face the reflection in the looking glass, searching until the familiar gleam of determination met her. She was ready then to face the day.

The long list of chores and duties began to fall into place as she descended the stairs, mentally trying to arrange an orderly schedule. The Yankees would be wanting their breakfast; the ground would be dry enough for turning; if she and Andrew and Sally could force the old mule Nemesis out of her stall and get her behind a plow . . .

Breakfast proceeded much as the morning before, except that Ambrosia kept her eyes carefully away from the Yankee's. It was only when the major was leaving the dining room that Ambrosia realized that she would need his permission to work in the fields and so reluctantly stopped him. "Major Rambert?"

He turned inquiringly and she could feel the color fading from her face as she met his eyes. "I will need your permission to spend the morning away from the house." The words came in a rush, but she somehow managed to survive the self-consciousness during the next few moments while he questioned her about exactly where she would be and what work would be done. Apparently she answered the inquiries to his satisfaction, and permission was granted.

Ambrosia took eagerly to the taxing, physical tasks that lay before her, glad for the momentary escape the work offered her troubled mind. The sun rose bright and hot in the sky as she and Andrew and Sally took turns guiding the plow or yanking persuasively on Nemesis's bridle to keep her proceeding on a straight path. The work was hard and tiring for the body but pure refreshment for Ambrosia's soul. In another few weeks it would be time for planting. And the seedlings would grow strong and green in the fertile soil, in spite of war and death. And by the time the harvest came, General Lee and his Confederate Army would have driven the Yankees far from the South. Ambrosia's blistered palms grasped the worn plow handles more firmly as her feet stumbled determinedly on the freshly turned ground. Her green eyes caught sight of the manor house as she made to begin a new row, and she paused for a moment to lift her head with pride. The house her father built still echoed the greatness of yesterday. As long as it stood it was easy for her to believe that someday, everything would be as it once had been. She only had to be strong enough, brave enough to hold on to what was left of the dream.

Ambrosia was so tired by dinner time that she could hardly taste the fare Sheba set before her, or care that the Yankees had eaten the same thing an hour before. She was surprised when Sheba told her that the major wanted to see her, and in spite of her weariness she felt a cold dread building inside. The remainder of her dinner was left untouched on her plate as she rose, tucking a loose strand of her hair into the knot at the nape of her neck, trying to force the light furrows of fatigue from her brow. She hesitated before entering the parlor to square her shoulders and hold her head high, to hide the anxiety she felt at the prospect of facing him again. When she entered the room, Ambrosia found the major bent low beside Corporal Laird. He acknowledged her with a brief glance, then continued prodding the swollen area about the gash in the corporal's abdomen and blotting the yellowish drainage which oozed from the wound. Ambrosia hesitated, still wondering why he had sent for her since his gesture had not been an angry one. She watched him work at cleansing the wound, marveling again at his skilled, precise movements. A moment later she went to get the healing box from the parlor table, then knelt beside him, not at all sure he would welcome her interference. She removed a small jar from the box and opened it, her hand trembling a little as she offered it to him. "This will help heal the infection," she said as matter-of-factly as she could manage.

Drayton paused to lift inquiring eyes, studying her face for several moments before he accepted the jar of salve. Scooping a small amount on his fingertip, he tested the consistency and the smell, guessing at its contents. "It's a mixture of brown sugar and honey and a bit of tallow," Ambrosia informed him coldly, angered that he did not trust her word, though admittedly he had good reason not to. "I've seen it work on worse wounds. Mammy used to swear by it."

Drayton hesitated, searching her green eyes for another long moment before he moved to apply the salve to the infected area. Laird's eyelids fluttered heavily and he mumbled something unintelligible as Drayton used the last of a long strip of linen to rewrap the wound. The corporal quieted when Drayton tucked a blanket about his shoulders and settled him on his makeshift pallet. Ambrosia came to her feet when the major did, her eyes wary, her stance cautious. "You sent for me?"

"I am in need of more bandages," he told her in an authoritative tone. "And your assistance, if you are willing," he added more gently.

Ambrosia was surprised and pleased by his request. She gave a brief nod, then went to get the linens which had been laundered the day before, and returned to help him rebandage Laird's leg wounds. The thigh was swollen and very much inflamed, but there was no strong odor to indicate gangrene. Ambrosia watched with satisfaction as Drayton applied the salve she had recommended to these wounds as well. Without a word he finished with Laird and moved on to the young blond soldier.

It was not really necessary to examine the boy's wounds, for a single look at the unnatural brightness of his cheeks in an otherwise grayish countenance, and at the constant, aimless movement of his head told Ambro-

sia more than she wanted to know. Drayton stared at the
bandage for a moment, then lowered the scissors and replaced the blanket. There was no sense in putting the boy
through any more agony, though he was probably beyond
any awareness of pain by this time. Drayton's face hardened as he felt the boy's brow and went through the motions of caring for him as if there were reason to hope. He
had known that this would probably happen, even as he
had wielded the knife. But he had had no choice; he had
been forced to gamble with full awareness that either
way, Jamie would probably lose his life. He was hardly
more than a child, Drayton thought bitterly as a helpless
frustration broke free inside him. A doctor's skill and
knowledge had not been enough to save his life.

Ambrosia's frown deepened as she stared at the young
soldier's face. Jamie, one of the men had called him. He
was only a boy, much too young to die. And he was so
much like Ledger with his youthful face and blond hair.
She closed her eyes and shook her head. She did not want
to think of Ledger now.

Her eyes slid to the major's face. "I'll get some cool
water. I've seen a sponging bring down a fever," she
told him hopefully, her eyes searching his face for some
encouragement.

Drayton withdrew his hand from Jamie's brow and
evenly met her eyes. "Sometimes it does," he said
softly. "But this time it won't."

She felt her lower lip tremble as their eyes locked, the
hard truth in his quiet words striking her full force. This
boy was going to die. Thousands of other Yankee soldiers had died too, and Ambrosia herself had wished
death on thousands more. But they had been nameless,
faceless Yankees, while this one had a name and a face
and a child's head of curly blond hair.

"When we've finished, you can sponge his brow,"
she heard Drayton saw in a low, gentle voice. "It might
give him some relief from the pain. We have nothing else
for him."

Ambrosia swallowed hard and did not move at first when Drayton rose and went on to the Rebel soldier who had fought him on the table. Slowly, wearily she followed.

The Rebel's leg was draining well, but the man had bled much more than the others and still showed no sign of regaining consciousness. Drayton glanced toward Ambrosia as she knelt beside him. "This one will benefit from a cool sponging as well, and perhaps a sip of water later on." Drayton turned abruptly to snipping away the soiled bandage, applying the salve and binding it tightly with clean strips of linen which Ambrosia efficiently supplied. When he had almost finished, he watched her leave to fetch a basin of water and return to press a cool compress to the young blond soldier's brow. It was only then that Drayton noticed her hands.

They were lovely hands, small and delicately boned with long, tapering fingers. But the tender flesh had been cut and blistered, her palms scraped raw by the hours she had spent behind a plow. Drayton's eyes lingered on those hands, then rose to study the eyes that had so often reminded him of a panther's—cool, cunning, and dangerous. But there was only compassion in those eyes now, a compassion that touched Drayton deeply.

Ambrosia held back a sigh of anguish as her fingers brushed at a soft blond curl that had fallen across the dying boy's forehead. He was quiet now, and perhaps more comfortable. There was so very little she could do for him. She closed her eyes for a moment, then struggled to her feet, feeling a new heaviness in her limbs and a lightness in her head. She swayed, and would have fallen if Drayton's arms had not been there to steady her. "It's been a long day," he said softly. He was noticing for the first time the shadows beneath her eyes and the unconscious lines of fatigue that pulled at her brow. "I'll finish here now. Thank you for your help."

Ambrosia willed herself to straighten and was extremely grateful that Drayton released her when she did so. It took a great deal of effort just to make the proper exit from the parlor, and even more to mount the stairs without stumbling. She knew, somehow, that his eyes remained on her until she was out of sight.

Once in her room, Ambrosia dropped into bed without even shedding her clothing. She fell immediately into an exhausted sleep.

For a long time after she left him, Drayton continued the work Ambrosia had begun, sponging the feverish men and periodically offering them small sips of water. When they were all sleeping peacefully, he spread a blanket on the floor near Laird and did his best to catch a few moments of sleep himself.

It seemed to Drayton that he had scarcely closed his eyes when a sound in the hall made him snap to attention. In a single movement, he rolled and lifted himself on his forearm, his revolver cocked and aimed at the doorway. A moment later he relaxed, letting out his breath and lowering his gun. It was Crawford. The layers of heaviest sleep cleared from his head as Crawford approached him. His expression was grim.

"I've spotted fires, Major. About five, maybe seven miles from here." Drayton glanced at him hopefully, but Crawford shook his head. "They ain't campfires, Major."

Major Rambert rose and quickly checked Laird and the others, making sure that the prisoners were both bound securely and sound asleep. Then he followed Crawford up the stairs, all the way to the tiny, winding steps that led to the cupola. Once in the cupola he took up the field glasses, but they were unnecessary to see what Crawford had reported. Huge tongues of flame leapt bright and orange against the velvet blackness of the night. Drayton let out a pensive breath and slowly faced Crawford.

"Kilpatrick," Crawford guessed, naming the worst of all Union scavengers. General Kilpatrick was Sherman's right-hand man, a leader who blatantly and triumphantly encouraged his soldiers to steal or destroy everything that lay in their path.

"Either him or a few of his close friends," Drayton answered as he lifted the glasses and took a second look, hoping for a glimpse of something more than shadows and flame and billowing smoke. But the night was moonless and otherwise pitch-black. He gnawed at his lower lip, wondering just how long it would take them to reach Heritage.

"I figure them here by tomorrow noon," Crawford said, mirroring his thoughts. "They'll probably have a wagon, so's we can transport the wounded."

Drayton vented a sigh and leaned heavily against the sill, his fingers kneading at the tension beneath his brow. "Get some rest, Crawford. I'll take the watch."

Crawford gave a grateful nod and eagerly headed for the stairs.

"Crawford?"

He turned, lifting an inquiring brow.

"Keep a close eye on Laird."

Crawford gave a short nod, then hurried down the stairs.

For some time after he'd left, Drayton stared numbly at the fires which roared uncontrollably in the distance. Crawford was right. They would be able to transport the wounded. By tomorrow noon Laird and Clark and the Rebel prisoner would likely be on their way to an army surgeon's care, and Drayton's responsibilities as a doctor would be finished. Tomorrow at noon he could go back to being a soldier and put to rest the memories that haunted him these past days. He ought to feel relieved. But a part of him screamed in outrage against the rest of what would happen, once that kind of soldier arrived at Heritage. And a part of him could not but wonder what would happen to them—to the loyal blacks who lovingly called this place home, and more especially, what would happen to her. She did not have the good sense not to defy them, and they were not accustomed to meeting resistance. He let out a lengthy breath and shook his head, certain that she would fight them, and just as certain that they would destroy her without a second thought. And though he really didn't understand why, he couldn't bear to see it happen. He lifted the field glasses one last time, trying to think of some way he could prevent it.

It was still a few hours before daylight when Drayton left the cupola and quietly descended the stairs to the parlor. Crawford was snoring loudly when he entered the room and continued to do so as Drayton strode slowly past him, silently making his way to Josiah's side. The black man started violently when Drayton clamped a hand over his mouth and slipped an arm about his rib cage. After a few moments of fitful struggling, Josiah settled down and Drayton gradually released his hold. Drayton drew a knife from his belt and sliced through the heavy rope bonds at Josiah's feet, leaving his hands bound behind him. With a jerk of his head, Drayton directed the black to the hall, then got up and led the way through the maze of sleeping men. Josiah eyed him suspiciously and considered making a ruckus, then thought again. Something made him more curious than frightened, and he wanted to know why Major Rambert would set him free quietly, in the middle of the night, when he had only been taken prisoner the day before. He followed Rambert out of the parlor, then through the front door and onto the porch. The air was cool and moist, but it smelled strongly of smoke, and the smell made Josiah wary about following the major too far from the house. He stopped, intending to go no farther. A glance at the major told him he would find no argument.

Major Rambert leaned his weight against the porch rail as he silently considered the shadowed land which spread before him in the darkness of the night. He seemed deep in his own thoughts for a time, then abruptly he turned and met Josiah's eyes. "I need to talk with you, Josiah."

"I'm lis'nin', suh." Josiah's eyes were steadfast on Rambert's.

"Have you ever heard of Kilpatrick's cavalry?"

The black gave a short, mirthless laugh. "I've a lot more 'n heard of them, Major. I've seen a few of the places they foraged. Ain't nothin' left of nothin' 'cept smoke and ash."

Rambert nodded, then turned away to brace his hands on the ornate iron rail which was in sore need of paint. "They'll be paying a visit here, Josiah."

"That what we're smellin'?"

The major nodded.

Josiah's voice betrayed his concern. "When?"

Drayton turned to meet the dark brown eyes. "Soon. Tomorrow morning . . . maybe noon."

Josiah's gaze grew distant and sad for a moment, then lifted to meet the major's once more. "Why're you tellin' me all this?" he asked bitterly. "Ain't nothin' I can do."

"Turn around." With a skeptical frown, Josiah did as he was told. Once again Drayton withdrew the knife from his belt, this time severing the ropes that bound the black man's hands. "You're a free man, Josiah."

Josiah said nothing as he rubbed briskly at his wrists, easing the painful tingle as the blood began to flow freely into his hands. He made no move and asked no questions.

"You're a free man, Josiah," Drayton repeated. "But you're still bound to this land and to the Lanfords. Just as surely as if you were blood kin."

Josiah straightened his spine proudly. What the major said was true.

"Miss Lanford is going to need your protection and your help when I leave here with my men, even if no other Yankees ever come to this place."

Josiah nodded, but his eyes were distrustful.

"Is there a place nearby where you could hide yourself? A place where you're certain you won't be found? Somewhere away from the house?''

''I know of a place. I know lots of places. But—'' His voice broke off as Drayton abruptly tossed him a small leather pouch of coins which he caught with both hands against his chest. Josiah's eyes were wary as he withdrew a coin from the pouch and bit on it, then those same eyes widened in surprise.

''Bury them,'' came the terse command. ''And don't leave any trace of fresh turned ground or they'll find them.''

''But why?'' Josiah did not have the words out of his mouth when the major handed him the gun he had confiscated the day before, fully loaded. Josiah stared at it in stunned silence. Drayton turned away and stretched a hand toward the door latch.

''Major?''

Drayton paused but did not turn to face him. He already knew what the black man would ask. ''Why're you doin' this? Why? You're one of them.''

''Yes,'' he said after a long moment. ''I'm one of them.''

Chapter 6

As the sun rose bright and clear on the horizon, Ambrosia woke and bounded to her window, her heart pounding in her breast, her breath coming short and fast. The sight of the huge gray cloud of smoke clinging to the low, moist morning air filled her with fear and revulsion. The Harrington place, a plantation not ten miles from Heritage. It must have been burned sometime during the night.

Ambrosia clenched her fists and pounded them hard on the sill, wanting to scream her frustration, wanting to break everything in sight with her bare hands just to prevent them from destroying anything more. For a fleeting moment she saw her father, as clearly as if he were standing beside her. His gray uniform was crisp and new; brass buttons gleamed in the morning sun; epaulets flashed light; the wide-brimmed, yellow-plumed hat was tilted slightly back on his handsome head. But the expression he wore was not from any memory. His eyes had lost their arrogant self-assuredness and bore a look she had never seen before. It made him seem old and terribly sad. She hurriedly forced the image from her head. She turned away from the window and quickly changed her soiled clothing, wanting to get on with the day, anxious to do what work was to be done. Thank God there was work to be done.

The parlor was quiet when Ambrosia came down the stairs. When her eyes searched the room, Major Rambert was nowhere to be seen. She held back a cry of shock as her eyes fell on what had been the young blond soldier's bed. It was empty. For a long moment she stared at it, biting her lip hard before she could pull her eyes away.

Private Crawford was snoring loudly in the corner, and Josiah—Ambrosia's eyes darted frantically about the room. Josiah was gone. She half turned to leave the parlor, frowning as she tried to think of some reason for his absence. Perhaps the major had taken him to help with the burial, or—

She stopped short, suddenly realizing that the soldier named Laird was waking, squinting and straining to see her, as if he were confused by what he saw. She knelt beside him, resting her palm lightly on his brow. Her eyes brightened. The skin was damp with perspiration, but not dangerously hot. She moved to get him a dipper of cool water, then lifted his head and gave it support as he sipped at it gratefully. He sighed and fell wearily back when he had finished.

"For a minute . . . I—I thought you were Grace," he forced out hoarsely.

Ambrosia shook her head. "I'm sorry, Corporal."

Laird gave a weak smile. "No need. You're a lot prettier than Grace."

Ambrosia felt her cheeks flush at the unexpected compliment. "I'll go and fetch you some broth from the kitchen," she said rather brusquely.

Laird sighed and closed his eyes wearily. He opened them again a few moments later when Drayton appeared in the doorway. The corporal gave him a sheepish grin, which prompted a look of pleased surprise on Drayton's face.

"You're awake early. How's the leg?" he asked as he stopped to check the patient's brow.

"Hurts like hell, thanks to you," Laird returned

promptly. He brushed the major's hand tersely from his brow. "And somebody a lot prettier than you's already given me a clean bill of health."

"Oh?"

Laird gave a nod. "Pretty, green-eyed little cat. Hasn't told me her name yet."

"It's Ambrosia Lanford. *Miss* Lanford to us Yankees. And I'm sorry to inform you about as loyal a Reb as you're apt to find anywhere. Every drop of blood in her veins is pure Secesh."

Laird paled and grimaced as a sharp pain took hold of him. "Well, I'm beholden to her, Secesh or not," he forced out, trying hard to smile.

"I wish I had something to give you for the pain, John. But there's nothing here. Not even whiskey."

Drayton's eyes lifted as Ambrosia entered the parlor with a tray of steaming broth. Drayton rose to take it from her and began to spoon-feed Laird in spite of his feeble protests. Only when he had finished did he notice that Ambrosia still stood nearby, her eyes troubled and questioning.

"Where is Josiah?"

Drayton's eyes narrowed coldly in a way that made Ambrosia want to cringe. "I needed his help this morning with burying Jamie. And I made a mistake of turning my back on him while he still held a shovel." He rubbed the back of his head.

Ambrosia's eyes mirrored her disbelief. "He—he escaped?"

Drayton glared at her, then turned away, signaling that the conversation was finished. Ambrosia would have smiled at that, but something in the story did not quite ring true. Rambert was not the type of soldier to have been so careless with a prisoner, and she doubted that he had ever turned his back on anyone in his life. But her inquiring eyes only brought her a second angry glare from Drayton that made her relief take precedence over her curiosity. Josiah had somehow escaped, she assured herself, and he would hide himself somewhere until the Yankees left. She was glad he knew the land well enough to do it.

It was almost noon when they came, descending on Heritage like vultures on the carcass of a freshly slain animal. There were fifty or more of them, their horses' hooves pounding as they all raced madly for the house. War whoops and yells shattered the peace of the warm morning. After spending the greater part of the morning behind a plow, Ambrosia was in the kitchen when the first sounds were heard in the distance. She froze, her eyes meeting Elly's, then Sheba's, before she could mask her terror. No one spoke, but fear hung almost tangibly in their silence.

Slowly, Ambrosia wiped her hands on her apron and proceeded with a calm, measured stride to the house with Sheba, Elly, and Sally close at her heels. Ambrosia headed instinctively for the parlor where she had seen her shotgun just a few hours before. She paused in the hall, seeing the major's broad back before the window. Her gaze flickered over the shotgun which was propped in a nearby corner. She had seen the major unload it when he confiscated it two days before, but it could still be used as a ploy. Yet the growing commotion told her that there were far too many of them to be held off with a single unloaded gun. Her eyes met Drayton's momentarily when he turned away from the window. She straightened haughtily and left the room. She would never play the part of a defeated, helpless woman, no matter how many of them came here, no matter what they did. If she could not meet her enemy with violence, then at least she could meet them with courage. It was the one part of her they could never defeat.

With a cool, determined stride, Ambrosia made her way to the door and stepped out onto the porch where she stood straight and unyielding as an unarmed guard. The scene which spread before her was like a nightmare, and a part of her immediately went numb. Blue-coated soldiers rode rampant over the land with utter disregard for paths and fences and even livestock. Several men galloped over the freshly turned field Ambrosia had left a few minutes before, swinging their sabers to strike at the smooth handles of the plow, laughing raucously as large chunks of wood flew in every direction. Others seemed to draw a perverse pleasure from chasing and slaughtering the chickens or leaving ugly, deep scars on the tall, stately oaks which lined the drive. One soldier was already calmly reloading a revolver he had just emptied into a harmless old hound.

For a moment Ambrosia thought she would be sick. Her hatred twisted her stomach as she watched a spectacle she could never have envisioned in her worst nightmares. The blue-coated butchers were everywhere, rushing in a hundred directions at once to desecrate everything she held dear.

She steeled herself as another group of soldiers approached the house, these in a more orderly fashion, followed by a parade of horse-drawn wagons and carts. A short, rotund colonel at the head of the group raised his gloved hand as a signal to those behind him to stop. He and another man who wore no uniform advanced to the edge of the piazza where Ambrosia stood. Ambrosia guessed the colonel to be fifty years of age, though in truth he was much younger. His round, drooping face was lined in a perpetual scowl, and a full, gray beard could not disguise the lax curve of his mouth. The second man was at least a score of years younger, and might have been considered handsome but for a long, disfiguring scar which drew far too much attention from his even features. Bright, black eyes and a rather dashing handlebar mustache only served to reinforce the fiendish, sinister quality of that scar. He was a well-built man of average height, his shoulders tapering to a trim waist which was accentuated by his tailored coat. The black eyes glittered with arrogance as they flashed over Ambrosia, his mouth curving upward in a knowing smile. She lifted her chin even higher and her eyes darkened to a stormy gray. Her gaze did not waver when the door behind her opened and the major stepped beside her on the veranda.

"Colonel Reed." Drayton saluted the senior officer but something in his stance, his tone, lacked pleasantness and even respect. Ambrosia's eyes wavered then, and she was surprised to see Drayton's right hand pointedly caressing the smooth handle of his revolver.

"Major Rambert." The colonel gave a return salute and copied the major's tone. The older man nodded his head toward his companion. "This is Julian Bardo, correspondent for the *New York Herald*. Mr. Bardo is doing a story on me."

"We met in Atlanta," Drayton returned coolly.

Bardo's lips curled slightly as he caressed his scar. "Under different circumstances," he said slowly, remembering the woman Drayton had taken from him, remembering too clearly the way the man fought. "Fancy finding you way out here in the middle of nowhere. I would have thought a hero like you would prefer the thick of battle to the unpleasant task of foraging."

Ambrosia saw Drayton smile, but at the same time she sensed the tension coiling within him. When he spoke again it was not to the man named Bardo. "I'm afraid that my preference has earned me and two of my men a short stay here, Colonel. We were wounded in ambush day before last, and these people were kind enough to take us in."

Again Bardo gave the ugly little smile. "We're very glad to hear that, Major. The colonel and I have met up with very few cooperative Rebels hereabouts."

Drayton's eyes wandered pointedly over the countless acts of destruction taking place even as they were speaking. "I don't suppose you have," he commented with sarcasm.

The colonel cleared his throat almost nervously as

Drayton's fingers curled unconsciously about the handle of his gun. "We will be taking temporary shelter here, Major. There looks to be enough food to give my men a decent meal or two." He twisted about in the saddle and gave the men a signal to dismount. A young soldier hurried to take the reins of his and Bardo's horses as they did the same.

Bardo eyed Ambrosia steadily as he mounted the steps, staring at her as if she were a slave on an auction block.

"There won't be enough for even one decent meal if you don't stop your butchers, Colonel," she said as the older man made to enter the house.

His eyes lifted to face her and he forced a smile. "I apologize if my men seem overly enthusiastic, Miss . . . ?"

"Your men seem to be animals, sir," she retorted. "And you seem to lack the authority to control them."

The colonel's smile vanished and his eyes bulged with anger. He would have slapped her without a second thought had she been alone. Like most of the Rebels she needed to be taught a lesson in respect. But something in the way Major Rambert stood beside her made him think twice about beginning that lesson just now. He let out a calming breath and turned abruptly away from her, lifting his revolver and firing several shots in the air.

It took several moments to get everyone's attention, for the shots blended with those from every corner of the plantation. But quickly a strange silence fell, except for a few squawking chickens and barking dogs. The obvious agitation in Colonel Reed's voice seemed to bring every man to attention. "I have just been reminded that we are 'guests' here, men. Major Rambert here has just assured me that the people in residence will offer full cooperation in seeing to our needs." Many of the soldiers stared at him as if he were going mad. But no one made a move to challenge him; no one said anything.

"I want you all to try and take advantage of the hospitality being shown us, and to refrain from undue destruction of private property." He lifted his chin and let his eyes roam over the land, seeming to catch the eye of each and every soldier, effectively emphasizing his words. He turned back to Ambrosia. "I will expect a meal prepared and served for my men within the hour," he ordered tersely. Turning on a heel, he entered the house, drawing off his gloves and handing them to the young soldier who diligently followed him.

Ambrosia stood there for a moment, still unaccustomed to responding to someone else's orders. But Bardo's hungry black eyes forced her to make a quick decision. She pivoted and headed for the kitchen.

A meal was readied from the nine chickens and the cow that had been slaughtered before Colonel Reed had put a stop to the destruction. Divine Providence, Ambrosia believed, had saved the other cow. It seemed a bitter irony that this was the largest meal Sheba had prepared since before the war. She flew about the kitchen, groaning as "Miz" Ambrosia herself laid out Lucille's finest china and silver for a pack of filthy Yankees that smelled of smoke and killing. Shaking her head in consternation, she filled a large old chipped pot with a bitter brew of acorn coffee for which there was no sugar and not enough cream. And everything Sheba prepared, everything that was carried from the kitchen, reminded them all that there might never be enough of anything ever again.

Most of the men were served their food from the kitchen door, but the officers and Bardo enjoyed a leisurely supper in the dining room. Colonel Reed had taken a seat at the head of the table, Bardo to the right of him, his black eyes following Ambrosia throughout the meal like those of a wildcat stalking a deer. The last of the men were finishing with their meal when Julian Bardo took out a cigar and ran it thoughtfully under his nose. His eyes never left Ambrosia's face even as she began to clear the table. "Miss . . . Lanford, isn't it?"

Sally dropped the plate she had just picked up and was wide-eyed with fright at the mere sound of his voice. But Bardo was not speaking to her, and his eyes hardly left Ambrosia's face, even when the china shattered to the floor. Ambrosia gave him a short nod, then continued to stack the plates and collect the silverware. It intrigued Bardo to see that her hands were perfectly steady. Everything about this woman intrigued him. "Sit down here. I want to talk with you."

Her eyes reflected her astonishment at the request. He lit his cigar and took a long draw on it, nodding his head toward an adjacent chair. "The colonel doesn't mind, do you, Colonel?"

Colonel Reed gave a contented sigh and patted his stomach. "By all means, Miss Lanford. Join us."

"I want to ask you a few questions for a piece I'm planning to do," Bardo explained. " 'A Loyal Southerner Welcomes Union Liberators,' I thought I might call it."

Ambrosia's eyes flicked over the chair as she struggled hard against the urge to slap his face. "Union liberators," they called themselves. How ironic that Josiah, who had been a slave, was now a fugitive from the Yankee "liberators." "I can talk just as well standing up, thank you," she said finally.

The colonel's eyes narrowed and there was a tense silence, angry and dangerous. Then the colonel kicked sharply at the chair Bardo had indicated and it leapt away from the table. "Sit down."

Ambrosia hesitated. Sally hurriedly gathered a small stack of dishes and made her way clumsily from the room, praying she would not faint before she reached the kitchen. It was her movement and the reminder that there were others in the house to consider, others who might suffer the consequences of her actions, that made Ambrosia take a seat. With a smile of thanks, Colonel Reed accepted a cigar from Bardo and drew on it leisurely, as if to calm himself. Bardo pushed his chair back a bit from

the table and impudently stretched his legs before him.
He made no move to take out pen and notepad. He took
another draw on his cigar. "How many slaves did you
have on this plantation at the start of the war?"

"Nearly four hundred."

"And you now have . . . how many?"

"Three."

"The war must have altered your way of life considerably, Miss Lanford."

Ambrosia's eyes touched briefly on her stained homespun gown, her ruined hands. She said nothing.

"What of your family? I caught a glimpse of a white
woman a little while ago. Is she your sister?"

"No."

Julian raised a brow. "Well, then, who is she?"

"Her name is Mrs. Partkin."

"Ah. That explains her reluctance to socialize with us,
if her husband is a loyal Confederate—"

"She is a widow."

"I see . . . And you? Have you no family? No parents? No brothers off fighting the war?"

"I don't see where that's any of your business."

Ambrosia ground her teeth as Bardo flicked an ash
carelessly to the floor. "Ah, but it is my business, Miss
Lanford." Bardo smiled and let his forefinger trace the
long scar to the side of his nose. And for the first time,
Ambrosia saw his eyes meet Major Rambert's. "I find
you a most interesting story," Bardo went on. "Particularly since you've been so accommodating to the major
here."

Ambrosia frowned, looking from one man to the other,
sensing a deep, personal antagonism between the two
without understanding it. She tried to guess at what game
Bardo was playing and decided quickly that it had been
carried quite far enough. "I'm very busy, Mr. Bardo."
She rose from her seat. "If you will please excuse
me."

"Sit down, Miss Lanford. You aren't too busy to talk

with me." It was the colonel's voice, low and hostile. She slowly dropped to the chair in compliance. "How many bedrooms are in this house?"

"Eleven. And there is a small area on the third floor that—"

"See that the eleven are prepared for me and my officers." The colonel stood, his tone indicating that the conversation was at an end.

Ambrosia stood also. "Mrs. Partkin and I occupy two of the rooms, Colonel. Certainly you don't mean for—"

"I most certainly do mean exactly what I said, Miss Lanford. I will retire before sundown. I expect you to have everything in order by then." He gave a short nod and strode stiffly from the dining room.

For a long moment Ambrosia stared after him in stunned silence. "You are welcome to share quarters with me," Bardo offered softly.

Ambrosia's eyes flew to his face. "I'd sooner share quarters with a snake."

She saw his face tighten in surprise and felt a tiny measure of satisfaction. She whirled and left the room, not giving him a chance to say anything more.

The table was left cluttered with dishes while Ambrosia and Elly hurriedly emptied their rooms of all personal belongings. Sally, Andrew, and Sheba helped carry clothing, jewelry, and the few breakable keepsakes to Jackson Lanford's study. Ambrosia also ran rummaging about the other bedrooms, flinging the last few of her mother's gowns over her arm, gathering up anything that might be broken or easily stolen. Despite her haste and concentration, a noisy disturbance drew her attention to the window. She leaned out the window and listened, feeling an eruption of bitter indignation as she sorted out the various sounds of men's drunken laughter and shouting, and the old mule Nemesis's braying and whining. The sounds were coming from the stable.

Ambrosia felt her temper rising as the noises contin-

ued, as the soldiers became more boisterous, and the
mule's braying became sharper and more pathetic. They
were torturing a poor, dumb animal, the bastards! Impul-
sively she tossed the gowns into Sally's arms with a terse,
"Finish here," and headed determinedly for the back
stairs. The soldiers had been ordered to leave the animals
alone and some of them were deliberately defying that order. At the foot of the stairs she brusquely passed by Andrew, whose arms were so laden that his tired brown eyes
barely managed to peek over Elly's things. Ambrosia
said nothing to him, but Andrew noticed her purposeful
march and the look in her eyes, and hurried to relieve
himself of his packages so that he might discover the
cause.

Ambrosia was almost running when she reached the
stable door and lifted it enough to slip inside. The interior
was dark and cool, and it took a moment for her eyes to
adjust to the light. The soldiers, four of them, all obviously drunk, had tied the mule to a supporting post and
were beating her unmercifully, laughing at how high she
kicked, at how loudly she brayed after each stroke of the
lash.

"Untie that mule." Ambrosia's order was so sharp
and so full of authority that the soldiers jerked to attention and stared at her dumbly for what seemed like an
eternity. The one who held the whip was the first to realize that she was alone. He made his way unsteadily toward her, and she had to brace herself to keep from
backing away. He was an ugly man, his expression brutal
and dangerous, and he reeked of strong whiskey. "I said,
untie the mule," she repeated through clenched teeth.
"Colonel Reed gave orders—"

"Now ain't you a feisty little thing!" he taunted as he
moved to block her only exit and to make sure that no one
else was with her. She felt a tingling of fear when she too
realized that she was alone now with these men, and too
far from the house to summon help. She struggled to
square her shoulders, leveling a bright, narrow glare on

the man with the whip. She was not about to let these cowards sense that she was afraid.

"What d' ya say, boys? Ain't she spunky? Kind o' like the mule we's tryin' t' teach some manners to, ain't she?" The man smiled at her, displaying an uneven row of tobacco-stained teeth. "We might jus' have t' teach her some manners too," he said thoughtfully, fingering the handle of the whip, which he cradled close to his chest.

"She shore is prettier 'n that mule, Caleb." It was the youngest of the four who said it, a tall, gangling youth with sparse brown hair. He immediately blushed when Ambrosia looked at him, and lifted a bottle of clear liquid to his mouth, letting a good bit of it dribble down his chin.

The other three men let out loud guffaws at his embarrassment. "You're right 'bout that, Jesse," said one when the laughter died away. "She shore is prettier 'n that mule."

There was something in the man's tone and something stronger in his eyes that made Ambrosia tremble for all her outward calm.

"A man's gotta be jus' as firm with a woman as wi' a mule," Caleb advised broadly, letting his fingers feel the long strip of leather. "She has t' know from the first who's in command."

Caleb's smile faded abruptly and Ambrosia heard a sharp cracking sound as the whip wound its way tightly about her shoulders. It was another split second before the pain registered, a hot, sharp sting of leather cutting her skin through the heavy fabric of her dress. Caleb smiled, pleased with his initial show of power. He jerked the whip back with such force that Ambrosia fell to her knees.

By this time the shock had receded, and Ambrosia rose swiftly and flew at him with every ounce of her strength. "Filthy Yankee swine!"

The cry sprang from her lips as she kicked hard at his

leg and pulled tenaciously at the whip. He wrenched it away easily but let out a groan and hopped on a single foot for several moments. Ambrosia twisted and lurched at him a second time, sinking her teeth deep in his hand and making another valiant attempt to get the whip. Caleb yelped aloud and his cohorts chortled with amusement as he pushed her roughly to the ground and sucked on his injured fist.

"Looks like she's got lots o' learnin' t' do, Caleb," one of the men teased, taking a generous swig of whiskey.

Caleb's jaw tightened as Ambrosia half rose, the hatred bright and defiant in her green eyes. Her lip curled in a murderous snarl as she faced him, wanting more than anything to kill him. She would kill him! She would! She would never cower before him like a helpless victim! But she was hardly on her feet when the thin strip of leather snapped loud and keen, laying open a bright stripe of blood across her back, making her body jerk with the impact, sending her to her knees again. Breathing hard, she instinctively crouched low and turned away, covering her face with her hands. She was suddenly trembling with fear as she braced herself for the next assault, her bravado dissolved in a wave of pain and panic.

Caleb drew a deep breath and lifted his expanded chest proudly. He had made his point. With a clearly victorious step he moved to hand the whip to the man who had chided him a moment before. Then he pulled Ambrosia to her feet, wrenching her arms tightly behind her back. She began to struggle immediately, somehow managing a sharp jab at Caleb's ribs when one of her elbows was momentarily freed. The others chuckled at the maneuver, but as Caleb fought to catch his breath, his patience ended. His grip was like iron when he caught her arm again. He pulled it behind her back so high that she had to bite her lip hard to keep from screaming out with pain. Caleb yanked her back against his chest, and held her there so tightly that she could scarcely breathe.

"Yer learnin' her real good, Caleb."

Caleb's eyes drifted slowly over the admiring gazes of the other men, who nodded in agreement. "Jesse," Caleb began, speaking to the youngest. "I think it's time you learned yourself a lesson too."

Jesse's youthful, pockmarked face was all attention.

"It's time you proved t' the rest o' us you're more 'n jus' a boy. An' you can prove it right here 'n now, wi' this filly here." His voice broke off as Ambrosia twisted furiously, and he struggled to hold her steady.

Jesse blushed a deep pink and his eyes flashed over Ambrosia's face. He gulped. "Caleb—y—ya can't mean fer me!— Not wi' her!" He glanced about helplessly, and one of the other soldiers came to fling an affectionate arm about his thin shoulders.

"Had my first woman in a barn," he said proudly.

"Ain' nothin' wrong wi' a barn," the other added with a shrug and a hiccup. "Keeps a mare from fergettin' her place."

Caleb growled as Ambrosia managed to deliver a vicious kick to his shin. "Come on, boy. I can't keep her tethered ferever."

"But—but—she's one o' them quality womenfolk, Caleb," he argued desperately. "She ain't like—like—"

"She's Secesh, boy!" Caleb snapped back. "Secesh!"

Ambrosia twisted her neck to spit at him, and he immediately threw her to the ground. She reeled on impact, a sharp tongue of fire flashing through her head as the toe of his boot struck at her temple. With every bit of strength remaining inside her, she struggled to rise. But suddenly there simply was no strength. Her face fell abruptly against the hay and dirt, and for a moment she felt nothing. Nothing.

"Ain't no Secesh woman what's quality," Caleb grunted.

Jesse winced as Caleb slipped his boot beneath her shoulder and turned her roughly over on her back. The pain that shot through her head made her face contort and without realizing it she let out a small, helpless cry. "What's the matter, boy? Afraid o' a filly wi' spirit? Afraid t' be the first?"

Jesse swallowed hard, his eyes leaving the expectant faces of his peers to drift hungrily over the firm curves of Ambrosia's breasts, to linger on the slender, shapely leg exposed nearly to the thigh. His breath quickened and he felt a tightening in his groin.

Caleb smiled knowingly. "Ye're man enough, boy," he urged, taking a flask of whiskey from one of the others and handing it to Jesse. The younger man gratefully drew a long sip to bolster his courage. He wiped his mouth with the back of his sleeve and began fumbling hurriedly with the fastenings of his trousers. "Don't be too long, boy!" one of them warned as Jesse mounted her and tore at her bodice. "Save somethin' fer us!"

The three spectators hooted and laughed at the youngster's clumsy, spasmodic movements and mimicked his heavy, loud panting. Ambrosia tried desperately to rise above the deep, velvet darkness which had engulfed her, but the dizziness, the pain, the persistent, cloying remnants of unconsciousness refused to be shaken off. And something inside her could not begin to face the hard reality that was flowing slowly into her mind. A cold knot of revulsion twisted angrily in her stomach at the oppressive closeness of hot, sweaty flesh; at the clawing, prodding fingers that dug roughly into her breasts; at the pervasive, overpowering odor of breath soured by strong whiskey. She raised her hands to claw at his eyes and twisted away from the mouth that covered hers. Jesse cursed and slapped her hard across the face.

Stunned by the impact of the blow, Ambrosia lay limp and quiet as he struggled with her skirts and forced a knee between her thighs. His thick tongue plunged deep in her mouth, until she could hardly restrain the urge to vomit. She clamped her teeth hard against his tongue, immediately tasting his blood. Jesse shrieked with pain and drew back, but not enough to allow her escape. She lifted her shoulders, but he grasped at her head with trembling hands clamped hard over either ear, meaning to slam her head repeatedly against the ground.

Suddenly a deafening explosion roared in Ambrosia's ears and shook the very ground on which she lay sprawled. The man who was upon her loosened his fingers from her hair, convulsed, and made a futile attempt to rise. He managed to raise only one knee before dropping in a bloody, lifeless heap, his limp arm falling possessively about Ambrosia's shoulders.

Even before Jesse fell, a second shot rang out, then a third and a fourth. Ambrosia's eyes were wide and glassy as she struggled from beneath her attacker, the sounds reverberating in her pounding head.

Her eyes met the Yankee major's, but it was a long time before she recognized him. Even as he knelt beside her and helped her to her feet, she was in such a state of shock and confusion that she trembled and nearly fainted. It came to her in a frightening rush that Major Rambert stood beside her, carefully dividing his attention between her and the men who had beaten her. A quick glance told her that the one they called Jesse was dead, a gaping hole in the back of his head. She turned away from the sight and buried her face in Drayton's broad chest, muffling a tiny sob of relief and feeling like a frightened child waking from a terrible nightmare. It did not matter at that moment that he was a Yankee too. His arms offered shelter that she desperately needed, and she could not bring herself to relinquish the safety she had found there. Her fingers clutched tightly at his tunic when the stable door was flung aside and at least a score of Yankees, all brandishing their weapons, stormed inside.

Colonel Reed, a fire leaping in his narrowed blue eyes, paused at the threshold to survey the scene. He marched slowly, arrogantly toward Major Rambert. "What is the meaning of this?"

One of the wounded men stumbled forward, his hand

pressed to his blood-splattered shoulder. "We was only funin', Colonel," he whined like a boy heading for the woodshed. "We didn't mean no harm."

Another soldier who lay on the floor wrapped his arms about the bullet wound in his abdomen. "He—he tried t' kill us!" he forced out hoarsely. He doubled over in pain and rolled to his side.

Caleb struggled to his feet, heavily favoring the leg which had been stung by the major's bullet. "He killed Jesse in cold blood, Colonel. Hardly more 'n a boy, an' 'ere he lies wi' a bullet in th' back o' his head."

Julian Bardo, who had remained safely behind the colonel until now, stepped forward to examine the boy's body. "Shot in the back of the head, Colonel. Just like the man says."

The colonel's eyes drifted over the boy, who lay in a growing pool of blood, then slid expectantly toward Major Rambert. "Well, Major?"

Ambrosia felt him tense, felt his arm tighten more securely about her waist, but her knees quaked so beneath her that she had to concentrate hard just to remain on her feet.

"I'm afraid your soldiers . . ." He paused for emphasis, letting his icy blue eyes rake over the three who still lived, ". . . had it in their minds to assault our kind hostess, Colonel. I'm sure that's not what you had in mind when you gave orders to enjoy the hospitality." His voice was low and calm, almost a purr. Yet the violent anger within him was a powerful, living thing, and the force of it made Ambrosia shudder.

Caleb attempted a wan smile as the colonel's blue eyes slipped inquiringly to his face. "We was jus' funin' a little, Colonel. Didn't mean no harm." The colonel's face remained hard, and Caleb spread his hands in supplication. "We wasn't gonna hurt th' filly, y' understand, sir. We jus' was gonna learn her some manners."

The colonel was unmoved by Caleb's words until Julian Bardo rose and took up their defense. "It seems to me, Colonel, that this man and his friends were slightly out of order. But this has been a long, hard war and as the private said, the men meant no harm.''

Colonel Reed's eyes shifted to Drayton. ''You shot a man in the back of the head, Major,'' he said slowly. ''There was no good cause for killing him in cold blood.''

Caleb's eyes lit with victory and he drew a sigh of relief. He just might have his fun with the bitch yet and see the high-and-mighty Major Rambert's neck stretched as well.

''I have no choice but to take you into custody, Major,'' the colonel said tersely. He turned on a heel and made to leave the barn.

''Don't you, sir?'' A tiny click and the surprised gasps of several men caused Reed to whirl about again. He had discounted the fact that Rambert still held his revolver. Now it was aimed at him, point-blank. He knew all too well that one bullet would put Rambert in total command.

''I don't intend to be taken into custody, Colonel. Not for preventing your soldiers from perpetrating a crime against a civilian.''

The colonel stood still and silent, his labored breathing and clenched fists the only sign of his agitation.

''If you take a moment to look at the lash marks on her back, you will realize that your men intended serious physical harm.'' Drayton paused as the colonel's eyes flicked over the small figure huddled against Rambert's broad chest, at the bloodied stripes across her back where the whip had torn the coarse fabric of her dress. His eyes returned to Drayton's. ''I sincerely doubt that any court,'' he went on softly, ''military or civil, would equate being 'slightly out of order' with the crime of rape.''

Colonel Reed's eyes darted momentarily to Bardo. There was a raging hatred in the scarred face, but no intention of crossing the major. The men who stood behind the colonel now were of the same mind. Some would have raped the woman without a second thought, but none wanted to challenge a man of Drayton's reputation. Particularly when he held a revolver in his hand.

"Sergeant Rykert."

A tall, balding man snapped to attention. "Yes, sir?"

"Privates Bagly, Turner, and Angus are under arrest. They are to be kept under constant guard until they can be sent to the surgeon."

His eyes remained locked with Rambert's, ignoring the wounded men's protests of innocence as they were taken into custody, keeping close watch on the gun that was yet leveled on his chest.

As the rest of the soldiers began a wary retreat from the stable, Bardo's voice rang low and threatening. "You won't get away with this, Rambert. You killed a man in cold blood, and I intend to write a story that will ruin you." He smiled. "And I'll have fifty eyewitness accounts to back me up."

Rambert gave a shrug. "Print what you like, Bardo. I've no desire to be one of your paper heroes."

Colonel Reed stiffened at the obvious affront. "Your conduct has been questionable at best, Rambert," he admonished sharply when he found his voice. "I would advise you to remember who's in command here."

"I'm very much aware of who's in command, Colonel." Drayton's eyes flicked significantly over Bardo.

The colonel's face went livid and his mouth tightened into a thin, white line. Letting out a furious breath, he whirled and marched stiffly from the stable.

Bardo's black eyes narrowed as he watched the colonel's retreat. He turned to face the major, his forefinger tracing idly over the scar at his cheek. "I'm going to write my story, Rambert," he said softly, slowly. "And I'm going to see that you pay for this. If not in one way . . . ." His eyes moved pointedly to Ambrosia before meeting the major's again. He smiled, then turned and was gone.

Ambrosia clung to Drayton's coat and dared not open her eyes through the entire exchange. She was only vaguely aware that the voices stopped, that there were sounds of retreating soldiers, groans of the wounded men as they were removed none too gently by the others. She started in terror at the final slam of the wooden door against the side of the stable.

When the last of the noises had died away, Drayton slowly lowered his revolver. His eyes were still alert in the semidarkness for any who might have remained to challenge him. He let out a long breath as he cautiously placed the gun in its holster, his full attention shifting then to her injuries.

"Ambrosia?" He whispered the name, caressing it with softness as he gently uncoiled the white fingers that gripped too tightly to his tunic. She fought him for an instant, her eyes opening wide and dazed as he firmly drew back to look at her face. "It's all right. They've gone. There's nothing here to hurt you."

The blank stare faded slowly from her eyes, but with reality came a tremor of barely restrained emotion echoing through her. She swallowed hard and looked away from him, instinctively trying to break free of his embrace now, wanting to sob her humiliation, her revulsion, her fear, but certainly not wanting a Yankee to see her.

"You're hurt." He held her fast and raised cautious fingertips to touch the bruise at her temple.

She turned away, her spine stiff and rigid with resistance. "Let go of me."

Her voice was so cold and final that he was taken by surprise. He released her, scowling darkly as she stumbled but a few steps and reached blindly for the side of the nearest stall. A single long stride put him beside her again. He began to examine the flesh wounds at her back, ignoring her weak, disjointed protests. "You're covered with dirt and mud and God-knows-what. These wounds will fester quickly if they aren't cleaned."

"I can take care of myself, Major." She jerked away from his hand. Her movement caused the room to lean sharply to one side, then to the other. She gripped the wooden post and tried to steady herself, but she continued to sway until she was leaning her full weight against it, seeing long, blurry images that refused to right themselves.

Drayton swung an arm beneath her knees and a second about her waist, easily lifting her from the floor. Her arms flew tightly about his neck and she braced herself against the nausea that rose in her throat as he carried her across the stable.

Just as he reached the door, he stopped short. He dropped her feet to the ground and drew his pistol in one sweeping motion. Ambrosia grasped tightly to his coat and hid her face in her hands as the hinges let out a soft groan of protest. A gnarled black hand eased the door slowly open from the other side, and two dark eyes peered anxiously through the crack in the door. The major relaxed his stance and returned his gun to his holster. "It's all right. It's only Andrew."

He lifted her again and proceeded briskly toward the house, giving a reassuring nod to the wide-eyed black who held the door ajar, then stumbled clumsily after them in an attempt to match Rambert's long-legged stride. The sudden coolness of the twilight air worked to clear Ambrosia's brain, and her hand swiftly left his neck to close the gaping bodice of her gown. She hazarded a look at him, then looked to where he was taking her. "I am capable of walking."

He tossed her a skeptical glance, not slowing his pace in the least. "Put me down, Major." She squirmed and forced him to meet her glare, swiftly becoming angry at having her demands so easily dismissed. "I told you to put me down."

He tossed a glance over his shoulder and allowed Andrew to catch up, all the while resisting Ambrosia's struggles to regain her feet. "I said, put—"

"I fully intend to," he returned with curt finality. "As soon as we get where we're going." They were nearing the rear entrance to the house, and Andrew scrambled forward to get the door. Major Rambert made for the back stairs but was stopped by Ambrosia's shriek of protest.

"No! Not up there!" She let go of her torn dress to press both fists against him in earnest. "Colonel Reed requisitioned all the rooms upstairs for himself and his men."

Drayton frowned and looked up the stairs, then evenly met her eyes. "Where are your things?"

Ambrosia lifted her chin and turned her head. "Put me down."

"Where are your things?"

She winced and bit her lip at his hard, demanding tone. "In Father's study," she said in a small voice.

Drayton made his way to the study, which he found cluttered with clothing and linens and sundries, so much that Andrew had to clear off a chair for him to put Ambrosia down. "Go and fetch the healing box, and some bandages from the parlor," Drayton ordered as he deposited her gingerly on the chair. "And bring a fresh pitcher of water."

"Bring Sheba back with you," Ambrosia called after him.

Major Rambert raised an amused brow as she flashed him a distrustful glare. "You seem to be feeling much better."

She turned her head away, not wanting to meet his eyes as he lifted a pile of Elly's undergarments from the corner of the desk and tossed it aside. "Would you care to tell me what you were doing out there? In the stable? All by yourself?" His amusement had fled now and he was angry. She could very easily have been killed if Andrew hadn't informed him of what was happening, if he had arrived just a few moments later.

Drayton half stood, half sat on the cleared edge of the

desk, leaning forward expectantly and letting a long, muscular arm dangle leisurely across his knee. Ambrosia sat, tight-lipped and rigid, fully aware of his anger, both her hands holding fast to her torn bodice. The space of silence lengthened. Drayton's anger grew stronger. She needed to learn a lesson from this. The next time, he would not be here to protect her, and he did not want to think what might happen to her then. "You seem to have a way of seeking out trouble, Miss Lanford," he began.

"Seeking out—!" She sprang to her feet, but her head rolled with the sudden movement and she was forced to sit down again. She drew a deep breath and braced a single hand on the side of the desk. "Yankees are the trespassers here, not I! Am I to watch as they torture and kill a helpless animal? This is Lanford land and it always will be, Major. It is mine, and I am free to do what I please here." She lifted her chin haughtily and gave him a condescending glare. "Drunken, thieving, bloodthirsty bluecoats and your self-righteous abolitionism! May you all burn in hell!" she muttered.

"Heah's de box, Majah, sah," Andrew announced as he clumsily opened the door and headed straight for the Yankee. "An' ah brung d' watah too."

Ambrosia's head shot up and her eyes swiftly searched the doorway. "Where's Sheba?" she demanded sharply.

"Sheba?" Andrew repeated with a blank stare.

"I told you to fe—"

"Thank you, Andrew." Drayton accepted the box from Andrew and pointed to the space on the desk where he could place the pitcher of water. "I will take care of everything here."

Ambrosia's eyes widened as the black gave a meek nod and made to leave. "Oh, no you will not! I will not have you giving orders to my people, Major. They listen to me! I will not have it!"

Even as she spoke, Drayton was placing an arm about Andrew's stooped shoulders and leading him to the door. She caught the general drift of what he was saying all the while he walked the old man, explaining to him about blows to the head and befuddled states of mind and dizziness. Andrew listened and nodded in agreement, ignoring Ambrosia's angry string of protests which continued nonstop until he left the room. Drayton closed the door behind him. Then she stopped in midsentence. The silence fell instantly and uneasily.

Ambrosia's eyes hardened as she met his cool blue eyes. "I am not amused, Major."

He gave an innocent shrug and approached her. "I'm merely intent on returning a favor. You tended my wounds the other night."

"That's a favor I neither want nor need returned," she retorted.

"Forgive me, Ambrosia, but I am of another opinion." His eyes were dark and serious. "I cannot bear the thought of your back being permanently scarred . . . or worse . . ." He came to stand at the side of the chair and placed the healing box on a stack of blankets nearby. Ambrosia considered bolting for the door, but there was still a fuzziness to her vision, and her head was beginning to throb. She clutched tightly to her bodice with both hands and made up her mind to endure whatever torture he had in mind with dignity. She closed her eyes and held her breath as he ran long, lean fingers through her hair, pausing to test the swollen area just above the ear. "You took quite a bump," he told her as he continued to examine the area. "It will probably pain you for a week."

"Thank you," she said icily.

She relaxed a bit when he stepped back from her but frowned darkly when he stepped close again, a scissors in his hand. His fingers took hold of her shoulders and turned her at an angle, paying little heed to the hot protest that followed. Catching both her wrists firmly in one of his hands, he lifted the scissors to cut open the back of her dress. He accomplished this in a single movement, then laid the scissors aside and struggled to hold her still so that he might gently separate the garment from the wounds. But she wanted no part of his ministrations. She wrenched and twisted and managed to thwart him quite effectively until his temper snapped. With a brisk, "Stop it!" his grasp on her forearms tightened abruptly, and he jerked her to a stunned silence of which he took immediate advantage.

Pulling the tatters of dress and chemise from her shoulders and leaving her to protect her modesty as best she could, he began to work with a moistened cloth, to loosen the bits of fabric and dirt from the deep slashes the whip had left on her back. He winced as he tore at the already tender wounds, though Ambrosia remained silent and gave no sign of the pain his work caused her. When he finished cleaning the wounds and applying the salve she had recommended for Laird a few days before, he set himself to binding them with a long roll of linen. He pulled the remnants of her bodice from her hands to draw the linen strip about her ribcage, leaving her to endure a humiliation that was far worse than the pain. Though his hands continued their precise movements with studied indifference, more than once Ambrosia felt his eyes linger on her naked breasts, and she felt her cheeks flaring hot and pink whenever his fingers grazed her skin. She bit her lip hard and squared her shoulders.

"You seem to enjoy humiliating me, Major." Her voice was low, her tone much subdued.

Drayton paused and cocked his head in surprise. "I have yet to see you humbled, Miss Lanford."

She turned her head then to search his face. There was no trace of amusement in his eyes. She looked away, her pride somehow soothed by his response. For a moment she was silent. "The man Bardo," she mused aloud. "He hates you for some reason."

Drayton gave a short laugh. "The feeling is a mutual one."

"He threatened to write things that would ruin your reputation."

Drayton knotted the bandage, then met her eyes. "It doesn't matter to me what he writes."

It was obvious to Ambrosia that he spoke the truth. She held his eyes a moment longer, then looked away and was silent for another moment. "Why did you stop them?"

He did not answer immediately, so she twisted again to face him. "Why?" she repeated, holding his eyes.

He shrugged and turned his attention to clipping the ends of the bandage. "I don't know."

Ambrosia stared at him a bit longer, then let out a long, thoughtful breath and looked straight ahead. "It might have meant your life, Major," she reminded him softly, pointedly.

Drayton closed the jar of ointment and set it aside, replacing everything neatly in the box and closing the lid. He rose then and rounded the chair, coming to stand before her. He bent low, placing an arm to either side of her and leaning his weight on the chair. Ambrosia's fingers tightened instinctively on the ruined fabric she had lifted again to cover her breasts. "Is my life of value to you, Ambrosia?"

"N-no Yankee's life is of value to me," she managed in a hushed voice. She turned her face away from his small, taunting smile, feeling the heat of his breath on her cheek, feeling the thudding of her heart with his closeness. She pressed her back hard against the back of the chair, heedless of the discomfort, wishing only to avoid his powerful masculine presence. His fingers caressed her jawline from her bruised temple to her chin, pausing to tilt her face upward, forcing her to meet his gaze. His eyes were intent, a clear, vivid blue. "Are you quite certain of that?"

She pushed his hand away, but he merely caught her fingers and pressed his lips deliberately against them. Ambrosia shivered and tried to retrieve her hand, not liking the way her breath caught at his touch, afraid to meet the question those dark blue eyes continued to pose. He held fast her hand, turning it, sighing as he contemplated its cuts and blisters, pulling it again against her will toward his lips, tenderly pressing a kiss to its palm. Ambrosia's last shred of composure flew, and something warm and new broke through to the innermost reaches of her heart, touching her in a way she did not want to be touched. Another man had kissed her thus, so very, very long ago. How long she had waited for it to happen again, though she had never admitted it to anyone, not even herself.

"Ambrosia . . ."

He whispered her name, his mouth descending slowly toward hers, so slowly that an eternity passed before it reached its destination. In those long, endless moments, the dim spark of warmth grew inside her, flaring bright and hot with the magic touch of his lips. Stronger, much stronger than her hatred or her fear. Her senses cried out with a heightened awareness as his fingers slid possessively up her arm, bringing her to her feet, pulling her into an intimate embrace. He had intended only a brief, proper kiss. But he had not been prepared for the desire that washed over him with her compliance. His mouth was moist and playful as it moved deliberately over hers, becoming more and more serious as he sensed her willingness. A small, trembling hand slipped against his chest, letting the tattered gown fall from her grasp. Then another hand, until her palms were flat against the great expanse, feeling the warmth, feeling the racing of his heart. His kiss became aggressive then, his tongue slipping cleverly through her lips, probing, tasting, plundering, bringing a rush of memories, very recent and very repulsive. Suddenly horrified at her nakedness, she gasped and stiffened as he moved to cup her breast. She pulled away and tried to cover herself, not really understanding what had happened, wondering how she could ever have allowed him such liberties. He felt the change in her at once and carefully searched her face.

She swallowed a large lump in her throat and forced

herself to face him. "You are no better than they," she spat at him, hating the bitter taste of the words. "Your life is worth nothing to me! Nothing!"

She was breathing hard, wishing that he would release her quickly, wishing that she could ignore the warm, strong feel of him against her, wishing that she could forget the kiss he had pressed to her palm. For a long moment she waited, tense and afraid of his next move. It would be all too easy for him to prove her a liar, and she had never been so afraid of being caught in a lie as at this moment.

But his face wore an odd expression, regretful and distant, until suddenly, the cool, impenetrable mask fell again. "My apologies, Miss Lanford," he said almost lightly. There was a slight mocking ring to his tone, and she wondered briefly if he meant the taunt for himself as well as her. She felt a twinge of guilt for her lie, and even sorrier that she could not hate him as she would have liked to.

A brief knock at the door startled the major to a proper distance and caused Ambrosia to fall limply into the chair and make a futile attempt at covering herself. Sheba entered the room a moment later and hesitated when she saw Major Rambert. She struggled to balance a pot of herb tea and a cup on a tray when her hands began to tremble. She was keenly aware of the uneasy silence, and as the major made a hasty departure, she noticed that Ambrosia fingered nervously at the remnants of her gown and stared dazedly straight ahead.

Without asking if she wanted it, Sheba poured her a cup of the tea and set it beside her on the desk, then went to get a comforter recently taken from upstairs to cover Ambrosia's bare shoulders. Ambrosia raised her eyes briefly when Sheba offered it to her, managing only the weakest of smiles in gratitude for her concern.

"Go and get the others now," Ambrosia told her. "We shall all sleep in here tonight."

Sheba pursed her lips and shrugged, then made to

leave the room. But as she chanced one last curious glance at Ambrosia and found her staring numbly at her opened hand, she wondered exactly what the Yankee major had said and done besides caring for her wounds.

Chapter 7

Morning dawned gray and threatening, as if winter wished to offer one final stand against the coming of spring. Just after the grayish light took hold, Hunt, Essex, and Riley returned to Heritage along with a dozen men from their regiment and a wagon to transport their wounded back to the regiment surgeon.

Ambrosia rose with the dawn and hurried to help Sheba prepare a breakfast for the soldiers, which emptied the last of their foodstores. All through the preparation Ambrosia did a mental accounting of damages and losses, and tried to imagine rationing what little had been buried over the following weeks. But she could not allow herself to dwell on despairing thoughts, not when the soldiers were preparing for departure, not when the wounded and prisoners had already been carried out of the parlor to the waiting wagons. The Yankees would be gone soon and life at Heritage would go on. To Ambrosia, that was all that really mattered.

Ambrosia was in the kitchen when Sergeant Rykert approached her, summoning her to the parlor on a matter of some urgency. She responded promptly, hoping only that neither Colonel Reed nor Major Rambert had decided to delay his departure. The moment she stepped into the house, she froze. Soldiers were rushing everywhere,

grabbing everything in sight, stuffing pockets and bags
with a mad fervor. One was removing miniatures of her
grandparents from the wall, several others were opening
and emptying drawers and cabinets. A few were even
fighting over the larger pieces of furniture. Ambrosia
stared in horror, then almost ran to the parlor, hoping that
it would not be too late to stop them. At the threshold of
the parlor she froze a second time, her eyes mirroring her
shock. There too soldiers were roaming wildly about,
pulling tables across the floor, even rolling up the threadbare carpets. In the center of the room stood Colonel
Reed, Julian Bardo, and the Yankee major. The colonel
wore a slight smile, as if he relished the words he spoke
to Major Rambert, all the while holding a cigar clamped
between his teeth.

". . . And my orders do not concern you, Major. I
will not tolerate any interference."

His smile widened then, and he removed the cigar
from his mouth. "Ah . . . Miss Lanford. I've been waiting to speak with you."

Ambrosia tried to calm herself as she strode toward
him, wondering why he was suddenly in such a good humor. "What are your men doing, Colonel?" she demanded tersely. "I was under the impression that you
gave orders—"

"I gave orders for my men to enjoy the hospitality,
Miss Lanford," he interrupted shortly. He blew a large
cloud of smoke and watched it rise, curling to the fancy
plaster ceiling. "But at the time I gave those orders, I had
no idea of your anti-Union sentiments. Indeed, Major
Rambert lead me to believe that you were a loyal citizen."

Ambrosia stared at him in disbelief. This was South
Carolina, and she was a Lanford. How could anyone
have thought for a moment that she was less than a Confederate?

He flicked an ash to the floor and raised an expectant
brow. "Do you deny it?"

Her green eyes flashed as she lifted her chin. "Deny what?"

"That you support the rebellion. That you are a Confederate sympathizer?"

Had Ambrosia been only slightly less shocked, she would have laughed in his face. "Shall I also deny my name, Colonel?"

Colonel Reed met her glare for a long moment, then turned his back and paced a few steps from her. "Mr. Bardo found two Confederate flags in the house," he stated matter-of-factly. "And several thousand dollars worth of Confederate bonds were also found, buried in the yard." He whirled to face her, his eyes narrowed in accusation. "Do you deny ownership of these items, Miss Lanford?"

"I deny nothing."

"Am I to assume then, that you refuse to take an oath of loyalty to the Union?"

Something in Drayton's eyes cautioned her against the retort she almost flung back at him. She calmed herself and spoke slowly. "None of this is justification for stealing, Colonel."

"I need not offer any justification to the enemy!" he barked.

In spite of what had happened the night before, Ambrosia's gaze flew anxiously to Drayton's face. She was suddenly afraid of what was happening, afraid of losing everything. And though she hated herself for admitting to any such fear, and even more for seeking his help, her eyes silently sought the favor. Colonel Reed followed her gaze. "Major Rambert has no authority here," he reminded her shortly. "I am in charge."

She stared at Drayton a moment longer, searching desperately for the protection he had offered her before. But his eyes were hard now, except for what might have been a tiny spark of pity. She watched numbly as he turned to give a curt salute to the colonel, then left the room with a quick, angry stride. And suddenly she knew. He had tried. He had pleaded her case and lost, and he would fight no more. She felt a cold prickling at the nape of her neck at the realization. She was alone now and powerless.

The colonel rose to his full height and drew a long puff on his cigar as he watched Rambert's exit. But it was the other man, Julian Bardo, who seemed more eager to gloat over his victory. He clasped his hands behind his back and stepped toward Ambrosia. "Perhaps you have learned a lesson in all this, Miss Lanford."

She stiffened and jerked away from him.

He smiled and stepped close again. "The next time you must be more careful about choosing a protector. I could have saved you from all this. . . ." He gestured about with his hand. "But you chose Rambert. And now you will lose everything."

Ambrosia whirled and slapped him across the face as hard as she could. Everything was dead silent for a long moment then as every eye in the room riveted on her and Bardo. Slowly, he lifted his hand to touch the red imprint that had appeared on his face, feeling the hot sting of the impact in disbelief.

The colonel tossed his cigar angrily to the floor. "You have half an hour to take your people and evacuate the house. I have orders to see it, and any other haven for Rebels, destroyed to the last timber."

Ambrosia felt a tear slip over her cheek, for all her efforts to hold it back. If she had had a gun, she would have shot the colonel and Bardo dead, and died willingly in exchange for seeing their blood. But she had no weapon, no way to fight so many, no way to prevent the slaughter of everything she held dear. She had only a tiny remnant of her pride.

Without a word she left the parlor and went to salvage what little she could that had not already been stolen and to somehow tell the others what she had been told.

The morning remained dark and gray, and a chilly, intermittent drizzle began as the noon approached. Ambrosia stood tall and silent beside Elly and the three blacks, her eyes dark and distant, watching the soldiers load up the last of the livestock, watching them carry off shovels and tools that might have meant a chance for beginning again, watching the men destroy what few things they did not take. She was overcome by bitterness as she watched Crawford and Riley and several of Major Rambert's men helping themselves to a share of the spoils as well. The major said nothing to stop them, and her hatred and bitterness grew. She met his eyes only once, briefly, but long enough to see the resignation in them, long enough to ignore the regret. She clenched her fists tightly to restrain the desire to scream at him, to hurt him, to destroy a part of him. Ambrosia lifted her eyes to the screaming soldiers who eagerly snatched up torches from a great bonfire at the front of the house. They ran like scores of fiery demons to spread their senseless destruction. Draperies, shutters, rugs, banisters, bookcases—all were set aflame. Then the shed, the springhouse, the carriage house, the kitchen, the stable . . . The fire was everywhere.

For a time, the great house seemed immune to the flames, standing proud and aloof, even as the bright redgold tongues licked voraciously at its every corner. Then one after another, windows cracked and exploded. The interior became an inferno as the hungry flames sought to feed on the fresh, cool air outside. The dream that was Heritage was dying before Ambrosia's eyes, leaving her alone and empty.

Huge clouds of smoke mushroomed all about the flames, and a strong, acrid odor clung to the humid air. The flames roared high and almost glorious as they consumed the cupola, crackling and gasping and relentlessly devouring. When the cupola fell and the largest part of the roof collapsed, Colonel Reed gave orders for his men to depart. As soon as they had gone, Rambert turned quickly and also led his men away. Only after the last of the Yankees rode out of sight did Ambrosia collapse in a small, convulsing heap to sob in utter helplessness as the fire ran its course.

The fire burned out of control until nightfall, when it began to rain in earnest. By then the grand walls of Heritage lay crumpled, fallen in defeat. Only a few brave tongues of orange managed to flicker into the darkness of the night, mingling their hissing and popping sounds with the gentle patter of raindrops. Ambrosia sat silent and oblivious to all, the rain cold on her hot cheeks, the wind sending shivers through her that echoed the cold ache in her soul. When darkness fell, the others thought to find shelter in the nearby woods, but Ambrosia refused to move. Andrew remained by her side throughout the night.

The first light of dawn illuminated the hills of Heritage with a bright golden glow, but the highest hill stood scarred and blackened, like a spectral reminder of a life that had once been rich and full and beautiful. Ambrosia's eyes were glassy and unblinking as they fixed on the ruins, refusing to believe. Her expression did not alter the slightest bit, even when Josiah crouched to the ground beside her, though his appearance had surprised the others.

"You all right, Miz Ambrosia?" he asked solicitously. "They didn't hurt you, did they?"

Her eyes left the shadowed ruins for a moment to gaze dumbly at his worried face. She said nothing, her eyes moving to the remains of the house once more. Tears flowed freely down her cheeks, though she sat utterly silent, as if unaware of them. Josiah sighed and glanced uncertainly up at Sheba, who gave a helpless shrug. It was Andrew who came to Josiah's aid, bending his cramped old legs to kneel beside her on the opposite side, putting his calloused, gnarled hand against her cheek. "Miz Ambrosia? Miz Ambrosia?" He prodded her until she met his eyes. "We can't stay heah, Miz Ambrosia. Ain' nothin' lef' fo' us heah. We gots t' go fin' us a place t' stay."

Her eyes flickered with momentary recognition, then she turned away. "You are all free to go," she told them in a hushed voice. "I—I cannot offer you a home any longer."

Josiah and Andrew exchanged a quick glance, then looked to Sheba and Sally who shook their heads determinedly. Only Elly drew a ragged breath and faced them with timidity. The big house was gone now. The Lanford name meant nothing anymore.

"Ain't nothing to keep us here," she insisted in a tearful whimper. "We'll all die if we stay here. It's cold and wet—we'll die!"

Ambrosia faced her with eyes which seemed suddenly old and faded. "You are free to go, Elly," she said with a strange indifference. "Your brother's place isn't far from here. Everyone is free to go."

Elly's face brightened a bit, but her eyes slipped uncertainly over the slaves who stood by Ambrosia so loyally. It made her feel guilty to be leaving, but survival was more important to Elly than any qualms of conscience. She turned abruptly to gather up the few personal items she had salvaged from the house. And then she was gone.

The blacks shook their heads after her while they stood steadfastly at Ambrosia's side. But there was an uneasy anxiety among them about what was to be done. For the past two years Ambrosia had given them orders, and they had been utterly dependent on her directions. Only Josiah had been on his own long enough to determine that breakfast was the first immediate need to be satisfied, and he left to find some small game. His initiative seemed to spur the others into action. Sheba and Sally went to dig up the provisions that had been buried weeks before, which proved quite a task without a proper shovel. Andrew gingerly poked about the remains of the kitchen, eventually locating a heavy old pot under the smoldering debris. It was badly dented but still serviceable, and it gave him reason to hope that there might be more.

It was some time later when all the scavengers converged and were able to put together a meal. No one spoke of what would be done afterward; no one spoke much at all.

When Josiah offered Ambrosia an old, misshapen tin cup filled with stew, she glanced without interest at it, then looked away.

"Eat, Miz Ambrosia," he urged, placing the cup firmly in her hand. "You starvin' t' death ain't gonna' bring back what's gone."

"Nothing will ever bring it back," she said softly. Ambrosia looked up at him with tortured eyes and slowly shook her head. "Nothing."

Josiah closed his eyes and sighed, then moved the cup with renewed determination toward her mouth. "Eat first. Massah Jackson always said a man thinks twice as good on a full stomach."

Ambrosia twisted away from the cup and her eyes clouded with tears. "There's nothing to think about anymore, Josiah. Nothing left to hold on to. Nowhere to go—" Her voice caught and she covered her face with her hands, ashamed of her tears. She did not want to cry but there was nothing left of strength inside her to stop it. All the memories of yesterday, all the dreams of tomorrow lay before her in ashes.

Josiah fumbled clumsily with the cup for a moment, then managed to rest a timid hand on her shoulder. "We still have folks, Miz Ambrosia. Miz 'lissa an' Massah Ledger, they'll take us in. But we can't stay here."

Ambrosia sniffed back a fresh onslaught of tears and wiped roughly at her cheeks with the back of her hand. The thought of leaving Heritage was unbearable, of running to her sister for help even worse. But the mention of Ledger's name made a tiny seed of hope take root in her deepest despair. Ledger . . . she closed her eyes and remembered the youthful, handsome face framed with thick, golden hair; the flashy, reckless smile; the clear, blue eyes so like a spring sky. Moments before she had believed that everything she loved was gone. But Josiah reminded her of what her heart had never really forgotten. She loved Ledger most of all.

She opened her eyes and drew a long, unsteady breath as she gazed at the smoldering ruins one last time. She turned away. Father was dead. The house was gone. The means of rebuilding had been destroyed. Yet there was still something of hope left inside her. Her eyes fell on a small splash of purple in the greening grass and were fixed on it for several moments before she realized what it was. She bent to touch the tiny violet, which had braved the wet, chilly night to blossom so much earlier than any of the other flowers. Ambrosia plucked it from its tiny stem and touched it to her cheek.

"Miz Ambrosia?"

She sighed and raised newly confident eyes, finally accepting the tin cup of stew. She would need strength to make the journey to Charleston on foot, without any money or provisions to speak of. And God only knew what they might find when they got there. She pushed that thought aside and began to eat in earnest, instructing the others to do likewise. They would all need their strength for what was to come.

Part Two

Charleston
April 1865

Chapter 8

The late April sun was a blaze of white gold as it rose above the city of Charleston, though the air was still pleasantly mild and the breezes cool. Ambrosia waited until Sheba unlatched the heavy wrought-iron gate, then swept impatiently past her onto the street. She paused for a moment, letting her eyes scan the long row of houses, each bearing disfiguring scars of the shelling in the harsh sunlight, each sadly in need of patch and paint. The houses were all tall and thin and stood at right angles to the street, each protected by a surrounding brick wall or wrought-iron fence. Some houses were pink, green, or yellow, colors which only made their current state of disrepair all the more apparent. All was strangely quiet.

The war was over; the South had been brought to her knees and had finally admitted defeat at Appomattox Court House weeks before. And though the hatred and bitterness inside Ambrosia raged stronger than ever against the Yankee victors, she had come to accept the fact that the Confederacy had been defeated on the battlefield. It was not right; it was not just. But she had learned many years before that right and justice were not always victorious. Still, life went on. It was a very different kind of life, a life of hardship, of poverty. But at least there was hope of changing those things. At least there would be no more killing and burning.

Ambrosia drew a deep breath and closed her eyes for a moment. There was so much to be rebuilt, so much that had been lost in those terrible four years. She opened her eyes and tried to shake off the uncertainties that clouded her mind. The men were coming home, more and more of them every day. Yet no horses were tied to the iron hitching posts which edged the streets; no carriages traversed the pockmarked roads. The high-spirited, pure-blooded stallions and expensive carriages which had once clogged Charleston's streets were things of the past, luxuries the proud gentry of this city could no longer afford. And Ledger . . . Ledger! Ambrosia repeated the name over and over in her mind, as though it could somehow take away the sights and smells of war that surrounded her. But then her eyes dimmed and her brow drew into a worried frown. Many, many soldiers had returned to Charleston these past weeks. Ledger had not. And Melissa had not heard from him, not a single word in months.

Ambrosia drew deeply of the fragrant air, heavily scented with flowers and the lingering tang of smoke. She needed to get away from the Bowman house, from the crowded quarters and the endless discussions of what had gone wrong with the world and what else was apt to go wrong. The proper folk of Charleston, for the most part, still kept to their houses and with good reason. Just two weeks before, the news of Lincoln's assassination disrupted the uneasy peace that Federal occupation had brought in late February. For nearly a week Union troops struggled to quell riots, looting, and destruction brought on by hundreds of disgruntled Negroes who had flocked to Charleston in the hopes of claiming confiscated lands. There was no land to be claimed here in the city, despite rumors to the contrary. And the thousands of newly freed slaves pouring into Charleston only threatened famine and more destruction for a city that had been ravaged by four long years of war.

Ambrosia sighed and began walking, noticing the tiny bits of glass that sparkled in the street. The larger pieces of glass and debris had already been cleared away by Federal troops. And the Yankees had forced order on the madness of the past weeks at least, she admitted silently as she passed a pair of patrolling soldiers. The two turned a curious eye on her and watched her make her way up the sidewalk for several moments before resuming their walk. She was a striking woman, even in black, obviously high-born. An observer could sense it in her stride and bearing, even if the huge Negress had not followed dutifully, protectively behind her with the look of a mother hen. The soldiers were surprised to see such a woman out so soon after General Sickles's order barring citizens from the streets had been lifted.

Ambrosia paused uncertainly at the corner of Broad and Meeting streets, then continued on though most of the residences beyond the intersection had been taken over by Union officers. The Bowmans, like many Charleston families, shared their home now with homeless relatives, all crowding into the small house on Meeting Street, trying their best to make do. Though Ledger's mother had managed a smile and a generous welcome for her daughter-in-law's kin, Madeline Bowman had not been overjoyed at the prospect of another mouth to feed, to say the least. The loyal Negroes Ambrosia had brought along helped make her arrival slightly more palatable. At least they could collect the food rations handed out daily by the Freedman's Bureau and keep meager fare on the table.

Ambrosia had not mentioned to anyone the gold coins Josiah had given to her, and she did not intend to. She had been furious when he had told her the truth about what had happened, furious about accepting charity from a Yankee, especially when that same Yankee had a hand in reducing them to the poverty they now endured. But her anger had subsided with the admission of cold reality. They had been left homeless and utterly destitute, and four loyal former slaves, who now shared quarters with the Bowman's handful of remaining servants at the rear of the Bowman house, were dependent on her for their survival. She had decided then and there that they would indeed survive, that they would someday return to Heritage and rebuild what had been lost. Even after the journey, she had sixty dollars in gold left in the leather pouch, sixty dollars she did not intend to waste on food as long as they were not starving.

She stopped for a moment and lifted her eyes to scan the shell of a huge brick building destroyed by fire years earlier. Stark, smoke-darkened arches rose from the rubble, supporting nothing more than a memory of what had been. Ambrosia lifted her chin and slowly moved on, her eyes becoming accustomed to the destruction all around her, her steps becoming firm and resolute. If she were ever to be able to leave this place, if she were ever to be able to return to Heritage, she would have to have more than sixty dollars. And that would mean she would have to find work—certainly no easy task in this city where the only jobs were army or government bureau jobs, both of which required applicants to take an oath of loyalty to the Union. Ambrosia knew of many proper women doing needlework and sewing, but she had almost gone mad trying to fill her hours with such work these past weeks. There were other women who had taken the oath in order to get positions teaching the children of Union officers stationed now in Charleston, or even teaching Negro children. The Yankees paid a decent wage. But Ambrosia could not bring herself to take the oath, not when she considered what her refusal to do so had cost her just two months before, not when she considered that her pride was the only thing she had salvaged from Heritage's ashes. She could never betray the flag her father had died to defend.

She sighed as she continued her walking, knowing that

her chances of finding any kind of employment were almost nonexistent. But she had needed so to get out of the house, to be by herself for a little while, to be free of the stifling, crowded rooms always buzzing with gossip and conjecture, and even from the garden that had imprisoned all its beauty behind high walls and gates. She had never been close to Melissa, and with the forced confinement and the recent news of the burning of the Bowman plantation on the Ashley River, Melissa's incessant whining and pessimistic remarks drove Ambrosia to her breaking point. Ambrosia was accustomed to being on her own, to walking alone about the wide, open spaces of Heritage, and to a life which demanded all her strength and will. She was a fighter by nature, and helplessness was something she could not bear to live with. In the Bowman house these days there was nothing to do but sit and wait for news of Ledger. Ambrosia felt every hour of confinement eating away at her courage, her resolve, her spirit. And in that she was not alone. Even Sheba had given in to tears this past week, and it was no wonder, the way she was bossed about the Bowman's kitchen and made to feel like an unwanted servant. The old black woman had been in command of her own kitchen too long to adjust to being an ordinary menial again.

Ambrosia halted abruptly when a large woman with flaming red hair stepped from a newly painted building, struggling almost comically with a hammer, nails, and a large wooden sign. Ambrosia cocked her chin curiously and stared as the garish, overdressed woman attempted to fix the red-and-white, hastily painted sign beside the door. The woman drove a single nail with twenty swings that Ambrosia could have tacked in two, then backed up into the street and admired her handiwork. The redhead studied it for a moment, walking a few steps to the right, then a few steps to the left, then grinning and giving a short nod of approval. She returned to the sign and put in another nail.

Ambrosia swung her skirt to the side and made to step

around the woman, who still blocked the sidewalk. But she suddenly thought better of it and peeked into the shop. Her eyes widened at the clutter and confusion which crowded every inch of space in the large room. Crates were stacked precariously one atop another, papers were strewn everywhere, and items just unpacked were tossed in haphazard piles, while shelves and counters stood completely empty. The woman left her sign and followed Ambrosia into the shop, catching her look of astonishment.

"I'm afraid things aren't too organized yet," she apologized with what struck Ambrosia as a horrible Northern accent. "But if you'll just tell me what you're looking for, I'll probably be able to find it . . . somewhere."

Ambrosia turned to face her and gave a shrug. "Actually, Miss—"

"It's Mrs. O'Neal. I'm a widow woman now, nigh on a year."

Ambrosia politely inclined her head in acknowledgment. "Actually, Mrs. O'Neal, I was merely . . . er— browsing. . . ." She couldn't help but frown at the disorganization as she spoke, and Maggie O'Neal snorted with frustration and turned away. This woman wore black, as almost all of them did. And the threadbare look of that dress gave her little hope for a sale.

After years of working in her husband's small shop, Maggie O'Neal could recognize a good prospect from a bad, though she generally treated everyone with the same amount of attention. As her husband often used to remind her, one never could tell for certain what someone carried in his purse. And besides, Maggie was a naturally sociable person who enjoyed chatting and saw no virtue in enduring lonely isolation, even during her time of mourning. Her husband's death had been sudden and untimely, just after they had made a commitment to sell their store and go west, a commitment that left Maggie with considerable capital and considerable uncertainty. From what she'd heard the West was no place for a lady alone, and she had not been thrilled with the prospect of living in some tiny, forsaken prairie town *with* a husband much less without one. So she had decided on Charleston just a month or so before, when the excitement and gossip about the recapture of Fort Sumter caught her fancy.

For Maggie this was a place to start over fresh, to be her own woman, and (though she wouldn't admit it), to capitalize on the needs of a conquering army as it occupied this city that had almost been destroyed. Army men were good customers, she knew that well enough. What Maggie did not know and what she had not really thought about before was the initial trouble it took to set up shop. She had arrived in town with two wagonloads of salable merchandise, found a place, and nailed up a sign. But the tasks of organizing, of recording what merchandise she had, of setting up books was completely beyond her. That had always been her husband's responsibility. And she didn't know where to begin.

Ambrosia picked her way gingerly through the store, scanning an abundance of merchandise the likes of which she had not seen since before the war. There were pots and pans and trinkets and farm tools, but the bolts of cloth propped in one corner were what caught her eye, the bright, soft fabrics of blue and green and gold which almost beckoned the touch of her hand. Instinctively she leaned forward and brushed them with her fingers, thinking how long it had been since she'd felt yards and yards of fabric swirling in graceful folds about her feet, suddenly remembering how wonderful it had been to wear a soft, feminine gown, to watch Ledger smile, to dance with him . . . It had been years since she'd thought of music and dancing and pretty gowns, since she'd thought of anything beyond survival.

"A—hab!"

Ambrosia started as Maggie let out another screech. "A—hab!"

Belatedly a young, gangly black wearing ill-fitting, tattered clothing shuffled slowly through the maze of boxes and stood before Mrs. O'Neal, scratching one shoulder. "Yes'm."

"Have you come across those spools of blue thread yet?"

The Negro stared at his bare foot as he moved it idly over the planked floor. "No'm."

"Well, hurry and find them. The general's wife will be here at noon and I promised her I'd have them for her."

"Yes'm." The black turned and retraced his steps, moving no more quickly than he had when he answered the initial summons. Maggie snorted and bit her lip in frustration, but she straightened immediately and forced a smile when she noticed Ambrosia's interest. "That Ahab! He'll be the ruin of me and this shop before I even begin!" She stepped closer and her smile widened at the prospect of making a sale. "Beautiful cloth, isn't it? And with your eyes . . ."

Her salesmanship was lost on Ambrosia, who was still eyeing Ahab as he moved slowly about the back room.

Maggie watched Ambrosia closely, wondering why this young woman seemed so interested in him. "He's the fifth man I've hired and the best of them so far," she admitted. "At least he's shown up three days in a row without the smell of liquor on his breath. But—well, he's not exactly the most ambitious fellow in Charleston, either. And you can see how much there is to be done." She waved a hand about her at the boxes and clutter, then forced another smile and pointed out another bolt of cloth, this one blue. "That would go well with your eyes too."

Ambrosia looked at the cloth with renewed interest, though her mind was not on buying fabric. "You're probably looking for some hardworking, reliable help, then." It was a statement more than a question.

"I'm beginning to wonder if there is such a thing in the South!" Ambrosia lifted an indignant brow. "Oh, I'm sure there are hardworking gents hereabouts," Maggie hastened to explain, "but most men would rather starve before they'd take orders from a woman."

"I sympathize with your dilemma, Mrs. O'Neal," Ambrosia returned politely. Her thoughtful expression became serious as she added slowly, "I can also help you solve it."

"You can?"

Ambrosia gave a short nod.

"How can you do that?"

"By working for you."

Maggie's hopeful eyes grew wide with shock as they flew up and down Ambrosia's diminutive form. She was an attractive girl in an odd sort of way, but small and frail-looking, and Southern gentility was branded plainly on her every word and gesture. She was probably wonderfully gifted at parlor conversation and sewing samplers, and terribly talented at pouring tea, Maggie thought. But she would certainly not be capable of the sort of work a job here would require. "I'm not interested in hiring a woman," Maggie told her bluntly.

"But, Mrs. O'Neal, you admitted your need just a moment ago."

"I said I needed a man. This is heavy work, Mrs.—?"

"Miss Lanford."

Maggie rolled her eyes. The woman had never even been married and probably couldn't add two and two. "There are things here that only a man could move, Miss Lanford."

"My man Josiah will help for a few days, until I can get things organized. And then I ought to be able to—"

Maggie vehemently shook her head. "You must understand, Miss Lanford," she insisted firmly, "that most of my customers will be Union soldiers and soldiers' wives and—and other people with whom I—I'm sure you would rather not associate," she added, flustered. She didn't quite know how to tell a proper woman that she welcomed the business of prostitutes as much as any other kind.

The argument gave Ambrosia pause, but only for a moment. "I am willing to associate with whomever the position requires."

Maggie searched the woman's face and knew that she meant every word she said. Still—a Southern gentlewoman working for her? The idea was preposterous! "I'm sorry, Miss Lanford. But the answer is still no."

"We will discuss salary at the end of the week," Ambrosia informed her, peeling off her gloves and untying her bonnet, both of which she handed to a stunned Sheba. "That will give me ample time to prove to you what a mistake you almost made."

Maggie was rendered speechless for an instant and considered calling the authorities and having the woman removed. But something inside her admired Ambrosia's persistence, even while it made her angry. And besides, she had little to lose by letting the woman work for a week and everything to gain. She stared, much agog, as Ambrosia sent her woman after that man Josiah, and then began to gather up the empty boxes and packing material that had been strewn carelessly about the floor. Maggie vented a bewildered sigh and shook her head, wondering how she had gotten herself into this situation and not at all sure she liked it. But there was little to be done about it now beyond waiting and hoping, and watching that the girl didn't steal her blind. It was important too that she get on with the business of making money. "A—hab! Ahab! Have you found that blue thread yet?"

Chapter 9

It was Ambrosia who discovered the thread, and not until the middle of the following day. By then Maggie was already in awe of the petite woman who worked as hard as any man, lifting boxes nearly as large as herself and organizing everything with an efficiency Maggie couldn't help but admire. One week later, after they had worked out a modest salary arrangement, Maggie was amazed when Ambrosia presented her with a complete account of all inventory, neatly penned and alphabetized. Each day after closing, Ambrosia stayed an extra hour or so to be certain that the accounting was kept up to date. In very short order she had earned herself a secure position by making herself invaluable to Maggie's business.

But there was a cost attached to the job that Ambrosia had not really considered. It did not take long for word to filter back to the Bowman household that Ambrosia would no longer be welcome in the homes of Melissa's friends. The fact that she, an unmarried woman, was employed as a common shop clerk was scandalous in itself, particularly when so many good men had returned home and had no hope of finding work. But the fact that she was employed by a Yankee woman and dealt with Yankees herself—well, it was more than the proper women of Charleston would stand for, even if her name was Lanford. The women would shake their heads and cluck their tongues in dismay every morning as she made her way up Meeting Street, the black woman Sheba following just a step behind her. Madeline Bowman was chided for permitting such conduct, and she was counseled to rid her home of any guest who would dare exhibit such untoward behavior. While Madeline made no excuses for Ambrosia, neither did she voice her objections to the girl's employment, for it put the first hard cash into the family coffers in many long months. Ambrosia was family after all, she would explain to her disapproving friends. The girl had no one else and could hardly be turned out into the streets.

Melissa was not so kind in her treatment of her sister and let everyone who would listen know that she disapproved heartily of Ambrosia's conduct. Yet it was not so much outrage she felt each morning when she watched Ambrosia rise and ready herself for the day's work. It was jealousy. Ambrosia had found a reason for going on, while Melissa felt as if she had none. The gracious, lovely way of life she had come to Charleston to enjoy was gone now. The opulent parties, the outrageously expensive gowns, the thrill of being admired by scores of dashing young men had all vanished into the past. Her world was filled with want and hunger and withered old women dressed in rags, and men who had come home maimed and defeated. How could they have been beaten? she wanted to scream. They had been so eager to taste Yankee blood, to prove their bravery on the field of battle. They had all been such fools, she thought. And now they were broken men. The anguish of war was there in their eyes.

Melissa was frightened that Ledger might never come home, that she would be left widowed like hundreds of other young women with little hope of finding a husband among the few respectable whole men who had returned. But she was even more frightened that he would return old and defeated like the rest of them. She couldn't bear to think of living the rest of her life with a defeated man, a man who could never again give her the life she deserved. How she envied Ambrosia her youth and her freedom. She had no one to answer to, nothing to lose by associating with the Yankees.

"Papa would have disowned you in a minute if he had known!" she cried bitterly one morning as Ambrosia tied her worn bonnet under her chin and prepared to leave for work. "And when Ledger comes home, he'll throw you out on the streets without a second thought!"

Ambrosia paused for a moment, meeting Melissa's eyes with a stony, unaffected silence that disguised the anxiety she felt at the threat.

As always, her cool manner placed Melissa at a disadvantage. Melissa could not begin to understand what went on behind those catlike green-gray eyes. But she knew that Ambrosia was clever as a fox, that no matter what happened she could work things to her own advantage. The Confederacy had hardly conceded defeat before Ambrosia allied herself with the victors. How easy it would be for her to find a husband from among the hundreds of young Yankee soldiers here in Charleston! Men with money and hope for the future . . .

The bitterness burned inside her as she watched Ambrosia leave the house. Melissa was hopelessly trapped here, a married woman waiting for her husband to return, with little hope that anything would change when he finally did. She never realized that Ambrosia was caught in a similar trap, hoping and praying for the same man's return with no hope that anything would change when he came home.

The month of May passed quickly for Ambrosia, her newfound work keeping her well occupied from early morning till sundown. She grew accustomed to the demands of her position, though there were certain aspects of the work she despised, like catering to the more difficult officers' wives, or forcing a polite nod to women who wore face paint and heavy perfume. What she hated more than anything else, however, was listening to the gossipy comments Maggie made about everyone who happened to cross the threshold of the emporium. It shocked Ambrosia the way Maggie could bustle about sweet-talking and cajoling a female customer as if she were a dear friend, then proceed to rake her across the coals the minute she was out of earshot. And the way she flirted with the men was utterly appalling. No matter whether he was a blushing lad or an old codger, Maggie's hand would rest coyly on his arm, her lashes would flutter, her breasts would brush accidentally against his sleeve, and her high-pitched giggle would carry throughout the store.

Ambrosia despised Maggie's natural duplicity and remained aloof and even cold when her employer made overtures of friendship. Her behavior, in turn, made Maggie feel uneasy and inferior, and oftentimes caused her to be short-tempered or bossy to prove that she was neither. She seemed to enjoy ordering Ambrosia about in front of customers, calling her by her first name like a common servant, sending her to fetch this or that or demanding to know why certain things hadn't been unpacked or properly displayed. But somehow Ambrosia usually managed to do more and say less than Maggie expected, which confounded the older woman as much as anything else. She watched over Ambrosia with a mixture of relief and reluctance, allowing the girl to take over most of the bookwork and trusting her to handle sales when she was out or when the store was extraordinarily busy. But she let Ambrosia know at regular intervals that she had no talent for selling and berated her for her lack of rapport with the customers. So it was that the emporium became the scene of an unspoken and oftentimes hostile truce that it behooved both women to keep.

May drew swiftly to a close and business at O'Neal's Emporium was stronger than ever. Newly arrived officials of the Freedman's Bureau and their wives, along with the wives of men in the occupational troops, made up the majority of Maggie's regular clientele, since they were the only people in Charleston with money to spend these days. It bothered Ambrosia to see the victors prospering so on the spoils of war while families like the Bowmans and the Lanfords remained closed up in their scarred homes, relying on their servants' rations from the Freedman's Bureau for their next meal. It seemed cruel and unfair, just like all the destruction of the war. And the injustice made it harder for her to mask the bitterness she felt whenever a Yankee came into the shop with a fat purse. But there was nothing she could do to change what was, and she was learning to survive on what was left behind. It was a more difficult kind of survival than before, because a part of her had died with her father, another part had perished in the flames at Heritage. But there was still tomorrow and a hope of rebuilding Heritage, of returning to the land she loved and working it, once she saved enough for tools and seed. And there was still hope that Ledger would come home.

Ambrosia found herself living through one day at a time, anxiously awaiting his return. She was certain that his arrival would change everything, that his smile and his constant joking would make everything seem brighter, less somber, and that his presence would make her strong enough to go on. She only hoped that he would not lecture or threaten her or shake his head in shame the way Melissa did, that he would not demand that she quit her job or leave the Bowman house for the sake of propriety. She liked to imagine that he would admire her ambition and tenacity and share her stubborn will to survive and rebuild in this new South run by Yankees; that he would notice just how much she had grown up.

It was late one afternoon during the last week of May. Ambrosia was unpacking and taking account of newly arrived inventory in the back room when Maggie's high-pitched screech interrupted her concentration. "Ambro-sia! Ambrosia!"

With a sigh she promptly left her work to answer the

summons. The day had been busier than most, and she assumed that Maggie wanted her to help with an impatient customer or keep an eye on a suspicious-looking browser. But as she glanced about, making her way to the front of the store, she was surprised to see it empty. There was only Maggie and a single Union soldier. Her eyes flicked over the soldier when he half turned toward her. She froze and fought back a gasp of shock.

For an instant Drayton's cool blue eyes widened in similar surprise, then warmed as he gave her a brief but thorough perusal and a slight nod of approval. Ambrosia's eyes narrowed in contempt.

"Ambrosia!"

She hastily directed her attention to Maggie.

"Have you unpacked the fresh tobacco yet?" Maggie demanded impatiently. "The major here is very particular about his cigars." Maggie's voice softened and her hand rested familiarly on his arm. She smiled sweetly up at him, but her smile was less warm when she realized that Ambrosia was staring. "Well? Is it unpacked or isn't it?" she demanded irritably.

"Yes. I'll get it right away."

Ambrosia hurried to the back room and emerged a few moments later with a large humidor. She purposely avoided Drayton's eyes yet was unable to will away the knot in her stomach or the hot blush that crept into her cheeks. She gave Maggie the humidor, flashing him a glare that reflected her resentment before she hurried back to her work, away from the prying eyes that made her feel so uncomfortable. But even when she was alone in the back room she was unable to concentrate on anything she tried to do. She was suddenly full of emotions that defied control, of hatred and anger and frustration. She never wanted to see him again, not after what he had done. And her pride didn't want him to know that the proud Miss Lanford had finally been humbled to working like a servant for a common Yankee woman.

She tossed her pen aside and glared at the tall stacks of

crates and boxes she had planned to unpack in the next hour, before Maggie could scold her for not doing her job. Damn them all! she thought as she kicked at the tallest stack. She sucked in her breath and leapt forward to steady the column when the boxes teetered precariously overhead. For several moments she swayed this way and that with the unsteady movement of the boxes. When they finally settled themselves, she let out a long breath of relief and closed her eyes. She was tired. It had already been far too long a day. And the tension inside her was making her close to losing her temper, something she had never done in front of Maggie and never intended to do. She had to get away before these Yankees drove her mad, she thought indignantly. She needed to be alone, to get a good night's rest before she faced all of this again. She glanced about the room, wondering if Maggie would even consider allowing her to leave early. Perhaps, if she promised to come in very early the following morning, if she promised to finish unpacking everything before the store opened . . .

Ambrosia found Maggie at the front counter staring wistfully into space. When she asked permission to leave, Maggie merely gave a vague nod, never bothering to question her as to her reasons. She seemed far away, distant and dreamy, and Ambrosia knew enough to take advantage of her preoccupation. She gathered up her things and tied her worn black bonnet under her chin, anxious to go before Maggie came to her senses or had a chance to change her mind. Ambrosia was so intent on making a quick exit that she gave no thought to going home unescorted. Sheba would not arrive at the shop to accompany her home for at least another hour, and she wasn't about to wait, no matter what propriety dictated. It was still very light out and the streets were still very busy, besides the fact that the Bowmans' house was not very far from the shop. But she had barely stepped out of the emporium when she realized her mistake.

She saw Major Rambert at once, leaning against the

very next storefront, leisurely puffing at one of his expensive cigars which he tossed aside immediately as he moved to block her path. His dark blue uniform was crisp and new-looking, and his trousers no longer carried the yellow stripe of a cavalry officer, so he was obviously with the occupational troops. Her eyes traveled upward slowly, from his polished black boots to the row of shiny brass buttons at his broad chest to his handsome, sundarkened face. He touched his hat in an abbreviated salute. "Miss Lanford."

She eyed him as coldly as she could for a long moment, heedless of the people who pushed by her. She despised him and all that he stood for. And more than anything else she wanted him to know that she would never forget what he'd done.

"I intend to pay you back, Major," she said curtly.

He raised a puzzled brow. "Beg your pardon?"

"The money you gave Josiah," she snapped. "I intend to pay it back. Every cent of it."

Drayton vented a sigh as he drew a hand thoughtfully over his chin. She wore a black dress that was threadbare and mended in a dozen places, and a pair of shoes which, while a definite improvement over her last pair, must have been purchased secondhand. Yet her message was clear. She wanted no part of his charity. And he knew enough to honor her pride. "If you insist, Miss Lanford."

She let out her breath and relaxed somewhat. She had expected an argument and he had not given it to her. She looked at him a moment longer, then stepped around him and made for home. But instead of allowing her to pass, his hand touched lightly to her arm and he took up walking beside her with the obvious intention of seeing her home. Ambrosia tensed at his touch but decided to ignore him. Her feet carried her quickly toward her destination. But suddenly she was aware of a gasp of outrage, and she lifted her eyes to meet the haughty looks of condemnation from a pair of Madeline Bowman's closest friends. The women drew themselves up arrogantly as they stepped aside and allowed Ambrosia and her Yankee soldier to pass. Ambrosia tossed a glance over her shoulder to be certain the two ladies had continued on their way, then stopped abruptly and turned to Drayton, her feet braced apart, her hands on her hips. "Just what do you think you're doing?" she demanded.

He gave an innocent shrug. "I'm waiting for you to explain how you're going to pay me back."

She narrowed her eyes. "I still have most of the money left, Major. I'll give it to you today, if you insist. . . ."

"I don't." Drayton placed a hand to her elbow and urged her to begin walking again.

". . . and as for the rest of it, I am employed at the emporium. I'll pay you what I can over the next few weeks."

"I'll trust you for it."

She flashed him an accusing glare. "I suppose you've stolen enough in the last four years to be quite comfortable without it."

This time it was Drayton who stopped short, his grip on her arm tightening ominously. Ambrosia felt herself tensing as she faced the anger in his eyes, but she was every bit as angry as he. And he held no trump card here, in broad daylight on a Charleston street.

"I am not proud of what happened," he said at length, the words coming with difficulty.

"Is that an apology, Major?" she inquired with a cold smile, her indignation overriding her better judgment.

His blue eyes burned wildly for an instant. Her barb had met its mark quite accurately. Then, to Ambrosia's surprise, he let out his breath and began walking again in silence, his hand at her elbow. For some reason she didn't really understand, she gave him no further argument.

"What brought you to Charleston?" he asked after several moments.

"That's none of your business," she retorted. There

was a space of silence. "My sister lives here," she relented. "She married a Bowman, just before the war."

He gave a nod. He'd been with the occupational forces long enough to recognize the name of one of Charleston's prominent families. Again there was silence.

"Corporal Laird . . . is he—did he recover?"

Drayton gave her a smile. "He was barely even limping the last time I saw him. He's home by this time, I suspect."

Ambrosia said nothing, but she was clearly pleased with the news. She stopped, indicating a tall, wrought-iron gate. "Here."

His eyes flashed over the long, narrow building, and Ambrosia was acutely aware of the peeling paint; the once neat, squared shutters that had been damaged in the shelling; the boards that temporarily covered several broken windows until new glass could be paid for.

"Wait here. I'll get your money." She turned quickly and entered the garden, giving him no chance to protest. Drayton paced uncomfortably before the gate, catching glimpses through the wrought iron of the garden, the shady piazza, the house. It was obvious that the Bowmans were in dire financial straits, as were most of Charleston's finest families. But like the others, they would die before accepting charity from a Yankee.

Several moments passed before Ambrosia reappeared, hurrying, breathlessly clutching the same soft leather pouch he had given to Josiah over two months before. "It's all there, except for thirty-three dollars," she said as she tossed it at his chest. He caught it easily, without thinking, his eyes never leaving hers. "I'll pay you back the rest as soon as I can. I'm paid every other Friday." Her tone was curt, businesslike.

He held her eyes for a moment longer before she turned away, closing the gate securely behind her without another word. Drayton started to say something, then bit back the words as his long, tanned fingers kneaded pensively at the leather pouch. The look in her eyes made any words an effort in futility. She hated him, blamed him for what had happened to her home. And though he had not been directly responsible, he also blamed himself. He let out a short, frustrated sigh and tossed the pouch in the air, catching it thoughtfully as he walked away. He did not see the cautious glance Ambrosia threw over her shoulder, or know that she paused at the door to stare after him.

"Who was that?"

Ambrosia whirled about as Melissa's voice startled her. "No one you know."

Melissa looked hard at Ambrosia's face, then at the gate, then at Ambrosia again. "I saw him, Ambrosia. Now tell me who he was."

Ambrosia sighed and tucked a strand of hair wearily behind one ear. "His name is Major Rambert, Drayton Rambert." She reached for the door latch, but Melissa caught hold of her arm and prevented her from going in.

"Drayton Rambert?" she repeated excitedly. "Is he any relation to the Draytons on the Ashley?"

"I haven't the slightest idea. As far as I'm concerned, he's just another dirty Yankee."

Melissa's pretty features hardened with suspicion. "Then what are you doing with him, little sister? And how did you come to owe him money?"

Her green eyes bore not a trace of emotion. "That's none of your business."

Melissa's blue eyes narrowed as her hand cracked hard across Ambrosia's cheek. Ambrosia deserved that and more for selling her reputation, for taking work in that Yankee store. Everyone talked about her and shook their heads after her every day when she walked up Meeting Street. It was humiliating to have a sister who was no longer received, who had given up respectability for a few Yankee dollars. But it was so much more painful to watch her getting everything Melissa wanted by doing so. Ambrosia had grown up. She was no longer the homely, skinny girl who couldn't catch a single beau.

That Yankee major who had just left here was incredibly handsome, and he had looked at Ambrosia in a way Melissa knew all too well. It had been a long time since a man had looked at Melissa that way . . . much too long.

Ambrosia lifted her fingers to her hot cheek, and her eyes were wide with shock and disbelief. Without a single word she reached again for the door latch.

"Just wait until Ledger comes home!" Melissa flung after her. "He'll throw you out on the street! He'll make you sorry for everything!"

The threat made Ambrosia hesitate for a long moment before she hurried up the stairs to her room.

Chapter 10

The June day had been uncomfortably hot and the store unusually busy. Ambrosia was just beginning work on the day's accounts when Sheba appeared, ready to escort her home. With hardly a glance Ambrosia waved the black woman to a seat, mumbling a promise that she wouldn't be much longer. Several moments had passed before Ambrosia noticed that Sheba had not taken the seat at all, that instead she stood before her, nervously wringing her short, plump hands. Ambrosia stood abruptly and put her pen aside. "What is it? What's happened?"

Sheba's head jerked up and she reluctantly met Ambrosia's eyes. "He home, Miz Ambrosia," she said quietly.

Ambrosia held her breath, feeling a knot of apprehension tightening in her stomach. Her eyes demanded the rest of it.

"Massah Ledger, he—he been hurt," she admitted reluctantly. "He been hurt real bad."

The hope in Ambrosia's eyes died and her gaze became glazed and distant. It could not be. Ledger—the young horseman who had flown magically over the high stone wall, his blond curls framing a face so warm and beautiful and alive, his blue eyes so young and confident

151

. . . Ambrosia closed her eyes and let out a lengthy breath, leaning her weight against the desk, wondering if she could bear to face a tattered remnant of what he had been. She bit her lip hard and slowly closed the book she had been working on. With a vague excuse to Maggie, she left the store.

The early evening air was moist and cool after the heat of the day. She hurried along the street with Sheba panting behind her. The black woman did her best to slow Ambrosia down, to prepare her for what was to come. But her efforts were in vain. By the time she reached the wrought-iron gate, Ambrosia had disappeared into the house. Sheba sighed heavily and shook her head. By now she knew the worst of it.

The house was quiet when Ambrosia hurried into the parlor. There was none of the usual bickering or gossip, no deliberately cutting remark from Melissa to herald her coming home. For a moment Ambrosia thought the room empty. The shutters had been closed against the sun and were still closed, though evening shadows had begun to fall. She half turned to leave, then caught sight of the figure curled up in a chair, her face hidden in her hands. "Melissa?"

Melissa's head lifted the slightest bit. She let out a little cry and faced away. Ambrosia frowned and walked slowly to her side, bending low and staring hard at her face. "Melissa?" Her voice was thin and shrill as she took in the terrible change in her sister's face. "What's happened to him? Tell me what's happened!"

Melissa stared at her for a long moment, then looked away. Her voice was low and hard. "I wish he'd died."

"No!" Ambrosia shook her head and slowly backed away. "Don't ever say that! You mustn't ever say it! You ought to thank God he's come home to you, no matter what."

Melissa's eyes flashed cold and accusing. "You haven't seen him. Go look at him, little sister," she spat bitterly. "Then come back here and tell me how lucky I am to have a husband. Tell me how grateful I ought to be—'' Her voice broke off and she covered her face with her hands and sobbed.

Ambrosia clenched her teeth against the growing panic. She turned and made her way from the parlor, her steps hesitant, heavy as she ascended the stairs to Ledger's room. She drew a deep breath and gathered her resolve as she rapped on the door and waited. A moment later Madeline opened the door, her face drawn and pinched and aged several years since that morning.

''Can I see him?'' Ambrosia tossed an uncertain glance over Madeline's shoulder.

''He's resting just now,'' Madeline whispered. ''I think it would be better if you waited till morning.''

Ambrosia's face fell. Of course she had no right to see him. She made to turn away.

''Who is it, Mother? Who's there?''

Ambrosia stopped at the sound of his voice.

''It's Melissa's little sister, dear,'' Madeline answered.

''Ambrosia?'' Ambrosia's heart soared at the excitement in his tone when he said her name. ''Ambrosia's here?''

''I told her you were resting, dear.''

''It's all right, Mother. Let her in.''

Reluctantly Madeline eased the door ajar and allowed Ambrosia to enter. The room was dark, the shutters closed, the draperies pulled shut. Only a low burning lamp in the far corner of the room gave off a shadowy light. ''Ambrosia? Is it really you?''

Ambrosia smiled and made her way quickly toward the chair where he sat, a comforter spread over his lap. Even from across the room, it was apparent that he had lost a leg. But Ambrosia had seen many men with missing legs or arms. They had become a fact of life since the war. She bent to take his hand. ''Ledger—''

He turned his head to face her and the light from the lamp fell across his face. Ambrosia froze.

"Ambrosia?" His voice was so full of concern for her that she thought she would be sick. She could not even bring herself to answer. For a long space of time all was silent as she stared at his face in disbelief.

"Melissa didn't tell you, did she?" he said finally. His voice was much different now, bitter and sad.

Ambrosia blinked back a tear and shook her head. No. Melissa hadn't told her that he'd lost a leg, or that his face had been so badly scarred she would never even have recognized him. She forced herself to speak, willing away the trembling in her voice. "Sh—Sheba told me that you had been injured . . ."

"Injured?" He gave a short, brittle laugh. "An inadequate term for what little is left of me, wouldn't you say?"

Ambrosia swallowed hard and lifted his hand firmly in her own. The scars were there too, dark pink and raised, terrible, ugly scars. "Ledger . . ." Her throat was so tight and dry that she could scarcely speak. She knelt beside the chair, using the time to compose herself. "Ledger," she began again, more steadily this time, "all that really matters is that you've come home. Thank God you're home!" She saw him smile a little at that, a sad kind of smile she had never seen before. "You can't know how I—how we prayed for you to come home."

The smile disappeared as he lifted his hand to the thick scars that had transformed his once handsome face into an ugly, disfiguring mask. "Like this?"

His voice was so full of despair that Ambrosia could no longer hold back her tears. Slowly she moved to touch his face, her trembling fingers traveling gently over the thickened patches of skin which drew his eye and brow down in an odd, unnatural angle. "I—I prayed for you," she whispered brokenly. "And you are here. All of you that matters to me. Your mind, your heart, your soul . . ."

Ledger felt her tears on his hands and struggled to hold back his own. He sighed raggedly, turning his head to kiss the fingers at his cheek. "Don't cry, Ambrosia," he pleaded softly. "I've had my fill of tears these past months. Tears and pity . . ." He closed his eyes and let out a long, weary sigh. "They all thought I was going to die. Sometimes I think it would have been better if I had."

Ambrosia sniffed and wiped the tears from her wet cheeks. She had seen too many men give up their will to live after losing a limb, or being disfigured, men would could not face a life of being endlessly doted upon and pitied. Or even worse, uncomfortably ignored. She silently vowed that she would never be a part of that. Her voice came strong and clear. "How did it happen?"

Ledger opened his eyes and met her even gaze with some surprise. "I got in the way of a Yankee shell. At least that's what they told me afterward. I don't really remember anything but the first loud blast, and the pain." He grinned, a shadow of the wide, boyish grin she had once known. "Do you know, you're the first one to ask me that since I came home? The first to do anything besides cry and make attempts at silly conversation." He paused, and his eyes were touched with warmth. "I shouldn't really be surprised. You're the only completely honest woman I've ever known." He tightened his hold on her hand. "You haven't changed at all, Ambrosia."

Ambrosia struggled to hide her disappointment. Couldn't he see that she had changed? That she was a woman now, not a child. "I—I've grown up," she said softly.

His eyes drifted briefly over her before returning to her face. He smiled, this time without sadness, though the scars pulled stubbornly at his skin. "Yes. You have grown up. You're a beauty, Ambrosia."

She tried to smile in return, but his eyes made her long for so much more than the touch of his hand. She swallowed hard and searched about uneasily for something to say. "Did Melissa tell you I've been working?"

"Doing what?"

"Oh, a little of everything, really. I work in a shop a few blocks north of Broad, mostly keeping track of the stock, though sometimes, when Mrs. O'Neal is busy, I—"

"Mrs. O'Neal?"

"Maggie O'Neal. She's the widow lady who owns the shop." Ambrosia bit her lip for a moment before she added, "She's a Yankee, and most of the customers are Yankees too." She waited, but Ledger made no comment. She gnawed at her lip and plucked nervously at her sleeve. "Some of your mother's friends don't approve of my working there."

"Oh? Why not?"

"They don't think it's right that I associate with the enemy, no matter what my motives."

"And what are your motives?"

"I'm going to save up enough to rebuild Heritage. Not the way it was before, perhaps, but enough to make a new start."

Ledger gave a short laugh and patted her hand. "You'll do it too. I know you will, if anyone can."

She let out her breath and smiled. He understood.

"Does she pay well? This O'Neal woman?"

"Twenty dollars a month."

Ledger gave a low whistle of admiration. "I'm impressed. Though you're probably worth every cent." Ambrosia's smile widened at that. "And I can understand why some of the women are up in arms over it. They're jealous! You can afford to buy all those stylish gowns the Yankees are wearing while they're stuck in rags," he teased. "Not that any of them would be as handsome as you in a new gown, mind you . . ."

"Ledger!" she cried in exasperation, but her eyes were shining with pleasure. "I told you I'm saving for the future. I haven't spent a dime on clothing—"

"Then you must be building quite a nest egg."

"Well . . . I do give some money to your mother," she told him. "And some of it . . . well, I have a debt that—'' Ambrosia stopped short and turned her head, suddenly conscious of Madeline's presence in the room. To her surprise Melissa was also there, her eyes burning with a hatred that made Ambrosia self-consciously pull her hand from Ledger's.

''I hope you aren't tiring yourself, Ledger,'' Melissa said in an overly solicitous tone.

''I—I was just leaving,'' Ambrosia told her, rising from the floor.

''Don't hurry off on my account,'' Melissa mouthed with a falsely sweet smile.

''I'm not. It's just that—as you said, Ledger should not tax himself.''

Ambrosia drew a lengthy breath and attempted a smile, aware that Melissa's narrowed eyes followed her every move. ''Sleep well tonight,'' she said softly, pressing her fingers to his arm. ''It's good to have you home.'' She straightened slowly and withdrew her hand, her heart aching to say so much more. With a small sigh and a quick glance at her sister, Ambrosia left the man she loved to his wife's care.

Chapter 11

The long days of summer slipped slowly by, passing in a much different fashion than Ambrosia had planned. Ledger grew stronger as the time passed and was able to move about the house on a pair of crutches loaned him by one of Madeline's friends. But there was little to occupy his time, since he refused to leave the house. Ambrosia was keenly aware of the hours he spent alone in his room, staring at the four walls. The few occasions when Madeline managed to coerce him into visiting or socializing, the drain on him was all too apparent. He was quiet and brooding for days afterward, hardly spoke a word, and even refused to eat. Worst of all was Melissa's cold indifference to his loneliness, his despair. It tore at Ambrosia's heart to hear her complaints about being shut up in the house, to hear her whine and cry about all the things she couldn't afford to buy. It was obvious that Ledger felt responsible for his wife's unhappiness, and even more obvious that Melissa could not bear to look at him.

Each evening when she returned home, Ambrosia would spend time with Ledger, filling the parlor with exaggerated stories about the Yankees she'd seen that day, or coaxing him into telling tales about the days before the war, or simply sitting beside him in silence. He confessed to her, after a while, that she was the only visitor who could endure the silence with him. Ambrosia cherished the compliment. She was grateful that Madeline and Melissa sometimes found other things to occupy their time, leaving her and Ledger alone. She was far more comfortable when she was alone with him, freer to say what she thought, freer to smile and laugh with him. It was almost like she had always dreamed it might be, the sharing, the closeness. She had never felt free with anyone before . . . and she had never felt loved.

One evening, when they were alone in the parlor, Ambrosia presented him with a small wrapped package. "Open it," she ordered laughingly when he left it lying in his lap and continued to stare at it. "I bought it for you."

With a quick look at her that seemed a mixture of pleasure and annoyance, Ledger took up the package and excitedly pulled at the string. A moment later the paper fell to the floor, and Ledger lifted a worn leather-bound volume, which he examined with utmost care.

"It's a collection of the works of John Donne," Ambrosia told him.

He gave her a small smile. "So I see."

"He was one of Father's favorite writers. I thought you might like to read some of his works and maybe—" She hesitated, biting her lip before she gave a timid shrug. "And maybe try to write some of your own thoughts down." She gave a shy smile. "There's paper in the back leaf."

"Ambrosia," he scolded with an affectionate smile, "you shouldn't have spent your money on me. And a book! You know I've never been the scholarly type."

She grinned. "I know. But you've spent so much time in your room lately, Ledger. And—and you have so much to share."

Uncomfortable at the compliment, Ledger laughed aloud and shook his head. "A book," he chided her again. He cleared his throat noisily and flattened his hand against his heart, flipping through the pages until he found a most solemn looking text. He raised his voice to a high-pitched squeal and read it aloud in an overly dramatic British accent.

" '. . . Who bends not his ear to any bell which upon any occasion rings? but who can remove it from that bell which is passing a piece of himself out of this world?' "

He flashed Ambrosia a playful grin which widened when she giggled, then went on. " '. . . No man is an island, entire of itself; every man is a piece of the continent, a part of the main. If a clod be washed away by the sea, Europe is the less, as well as if—' " He stopped, the meaning of the words suddenly penetrating his mind, suddenly driving all levity from his voice.

" 'If a clod be washed away by the sea,' " he repeated softly, " 'Europe is the less, as well as if a promontory were, as well as if a manor of thy friend's or of thine own were . . .' " His voice trailed off for a moment, then began again, slowly, with a wealth of feeling in each word. " '. . . any man's death diminishes me, because I am involved in mankind . . .' " He stopped again and was silent for what seemed like a long time. Ambrosia watched the emotions play across his face, wanting more than anything to touch him, to hold him near. She smiled softly when he met her eyes, the surprise and confusion still evident in his expression. "It—it's strange to find so much truth in so few words," he said finally.

Ambrosia nodded, then watched as he swiftly turned the pages of the book, letting his eyes scan a verse here, a line there. A few moments later he closed the book and ran his fingers slowly over the worn leather binding. "Thank you, Ambrosia. I shall treasure this always."

He did not meet her eyes again, even when she rose and came to touch his hand, to bid him a good night. There were times, like this one, when he could not bear to look at her, when he could not bear the sight of her beautiful face or the innocent love in her eyes. It was always there, so clearly, just as it had been there that night at the Woodard's party so many years before. Only now Ledger realized what a fool he'd been to call such love childish, what a fool he'd been not to realize that he had loved her too. He'd been a boy then, so sure and confident. And blind. And his blindness had cost him everything, just as it had cost her.

Ledger closed his eyes and sighed as her soft footfalls sounded on the stairs. He might have been able to reconcile himself to this terrible, broken body if it hadn't been for Ambrosia. But she forced him to hope and refused to allow him to retreat into a world of self-pity and despair. She believed that in spite of all that had happened to him, he was still the same man who bravely jumped the fence at Barhamville Academy six Saturdays in a row. And whenever she was with him, she made him believe it too.

But the cold, hard truth of the situation wore heavily on Ledger's conscience. Ambrosia was young and beautiful, and he was no longer either. And he was a married man. He loved her deeply, but he could offer her nothing. And because he loved her, he could not bear the thought of watching her waste her life away, working at O'Neal's Emporium sunup to sundown, wearing her mended black gowns and buying him little gifts with her hard-earned money. Someday he would have to tell her in no uncertain terms that she was a fool for loving him, and then he would have to watch her leave.

Ledger stared distantly at the book she had just given him, wondering if he would ever be able to summon the courage to do what had to be done.

Chapter 12

Throughout the hot, humid days of summer, O'Neal's Emporium enjoyed a thriving business. More and more often Ambrosia was called on to wait on customers, a task at which she became adept and began to tolerate with less distaste. Much to her surprise, several of the younger soldiers and not a few older ones intentionally sought her help with their purchases rather than Maggie's, sometimes complaining of the older woman's loose tongue or her overly bold sales techniques. Ambrosia did nothing to encourage such complaints, but neither did she say anything in Maggie's defense. To her they were all Yankees, one the same as the next. She merely did her job and remained indifferent to their feelings, polite but totally aloof and clearly disinterested in cultivating a friendship.

It was late one afternoon when Ambrosia collected her pay for the last two weeks of August. She counted out the money, setting aside the six dollars that would pay in full her debt to Major Rambert. He was a regular at the emporium these days, though Ambrosia had never once waited on him. The moment he set foot in the place, Maggie flitted about him like an oversized moth about a flame, smiling and posing and acting as silly as a schoolgirl at her first social. Ambrosia was actually embarrassed to witness such tactics, particularly since Major Rambert ignored them. But she was glad that Maggie's infatuation kept her from having to deal with the major at all in the store, since he was difficult enough to handle every other Friday, when he met her after work to collect on the debt.

He was always waiting for her when she left the shop, and always insisted on escorting her home in spite of her protests, in spite of Sheba's initial frowning disapproval. Ambrosia could not begin to understand him. He was certainly not like the homesick young soldiers who came to the emporium to stare at her with large puppy-dog eyes, hoping for a quick pat on the head. She doubted if Drayton Rambert had ever been that young or that naive. He said very little to her and seemed as comfortable with the silence as she. Still, he made her feel tense, as if she were flirting with something volatile, something dangerous. There were times when he would rest his hand lightly on her elbow, or briefly touch her back as he guided her along Meeting Street, and Ambrosia would find herself remembering the feel of that hand, warm, caressing against her cheek. The slightest touch and she would blush and be forced to lower her head so that he would not notice, feeling every bit as foolish as Maggie, and every bit as obvious. It was not a feeling she enjoyed.

But this day would mark the end of it. The six dollars would pay her debt in full and she was anxious to have the thing over and done with. She said a brief good night to Maggie and left the store in high spirits, even managing a polite nod to the major when he joined her. Her good mood vanished when Sheba bid him a hearty "Ev'nin, Majah!", reminding Ambrosia that the old black woman had come to like him for some reason and to insist that he was a gentleman, even if he was a Yankee. Irritated now, Ambrosia hurried along the street until she was almost running, weaving in and out of the crowds of people, not caring if the major or Sheba were close behind or not. Let them enjoy each other's company, she thought as she approached the house. She would wait for them, pay her debt, and be free of him for good. She reached the Bowman house, whirling about, expecting to see Major Rambert and Sheba still some distance up the street. She drew a sharp breath when she discovered him right at her heels, while Sheba was nowhere in sight.

"Were you trying to lose someone in the crowd?"

Ambrosia colored and lifted her chin, feigning concern as she craned her neck to look for Sheba. It was just like him to know exactly what she was thinking.

Drayton leaned his back against the tall stone wall and crossed his arms comfortably across his broad chest. "She ought to know the way home by now, shouldn't she?"

Ambrosia felt her cheeks growing hot and pink but she said nothing. Instead she opened her worn reticule and thrust the money at him with a triumphant gleam in her eye. He straightened and took the money, his eyes never leaving Ambrosia's. She grew uneasy beneath his gaze, though she didn't know why, except that he had always been able to make her feel uncomfortable, just by looking at her. "I—It's all there," she said hastily. "The debt is paid in full."

He said nothing. Ambrosia's mouth went dry as he continued to search her face. She swallowed hard and faced away, pretending to look for Sheba again, hoping that he would leave. He did not. She lifted her hand to unlatch the gate. His low, vibrant voice stopped her.

"I want very much to see you again, Ambrosia."

She whirled to face him squarely, her eyes fixing to his face in astonishment. For an instant she thought she would faint from the shock. She could not believe what she had just heard.

He raised a mildly curious brow and the curve to his chiseled mouth softened, hinting a smile. "Does it come as such a shock to you? That I should desire your company?"

For a long moment, Ambrosia stared at him in speechless amazement. "If I am shocked, Major," she began in a thin voice which grew stronger and more brittle with every word as the indignation exploded inside her, "it is due to your incredible gall! You desire my company? After what your men did to my home? After what you helped to destroy?" Her eyes flashed with hatred and bitterness. "After what your people did to my father? And Ledger—" Her voice caught as she spoke the name, and her eyes brightened with moisture. She blinked away her tears and drew a short breath, oblivious to the regret so apparent in his blue eyes.

When she spoke again, her voice was low, each word emphatic. "I want nothing further from you, Major. Nothing. Not your charity, and certainly not your company."

As if to punctuate the finality of her statements, Ambrosia threw open the gate and closed it soundly behind her again without ever looking back.

In a bedroom on the second floor, Melissa stood near the window, watching, listening to all that occurred. The handsome Yankee had made a polite request to call on her sister, and her sister had scornfully turned him away. What a little fool she was, Melissa was thinking, to allow such a prospect to slip through her fingers. She sighed wistfully and fingered the curtain as she watched him walk away. She thought of the men who had once come to court her, boys most of them, with foolish boys' dreams that had been crushed by the reality of a long, terrible war. Something told her that this Major Rambert was nothing at all like the boys she had known. There was a strength to him, a self-sufficiency, a cynicism that would surely laugh at the foolish dreams of youth.

A jealousy rose within her, distorting her perfect, angelic features as she heard the sounds of Ambrosia's footsteps on the stairs. It was unfair! It was all so unfair! There was nothing left in Melissa's life beyond duty and loyalty to a husband who was nothing but a helpless cripple, a millstone hung about her neck. She could not bear the thought of existing like this much longer. She gave an angry tug on the threadbare curtain and turned away. It would not be this way forever, she vowed silently. Somehow she would find a way out of this trap. Somehow she would find a whole man with money who would take her away from this and give her the life she deserved.

Chapter 13

The days grew shorter, the breezes sharper, the nights cooler. Autumn had come to Charleston. A summer of relatively peaceful occupation had passed. President Andrew Johnson, acting in accordance with Lincoln's original plan for "Reconstruction" of the Union, did his best to restore home rule to states where a fair percentage of whites had taken an oath of loyalty to the Union, then to allow these newly organized state governments, once they had passed resolutions disavowing both slavery and secession, readmission to the Union.

Moving with all possible speed, Johnson appointed B. F. Perry provisional governor of South Carolina in June; and Perry, in turn, called for an election and a constitutional convention to be held in September. The ratification of the Thirteenth Amendment and the framing of the new state constitution that same month lead many to believe that South Carolina would return to legislative normalcy by the end of 1865. But there were also rumors of trouble to come, rumors that the Republican Congress scheduled to meet in Washington in December would demand much more than the president before allowing any Southern Democrats readmission to Congress. Allegations were made concerning Johnson's Southern sympathies, and editorials in Northern newspapers rang with

167

bitter demands for vengeance. Most Yankees believed that the South must pay for the loyal lives lost in four long years of war.

Ambrosia sighed thoughtfully as she arranged a dozen delicate glass bottles of perfume on the counter. The change of season reminded her of home. It would be cooler there, the harvest she had planned last spring would be over now. Trees would be ablaze with color, the dry corn stalks would rustle pleasantly in the wind as she walked by, drawing on the clean, morning air. Autumn had been a special time at Heritage, a time of reward for the long, hot days of hard work, a time to rejoice in the generous yield of the dark, fertile earth. A taste of winter would edge the nights, but the days would be yet pleasantly warm, the skies a deep, cloudless blue. How her soul longed for the sights and the smells of home, for the peace she had known in belonging to the land! And as autumn touched her golden finger to the green riches of summer, Ambrosia could not help but remember what had been at Heritage, and what would never be again.

She had gone to a lawyer just yesterday, only to be told what she had known for some time. The land at Heritage had been confiscated as abandoned land and would be held until December or until payment of back taxes were made, whichever came first. In a few short weeks, those taxes would come due, and Ambrosia could not begin to pay them. She was not alone. She could almost feel the despair of the people she passed as she walked along Meeting Street, the heartache of losing the small bit of pride the war had left to them, of losing home. She shook her head quickly to dispel the memories as a thin old woman dressed in a threadbare black gown entered the shop. Maggie had gone to the bank a few minutes before, and Ambrosia was responsible for waiting on customers while she was gone.

Instinctively Ambrosia's brow drew into a frown of sympathy. The woman was obviously destitute. Ambrosia was sure that she had nothing to spend. She turned her attention to the small glass bottles, tossing a sidelong glance at the old woman who hungrily eyed the thick bolts of colored cloth as she passed them. Ambrosia was surprised that she did not pause to touch them. They usually did. The woman approached the counter and shook her head with a sigh. "Ambrosia Lanford."

Ambrosia stared at the small dark brown eyes, the furrowed brow, the thick silver hair. There was something strangely familiar about the face, but it took a long moment for recognition to dawn. "Elisabeth Woodard!" she whispered in awe. "My heavens! Is it really you?" Ambrosia tried to hide her shock at how much Elisabeth had aged in four short years.

Elisabeth gave a small smile and nodded. "It certainly is. And you—you've changed a bit yourself, Ambrosia," she added pertly, sounding very much like herself, "though it seems your changes are for the better."

"What brings you to Charleston? Is Mr. Woodard here?" Ambrosia was sorry the moment she asked the question. It was apparent that Elisabeth had to struggle with her grief.

"Daniel passed on several months ago," she said quietly. "And I came to Charleston to be with friends . . ." She toyed nervously with the mended lace fringe on her faded glove. "I suppose you heard what happened in Columbia. I was almost grateful that Daniel wasn't there to see it." Her tone was bitter. "Drunken heathens! The devil take them all!"

Ambrosia was silent. Columbia had been burned, totally destroyed, just as Heritage had been destroyed. She knew exactly what Elisabeth must be feeling.

The older woman drew a long breath and straightened, abandoning the luxury of indulging in bittersweet memories. "I have a small house here," she told Ambrosia matter-of-factly. "It's all I have left, and I intend to keep it."

Ambrosia met her determined brown eyes and waited, hoping that Elisabeth would spare herself the embarrassment of begging for a loan to pay her taxes. Ambrosia had already turned every dime of her savings over to Madeline Bowman in the hopes of saving the Meeting Street house, admitting by her actions that Heritage was lost. She felt a part of herself dying every time she thought of it. But she was not alone. The Bowmans' plantation on the Ashley was to be confiscated for back taxes as well, barring a miracle. And so many, many others were in danger of losing the very roof over their heads.

Elisabeth removed a small bundle from her purse, her fingers clinging to it for a long moment before she opened it and allowed the contents to spill on the counter. Bright colors flashed from the rings, earbobs, and necklaces as the polished stones and precious metals caught and reflected the sunlight. Before Ambrosia said anything, Elisabeth peeled off her gloves and gazed wistfully at the large sapphire ring that glinted as she stretched her long white fingers. It was her wedding ring, Ambrosia knew, but the older woman abruptly twisted it and withdrew it from her finger. Her thin mouth tightened as she laid it with the other jewelry on the counter.

"I need to sell all of this, quickly, and at a fair price. I know the lot's worth at least a thousand dollars; I'm willing to part with it for half that much if I have to. But it's all I have left, and I'll need every penny it can bring."

Ambrosia's eyes fixed on the jewelry, not daring to touch it. Elisabeth was not the first to come here, desperate for money, trying to sell family treasures. But she was the first who had come to Ambrosia directly. Her green eyes lifted with regret. "I'm sorry, Elisabeth. But Mrs. O'Neal will never give you a fair price."

"I'm fully aware of that, Ambrosia. And neither will anyone else I've spoken with."

Ambrosia frowned her confusion.

"I'm asking you to sell it for me," Elisabeth told her bluntly. "I know you can get more than two hundred dollars, and that's all I've been offered for the lot. I'd rather starve to death than sell for that!'' she retorted, cocking her chin arrogantly.

"But, Elisabeth, I don't think I could—"

"I'm asking a favor of you, Ambrosia. You are in a position to help me. And while I certainly don't approve of what you are doing here, I'm not above asking you for help. To be perfectly honest, I have nowhere else to turn."

Ambrosia's eyes settled on the jewelry again for a long moment before she slowly shook her head. "Please try to understand, Elisabeth—"

"You might at least make an attempt before you refuse me. You owe me that much, Ambrosia."

Ambrosia bit her lip hard, but her eyes were unable to meet Elisabeth's. After a time she closed her eyes and lifted a hand to knead her troubled brow. Elisabeth waited in silence.

"Ah-h-hem . . ."

Both women started at the sound of an intruder loudly clearing his throat. Ambrosia's eyes flashed with annoyance as they found Major Rambert standing but a few steps away. Elisabeth dismissed him with a single glance, then promptly made to finish her business. "My house is on Charlotte Street—Josiah knows where. I shall come back here in two weeks' time if I haven't heard from you."

Without another word Elisabeth made her exit, leaving her jewelry on the counter and Ambrosia staring helplessly after her.

"An old friend of yours?" Drayton moved toward the counter and took the place Elisabeth had occupied a few minutes earlier.

She eyed him warily. "I don't see where it's any of your business."

He forced a tight smile. "It's not."

"How long were you eavesdropping, Major?"

He gave a shrug and eyed the jewelry. "Long enough."

Ambrosia made to snatch up the small pile, but Drayton was quicker. His fingers closed over it a split second before hers. She restrained his hand, her eyes doing battle with his for a long moment before she relented, allowing him to lift Elisabeth's wedding ring up to the light and examine it with a knowing eye. Ambrosia ground her teeth and waited impatiently for him to finish.

"Very nice."

She flashed him a haughty glare and opened an expectant palm, which he chose to ignore.

"I might be able to help you with this."

She narrowed green, catlike eyes. "I told you before, I don't want your help."

"Then what are you going to do with this jewelry?" he returned calmly, a single brow raised in challenge. "Would you allow the poor woman to lose her home? Would you see her starve to death, carrying these gems with her to the grave? Or perhaps . . ." he continued thoughtfully, again pretending to study the stone, "you have another purchaser in mind." His gaze lifted in time to see her mouth twist in anguish. She had no other outlet for the jewelry.

"A friend of mine is coming to Charleston on business next week. I think I could talk him into buying all of this for a fair price." He seemed almost amused by the resistance that flamed in her eyes. "Unless, of course, you don't trust me with it."

Ambrosia felt the color rushing to her cheeks and turned her back to him in confusion. The very thought of being indebted to him again, of accepting a favor from him, was enough to make her stomach churn. But it had not even occurred to her that he might betray her trust if she allowed him to take the jewelry. It had not even entered her mind! She scowled as she ran her finger timidly across the smooth edge of a wooden shelf. She was trapped. She had no choice.

"Damn you and your stubborn pride!" she heard him mutter suddenly. He followed it with a curse she was glad she didn't quite hear. She whirled to face him and watched in horror as he placed the ring emphatically on the counter with the other jewelry. Now he was riled, and she had ruined her only chance to help a friend who desperately needed her help. Her troubled eyes reluctantly met his then, and she saw his anger slowly die. "I—I am grateful for your offer of assistance," she managed, almost choking on the words.

"No, you aren't. You despise me for it." She lowered her eyes uneasily at the truth and he added, "But then, I don't really want your gratitude anyway."

She didn't know exactly what he meant by that, and she wasn't sure she wanted to know. She bit her lip and watched in silence as Drayton slipped the jewelry into his pocket.

Without a word he turned to leave and nearly collided with a flushed, breathless Maggie, who rushed to accompany him on his way out of the store. She fluttered her eyelashes furiously and twittered about her business at the bank. "And to think I almost missed you altogether!" Ambrosia heard her say as the two reached the door.

"Imagine that," the major returned dryly.

Maggie's flirtatious smile faded swiftly when he left, and she sighed wistfully as she began a slow return to the counter. It was only then that she set suspicious eyes on Ambrosia, who was quietly arranging perfume bottles on the counter, just as she had been when Maggie left her. Maggie frowned and studied her for a long moment, until Ambrosia felt the eyes upon her and looked up inquiringly. With a quick change of expression, Maggie dismissed the thought, turning her back on an uncomfortable Ambrosia to stare dreamily in the direction Major Rambert had gone.

Chapter 14

It had been six years since Matt Desmond had seen Drayton Rambert, but he was still able to pick him out in the lobby of the Charleston Hotel, a lobby crowded with Union soldiers and brashly talkative carpetbaggers. It took Drayton a moment longer to recognize Matt. A man of average height and build and a banker by profession, Matt Desmond had a quiet, congenial air about him that mingled well in spite of his conservative suit and somewhat sophisticated manners. Matt's brown eyes lit with recognition and his mouth broke into a smile as Drayton approached him and extended a hand. They appraised one another momentarily, then made their way through the various clusters of men in the lobby toward the comparative quiet of the dining room.

"How long are you going to be in Charleston?" Drayton inquired conversationally just after they had ordered dinner.

"Only a day or two more. To tell the truth, the place depresses me. It's nothing like it was before the war. But then," he went on thoughtfully as he poured a glass of wine from the bottle that had just been placed on the table, "there weren't nearly as many interesting investments here before the war. Now . . ." Matt took a sip of wine and gave a shrug. "Well, it's no secret that most loyal Confederates are desperate for money to pay delinquent taxes.'' He grimaced slightly as his eyes drifted pointedly toward the crowded lobby. ''I'm here to collect a share of the spoils for my bank, just like the rest of them,'' he admitted candidly. ''I suppose that's why I find the place so depressing. I've never before thought of myself as a vulture.''

Matt took another sip of wine and fixed a pleasant expression to his face. ''And you, my friend? What attraction does this fallen city of rebellion hold for you?''

''I have my position with the army,'' Drayton answered. ''I've been stationed here indefinitely.''

''And you've no thoughts of coming home?'' Matt countered in some surprise.

Drayton studied his glass for a moment, his eyes distant. ''I haven't really thought much about the future.''

Matt frowned, almost not believing what Drayton said. There had always been a drive, a purpose to everything he did. But that was missing now. So much was missing, now that Kathryn was gone. ''Rumor has it that your father left you quite an inheritance, Drayton,'' Matt said after a moment. ''A thriving carriage paint business, a lovely house in Gramercy Park . . .'' He watched Drayton's face carefully, expecting some flicker of interest. There was none. ''I heard you inherited everything Aaron expected to get, and that your stepbrother was fit to be tied when the will was read.''

Drayton's eyes hardened a bit. ''You're certainly well informed.''

''I speak with Warren Pierce every now and again. The last time we spoke, he seemed concerned about your stepbrother's having control over the business you've inherited.''

''He wrote me something to that effect.''

''And you aren't troubled by the thought of what might happen?'' Matt pressed.

Drayton gave a shrug. ''Warren's a competent lawyer. I'm sure he'll handle any problems that arise.''

Matt eyed him narrowly again, not quite knowing what to say. "If it were my inheritance—" he began.

"But it's not," Drayton broke in firmly. "And it's also none of your business."

For a long moment Matt considered saying what was on his mind. But something in Drayton's voice and manner made him think again. The waiter began serving them dinner, and Matt politely steered conversation to more general topics of politics and finance, purposely avoiding anything that might lessen his enjoyment of the meal. After all, Drayton was an old friend, not a client. Years ago they'd shared everything with one another, made secret pacts and even searched for buried treasure. The past was a bond between them even now, when they had chosen to lead such different lives.

"I need your help with something, Matt," Drayton admitted as they waited for brandy at the end of the meal. Matt lifted an inquiring brow and Drayton removed a small package from his tunic pocket and placed it on the table. "I have a friend who wants to sell these quickly, and at a fair price. But as you know, it's difficult to sell anything in Charleston for a fair price these days."

Matt glanced curiously at the small bundle that Drayton handed him, then unwrapped it and closely examined the collection of jewelry that spilled onto the table. He gave a slight nod of admiration. Whoever had owned the pieces had been quite wealthy once, and had exquisite taste. "This 'friend' of yours," Matt said slowly, "how much is she asking for the jewelry?"

"A thousand dollars, and she needs it within the next week. They're worth that much, you have my word on that. I'd buy the lot myself if there were more time. But my savings have all been invested in stocks, and it would take me longer than that to come up with the cash."

"And taxes are due the first of December," Matt inserted, fully aware that he held the upper hand.

"Yes."

"This 'friend' of yours," Matt began again with a sly

smile, "she wouldn't happen to be young and pretty, would she? And perhaps the reason for your staying on with the army here in Charleston?"

For a moment Drayton was silent. The question had caught him off guard, though perhaps he ought to have expected it from Matt. Always digging into everyone else's business and making it his own. Still, Matt's penchant for nosiness had little to do with the anger Drayton felt at the suggestion. For the first time, he wondered if it were true. "The owner of the jewelry is a sixty-year-old widow woman," Drayton told him succinctly, not liking the way he had so easily seen what Drayton didn't want to admit was there at all. "And the reason I'm staying here in Charleston is because I have orders to stay here, and a soldier follows orders."

The mischievous grin faded from Matt's face, though his eyes remained intently on Drayton. "I beg your pardon," he said unconvincingly. "I didn't mean to offend you."

"If you aren't interested in buying these—"

"But I am," Matt broke in, certain that he could sell the lot for a great deal more than a thousand dollars once he got back to New York. "I'll give you eight hundred dollars, cash. A fair price, considering the circumstances."

"Nine hundred, not a penny less."

With a half-smile of concession, Matt lifted his brandy in a toast. "To the poor old widow woman," he intoned. "May she spend her money wisely." As he sipped at his brandy, he wondered if the widow had a young, pretty daughter.

Less than one week later, Ambrosia returned to the house on Meeting Street one evening to find Major Rambert waiting for her, just outside the wrought-iron gate. He touched his hat in a polite gesture to Ambrosia, then Sheba, but his manner was one of business rather than congeniality. "I sold the jewelry," he told her simply, handing her a sealed envelope. And then he promptly bid her a good day. Ambrosia mumbled a halfhearted thank-you, which she was not certain whether or not he heard, then sent Sheba inside to fetch Josiah before she examined the envelope's contents.

Twice, three times she counted it, hardly believing her own eyes. The envelope was fat with Yankee green-backs, nine hundred dollars' worth. Nine hundred dollars—so much more than Elisabeth had ever dreamed of getting! For an instant, a temptation to take four hundred dollars, the amount she needed to pay the taxes on Heritage, gripped her hard. Elisabeth would never know and, in a way, she owed it to Ambrosia in return for the favor of selling the ring. Ambrosia would pay it all back some-day. But for now, she could save the land! She could re-build!

The long-dormant dreams tripped over one another as they rushed to quiet her conscience. But the reality of the situation could not be silenced by dreams that were so bruised and worn. Once it had been so easy to believe in a bright tomorrow; now she could not. She would never have the money to repay Elisabeth. Taxes were only a small part, anyway. There was no house, no crops, no slaves, no tools. Ambrosia sighed wearily as she closed the envelope. There was so little left of her that could afford to dream anymore.

"Sheba said you wanted to see me, Miz Ambrosia."

"Yes, Josiah. I need you to take something to Elisabeth Woodard's house on Charlotte Street right away." She thrust the envelope in his hand. "Don't dally. It's very important."

He fingered the envelope nervously and shifted his weight from one foot to the other. "I—I'll be needin' t' speak with you about somethin' else first, Miz Ambrosia. Somethin' really important."

Ambrosia's brow knitted with concern. "What is it, Josiah?"

"I—that is, Sally and me and Andrew, we've found

work." He gave an uneasy shrug and looked at the ground. "I—I'm sorry t' be leavin', Miz Ambrosia. But there's no work for us here. And pretty soon, they'll stop givin' out the food at the bureau, and the Bowmans' won't want us emptyin' their cupboards . . ." His voice softened as he met her eyes. "Besides, I'm a freedman now. I've got two strong arms and two strong legs, and I can work hard as any man. So I signed a contract that gives work for the next year."

"You signed a labor contract?" she repeated numbly.

He gave a nod. "Yes'm. And the contract's been okayed by the bureau man, too."

"For doing what? What kind of work?"

"Fieldwork, Miz Ambrosia. Ain't no other kind of work t' be had these days."

"But you aren't a field-slave, Josiah! You're a gentleman's valet—"

"And you ain't a common workwoman, Miz Ambrosia. But you're workin', all the same."

Ambrosia tried to hide her hurt at his remark. "What about Sheba?"

Josiah lowered his eyes and kicked at a pebble with his tattered leather shoe. "Sheba says she'll stay here as long as you do."

Ambrosia watched his normally noble posture sag in remorse. He felt he'd been disloyal to her, though in fact he had little choice. The Bowmans' house was crowded, and their few remaining slaves had made it clear they did not enjoy sharing quarters, or even duties, with "inland" people. She let out a sigh and touched her hand to Josiah's long, muscular arm. "You deserve so much better, Josiah. If only Father hadn't died! If only I could have—"

"No, Miz Ambrosia." He shook his head. "You did the best you could. We all did the best we could. It's just time for us to start all over again, I guess." He fingered the envelope again and gave a short nod. "Guess I'll be gettin' this over to Miz Woodard now."

Ambrosia watched him set off, plodding steadily up Meeting Street into the crowds of people, wondering bitterly if there was anything left in her life for the Yankees to take away. She had already lost so much. She bit her lip hard, forcing away her depression, fixing a pleasant expression to her face for Ledger as she entered the house. A warm feeling flowed within her as she did so. For him she could always find the strength to be brave. For him she could face a million tomorrows with her chin held high.

Major Drayton Rambert walked briskly away from the Bowman house on Meeting Street, his stride suggesting an important destination, though in truth he had none. He kept his eyes downcast, avoiding the constant reminders of war, of ruin, of destruction. The city of Charleston seemed to him a mortally wounded animal, struggling mightily against a cruel trap that had snared its throat, writhing, agonizing, waiting for death as the blue-uniformed buzzards circled eagerly about its head. For this city, these people, the war was raging as strong and bitter as it had for the past five years. Only now there was no hope behind their struggle. They were fighting now to hold on to what was left because it was a matter of dignity. They did not know how to surrender their pride.

And to what would the Southern aristocracy surrender? he asked himself as he strode along. To a confusing, self-serving tangle of bureaucracy? To the army, with its cocky soldiers and greedy officers? To the Freedman's Bureau, which, for all its good intentions, was constantly at odds with the army? To the corrupt Treasury agents who swarmed like hungry locusts on a prostrate state? To the Republicans and carpetbaggers, who were anxious to see the South punished for past wrongs as they helped themselves to a share of the spoils? It was no wonder that the hatred lingered in their hearts.

He drew a deep breath as he reached East Battery and slowed his pace, pausing to lean forward on the wooden rails. He stared at the water as it lapped gently against the

rocks below. It was a soothing sound. He sighed heavily.
For him, the war was over. The perverse comfort he had
found these past years in living on the edge, in walking
the dangerous line between life and death, had been lost.
He was trapped now by his work, having been deemed
far too "useful" to the occupational forces to be given
the assignment he'd requested in the West. He could read
and write and count, a fact which had earned him an office here in Charleston he didn't want, and an endless
stream of paperwork he abhored. Work details, requisi-
tion forms, official reports, the list was endless. And all
of it chained him to a desk and made him want to climb
the walls.

Drayton closed his eyes and rubbed the back of his
neck. There was more to it than his job with the army.
Matt had forced him to admit that much. And having admitted it, he realized just how much he loved her, and
how deeply she despised him in return. For the thou-
sandth time that hour he berated himself for being the
worst kind of fool. How had he let it happen—loving a
woman who could not begin to love him? Ambrosia was
nothing like the first woman he'd loved, nothing at all
like Kathryn. She had been warm and bright and smiling
and young. . . . He wondered if Ambrosia had ever
really been a carefree, smiling young girl. He opened his
eyes and stared at the swift current of the Cooper River,
flowing relentlessly, sweeping leaves and branches and
debris along with it. And Kathryn's image was swept
aside as he recalled a stormy night when another woman,
a small slip of a woman, had stood silently, courageously
beside him in an attempt to save the lives of three men.
Perhaps it had happened at that very moment, when she'd
looked at him with defiance and stood her ground. He
had known then that she was different, different in a
thousand ways. He could picture her diminutive form
struggling behind a plow, or pulling with all her might
against the stubbornness of an old mule. And he could
see her thin, delicate fingers, freshly bruised and cut,

pressing gently to Jamie Clark's brow, could see the care in her green-gray eyes as she bathed his hot skin with cool water, knowing that it would do no good, knowing that he would die. There was a rare kind of gentleness to her; and though she hid it carefully beneath pride and defiant anger, he had seen it then, seen it clearly. He knew little of the wounds her heart must have suffered, but he knew that some of them were deep, and he knew that she was afraid of being hurt again. Perhaps even as frightened as he.

But for him it was already too late. How many nights had he lain awake, remembering the way she had clung to him in the stable at Heritage? Or the small, precious moment when she had surrendered to his kiss, before she gathered her defenses to fight him as an enemy? Remembering that moment gave him a tiny shred of hope that she might, in time, come to care for him too. But he knew all too well that her hatred ran deep, to her very core. And he knew that nothing he could ever do would change the way she felt. With a sigh of resignation, Drayton watched the movement of a large branch as it floated smoothly atop the water and on into the bay. It was time to go home. It was time to stop running from the memories that haunted him, time to build a new life, a stable life. Letters arrived regularly from the lawyer handling his father's estate, advising him to return to New York immediately. But he still couldn't face the thought of returning to the life that had been, of confronting any part of a past he'd tried so desperately to forget. He turned abruptly away from the water, not wanting to think of the past, not wanting to consider a future without Ambrosia. He could not give up hoping, as long as she remained so close by, working at the store, living in the house on Meeting Street. Though it made him a fool, he could not give up hoping.

On the opposite side of the street only four houses down, a pretty young woman was standing at her bedroom window, staring idly at the people walking up and down East Battery. Mrs. Carolyn Craig, who had been a widow for nearly four of her twenty-two years, was bright, attractive, and flirtatious, and she had always gotten what she wanted from men. She had been the most sought-after girl in New York for a season and had broken scores of hearts when she married Thomas Craig. Tom had seemed so worldly and ambitious to Carolyn, who had wanted a fine house and more fashionable clothes than her parents could give her. But the marriage had been a terrible mistake, and less than a year after she took her vows, Carolyn was both relieved and grateful to see her young husband laid to rest, the victim of pneumonia. After months of being tied to a fiercely jealous man who was as close to a miser as Carolyn ever wanted to meet, widowhood had been a reprieve, a welcome second chance at life. Carolyn had enjoyed playing the part of the proper, grieving widow, all the while knowing she was as sought after and openly adored by men as she had been before. But she'd never found any man who could hold her interest for long . . . until now. When she had come to Charleston a few months ago to visit her late husband's aunt and uncle, she'd achieved immediate popularity and enjoyed the attention of dozens of homesick soldiers. A single, suggestive smile and men were fluttering about her like moths about a flame. But it was the one soldier who had hardly glanced at her that had made her stay months longer than she'd planned.

"Major Drayton Rambert . . ." she sighed the name aloud, wistfully wrapping her arms about herself as a shiver of excitement ran through her. He was far more handsome than any of the others, she thought, though it was not his appearance which held her attention. There was something so cool, so masculine about his manner, an intangible aura of danger, or violence, masked by a demeanor of perfect control. The moment she saw him she felt butterflies in her stomach. Tom's uncle had introduced them, as he had introduced her to a hundred other soldiers, and she had actually felt light-headed as Drayton politely repeated her name, his voice so smooth and rich and masculine. . . . But then he had turned away.

Carolyn frowned as the memory caused a pang of frustration to surge through her. She had failed so miserably where Drayton Rambert was concerned. She had tried everything to be noticed, only to be ignored. But there had to be some way to—

Her thoughts scattered as her eyes riveted on a tall, broad-shouldered soldier making his way along the street. When he stopped for a moment to gaze out at the river, she pulled aside the lace curtain and leaned forward for a better view, then hurriedly shrugged out of her silk dressing gown and into a hooped petticoat and pretty green print muslin gown. Muttering anxiously to herself the entire time, she struggled with the fastenings at the back of her dress, then paused for barely a moment before the looking glass before flying out of her room and down the front stairs. She purposely ignored the puzzled inquiry her late husband's aunt called from the parlor, and let the front door slam behind her with a bang. She scampered up the street in excitement. He was still there!

She paused, totally out of breath, just a few yards from him, considering his somber expression and working out a plan of attack. She was still standing there, considering, when he turned his head, straightened, and began to walk away. Her voice rose to stop him. "Major Rambert! What a pleasant surprise!"

Drayton whirled, then removed his hat and gave a polite nod. "Good evening, Mrs. Craig." He eyed her speculatively for a moment, noting that she was alone, that she wore no cloak or bonnet, that her cheeks were flushed, her dark brown hair smoothed, her blue eyes alight with a devilish glint. She fluttered long, dark lashes and turned her attention coyly to the river. "I can see we have something in common," she announced softly, feeling his eyes upon her and enjoying the feeling.

"Oh?"

She gave a nod and made a show of inhaling very slowly, letting her breasts rise high and full against the neckline of her gown. "I enjoy this place . . . the river. . . ." She tossed him a sidelong glance to be sure he had noticed before she added, "Oh, it's nothing like New York, of course, but I often come here when I need to think."

Drayton's eyes left her as he propped one foot on the bottom rung of the railing and braced both hands on the top. He was silent. She let her fingers creep slowly toward his hand, but refrained from touching him. She had seen forward women lose his interest with a single aggressive tactic, and she didn't want to do that. But it was so difficult to get his attention, and she had to make an impression now that she had it. "Do you miss New York?" she asked him suddenly.

"Sometimes."

Carolyn could hardly keep from frowning her frustration. At this rate, she would never draw him into a conversation. She drew a deep breath and decided to be bold. "Who is she, Drayton?"

He cocked his head to look at her and lifted a mildly curious brow. "Who is who, Mrs. Craig?"

"The woman you come here to think about," she returned bluntly. "And don't tell me it's not a woman," she hastened to add. "I know enough about men to recognize the look on your face."

"I'll wager you do," he agreed under his breath.

Her lips tightened angrily for an instant before she caught herself. She forced them into an attractive pout. "I—I remember your wife," she lied in a soft, wistful tone. "Of course, I was very young when she died, but I remember how lovely she was . . . and—and when my late husband's aunt mentioned your name the other day at tea, well, I—I know how much you must miss her." She did her best to conjure up a tear as she reached to cover his hand with her own. "Six years is a long time to mourn, Drayton. Life is so short. . . ."

His eyes fixed on the hand which covered his, a soft, lily-white hand with perfectly manicured nails that rubbed lightly, sensuously at his knuckles, then slipped into his palm. The movement was bold and very arousing to a man who had been without a woman for a long time. An open invitation. Drayton was very tempted to take her up on it, though he knew her late husband's uncle, Henry Bates, an official at the Freedman's Bureau, and though Carolyn was supposedly a proper young widow. She was definitely not the type he usually chose to dally with. Still . . .

Carolyn saw the sparks igniting in his cool, blue eyes and immediately backed off. Too much too soon. It had taken her two long months to get his attention, and she wasn't about to settle for a brief, physical affair. Not from Drayton Rambert. He was much too handsome and too rich, according to the rumors she'd heard. They said his father had left him a fortune a year or so ago. She had just about made up her mind that she would marry him when he asked, and she had no doubt at all he would . . . if she played her cards right. She was looking forward to playing those cards.

With a properly demure smile, she slowly withdrew her hand. "Will you be attending the Dalys' reception Friday next?"

His eyes narrowed knowingly as she changed her tactics. She was going to play games.

"I'm sure you must be invited," she bubbled with a coy smile. "Everyone is." She tilted her head just so. "I was hoping I might see you there, Drayton." She fixed a sweet, hesitant look to her blue eyes before she raised them to his.

He placed his hand upon hers and she shivered at the feel of his fingers, warm and strong against her skin. The slow smile he gave her was different from the one she had anticipated, cold somehow and calculating. But she found it wildly exciting. "Well?" she inquired breathlessly. "Will I see you there?"

His eyes were so intent that she nervously averted her gaze, only to hear a touch of amusement in his response. "There's a fair chance you will, Carolyn . . . a very fair chance."

Chapter 15

The month of November drew to a close, bringing an end to the hopes of many Southerners. Charleston swelled with carpetbaggers who generously arranged to buy property from destitute owners at half, even a third of its value, rather than see the government confiscate it for delinquent taxes due the first of December. Many elderly women and young widows with children were forced to accept whatever was offered them. Others waited and hoped for a reprieve until the hourglass was empty and they were forced to face reality. For the South there would be no mercy.

The first of December was the start of the busiest season of the year at O'Neal's Emporium. Ambrosia was on her feet the entire day, trying to keep up with the constant flow of customers as well as unpacking and keeping records of the newly arrived Christmas items Maggie had ordered. Ambrosia found it easier to work alongside Maggie these days, since the emporium was so busy and she rarely had the time to lecture Ambrosia about her cool response to customers, much less relate the latest gossip. It was just as well, since Ambrosia's emotions had been at their breaking point these past weeks, ever since the dream of rebuilding Heritage had been wrenched from her grasp. Today it was final. Today the taxes were due and would not be paid.

It was long after the sun had disappeared when Ambrosia finally finished the bookwork and put aside her pen with a sigh of utter exhaustion. Sheba, who had arrived at the usual time to escort her home, had taken a seat atop an empty wooden crate, shifting her weight uncomfortably every few moments and periodically shaking her head in disapproval. "You done miss suppah 'gain, Miz Ambrosia," she scolded as Ambrosia finally closed the book of accounts.

Ambrosia's fingers lifted to gently rub her tired, burning eyes. "I'm not hungry anyway."

"You's nevah hungry no more." She snorted as she abandoned her uncomfortable seat and came to stand beside her. "Prob'bly didn't hab no dinnah, eithah." When Ambrosia gave no answer, Sheba thrust out her bottom lip. "You works too hard fo' a lady. An—"

"Please, Sheba. No lectures tonight," she mumbled softly.

Ambrosia rose and put out the lamp, tying on her worn bonnet and throwing her threadbare cloak over her shoulders to ward off the evening's chill. She reminded herself that she had caused Sheba to miss her supper too, and still she could not help but be grateful for the long day's work, for the exhaustion. It had kept her from thinking about Heritage, which, as of today, no longer belonged to her. Acceptance of that came hard, though she had tried mightily to steel herself against the heartache.

She drew her cloak close about her as she hurried along Meeting Street, the cold wind echoing the despair that clutched at her spirit. The scent of a storm was in the air, and the night sky bore no trace of moon or star. Ambrosia reached the house and made her way into the parlor where Ledger, as was his custom whenever she missed supper, sat waiting in a large green chair near the window. She felt the need for his company tonight far more than the need for a meal, even though she had not eaten since early morning.

They spent time together every evening, though they were seldom alone with one another. A hand of cards or a word game or the simple conversation they shared made the minutes pass much too quickly. Often their eyes said far more than their words could say, particularly when Melissa sat nearby. And yet, there were strict boundaries to their behavior even when they were alone, a line over which neither Ambrosia nor Ledger dared to step. If she touched his hand, it was briefly, gently, always in what might be considered a sisterly fashion. If Ledger's eyes held hers, it was only a few moments before one or the other looked away. The friendship that had begun with two adolescents in the garden at Barhamville Academy had become something stronger, more mature. Though their conversations were confined to trivial matters, though Ledger's marriage vows placed hard and fast barriers between them, their relationship was deepening as each heart was drawn to the other.

Melissa, who envied Ambrosia her freedom and despised Ledger for condemning her to a life of poverty, seemed increasingly bitter and resentful of the closeness they shared, so Ambrosia was relieved when she entered the parlor and saw that Ledger was alone. Tonight at least she would not have to endure her sister's deliberately cutting remarks. She made her voice sound bright as she took the chair nearest Ledger, grateful for the quiet, grateful that for once, Sheba had hurried off to have her own supper without scolding Ambrosia about having hers. She politely asked Ledger about Melissa and his mother, who were attending an engagement party for the daughter of one of Madeline's friends. Ambrosia had not been invited; Ledger had chosen not to go.

"You're late getting home tonight," he remarked.

"We were busy today." She gave him a half-smile. "Looks like the Yankees celebrate Christmas same as we used to years ago, when we had money."

She was sorry she had said it the moment she saw his face fall. She oughtn't to have mentioned money or the fact that this Christmas there would be so little to celebrate. She hurriedly searched her mind for another topic of conversation. "Do you remember when you had the idea of tarring all the benches at the college because the dean refused you an extra Christmas holiday?"

He gave a faint, distant smile, very unlike the one she had hoped for. "You know I remember everything about those years," he said softly. "Everything." He sighed and struggled to his one good leg, propping a single crutch beneath his arm and turning so that he faced the window, though Ambrosia knew he could see little in the darkness. For once she could not bear the silence.

"The air smells of rain," she said quickly, to break it. "And the wind off the sea is stronger than it was this morning. I think we're in for quite a storm. And it will probably turn colder tomorrow, after . . ." Ambrosia faltered as he turned to face her, his eyes accusing.

"I've never known you to force conversation, Ambrosia. Why are you doing it now?"

Ambrosia stiffened for a moment, clenching her jaw against an angry retort. But the effort, after endless months of holding back so many feelings, proved too much. She needed so much to tell him! "Oh, Ledger!" she whispered. "What's to become of us?" She squeezed her eyes tightly shut, and her face contorted as she tried to keep from sobbing aloud. Her voice was filled with the tears she refused to cry. "Every day I see the Yankees beating us . . . taking away everything that's dear to us . . . until we haven't anything left to fight for—" Her voice rose suddenly and she shook her head, unable to go on, unable now to hold back her tears.

For a long time he said nothing. He had never seen her cry before. There had only been that small rush of tears when he had first come home. It hadn't been like this. It hadn't made her seem so small and fragile . . . and nearly broken. He watched her shoulders tremble with the force of her emotion, and suddenly he could bear no more. "Come here," he said softly, taking an awkward step toward her at the same time, leaning heavily on his crutch.

She rose and stepped hesitantly toward him, stopping carefully while still an arm's breadth away, stretching her hand uncertainly toward the one which reached for hers. For an eternal moment, they stood unmoving, their eyes locked, the barriers between them melting away as they continued to hold one another's eyes. Ledger drew her close until she was encircled by his arm, her head pressed against his chest. He held her closer, closer, touching the softness of her hair as he had wanted to do all these past months, pressing his lips to the top of her head as her tears continued to slip over her cheeks. "You're a brave woman, Ambrosia," he said softly.

He felt her arms tighten about his waist, but was unaware of her timorous smile as she remembered that he had spoken those words once before. She bit her lip hard and struggled to stop her tears as she heard the brighter note fill his voice. "Do you remember the way you climbed that tree and hid, just so that you could ask me my name?" She heard him smile. "You demanded it, if I recall, for another girl who wasn't quite as courageous."

She drew back, her eyes wide with surprise as they met his. "You—you remember that?" she asked in amazement, quickly wiping the tears from her cheeks.

He grinned. "I also remember that look on your face when I gave you that silly little flower. I could tell you hadn't had many men present you with bouquets, or you wouldn't have been so infatuated with my—er, gallantry."

"I was awestruck," she corrected gently.

"You were infatuated," he insisted. "It was written all over your face."

Ambrosia's smile vanished suddenly and her voice was small and childlike. "I was in love with you, Ledger. I'm still in love with you."

His smile faded and he started to speak, but she pressed a hand to his mouth to stop him. Slowly, carefully, she stretched on tiptoe and touched her lips lightly to his. Her lips were soft and warm, and they instinctively parted as he responded. Her heart soared.

But then he stiffened and turned away. "Ambrosia, don't."

She stared at his back as he took a step away from her, her eyes filling with tears once more. For that one, precious moment they had stepped across the line that had been drawn years before, and Ambrosia had tasted the dream she'd kept locked so long inside her heart. Though he turned away from her now, it was too late to go back. "You're the only thing that matters in my life anymore, Ledger," she said quietly to his back. She spoke slowly, giving each word ample time to echo in the silence of the room.

"Ambrosia, please . . ." He turned to face her again, his shoulders squared, his mouth set, though he could do nothing to still the pounding of his heart. What a fool he'd been to allow this to happen, to jeopardize what little they could have together rather than leave it alone. He had known that if he once took her in his arms, they could never go back. And now . . .

She stepped toward him again, her fingertips touching tenderly to the scars which covered his cheek. The words came hard. "I—I know that you have never loved me—"

He stilled the caress of her hand and pushed it roughly from his face. She was the only woman who could even bear to look at him now, much less touch him. And he loved her more than he had ever thought it possible to love anyone. The temptation was too much. If he did nothing to stop her, she would be in his arms again in another moment. He couldn't allow that to happen. "Ambrosia, you're still such a child!"

She flinched at the sharpness in his tone and stared up at him in hurt disbelief. "But I'm not a child! I'm not!"

The pain in her eyes made him wince. He had hurt her

deeply; he had never meant to do that. "You are if you believe that there could ever be anything between us. I have a wife, Ambrosia."

"How noble of you to remember that!" came the choked retort from across the room.

Ambrosia instinctively pulled away from Ledger, her eyes flying to the door of the parlor where Melissa stood beside a pale, distraught Madeline Bowman. For a long moment, the room was terribly silent.

"You brazen little hussy!" Melissa lashed out. "Playing up to my husband like a common street woman! After we welcomed you into our home! After we endured the scandal of your working for that horrible Yankee woman!" Melissa clenched her fists hard and her breasts swelled with righteous indignation. She crossed the room, expecting a rush of hasty explanations, of tears and apologies that she could fling back in her sister's face. But Ambrosia stood silent, her green-gray eyes somber and distant, her face an aloof mask. It was just like her, Melissa thought, to play the part of the injured party even when she was guilty as sin. How she hated that constant indifference, that arrogant shell Ambrosia always seemed to wear. There was never any sign of what she was feeling, if indeed she felt anything at all.

Melissa's jealousy grew stronger and more vindictive as she drew nearer to Ambrosia's impassive face. It was all so unfair, that Melissa Lanford should be tied to a useless, defeated man while still young and beautiful, and that her sister should be free to do exactly as she pleased. It had always been that way, for as long as Melissa could remember, ever since Father had taken her to Columbia when she was a little girl. Ambrosia always got everything she wanted. But she could not have Ledger! God only knew why she would want him now; his face was so ugly one could hardly bear to look at it. But he was still Melissa's husband, and now he had provided the perfect justifiable motive for Melissa's vindictiveness toward her sister.

Ledger stared out the window and said nothing, but Melissa noticed that his fingers gripped so tightly at his crutch that they had turned white. Her eyes narrowed, bright and hate-filled. "Whatever will your handsome Yankee major say when he hears you've been unfaithful to him?" she intoned sarcastically, her eyes remaining on Ledger's face. "When he finds that you're actually smitten with a crippled monster?"

Madeline Bowman gasped and nearly swooned, clutching the door frame for support. Ambrosia's eyes darted in panic to Ledger's face, which clearly reflected the accuracy of Melissa's blow. "You know there was never anything between Major Rambert and me." Her eyes searched for some sign of pity in the cold, hard lines of Melissa's face.

"Nothing between you?" Melissa scoffed. She met Ambrosia's eyes and flashed a falsely sweet smile. "I suppose it doesn't really surprise me to hear that the major didn't want you. Ledger didn't want you either, did he? Has there ever been a man who wanted you, Ambrosia?" she taunted.

Ambrosia's rigid stance crumbled slowly in the silence that followed, the last remnants of her hope slipping away as she waited in vain for Ledger to respond. He said nothing.

Has there ever been a man who wanted you? The words echoed louder and louder in her head, forcing Ambrosia to admit the truth. Ledger had never wanted her. . . . Never wanted her . . . Never . . .

Without a word, she turned to him, her face bright with tears. For the barest moment, she simply stared at him, her eyes pleading silently. He turned away. Suddenly she let out a sob and ran from the room.

Chapter 16

Drayton scowled as he turned away from the glass and tossed the hairbrush on the heavy oak bureau top. It had been a long time since he had gone to so much trouble for a woman, and his instincts warned him that Carolyn Craig wasn't worth it. But the alternatives—another night alone, or searching out a woman of the streets—seemed worse at the moment. At least Carolyn offered him an interesting challenge.

He straightened the gold braid at his cuffs, the epaulets at his shoulders, and worked the row of polished brass buttons that stretched over his chest. He fastened the buckle of a thick leather belt about his trim waist and gave a sharp tug at his tunic. Glancing again in the looking glass, he pulled on a pair of white gloves and scowled at his reflection once more. He grabbed his pistol and Hardee hat in a single motion, anxious to have this night over and done with. If Carolyn delivered anything near what she advertised, he told himself, then he ought to be able to forget everything and everyone else and concentrate on her alone, at least for a little while. That was all he really wanted at this point, to forget.

He tossed a heavy cape about his shoulders and hurried down the stairs, nodding a terse greeting to two of the three officers with whom he shared the house. Colonel

196

Beam, the senior officer of the group, came forward. He was a tall, graying gentleman, half again as old as Drayton, with keen eyes shrouded with heavy, drooping lids and a mouth perpetually set in a wry smile. Beam was a confirmed bachelor who had a habit of speaking his mind, but generally he cushioned his blunt candor with humor that made him pleasant company. "Oh-ho! Dressed to the hilt, I see."

Drayton paused to glance at his uniform, then gave a halfhearted shrug. "We seem to have the same tailor, Colonel."

"Better the same tailor than the same woman," he returned with a sip of his bourbon. "Join us for a quick drink?"

"No, thanks. I think I'll keep my wits about me tonight, if you don't mind."

"A wise move, Major," called Lieutenant Hayes from the parlor, "if you're planning to tangle with a female in the near future." The slurred comment indicated that Hayes had already had too much to drink himself.

"Going to the Dalys' tonight?" Colonel Beam inquired with a lift of his brow.

Drayton gave a nod. "And I intend to arrive early," he said with finality, jerking on his hat. "I'll leave you gentlemen to your drinks."

Colonel Beam landed a hearty smack between Drayton's shoulders. "Careful of Mrs. Craig," he warned with a conspiratorial grin. "She's had her eye on you for months now, Drayt."

"Thanks for the advice, Colonel," he returned with a cool smile.

Drayton scowled as he stepped outside, turning his back to the strong wind, lighting a cigar as he waited for the young private to bring his horse around. He almost smiled when he saw the youngster coming, struggling mightily with the reins of the stallion, who pawed nervously and danced sideways in spite of the boy's best efforts to be firm. Relenting, Drayton moved forward to grab the bridle and allow the white-faced lad to dismount. Drayton took possession of the reins and swung easily into the saddle. "Thank you, Private Reynolds."

"Will there be anything else, sir?" the boy asked, backing up a few steps and eyeing the horse warily.

Drayton drew a final puff on the cigar and glanced thoughtfully at the sky as he tossed it to the ground. "Leave a bottle of brandy in my room, in case I get drenched. Oh—and don't let me forget my meeting with General Saxton tomorrow morning. Eight o'clock."

Private Reynolds saluted with a hearty, "Yes, sir! Good night, sir!" then shook his head in wonder as the major reined the horse in a tight half-circle and took off down the street at an easy trot. He sighed wistfully, then hurried into the house to find some brandy.

Ambrosia ran from the Meeting Street house without a backward glance, not stopping until she had covered several long blocks and felt a sharp pain in her chest. She stumbled along a darkened section of the street as a howling wind whipped at her cloak and threatened to knock her down. The wind was so much stronger than it had been just a few hours before, and a few defiant raindrops pelted her cheeks, mingling with salty tears. She ignored them and continued on. She did not know where she was going. She did not care. She had long since passed the emporium when the thought struck her. She would go to the river. She was almost certain she could bargain for passage on one of the ships there. She didn't really care where it took her, as long as it was away from here. She only wanted to get away. She tried to think about where she might go, how far she might get on the twelve dollars she had in her possession, along with a few worthless items of clothing.

She drew her cloak close as the rain began to fall in a more regular drizzle, hardly noticing that the alley she was passing echoed of drunken laughter and shrill voices. The empty streets began to fill with Yankees even as the rain fell harder. Oblivious to the eyes which followed her progress, oblivious to everything but the terrible truth she carried in her heart, Ambrosia stumbled on.

Drayton reined his horse to a walk as a shadowy figure crossing the street caught his eye. There was something so familiar about the woman that he could not take his eyes away. He watched her for a moment, his chin lifting and eyes narrowing when a young soldier in fancy dress uniform stepped from a dark alley to block her path. She gasped and stepped backward, staring dumbly at the man, clutching at her cloak. The soldier closed the distance between himself and the woman, a dangerous glint in his eyes and a leering grin on his mouth. Drayton half expected her to scream. She did not. A common street woman, Drayton chided himself. He made to turn away, but something made him pause. The woman drew back abruptly then and attempted to sidestep the soldier. He moved to block her path again, his hand stretching boldly toward her and yanking at her hard. Drayton watched and waited. Perhaps they were merely discussing a price, but then again . . .

Ambrosia swallowed hard as the first tinglings of panic began at her spine. But she was too tired to fight, too numb to bolt and run from the danger, so she stood silent, unmoving—afraid, yet unable to react to her fear. She felt the cold sting of rain at her cheeks as the soldier caught hold of her and jerked her abruptly against his chest. He pulled roughly at her bonnet until it fell away, then raked his fingers through her hair until it flew about her shoulders. Her eyes grew wide and bright with tears. "No!" she whispered, her breath coming short and hard. "Please, no!"

Still unable to summon the strength to fight him, she began to scream hysterically. At that instant Drayton knew that it was she. He spurred the stallion hard and swung off, firing a warning shot that caused the soldier to start in surprise then freeze momentarily. The stallion's hooves thundered as he reared and took off down the street. The soldier's dark eyes darted anxiously about, seeking escape. He wanted no part of the gun-wielding stranger who rushed toward him. He pushed Ambrosia forcefully to the ground as he made a run for the alley. Drayton fired another shot after him, but the rain obscured his vision. The soldier went free as Drayton muttered a curse and hastened to Ambrosia's side.

She was crying softly, huddled in a near-fetal position, her hands held protectively over her face even as he called her name. She did not answer him. He took hold of her shoulders and lifted her, prying her hands from her tear-streaked face, studying her with concern. "Ambrosia, are you all right? Did he hurt you?"

It was a long time before the terror faded from her eyes. There was a tiny flicker of recognition before she faced away.

"What in the name of heaven are you doing here? On a night like this?" he demanded, his anxiety giving way to anger. "And where the hell is Sheba?"

She stared at him dumbly as he repeated his questions over and over again before the words registered in her mind. "I asked what you're doing—"

"I'm leaving Charleston," she mumbled stonily as she turned slowly to retrieve her bonnet and bundle of clothing. "I'm going to book passage on a ship. . . ."

His frown was dark and skeptical as he took the bundle from her trembling hands. "You certainly didn't pack much," he attempted lightly. "Are you planning a lengthy stay or merely a pleasure trip?"

Her face tightened. "I'm leaving for good, if it's any of your business." Her voice was tired.

"It's not," he admitted. "But there will be no ships taking on passengers on this night," he assured her. He moved to shield her as best he could from the rain and let out a lengthy breath as he helped her to her feet. "Come on. I'll take you home."

"No!" With a suddenness that startled him, she

snatched away from his grasp, the panic burning bright again in her green eyes.

"Ambrosia . . . ?"

"No! I can't go back there!" She let out a cry of anguish and shook her head violently as she backed away from him. "I can't! Not ever!"

He searched her face uneasily. "Where then?"

She lurched forward to grab blindly at her bundle and would have fled had he not taken hold of her arm and pulled her close. With a tiny cry of defeat, she fell limp and trembling against him, the fight in her totally spent. "I have nowhere to go," she choked out softly. "But I can't go back there. I can't . . ."

For a long moment he held her fast, not caring that the rain beat hard and cold against his back, drenching him to the skin. Then he made a decision, and in a swift motion he slipped an arm beneath her knees and lifted her like a child into his arms. He glanced about for some sign of the stallion, but the horse had long since disappeared. With a silent curse, he gave up hopes of finding the animal for the moment and hunched his back against the rain as he made his way toward home.

To his relief, the house was empty when he finally reached it, the other officers having long since left to pursue an evening of pleasant diversion. A lamp had been left burning low in the front hall near the staircase, as was the custom. Drayton passed it without stopping, continuing up the stairs to his private quarters. He nudged the door closed behind him with his shoulder and rather brusquely deposited a soaking wet Ambrosia on her feet near the fireplace. A single arm shot out to steady her when she swayed precariously, but he released her just as quickly the moment she regained her balance.

Turning his full attention to lighting a fire, Drayton quickly coaxed a tiny yellow-orange flame to curl about a small stack of kindling. He dropped a pair of thick, hardwood logs on the grate and watched for a time to be certain the logs had caught. He stared at the fire, unconsciously removing his belt and revolver and placing them on the floor, unbuttoning his rain-drenched cape, tunic, and shirt and peeling them off his broad shoulders. His mind was racing with a thousand questions. What was she running from? Why couldn't she go home? And what in heaven's name had made her so desperate that she would turn to him, a Yankee, for help? Not that she would ever be grateful, he reminded himself ruefully.

He glanced up at her, noticing at once that she still shivered beneath the cloying folds of a wet cloak, that her jaw still quivered slightly with the chill, that her eyes were a deep, brooding gray, like a dark winter sky threatening snow. There was something very changed about her face, he thought as she continued to stare indifferently at the fire. He scowled as a tremor made her shoulders shake with cold and put his musings aside. He rose and went to the carved cedar chest at the foot of the bed, from which he withdrew a light woolen blanket. She looked up at him blankly when he offered it to her and winced when his impatient growl broke the silence. "Get out of those wet things before you catch your death of cold."

She accepted the blanket with a mute nod, her strangely distant eyes meeting his for the barest moment before she stared at the floor. For a long time she stood there unmoving, the blanket clutched tightly in her hands. Drayton moved to the shadows of a far corner of the room and refrained from lighting a lamp. He turned his back to allow her some privacy. Moments passed.

She heard the thud of first one boot dropping, then another, the distant rustle of wet clothing being removed, the slap of each garment as it hit the floor. At length the noises registered in her mind and spurred her into obeying Drayton's order. She stepped away from the fire toward the protective shadows and laid the blanket over the arm of a chair before pulling shakily at the drawstring of her cloak. Her fingers were trembling so badly that it was several moments before the knot came loose. She shrugged it slowly from her shoulders and laid it carefully over the back of the chair. She turned toward the fire, the welcome heat of it causing her to shiver anew as her body struggled to regain its warmth. Lifting both hands to the back of her neck, she tried to work the buttons there. But the air in the room was chilled and her fingertips were still numb with cold. She fought an urge to cry as she pulled uselessly at the fastenings, her fingers slipping clumsily in spite of a concerted effort to hold them steady.

Drayton took his time donning a dark blue woolen dressing gown, then he turned, momentarily forgetting his resolution to respect Ambrosia's modesty. His eyes found her small trembling form in the shadows, her arms raised as she struggled in vain with the fastenings at the back of her dress. He drew a lengthy breath to strengthen his resolve before he crossed the room to help her. He was surprised when she offered not the slightest resistance.

He brushed aside her still-damp hair and brusquely loosened the buttons at the nape of her neck and on down her back, steeling himself against the hunger that rose in him at the sight of her thin, feminine undergarments, at the feel of her cool, velvet skin against his fingers. He forgot himself for the slightest instant, and his hands slipped beneath the wet fabric at her shoulders and lingered there before he began to draw off her gown. His breath quickened. Ambrosia stood stock still, finding a strange sense of reassurance in his move, though she also knew a fearful uncertainty. A moment later, when he muttered something under his breath and tersely pulled away, she frowned in hurt confusion.

It doesn't really surprise me to hear that the major didn't want you . . . The words came back to haunt her with a cruel, taunting ring.

She shrugged off her dress, her single hooped petticoat and pantalets, leaving only a damp shimmy clinging to her skin as she quickly reached for the blanket, which she gathered about her shoulders. She turned, her troubled eyes following Drayton across the room, watching as he lifted a full decanter of brandy from his bureau and filled a small glass. He took a long swallow.

Venting a pensive sigh, Drayton tossed a glance at her over his shoulder. He needed a good stiff drink. Several, actually. But there was only the brandy here, to ward off the chill. At least it did that much. He half filled a second glass, which he offered to Ambrosia. He purposely ignored the pleading, bewildered look in her eyes as she accepted it, abruptly turning his back and retracing his steps to the bureau.

Ambrosia blinked painfully as she took a long sip of the brandy, gazing forlornly at the thick amber liquid as the warmth slid into her mouth and down her throat. *Has there ever been a man who wanted you?* The words began to echo loudly in her head again, even as the fire in the brandy warmed her blood and made her feel light-headed. *Has there ever been a man . . . ?* Ambrosia cringed and covered her ears as the voice became louder and louder. *Has there ever been a man . . . ?*

Ambrosia opened her eyes slowly and drew a hesitant breath. The voices grew softer and finally subsided. She straightened with effort and stared at Drayton's broad back. Once, not so very long ago, he had looked at her so differently, with a strange kind of hunger that might have negated Melissa's words. She took a sip of brandy and tried to think clearly. Perhaps she had only imagined such a look. She knew so very little of men, of desire. Perhaps Melissa was right in everything she said. And Ledger, in calling her a foolish child. It was at this last thought that Ambrosia felt her throat sting with fresh tears. She stared at her brandy through a blur of moisture, then quickly drained the glass and set it aside. She hesitated, but only long enough to draw on the courage the strong draught offered her. She drew a deep breath. "Drayton . . . ?" Her voice was weak, tentative.

He whirled to face her, struggling hard to keep from choking on his brandy. She had never called him by his first name before. Her eyes were averted, but she looked extremely fetching dressed in little more than a thin blanket, her long, black hair falling in shiny waves about her shoulders, a smooth length of slender leg plainly visible where the blanket gaped open. He stared at her with careful scrutiny. She met his eyes and he somehow managed to mask his surprise as he lifted an inquiring brow. Her bottom lip began to tremble as she faced away from him to stare at her empty glass. "Have you . . . have you ever desired me?"

For a long moment he wondered if he was going completely mad. She was far too lovely standing there in the firelight, like a seductive gypsy maiden, the flickers of red and gold on her flawless skin, like something he had conjured up in his dreams. It was a vision that could easily drive a man to madness. He finished off his brandy and swiftly refilled his glass, never taking his gaze from her. Her large green eyes lifted to question his continued silence. No. He had heard correctly. If anyone was going mad, it was certainly not he. He walked slowly toward her, swirling his brandy pensively as he tried to guess at her mood, tried to imagine what kind of game she wished to play. Her breath quickened at his nearness and nearly stopped as he reached out to tuck a long, black lock behind her ear. His fingers lingered there in a light caress. "Have you ever desired me?" he parried.

His voice held a velvet softness which yielded her a precious hint of the assurance she sought, but not nearly what she had hoped. She swallowed hard, feeling that somehow a trap was closing neatly about her, that she would be caught no matter which way she turned. "I—I have been curious," she admitted in a strained whisper. She eyed Drayton's nearly full glass and instinctively reached for it, her bravado wearing thin. She took a single large gulp and returned it to him without raising her eyes, missing his smile as he raised the glass to his own lips and drained it in a single swallow. Curious, was she? He intended to find out in short order just how curious she was.

He leaned very close to her, setting his empty glass on the desk beside hers, his hand lightly, but intentionally brushing her breast. He heard her sudden intake of breath but she made no move to flee, no move to fight him. For whatever reason, he determined, she seemed quite curious enough.

"Ambrosia?" His voice was soft, caressing.

She could not look at him. The skin at the back of her neck began to tingle. He put a forefinger beneath her chin and lifted her face. She closed her eyes. His parted lips lowered to hers with warm familiarity, unhurried, experienced in their movement. She trembled. The tenderness of his kiss faded swiftly as his passion grew. His tongue probed lightly at first, then ever deeper into her mouth. While she clutched tightly at the blanket, her free hand groped hesitantly for his chest. She swayed toward him.

His head lifted slowly and he searched her face. There was something very different from curiosity in her response. Something deeper, something stronger. "Ambrosia?"

She reluctantly met his eyes. For what seemed like a long time, he tried to deny what he saw there, the sadness, the desperation, the fear. But it was too poignant, too haunting, almost like the look of someone about to surrender his last bit of life to death. It was a look that had nothing to do with curiosity . . . or desire.

"Tell me what happened tonight," he prodded gently. "What were you running from?"

She stiffened, her eyes suddenly hard and impenetrable. She turned away from him, and only his firm grasp on her forearms prevented her from fleeing. "Ambrosia—"

"No!" She twisted and pulled in a valiant effort to be free. But he jerked her tightly against his chest, jarring the breath from her lungs as her bosom pressed hard against him. Realizing she could not hope to escape him, her struggles came to an abrupt end. She closed her eyes and blinked at the tears which had again begun to fill her eyes.

Drayton heaved a weary sigh and gradually loosened his hold on her, placing a hand to either side of her face and gently brushing the tears with his thumbs. He kissed her then, with such tenderness and care that she unconsciously responded, her mouth warm and pliant beneath his. For a time he fought the urge to do what came naturally to him. He knew somehow that it was wrong. But he had waited too long for this, he wanted her too badly. Her hand trembled as the palm perched lightly against his robe and her lips parted slightly, until he even felt the tip of her tongue against his. The kiss deepened, the cool, sweet taste of her filled his mouth.

Tiny tremors of pleasure rushed down Ambrosia's limbs, and she sighed at the comforting dizziness which had silenced completely the taunting voices in her head. She tensed as his hand moved to break her fingers' tight hold on the blanket and allowed it to slip silently to the floor. He ran his fingertips lightly over her breasts, taking her breath away as he idly traced the worn ribbon and mended lace edge of her shimmy, tugging gently at the tiny bow until it fell free. She would have drawn away, but suddenly he was kissing her again, demanding more of her this time, his tongue thrusting urgently against hers until she acquiesced.

He murmured her name as his lips slid along the slim column of her throat, and again as he pressed a lingering kiss to the rise of silken flesh that strained against her loosened shimmy. With a half groan of frustration, his thumbs hooked beneath the straps and drew it from her shoulders, leaving her bosom fully exposed to his gaze. "You're beautiful, Ambrosia," he whispered as his mouth trailed downward. "You're everything a man could desire. . . ."

Ambrosia felt hot color shoot through her cheeks as she tried to cross her arms over her naked breasts. She had never expected him to touch her like this, to look at her with such undisguised hunger in his eyes. She was breathing hard and shaking, caught between the strange, sweet warmth she felt whenever she met his eyes and an instinctive need to defend her modesty. She was totally unprepared for what was happening to her, and the queer little shivers that raced everywhere in her body made her feel weak with confusion. Surely this was not what Melissa had meant by desire. Surely no gentleman ever dared to stare at a woman's nakedness, or touch her as Drayton was touching her now, and surely no proper woman would allow herself to take pleasure in anything like this. And yet Ambrosia did feel pleasure and reassurance along with fear—a terrible fear—of the power he held over her, of the control she was losing to his experienced seduction. She bit her lip hard to stop the cry that rose in her throat when he nudged her hands firmly aside and began to kiss her breasts. His mouth slid over the satin skin, his tongue circling, making deliberate suckling pulls at the nipples which throbbed in a response Ambrosia could not stop. His hands moved over the silken curve of her spine, pulling the chemise below her hips until it slipped silently to the floor. She gave a tiny cry of protest, but he stopped it with a hard, demanding kiss, a kiss that considerably lessened what remained of her resistance.

What seemed an eternity later his mouth softened and lifted. Ambrosia twisted her head and weakly tried to pry his hands from her back in a single last effort to stop what was happening. She felt so lost, so confused, so helpless, that she could not resist when his arms about her tightened, molding her softness perfectly to his strength, until she was aware of every inch of him, from his hard muscled thighs to his burning blue eyes.

"Please," he whispered hoarsely, "I need so to take you. . . ." His mouth was pressing intimately to her throat, her breasts, and she felt herself yielding to the gentle pleading in his voice. How could she hope to fight against what she brought upon herself, especially when she could no longer control even her own feelings?

Sensing her surrender, Drayton swiftly discarded his robe and lifted her into his arms, carrying her across the room, easing her onto the bed. Ambrosia closed her eyes tightly against whatever was to happen and struggled to place her mind safely in another time and place. A garden . . . so long ago . . . Ledger with his blond hair blowing about his beautiful, youthful face . . .

Ambrosia gasped as Drayton parted her thighs and was between them, touching, caressing, searching, slowly, urgently, making her tense, making her body quake until she forced herself to leave those feelings behind, to think instead of Ledger's smile, so handsome, so confident. . . . She bit her lip hard and turned away from Drayton's kiss, willing away the reality of him above her, probing, touching, making it so very hard for her to remember the gentle kiss Ledger had pressed to her palm, the tiny violet that he—

An intense, almost electric flash of pain was so sudden and so unexpected that she cried aloud, all images in her memory blurring and fading away. She bit her lip until she tasted blood and fought to remain still and silent, though she could hardly breathe. She understood pain. She almost welcomed it. It made the other feelings, the strange feelings of yearning, recede, and put her in control again.

"Ambrosia?" Drayton's voice was low and strained. "Ambrosia, are you all right?"

Ambrosia opened her eyes. He was searching her face anxiously and his fingers were smoothing a damp tendril of her hair from her cheek. She nodded slowly, wondering if it were over, wondering if he were satisfied. His eyes were soft as he gazed down at her, as he began to drop feather-light kisses all about her face until she felt her body quivering again with that same mixture of warmth and fear, in spite of the pain she still felt, in spite of the discomfort. He covered her mouth with a hungry, pleading pressure that caused her to arch her back in an instinctive struggle to be free, to stop the cruel invasion of the most intimate part of her body. But when she moved against him, his breath caught sharply and something within him seemed to snap. His shaft thrust deeper and ever deeper inside her, again and again and again, until he groaned in near agony and shuddered, then fell motionless and spent against her. She closed her eyes and sighed with relief. It was over.

A few moments passed before Drayton rolled onto his back and reached to gather her against him, drawing a blanket over them both. It was a long while before she felt comfortable lying close to him, after what he had just done. She was very aware of the hard swell of his chest, the crisp mat of hair beneath her hand, the slowing rhythm of his heart, the quieting whisper of his breath.

Drayton's eyes were troubled as he ran his fingers along the length of her arm, pausing to knead thoughtfully at the lovely curve of her bare shoulder. He knew he had not given her pleasure, knew he had not even possessed her in a way that meant anything, though he had been her first man. The knowledge made him feel empty and helpless, though the fault had not been his. He uptilted her chin to look into her eyes. The fear was gone, and the desperation. The indifference and the despair remained. He sighed and let his hand trace wistfully along the smooth line of her cheek, over her chin, her full, soft mouth. A frown flitted across her brow. He knew that his touch troubled her, that she would rather he left her alone. But he had no intention of letting her alone.

"What were you running from tonight?" he ventured softly, slowly.

Ambrosia's frown disappeared. Her expression became closed, distant.

Drayton sighed softly. "How long have you been in love with him?"

She lifted her head from his chest and frowned at him as if she didn't understand.

He drew a long breath and held her eyes. "Ledger. How long have you been in love with him?"

Her face paled at the mention of his name. With a sudden lurch she tried to break away from Drayton's hold, but he anticipated her move. His fingers gripped tightly at her shoulders and pinioned her easily behind him. He loosened his hold only some moments later when she stilled, turning her face away and blinking in vain against the moisture that filled her eyes. Her voice was barely audible when she finally managed to speak. "How? How did you know?"

He did not answer until she turned her eyes to question him. "You called out his name as I took you."

She swallowed hard and looked away again in humiliation. She was silent for a long time. "I'm sorry," she whispered.

He sighed and rolled over on his back again, drawing her into his arms. She wondered fleetingly why he showed no anger. Surely her mistake had wounded his pride.

"How long have you been in love with him?"

Ambrosia fixed her eyes on the steady rise and fall of his chest, finding the movement somehow comforting. "Forever," she admitted softly.

"He was your first love, then?" She did not answer that; she did not need to. "First loves always last forever," he told her quietly. He gave a reluctant smile. "The pain lasts almost that long too. But after a while, you learn to live with it."

The green eyes that rose hesitantly to study his face were openly skeptical. His smile deepened, a warm smile. "Is it so difficult to believe that I was in love once?" She lowered her eyes, considering.

"It doesn't help to run away from it," he went on after a moment, when she did not speak. "I suppose it's because you really can't run from yourself, no matter how far you go, or how hard you try."

She lifted her head. "Did you run away?"

His gaze was even and totally honest. "Yes."

"From what?"

His smile faded slowly, and for the first time since she'd known him he pointedly avoided her eyes. All the same she saw the sadness in them and heard it in his voice. "From the memories . . . from all that I wanted and knew I could never have . . ." He paused. "I lost everything when she died."

Ambrosia watched as dozens of emotions crossed his face at once, watched pain and vulnerability rise clearly in the eyes that had always been strong and resolute. There was something in his face, his eyes, his voice that reminded her of that first night, of the man who had worked so hard to save the wounded soldiers at Heritage. The memory made her reach instinctively for his hand, made her lace her small, white fingers carefully between his lean, tanned ones as she lay her head against him.

The gesture brought Drayton back to the present, and he looked down at her with a renewed longing for what might have been. She felt his gaze and lifted her eyes to meet it. He pressed a kiss to her hand, holding her eyes even as he lowered his mouth to meet her lips. His mouth lingered, his tongue gently played. When he met her eyes again, they were watchful, wary, perhaps even distrustful. But they were no longer sullen, no longer distant.

With deliberate slowness his mouth descended a second time, and the tenderness in his kiss became something stronger, something warmer and more intimate. Ambrosia's hand slipped unconsciously about his neck and pulled at the soft curling ends of his hair. His tongue probed inquiringly, then assertively into her mouth, lighting a tiny spark of warmth in some secret place within her, a spark that burned bright and hot as a part of her began to let go. A thousand feelings burst forth in a single splendid moment as he held her tightly and claimed total possession of her mouth, as she felt some unexplainable force eating away at a part of her, a part she had never surrendered to anyone, a part she wanted very much to protect. She tensed and struggled to regroup her defenses, but Drayton's hand was already moving to her breasts, gently touching, exploring, arousing, until the rose-tipped crests throbbed and hardened, aching for the feel of his mouth. With a cry of surrender, she grasped at his hair and drew him closer, wanting him to touch her, wanting to feel his body hard against hers. She was capitulating to a force she did not understand. And yet her spirit knew nothing of defeat at this moment; it felt strong and triumphant, even as she admitted to a need that was stronger than anything she had ever felt before. Hot tremors of longing flashed down her spine, and a fire seemed to be flickering everywhere inside her. Once, as a child, when she had nearly fallen from the top of a very high tree, she had known a similar dangerous elation as she swung uncertainly between the safety of her hold and serious injury. Now, as she opened herself to his most intimate touch, as she arched to allow him entry into the moist warmth of her body, something far in the back of her mind warned her that she was letting go to grasp for something every bit as dangerous. Yet she ached to relieve the tension that coiled tighter and tighter inside her, with each of his urgent thrusts. The pleasure was building, wave upon wave, until it exploded in a shower of heat and light. She let out a joyous cry of relief and elation as she clung to him, feeling his similar shuddering fulfillment within her and knowing fully now what it meant.

It was long moments later when the wild hammering of her heart stilled and her breath fell lightly, stirring the crisp hairs on his chest. There was a quiet peace born of their closeness now, born of the knowledge that each had reached the other in a simple, yet most powerful way. Yet, just before Ambrosia gave herself up to slumber, something deep in her heart warned her that nothing would ever be quite so simple and peaceful again.

Chapter 17

The morning dawned bright and clear, with rich yellow sunshine warming the chilled December air. Ambrosia squinted against the brightness which streamed through the nearby window, her eyelids blinking repeatedly as the lethargy of a deep sleep drifted stubbornly away. She frowned as she glanced anxiously about the strange room, then started as the man beside her stirred and tightened a long, muscular arm about her. He did not waken.

Ambrosia let out her breath and allowed her eyes to roam slowly over his broad shoulders; his thick, coal-black hair; the precise, angular features of his face. He seemed much younger now than she'd ever seen him look before, much less threatening than the gun-wielding Yankee soldier she feared and hated. His lashes were incongruously thick and dark as a child's against his tanned cheek, his mouth smooth, his sleep heavy and content. Once, a long time ago, he had actually been in love, she thought suddenly. And he had loved so deeply and so totally that he had lost everything when he lost her. They were alike in that respect. The thought made her feel a strange kind of affection for him, perhaps only because he had shared his hurt with her the night before, when she had needed to be comforted. Remembering had not been easy for him, of that she was certain.

Ambrosia laid her head back on the pillow and sighed as she stared at the ceiling, her fingers nervously clutching at the comforter. She remembered all that had happened, remembered the pleasure, the triumphant surge of her physical being as she surrendered herself entirely to his strength. She no longer felt any semblance of triumph. Suddenly she was filled with shame and guilt over everything she had felt and was still feeling. Everything that had happened had been wrong, terribly wrong. Whatever else Drayton Rambert might be, he was a Yankee first—how could she have forgotten that? Had she really been so afraid, so weak that she had needed reassurance from him? She, Ambrosia Lanford, who prided herself on her courage, had shown herself a coward last night. She bit her lip hard, remembering that the one thing Ledger had admired in her from the first had been courage. A sharp pang of regret tore through her with the admission that she had betrayed all that she was and all that she felt for Ledger, in return for an empty moment of reassurance from her enemy.

As if feeling her gaze upon him, Drayton slowly opened his eyes, only to see her look away. He regarded her steadily for a long moment, seeing the same, distant sadness in her eyes that he had seen the night before, recognizing it all too easily now. He raised himself up on one arm, his other still encircling her possessively. "Good morning."

His voice was soft and gentle, and Ambrosia felt a warmth flicker inside her at the mere sound of it, though she did not welcome the intrusion on her thoughts. She tossed him an impersonal glance and returned a terse good morning.

He smiled down at her. She colored and looked away. He raised a single annoyed brow, then scowled in frustration as he continued to look at her, as she continued to avoid his eyes. His patience waned. He bent suddenly to kiss her, smothering any and all protests with hard, bruising force that gentled only when she yielded to him. His hand moved instinctively to the softness of her breasts, his careful coaxing of them swiftly bringing the response he sought. Ambrosia's breath caught sharply as she threaded her fingers shakily through the short thickness of his hair, her mouth moving slowly, yet hungrily beneath his. And at that instant, every thought in her head fled but one. The muted sounds of footsteps on the stairs and in the hall did not begin to disturb her newly aroused passion. The sudden opening of the door was quite another matter. She bolted to a sitting position, clutching a blanket to her breasts.

"Seven-thirty, sir. Have to hurry if you don't want to be late for—"

Private Reynold's thin, freckled face went white as a sheet as his eyes met Drayton's furious scowl. Though his first impulse was to bolt and run, the private's gaze slid curiously toward the lovely bare shoulders beside his superior officer. For an eternal moment he stood there frozen, holding tight to a breakfast tray, staring at the perfect curved outline of her body through the thin blanket which covered her. His eyes traveled slowly upward, until they locked with a pair of familiar green-gray eyes. He promptly dropped the tray. It was the girl from the emporium! The pretty, uppity one he and about a hundred other soldiers had tried so hard to be friendly with. She was in bed with Major Rambert!

The loud clattering of scattering cutlery and breaking glass seemed to jar the private from his daydream. His long legs and arms scrambled in every direction at once as he dove after the tray.

"Private Reynolds!"

The low, articulate command made Reynolds snap to his feet in perfect attention. His face was red as a beet, neck to brow, and his gaze could find no safe place to fall. "Yes, sir!"

Drayton's eyes narrowed as he let out a breath through clenched teeth in a valiant attempt to control his temper.

The attempt failed. "Get OUT!" His growl reverberated through the room

"Yes, sir! Right away, sir!" Reynolds gave a crisp, almost comical salute, then backed up a step at a time, mumbling phrases of explanation and apology as he moved to the door. He whirled on a heel, then turned just long enough to toss over his shoulder, "And don't forget your meeting, sir."

There was a loud clank as he opened the door and smashed it squarely into a saucer and various pieces of silverware. The private stared at it for a moment, then scampered from the room without a backward glance.

Drayton's blue eyes continued to flash murderous sparks for several moments after Private Reynolds had gone. "Damn!" he muttered. "Of all the stupid, clumsy, inconsiderate, bumbling—"

His eyes caught sight of Ambrosia's face and his anger fled. Her skin was pale, her cheeks flushed unnaturally, her eyes once again distant and brooding as they stared at the door. For a moment he considered skipping the meeting with General Saxton, claiming illness or—but he knew that he could not do that. His meeting was urgent and could not be postponed. Rumor had it that these were the general's last few weeks in office, that his successor to the post of assistant commissioner of the Freedman's Bureau had already been named and would be installed within the month. And General Sickles, who was in the process of assuming the role of military commander of the district, had insisted that his officers show total cooperation with the bureau. Besides, Private Reynolds was not exactly the soul of discretion. The real reason for Drayton's absence would be all over Charleston if he missed that meeting, and he didn't want Ambrosia to face that kind of scandal. He took gentle hold of her shoulders and guided her head to his chest with a sigh, deeply troubled by the depth of her aloofness. He had so little time now to break through it. He lifted her chin until her eyes met his. "I have a meeting I must attend this morning. It won't take long.'' He touched his lips lightly to hers. ''I intend to make sure it doesn't take long.'' He ran a finger wistfully down her cheek and searched her face for a long moment. Nothing. No defiance, no anger, not a single spark of anything. She might have been a million miles away. ''Ambrosia?''

A dim flicker of some emotion finally touched her eyes.

''I want you to stay with me,'' he told her softly, taking hold of her hand. ''You know that, don't you?''

She averted her eyes and Drayton felt a cold knot of dread tightening in the pit of his stomach. She meant to leave him. To go on as if last night had never even happened. But he could never do that now. He could never let her leave like this, while her heart still ached with the pain of a love that couldn't be. She didn't know it, but she needed him every bit as much as he needed her. He had to fight to keep his frustration from igniting his temper. Anger had never been effective in dealing with her. But perhaps, if he spoke to her as he had the night before, she would listen at least.

''You can't run away from your heart, Ambrosia,'' he began earnestly, ''no matter how hard you run. The hurt will always be there. You need to wait it out, to give it time to heal, to give yourself a chance to begin again. . . .''

Her face was blank. He touched his lips to her hand and sought her eyes. ''Stay with me,'' he pleaded softly. ''Please. Just for a little while.'' He was afraid to ask for more, afraid to put aside any more of his pride to plead with her. If she cared at all for him it might have been different. But Ambrosia's coming here in the first place had nothing to do with what he felt for her. She had come out of sheer desperation. And he would have to hope that she stayed for the same reason.

He sighed as he released her and left the bed to wander about the room, quickly gathering up the clothing he intended to wear, hastily donning long, woolen undergarments and his blue uniform trousers before he went to the washstand and began to shave. Ambrosia watched him covertly, shivering as she huddled beneath the blanket in a futile attempt to retain the warmth of his body, berating herself for the yearnings that rose within her at the sight of him, at the graceful ripple of his muscles beneath his roughened bronze skin. She had never really noticed how devastatingly handsome he was before, how deep and blue were his eyes, how firm and square his jaw, how generous the chiseled curve to his mouth. There was something beyond the handsome line of his features now that was even more attractive to her, some unexplainable aura of manliness, of certainty, of command. It was something she felt more than saw, and it made her very aware of the knowledge he had of her body, of the ease with which he could arouse her. The simple meeting of their eyes had become a forceful, unwelcome reminder that she was a woman. A soiled woman now, she reminded herself with a surge of self-loathing. A Yankee officer's plaything that he wanted to keep "just for a little while." He knew her weakness much too well to want anything more than a few moments of pleasure with her. Indeed, what else did she have to offer him or any man? She was no different than the painted women who came to buy perfume at Maggie's emporium.

She watched him pull on his white blouse and over that, his dark blue, brass-buttoned uniform, becoming the soldier she knew so well. She wondered vaguely if he would want to buy her horrible new clothing that would proclaim what she was to the world. Or if he would flaunt her before his friends as some of the Yankees did their mistresses, the way gentlemen flaunt their finest horses or expensive jewelry. She did not intend to stay with him long enough to find out. Everything inside her screamed she would sooner die than let anyone humiliate her like that. No one must ever know what she had done. She would go somewhere where no one knew her, where she could take up her life again without anyone guessing at the truth. She could not think about where that might be, or about what she might do to support herself. She had found a job in Charleston; she would do so elsewhere. But she would never, ever allow herself to succumb to weakness again.

When he finished dressing he stood looking down at her, his hand running pensively over the brim of his Hardee hat as he tried to read her expression. "You must be hungry. I'll have Private Reynolds bring a breakfast tray up for you. He can leave it outside the door if you like."

"Thank you." She did not look up.

He stared away, his fingers circling the brim of his hat nervously. "I—I will leave some money on the bureau, in case you need anything. Anything at all—"

The sudden iciness in her eyes made his voice break off. She wanted nothing to do with his money. He ought to have remembered that.

He stretched a hand toward her cheek and ran his fingers regretfully over her smooth skin. "Ambrosia, I—" He stopped. Her cold, distant expression made him wary of saying anything more. He straightened and turned to leave, stepping over the ruined breakfast tray as he made his way to the door. He paused, his hand on the latch. "I won't be very long. We'll have plenty of time to talk when I get back."

"Yes." Her voice was hollow, without conviction. And he knew. She meant to leave the moment he was gone. Drayton let himself out and closed the door soundly behind. He heaved a long, weary sigh and leaned his back against the door for a long moment, thinking. He could not allow her to leave, not like this. He had to have time.

With a sudden thought, he hurried down the stairs to find Private Reynolds. He would have the private prepare the breakfast tray right away, and leave it at the door without disturbing her. But he would also put the private on guard. Under no circumstances was he to let the lady leave the house without an escort. And if she proved unmanageable and did live the house alone, the private was to follow her. He was not to say a word to anyone about who she was or what she was doing here, and he was not to let her out of his sight.

Within moments of his departure, Ambrosia left the warmth of the bed and padded across the cold wooden floor to the chair where she had left her clothes. She was relieved to find them dry. She retrieved her chemise from the floor, squelching an odd feeling of light-headedness as she straightened to tug it over her head. She swayed. She caught herself on the bedpost and waited for the dizziness to subside before she hurriedly continued dressing. She was certain that the leaden discomfort in her limbs would go away in time. It was merely that she had not eaten since early yesterday morning, that she needed something to fill her stomach. But she could not eat here. She would not take anything from Drayton in return for what had happened last night. Not even a bite of his ruined breakfast. Her eyes flicked bitterly over the money he had left on the bureau, too obviously payment for services rendered. She would have none of it. She finished dressing and wound her hair in a hasty knot, which she quickly covered with her limp, water-stained bonnet. The cloak she flung about her shoulders provided her a welcome warmth, and she was at once grateful for it. For some reason she could not shake off the chill that seemed to have penetrated her bones with the rain the night before. She sidestepped the remains of the breakfast tray, a strong wave of nausea sweeping over her at the sight. She held her breath and looked away, struggling to keep from retching. She closed her eyes tightly and waited for the feeling to ease. The moment it did, she scooped up her small, still damp bundle of clothing which Drayton had dropped just inside the door. She pressed her ear to the door and listened for several moments. Nothing. Opening it a crack, she slipped silently from the room.

Ambrosia made her way stealthily toward the stairs,

listening intently to several masculine voices that rose from the first floor. She tried not to think about what she would do if she ran into one or more of the soldiers. She stepped down one, two, three steps, then hesitated and peeked slowly over the curved banister. With a fist to her mouth to stifle a gasp, she whirled and hurried back up the stairs. Her eyes darted about for a place to hide. Panting hard, her heart pounding against her ribs, she flattened her back against the wall just inside the hallway. For the next few moments, she felt certain she would faint. She held her breath as Private Reynolds strode swiftly past her, bearing a tray nearly identical to the one which had spilled on the floor. Without waiting an instant longer, Ambrosia bolted from her hiding place and all but flew down the stairs, pausing only a half-second before she reached the landing to be certain no one was there to stop her. With a trembling hand, she eased open the front door and closed it slowly behind her, proceeding carefully until she had cleared the grounds, though her instincts screamed in protest at the precious waste of time. And then she was free. No one was even aware that she had gone.

Anxiety slowly loosened its grip as she hurried along the busy street, mingling with other nameless, faceless people. She wondered vaguely why her muscles were aching even worse now, why each and every movement seemed a test of will. She was only a few blocks from the house when she paused for a moment, tired and breathless. She leaned heavily against the side of a building she didn't recognize and tried to think of where she was. She was not very well acquainted with the northern section of Charleston, since most loyal Southerners now lived south of Broad. She stared at the sun and tried to determine which way to go to reach the Cooper River. A cold blast of air whipped suddenly about her as she made up her mind and turned east. She shivered, feeling her body break into an icy sweat. A lethargic heaviness seemed to settle in her limbs. She stopped and put a hand to her brow to ease the dull throb that had begun there. It seemed to grow worse with every step. She drew a deep breath and squared her shoulders. She had to go on, just a little further, just to—

Her vision blurred. She nearly fell as she groped for a wooden post and struggled to steady herself. But the fuzzy images of people and buildings that seemed to float in an eerie kind of circle refused to be righted. Ambrosia clenched her teeth and straightened her spine, aware of the people who brushed impatiently past her, knowing that she could not stop here. She did not even know where she was.

She forced her feet to take a few more steps. The sun had gotten so terribly bright that it hurt her eyes. She lifted an arm to shade her face from the painful light, feeling the heat of it in her head even as she shook with the cold. The perspiration beaded on her brow and upper lip, and sweat dripped down her back and between her breasts. Then abruptly, just as she stepped into the street, she felt her fingers loosen, felt her bundle fall from her hand. The light and the cold and all the blurred images were suddenly gone.

It was just after eight o'clock in the morning, but the streets were already crowded with people as the three prim and proper ladies, all struggling with their baggage, paused for the third time to check the address scrawled on a small piece of paper.

"The captain said to go *three* blocks before we turn to the right," the shortest, plumpest of the group insisted with a decisive nod of her head.

"We have gone three blocks," retorted the tallest, a pale, homely brunette who seemed at least ten years younger than the other two.

"Mary. Rebecca. Please." The soft reminder from the third woman brought immediate silence from the other two. "We have indeed gone three blocks," she confirmed patiently. "This is where we are to turn."

Pretending not to notice the scowl on Mary's face or the smug grin on Rebecca's, the woman stepped into the busy street, leaving the others to follow her lead.

"Told you so," Rebecca tossed over her shoulder as she sidestepped a puddle and followed in Susannah's footsteps.

Mary's little round face reddened with indignation as she gave a derisive snort. She was a good Christian woman, but Rebecca Gaines had a way of driving her to a righteous anger at least a dozen times a day. Mary's bright blue eyes shot daggers at Rebecca's tall, shapeless back for a moment, then lowered in heartfelt contrition. She scrambled to catch up with the two women, stepping directly into a large puddle as she did so. Each and every morning, Mary prayed for the strength to control her quick temper, particularly with regard to handling Rebecca. Rebecca was young, after all, she would remind herself, and no stranger to grief. She had lost her only child to cholera, and been widowed by the war after only three years of marriage. Her sorrow was still fresh and her bitterness too. Yet she had volunteered to come here, to Charleston, to teach the poor Negroes to read and write, and to save their immortal souls. Mary tried to keep that in mind whenever she found herself thinking uncharitable thoughts about Rebecca. She raised her eyes curiously to stare at a gaudy, wrought-iron gate, and the tall, brick wall which surrounded a lovely house. Many of the houses here were sideways, set at right angles to the street, rather than facing it. How very odd! Mary was thinking. And the colors—

"O-O-O-F!" Mary's breath was knocked abruptly from her lungs when she ran headlong into Rebecca's back.

"Why don't you watch where you're walking? Can't you see Susannah's stopped?"

Mary doubled over in surprise and pain at the impact. "I—I'm sorry. Wh-What's happened?"

"Someone appears to be ill," Rebecca told her matter-of-factly. "Apparently whoever it is, is lying in the street."

Mary gasped and began elbowing her way through the circle of curious people who had crowded around the collapsed woman. Susannah was already kneeling beside her, slapping her wrists and trying to rouse her. Mary began to order the people to back off, to give the poor woman some much-needed air. Susannah glanced up at her in concern. "She's burning up with fever."

The announcement quickly filtered through the crowd and caused it to thin almost immediately. Susannah and Mary seemed not to notice. "Does anyone know this woman?"

There was no response, save a few shrugs and the shakes of several heads. "We'll need help getting her to the house," Susannah said thoughtfully as she brushed a strand of wet hair from the woman's brow. She raised her eyes to the crowd and considered several faces which still hovered close about, seeking a man who might be willing to help. She addressed a kindly, older gentleman in a threadbare black suit whose arms looked able to bear a heavy load.

"Sir, this woman is in need of immediate care. Our destination is but a few blocks away. Could you possibly help us?"

Before she could finish, the gentleman was nodding and reading the address from the paper Mary handed to him.

"I know the place," he said. Without another word, he lifted the unconscious woman into his arms and proceeded toward the house with Susannah, Mary, and Rebecca close behind.

Chapter 18

The room was freshly whitewashed and the air smelled of strong lye soap, though the tang of recently burned hickory wood in the fireplace masked the odor somewhat. Ambrosia's eyelids fluttered heavily, once, twice, a third time as she struggled from a deep, cloying darkness toward the light. Finally, after a valiant effort, the light triumphed. Ambrosia squinted against the brightness as her eyes drifted about the room, lingering on a winter blue sky that sparkled cloudless through the polished glass windowpanes.

"Good morning."

Ambrosia started and turned her head to stare at a slender, attractive woman who sat in a nearby chair, her long, nimble fingers swiftly working a small crochet hook and thin gray yarn. "You're looking much better this morning. Are you hungry?" she asked pleasantly.

Ambrosia studied the woman's face for a long time, trying hard to remember who she was and how she had gotten here. But there was nothing at all familiar in the woman's face or her voice, or in this room. Nothing at all. "Where am I?" The words were low and scarcely audible as Ambrosia forced them through a sore, parched throat.

"You are with friends." The woman smiled. "You

are quite safe here." She put her needlework aside and rose. "You ought to eat something as soon as you feel up to it. It's been over a week since you've had anything but broth and—"

"A week?" Her eyes were dazed and disbelieving.

Susannah nodded. "Nine days to be exact. You have been very ill. But your fever is broken now. I'm sure you will recover."

Ambrosia's eyes slid to the window. Nine days. And she remembered nothing. Nothing after feeling that terrible pain in her head and falling in the street. She had been running, hurrying away from something. . . . She lifted her head to knead her brow, which throbbed mercilessly as the memories came flooding back. Ledger . . . Melissa . . . Drayton . . . Her cheeks paled and Susannah frowned with obvious concern. "Do you feel up to eating?"

Ambrosia's eyes flew to her face in near-panic as the question interrupted her thoughts. She was breathing hard, her blood pounding in her head. "What?"

"I asked if you'd like something to eat."

Ambrosia swallowed hard in an attempt to hide her confusion. She gave a small nod as her eyes grew distant and glazed as before.

"Good. I'll be right back."

Only a few moments later Susannah returned, bearing a tray. She was followed by an odd pair of women—one young, slender, and homely with a bitter, snippy kind of look to her; and the other short and plump, with shining cheeks and a jovial smile. Both stared at her with some amazement as she struggled to raise herself to a sitting position. Before she could do so, Susannah had deposited the tray in the older of the two women's arms and bent to arrange the pillows to support Ambrosia's back.

"Here we are," Susannah said as she placed the tray gingerly on Ambrosia's lap and took a seat on the bed beside her. Ambrosia stared down at the thick broth and generous slice of dark bread, feeling absolutely no appetite.

"I know you are probably not hungry," the woman told her. "But if you don't eat, you'll never get out of that bed. I can help if . . ." Susannah reached for the spoon, but Ambrosia brushed her hand away and took hold of it.

"Thank you," she managed, though she was repelled by the very thought of being cared for by anyone, especially a Yankee woman. Nine days! she thought again as she slowly, carefully raised a small bit of the broth to her lips. Her hand shook noticeably as she fed herself, but she gripped the spoon all the more tightly, until her fingers were white and cramped, and somehow managed to empty the bowl. Susannah moved from the bed to a nearby chair, sending the other women scurrying from the room with a single glance before she opened her prayer book and settled comfortably against the chair's back. A slight smile of satisfaction played about her mouth as she silently observed Ambrosia's brave efforts to finish her meal. Mary was right about this one. She would recover quickly.

Ambrosia let out an audible sigh of relief and let her head fall wearily back on the pillow. She had done it, finished the entire bowl. And she was utterly exhausted from the effort.

Susannah removed the tray immediately and rearranged the pillows so that Ambrosia could rest more easily. "You—You're from the North?" Her eyes were wary, with only a hint of begrudging gratitude.

Susannah nodded. "From Vermont. We—Mrs. Gaines and Mrs. Caldwell and myself, I'm Susannah Burton—we were sent here by the First Christian Church of Vermont to open a school for colored children."

It was all Ambrosia could do to restrain a scowl of disapproval. Charleston was full of Yankee do-gooders these days, anxious to save the souls of the newly freed slaves and make good little Yankees out of all of them.

They had destroyed everything else, Ambrosia thought bitterly, and now they wanted to redeem themselves by preaching the gospel.

"And what is your name?" came the clear, serene voice.

Ambrosia was torn between embarrassment at not having offered the information and reluctance to give it even now. "Ambrosia Lanford," she mumbled finally.

"Ambrosia. What a lovely name!" Susannah smiled warmly, even as Ambrosia looked away. "Your family is undoubtedly worried to death about you, Ambrosia. We would have contacted them, of course, but we had no way of—"

"I have no family." She looked very much like a child now, staring down at her fingers.

Susannah hesitated for a long moment, watching Ambrosia clasp and unclasp her hands. "Friends, then?"

She shook her head without looking up.

"There must be someone," Susannah insisted, remembering the names Ambrosia had called out in her feverish delirium. "You weren't here in Charleston all alone, were you?"

Ambrosia swallowed hard and felt the color rushing to her cheeks. She was not up to lying, to formulating a feasible story for this woman. Neither was she so ill and befuddled that she would divulge any part of her personal life to a total stranger. A Yankee stranger at that.

"I—I was leaving Charleston," she admitted slowly. "I was going to book passage on a ship—" She looked up anxiously. "Did you find my things?"

Susannah's brow creased in bewilderment. "Your things?"

"Yes. Some clothing and—and—They were tied together in a bundle. I was carrying it when I—"

Susannah slowly shook her head. "I'm sorry, but we found nothing. You must have dropped the rest of your things somewhere. I'm so sorry, Ambrosia. I wish I had known."

Ambrosia closed her eyes against tears of frustration and total despair. Now she hadn't a cent to her name, and after nine days, certainly no job to return to, no way to leave Charleston.

Susannah's hand lightly touched her arm. "Don't worry about the future just yet," she comforted. "Sometimes, the good Lord sees to it that we lose everything, just so we're forced to start fresh on the path He's chosen for us."

Ambrosia could not meet her kindly gaze. The good Lord had certainly seen to it she lost everything, she thought ruefully. But she doubted very seriously if He had made special plans for her life. She was a soiled woman now and hardly worth the Lord's special attention. She wondered briefly if the righteous Mrs. Susannah Burton would have bothered to nurse her back to health had she known the truth. And she wondered too what difference it would have made to anyone if she had been left to die.

"Ambrosia . . . ?"

With effort she lifted her eyes, eyes dark and gray and deeply troubled.

"Never mind," Susannah said, patting her hand. "We can talk later. You rest now."

Chapter 19

The day was warm and clear, and the gentle breezes hinted at spring, though it was yet mid-January. Drayton hesitated as he reached the wrought-iron gate, asking himself for the hundredth time why he was here, asking himself exactly what he planned to do if he found her, what he planned to say. He had no answers. It had been over a month now since she'd left, forty days of hoping and wondering and knowing that she would not be coming back.

At first he had been violently angry, more so because she had taken no money, had not even eaten a decent meal before she left. He understood well enough the message in her refusal to accept anything from him.

He had gone after her in a fury, checking every possible vessel she might have boarded, questioning everyone within a four-block radius of the river. His efforts had yielded him nothing. He returned to his room late that night and promptly drank himself senseless. He had done the same too many nights since. He was ready now to leave her memory behind him, to try to forget. But he could not do that without being absolutely certain she was completely out of his reach. He had to know for sure that she was gone forever.

Drayton lifted the brass latch on the gate, and it swung

open with a reluctant creak. He cocked his head and
stepped inside the garden, following a short path toward
three steps and a shaded piazza, where the sun's brightest
rays were filtered through trees and vines even in the
midst of a mild winter. Drayton stopped short just before
he reached the steps. His eyes paused on the figure of a
man who sat in a chair near the door of the house, on a
pair of crutches propped in the corner near the chair. The
man had been positioned to catch the sun's warmth, his
back toward Drayton, his face toward the shaft of light
that penetrated the piazza where a giant magnolia tree
had been splintered by a stray shell. He sat quietly,
unmoving, a worn leather-bound volume open in his lap,
his finger tracing idly over a single folded piece of paper
which might have marked the page. His head rested full
against the high back of the chair. After a short silence,
he lifted his head and turned to face Drayton. "Oh, I'm
sorry. I thought it was Sheba."

Drayton struggled against a gasp of revulsion as
Ledger turned to face him, as the sun fell fully on the horrible, twisted mass of scars that was his face. He was a
much younger man than Drayton had expected, but the
hardened pink and reddish skin that pulled and contorted
his eyes and nose and mouth spoke of war, and a lifetime
of hell. "I hope you'll pardon my intrusion, sir," he said
quickly, doffing his hat and stepping closer. "My name
is Major Rambert, and I am trying to determine the
whereabouts of Miss Lanford—Ambrosia Lanford. I was
told she resides here."

Ledger's hands stopped their aimless movement and
his face lost all trace of healthy color. Major Rambert—
Ambrosia had spoken that name the night she left. *You
know there was nothing between Major Rambert and
me. . . .* The words played over and over in his head.
Ambrosia. He glanced down at the folded paper in his
lap, a letter which had arrived just a few days before. He
did not need to open it; he knew it by heart. "Dear Mr.
Bowman," it began. "We are very much impressed with

the beautiful verse you sent to us and are most interested in negotiating a purchase of this and future work. . . ." The letter marked a new beginning, a chance at a new life. Ambrosia's leaving had marked an ending. She had given him everything, and he had given her only hurt in return. He closed the book slowly on the letter, his voice low. "She did live here . . . but she left. Over a month ago." A moment later he frowned and looked up at the major, so tall and handsome and whole. He almost wished that she had gone to him. He looked so able to protect her. Ledger didn't like to think of her being alone and unprotected. "Why did you want to see her, Major? She's not in any kind of trouble, is she?"

"No, no." Drayton's eyes fixed on the flagstone path that wound its way through the garden as he mouthed his prepared excuse. "Her employer, Mrs. O'Neal, expressed her concern to the authorities about Miss Lanford. Apparently she left her work without giving any kind of notice." He hesitated, shooting a sidelong glance at Ledger's face. "Would you happen to know where she might have gone?"

Ledger's hands began to caress the volume he held, running over the tattered binding. His eyes stared straight ahead and his voice came hollow and empty. "No."

"Perhaps her sister has had some contact with her in the past weeks," Drayton pressed.

"Melissa left Charleston shortly after Ambrosia did," Ledger told him quietly.

"Do you think they might have gone somewhere together?"

Ledger gave a small, unhappy smile. "No. I'm sure they didn't."

Drayton forced the disappointment from his voice and turned his hat in his hands. "I see. Well, then. I won't be troubling you any further, sir. I thank you for your time." He turned to leave.

"Major?"

He turned back, inquiringly. "Yes?"

"If—if you happen to find Ambrosia," he said haltingly, "that is, if you find out what happened to her . . . where she's gone, or . . ." Ledger swallowed hard and blinked against the sting of tears. "I—I would very much appreciate knowing she's all right."

Drayton gave a brief nod, taken by surprise by the man's obvious concern. "Of course."

"You won't forget?"

"No. I won't forget."

"Much obliged, Major Rambert," he said quietly, shifting the book to one leg and extending his right hand. "Sorry I can't get up without those damned crutches."

"No apologies necessary, sir," Drayton returned, grasping the hand firmly.

Ledger's eyes smiled then, a smile that almost made him seem a boy. "The name's Bowman. Ledger Bowman." Just as quickly the brightness vanished from his expression and the light in his eyes died. "I'll be waiting to hear from you, Major."

Chapter 20

Ambrosia's strength returned much more slowly than she anticipated. Even a full month after her fever had gone, she was unhappy to find that she tired after the slightest exertion, that she required much more sleep than she had ever needed before. It seemed a struggle to simply get up each morning, and even more of one to remain on her feet the entire day. Often the effort made her feel nauseated or set her head to throbbing until she feared she might faint. Yet she could not bring herself to accept any more charity from Susannah and the other women to whom she was already so heavily indebted. Especially since there was enough work to take up every waking hour of their time and hers too.

The house in which Ambrosia convalesced was in dire need of repair, as she discovered the moment she was up and about. Susannah had seen to it that she was given one of the two habitable rooms, which had been hurriedly scrubbed and whitewashed the very day she arrived. But the remainder of the rooms were sorry cubicles of falling plaster, deep cracks, or victims of a gaping hole in the roof. At Susannah's urgent request, the church had sent money enough to mend the roof and any structural damage, but the remainder of the cleaning and painting and general repair was left up to the women themselves.

Though she was hardly committed to the righteousness of the task the women were undertaking, Ambrosia could not bear to watch them labor while she sat idle, particularly since she needed so to regain her strength if she ever expected to leave here. She could not even consider remaining in Charleston after what had happened. Somehow she intended to get money enough to go elsewhere, to get far away from her past. She could not admit to herself that she might still be too weak from her illness. Ignoring Susannah's repeated objections, she began to work beside the three ladies, saying very little but always taking a full share of the work load and driving herself daily to the brink of total exhaustion.

Susannah watched with growing concern as Ambrosia's skin lost its newly achieved healthy color, as her cheeks grew thin, her features sharp, as the telltale smudges of purple-gray circled her eyes. The girl was working herself into a grave, and there seemed very little Susannah could do to stop her. Gentle reminders to eat well and rest more often had no effect on her behavior, and even firm instructions were met with excuses. She would never admit to being tired; she was never hungry; she never felt ill. And perhaps worst of all, no matter how open and honest the others were with each other, she never wanted to talk.

Conversation with Ambrosia was a constant struggle. Her responses were short, unemotional, unrevealing. Susannah wrung her hands in frustration and did the only things she could do to help this woman who seemed unwilling to help herself. Each morning, before they began the day's work, Susannah began assigning specific tasks to each woman, making certain that Ambrosia was kept busy, but seeing to it that her work load was light. Mary eagerly agreed to this plan, but Rebecca objected. As far as she was concerned, Ambrosia and the rest of them deserved to suffer for the war they had caused, a war that had cost Rebecca her husband. And if Ambrosia chose to live off their charity, then the least she could do was her share of the work. It made Rebecca angry that Susannah insisted on taking Ambrosia along whenever she went out to purchase supplies—she felt herself every bit as deserving of the fresh air and sunshine and was envious of Susannah's doting concern for Ambrosia. She made her feelings known with her ambiguous comments and cutting remarks.

On the occasion of her first outing, Ambrosia tried to disguise the fear she felt at the prospect of being recognized. She was relieved that they remained in the northern section of Charleston, which was crowded with Yankees and soldiers. There was not much chance of running into someone who had known Madeline Bowman or her sister, or even worse, her father. She was relieved, too, that she had never been friendly with any of the Yankees she had met at Maggie's. If she did see anyone who recognized her, she would simply turn away and there would be little chance of their forcing a conversation. She was only truly afraid of seeing Drayton again, for she knew that he would confront her, and she did not think she could bear to face him. So she lowered her head and kept her face concealed beneath her bonnet, and prayed that she would not chance upon him.

Susannah was very aware of Ambrosia's initial reluctance to leave the house and at first thought it might have something to do with Rebecca's obvious jealousy. But Susannah quickly noticed the way Ambrosia anxiously scanned the faces of people everywhere they went. Now and again, someone stared at her as well, their eyes narrowing as if in recognition. But no one ever stopped her, or spoke to her, and Ambrosia never said a word. Susannah wisely held her tongue and pretended to look the other way. There was little doubt in her mind that the girl had known people here, that she was terrified of meeting someone. It was only after several weeks of uneventful outings that Ambrosia's timidity began to fade somewhat, that she seemed almost comfortable walking beside Susannah, a wicker basket slung over her arm. Yet

Susannah noticed that her head was generally kept bowed so that the brim of her bonnet all but concealed her face.

It was a lovely spring morning in late February when it finally happened. Susannah was haggling with a woman over the price of a fresh-caught fish when she happened to flash a sidelong glance at Ambrosia. With a quick double take, Susannah stopped her bargaining midsentence and turned her head to follow Ambrosia's wide-eyed, panicked stare. For a long moment Susannah studied the man whose mere proximity caused the woman beside her to tremble with apprehension. He was tall, broad at chest and shoulder, with obviously well-muscled limbs that swelled beneath a resplendent blue uniform decked with gold and brass. There was something incredibly masculine about his dark, striking features, about the hard, bronzed ruthlessness etched in the aristocratic nose, brow, and chin. There was a confidence in the way he moved, the way he spoke to the woman at his side, his every gesture smooth, sure, and calculated. Susannah took an instant dislike to him, and to the pretty woman whose arm was linked possessively in his, whose breasts brushed him brazenly at every opportunity. Susannah did not like the cold, knowing gleam in his dark blue eyes, or the practiced, flirtatious way the girl flounced beside him. He seemed the type of man who would use a woman, then discard her without a second thought. A dangerous, heartless man. And as her eyes slid again to Ambrosia, who cowered close beside her, she felt a surge of pity. A Union officer. A few pieces of the mystery were beginning to fall into place.

Without a word, Susannah paid the full price the woman was asking for the fish, took hold of Ambrosia's arm, and hurriedly left the market.

A week passed swiftly by. Then another, and another. The Vermont First Christian School for Freedmen was finally ready to open. Large crates packed with books and supplies from the North arrived, and after three days of registration, advertised on placards and with handbills the ladies themselves had distributed, the school enrolled fifty children and seven adult students, all willing and eager to learn.

Susannah, Mary, and Rebecca were soon devoting long hours each day to educating their new charges. More and more, Ambrosia was left to do the necessary cleaning and cooking, tasks which she gladly assumed. She seldom did such work, however, without thinking of Sheba and wondering what had become of the black woman who had remained so loyally by her side only to be abandoned. She pushed the guilt firmly from her mind, reminding herself of the future, knowing that if she once allowed herself to look back with regret she would never have the courage to go on. She was adamant about finding some outside employment in addition to her work for the Christian ladies, and eventually enlisted Susannah's reluctant help in finding a job at a nearby boarding house.

It was with some shock that Susannah faced a snide comment from Rebecca one morning, just after Ambrosia mumbled a hurried apology and ran from the breakfast table. "I said," Rebecca repeated pointedly, responding to Susannah's inquiry with a sarcastic smile, "if I weren't so aware of that woman's impeccable Southern upbringing, I'd wonder if she hadn't gotten herself into a delicate situation."

Susannah's cheeks actually paled as she forced herself to face the possibility that Rebecca was right. She considered several things she had conveniently ignored until now. Ambrosia's constant nausea, her continued fatigue, and her lack of a monthly flow could no longer be attributed to the fever she had suffered in December. And she recalled that Ambrosia had spoken recently of leaving Charleston, had hinted once that she might even accept a small loan from Susannah to allow her to do so. Susannah had pointedly ignored the hint in the hopes that Ambrosia would reconsider and remain a while longer, at least long enough to stop running from whatever it was she feared, long enough to reconcile whatever it was she felt for the Union officer she had seen in the market that day. Susannah was certain that she had nowhere else to go, no one else to turn to. And whether she would admit to it or not, she needed someone to care for her. But now—a child! Dear God, a child!

"I will not tolerate such talk, Rebecca," Susannah said in her normal smooth tone, her blue eyes flashing an authority which neither Mary nor Rebecca ever thought to question.

Some time later the breakfast ended in silence. But it did not escape anyone's notice that Susannah's mind was far from the business of eating, or that for the first time in anyone's memory, she nearly forgot to lead grace after the meal.

"Is there any possibility you could be with child?" Susannah's voice sounded calm and serene as always in the empty room. No one would have guessed that she was quivering with uncertainty inside.

There it was. Out in the open. The question Ambrosia had feared for weeks now had finally been asked. She was almost relieved. At least Susannah had chosen to take her aside. At least the confrontation was a private one that allowed her to salvage some semblance of her pride. She met Susannah's gaze for a long moment before she lowered her eyes and gave a reluctant nod. She offered no excuse, no explanation.

"The father?" Susannah asked quietly.

There was no answer. Susannah had not really expected one. Still, she knew instinctively who the father was and would have wagered her last dime on the accuracy of her instincts.

"A man can be legally coerced into assuming his responsibilities in many such cases," Susannah began.

"No." Ambrosia's voice was firm and final.

"Ambrosia." She waited until the intransigent green eyes lifted to meet hers. "Did he threaten you?" she asked gently. "Or force you in any way to—to submit to him?"

An odd look came into her eyes, distant and sad. "No," she said softly.

Susannah heaved a helpless sigh. "Perhaps if you spoke with him then, told him about the child—"

Ambrosia's chin lifted and she stubbornly shook her head. "I'm leaving Charleston, Susannah," she stated quietly. "I'm leaving as soon as I have enough money to—"

"But where will you go?" Susannah burst out in exasperation. "What will you do? You will be all alone if you leave here, and with a child to care for! Who will help you when the baby comes?"

Ambrosia bit her lip. "Please don't worry," she pleaded. "I'm accustomed to managing on my own." She placed a small hand on Susannah's arm, the first gesture of affection she had ever shown the older woman. "You've already done enough."

She turned away then, pretending not to notice the tears that had filled Susannah's eyes, and quietly left the room.

Chapter 21

For the following two days Susannah fasted and prayed, asking God for guidance in dealing with a situation she had never faced before. She had lead a sheltered life until the war called upon her to respond to the needs of countless wounded soldiers, and the untimely death of her husband called forth in her a courage she had never dreamed she possessed. But she had not been so sheltered as to be ignorant of Ambrosia's plight. She had heard too many stories about women on their own, women who bore children without fathers. They were ostracized. Taunted. Hated for their mistakes. And oftentimes, forced to prostitution to support themselves.

Ambrosia was making a terrible mistake. A child needed a father. Even a bad father was better than none. At least the child would have a name. Yet Susannah did not know if she had the right to interfere. There was always the possibility that the man was already married. Her heart nearly stopped beating at the thought. If he were married, then there was little hope for the child Ambrosia carried. And Susannah's interference could only cause problems unless . . . Her eyes hardened. He could at least contribute in some way to the support of the child, she thought. If only she were certain the Lord wanted her to act in this matter. She opened her Bible, trying to re-

lieve the bitterness and hostility she felt for the man who
had caused such pain. "Bear ye one another's burdens,"
she read. Her eyes lifted and she pondered for a long moment. And then she was certain what needed to be done.

The following day, Susannah dismissed her class after
a short review of the previous day's lesson and left school
to visit Mr. Whittemore, a longtime acquaintance who
had served as Mr. Burton's chaplain early on in the war.
Mr. Whittemore had since been named assistant superin-
tendent of education by the head of the Freedman's Bureau and was in a position, Susannah hoped, to help her
locate the man she would describe to him.

Less than an hour later, she was hurrying off, armed
with the information she had sought. Major Drayton
Rambert. She had recognized the name at once when he
mentioned it. Drayton. Ambrosia had repeated that name
over and over in her feverish delirium. That, and another
name Susannah could no longer recall. She stopped to
catch her breath before the entrance of a large house, one
of several along South Battery which had been converted
into temporary offices for high-ranking Union soldiers.
She lifted her chin and mounted the steps, pausing before
a short, rotund corporal whose merry face seemed out of
place behind the cluttered desk. His full, ruddy cheeks
lifted above the confusion of the mountains of paperwork, and Susannah met a pair of lively brown eyes.
"Yes, ma'am?"

"My name is Mrs. Burton, Susannah Burton, and I am
here to see Major Drayton Rambert."

"Do you have an appointment with him, Mrs. Burton?"

"No, but—"

"Then could I ask what you need to see the major for,
ma'am?" the corporal inquired politely. He was accustomed to screening all visitors, though most of the walk-
ins demanded to see General Sickles immediately. No
one had ever asked to see old "Die-hard Drayt" before,
with the exception of Carolyn Craig, of course.

"It is a personal matter of some urgency, Corporal."

The corporal's thin brows shot up as his eyes flashed up and down Susannah's trim form. Mrs. Craig wouldn't like this at all. And she'd know about it before the day was out, the way she kept track of old Die-hard.

"Uh—a personal matter," he stammered. "Yes . . . well, I—I—I'll tell him you're here, ma'am."

The corporal left his desk and hurried up the stairs, racing down them again just a few moments later, red-faced and breathless. He paused before he descended the last three steps, straightened, and squared his shoulders importantly as he strode crisply toward Susannah. "Major Rambert said he isn't in."

Susannah stiffened, and her chin lifted haughtily. "He said what?"

The corporal's eyes flew open in embarrassment. "What I meant to say was . . . I mean, what the major meant to say was—that is, what he did say was that he won't—er, I mean, he doesn't—er, handle things like you." A confused frown flitted across his brow. "What I mean is—"

"Is the major in or isn't he, Corporal?" she interrupted frigidly, hoping to spare herself another rush of nonsensical explanations.

Feeling himself caught between the proverbial rock and hard place, the flustered corporal tossed a fearful glance over his shoulder and lowered his voice. "He's in, ma'am, but—"

"Then I'll wait."

Her cool blue eyes gave the corporal no hope. "Uh—yes, ma'am," he mumbled to himself as she turned away and took a seat. "You'll wait."

It was all of two hours later when an unsuspecting Major Rambert descended the stairs. Susannah bestowed a chilly stare on him as he handed the corporal a stack of important-looking papers.

"What are you whispering about, Corporal?" Drayton barked irately. "Speak up, man!"

The corporal's face became so red that it very much resembled an overripe tomato. "The lady, sir," he stammered quietly, nodding his head in Susannah's direction.

Drayton met her eyes briefly as she rose from her chair and waited expectantly for him to approach her. He looked away. "What about the lady?"

"It's Mrs. Burton, sir. The woman who wanted to speak with you. About a personal matter, sir."

Drayton turned to regard Susannah a bit more carefully, then scowled and lifted an envelope from the corporal's desk. "I don't even know the woman, Corporal," he said in a low growl. "I'm very busy. Now get rid of her."

Susannah overheard just enough of Drayton's order to decide she'd had enough of polite waiting. "I don't intend to leave, Major Rambert," she retorted as she moved to block his path. "I've already waited two hours. I'll stay here all day and all night if I must, but I will speak with you . . . *sir,*" she added sarcastically.

Drayton's brow arched a bit at her outburst. The woman was clothed in a plain gray dress with white collar and cuffs and wore a small silver cross just below her right shoulder. A religious woman of some sort, obviously. She probably expected a donation for a "worthy cause."

"I haven't much time, Mrs. Burton."

"Neither do I, Major," she snapped back. "And we do seem to be wasting quite a lot of it."

Drayton stared at her a moment longer. Feisty for a religious woman, he thought. He relented, sweeping an arm toward the stairs. "My office?"

She gave a short nod and proceeded stiffly up the steps.

"As I told the corporal," she began once she was comfortably seated in the chair Drayton had offered her, "I am here to speak with you about a personal matter . . . a matter of some urgency." She hesitated, avoiding his eyes as she added, "A matter of some delicacy."

Drayton took a seat at his desk and leaned back, inclining his head in curiosity. There was a short space of silence before Susannah spoke again, her voice calm in spite of her anger, in spite of her reluctance to broach such a subject with a total stranger.

"I will try to be brief, Major, but I think it best to begin at the beginning. I arrived in Charleston with two other women in December, almost three months ago. We were sent here by our church, to open a school for illiterate freedmen and their children, which we since have done." She shook her head. "I'm sorry. I disgress." She drew a deep breath and began again, the words coming faster, her voice trembling a bit. "The very morning of our arrival, while we were still trying to locate the house our agent had purchased for us, there was a commotion in the street. I hurried forward to see what it was, and I discovered a young woman, lying facedown in the street. I thought at first that she had stumbled and fallen, and in doing so, had struck her head. But I found instead that she was seriously ill, burning up with fever. No one seemed to know who she was or where she was going, so Mrs. Gaines and Mrs. Caldwell and I took it upon ourselves to care for her." She paused, searching Drayton's face for some sign he understood what she was talking about. His expression was indifferent. "She was very, very ill," Susannah went on hurriedly. "She required constant attention for several days. We even called in a physician, though Mrs. Caldwell and I have had years of experience in nursing—"

"Are you requesting a donation for your good Christian work, Mrs. Burton?" he interrupted impatiently.

"Certainly not, Major!"

"Then I don't see what any of this has to do with me."

"But you must know her, Major," she pleaded earnestly. "She called you by name. She was delirious, and I could not understand much of what she said, but I know that she called for you—"

Susannah stopped short at the sudden change in his

eyes. He had gone so pale it frightened her, and his expression was one of total vulnerability. He closed his eyes. "Ambrosia," he whispered.

For a long time he said nothing more. The silence in the room was poignant. His eyes opened then, and the pain and despair in them took Susannah completely by surprise. "She called for me, you said?"

Susannah nodded. "Many times."

He lifted his chin and hardened his expression, reminding Susannah very much of a small boy trying to be a man. "Is—is she dead?"

She resisted an urge to place a comforting hand on his arm. "She is very much alive, Major," she assured him. "She was very ill for a time, but she recovered completely from the fever."

Drayton let out his breath and ran a hand anxiously through his hair. He rose from his chair and paced nervously across the room, back and forth, back and forth, without a word. He was in dire need of a good stiff drink. Between his anger and his relief, he did not even know what he was feeling anymore.

She was alive. Thank God for that. He almost felt like he had died himself a few moments ago, when he'd thought her dead. With his back to Susannah he closed his eyes and let out a sigh while his fingers kneaded the tense muscles at the back of his neck. She was too strong to die, he thought, too much of a fighter. And yet, that night she had seemed so small and so broken. . . .

"There is more."

With a start, he whirled to face her, his eyes wide and somewhat dazed. "More?"

Susannah nodded. "Perhaps you'd better sit down again, Major."

He obeyed her order without protest, all the while regarding her warily.

"I have good reason to believe that she is in a family way."

Susannah watched him closely as she broke the news,

carefully trying to gauge his reaction. She expected the surprise, but certainly not the smile that began to play about his mouth, or the grin that eventually followed. He actually seemed pleased with the news.

"Did she send you here?" he asked abruptly.

Somewhat disconcerted, she met the hopeful gleam in his eye and slowly shook her head. The hopeful gleam faded, as did his smile. "She doesn't want to see me, does she?" His tone was edged in bitterness.

Susannah bit her lip nervously, and while she was still trying to think of how to respond, Drayton's fist struck the desk with a resounding thud. Her head snapped up.

"Then what the hell is she planning to do about the child?"

Susannah winced at his rather untoward choice of language. "Well," she began carefully, "she spoke of leaving Charleston—"

"Leaving? Is that all she spoke of?" he pressed none too gently. "She hasn't tried to end it?"

Susannah gave him a look of total bewilderment, as if he were quite mad. "End what?"

He let out a long breath and rose to begin pacing again, this time with crisp, angry steps, all the while muttering under his breath, "Of course she would not end it. She probably knows nothing of such things. And even if she did, she would not consider—" He stopped short and faced Susannah. "She would have left without even telling me?"

Susannah gave a helpless shrug and he began pacing again. She watched him uneasily. She wished she knew more about him, about what had been between Ambrosia and him. He was not responding at all as she had expected.

He turned to her suddenly, his eyes bright with anger, his tone demanding more than inquiring. "Where is she?"

Susannah frowned. "I—I must know your intentions before I reveal that to you, Major."

He glared at her. "My intentions!"

She nodded.

His mouth twisted in a cold sort of smile. "My intention, Mrs. Burton," he returned succinctly, "is to make Ambrosia my wife the moment I get my hands on her."

Susannah's eyes widened in amazement. Without a single word of prodding he intended to do the honorable thing. She let out a long sigh, relieved that she would not need to persuade him. He did not look to be the type who was easily lead. She withdrew a card from her pocket and gave it to Drayton. "This is the address of our school."

He glanced at it and then at Susannah. "I shall be forever indebted to you, Mrs. Burton."

He gave a polite nod as he took up his hat and gloves and made to leave. Susannah stood up and followed him to the door. "You—you're not going to her now?"

"Is there any reason why I should wait?"

"No, of course not. Only—" Susannah frowned as she hurried along beside him. "Only—only—"

He stopped at the top of the stairs. "Only what, Mrs. Burton?"

"She may not be there," Susannah said finally. "She spends a few hours every other day at the boardinghouse next door."

He snorted his displeasure as he drew on a pair of heavy buckskin gloves. "And what, pray tell, does she do at this boardinghouse?"

Susannah's voice was small. "A number of things she ought not to do in her condition."

He met Susannah's eyes with a fierce scowl, then jerked the brim of his hat low on his brow and marched down the stairs.

Chapter 22

The hall and stairway were in sore need of paint, the ceiling stained with recurrent water leaks, the plaster walls cracked and spotted. Ambrosia grimaced as she dipped the scrubbing brush into the heavy pail of water and glanced about the landing. She hated this place almost as much as she despised its new Yankee owner, who refused to make necessary repairs, who rented every inch of what had once been an elegant home to poor whites and drunkards and derelicts. Ambrosia was grateful she hadn't known the previous owners of this place or of the place that was now the Vermont Christian School. Too many fine people had been forced to leave Charleston, people who belonged here, people her father had known intimately.

She let out a lengthy breath through clenched teeth as the door slammed on the floor below and the telltale scuff of heavy boots was heard on the stairs. Zachary Skinner, the owner of the building and her employer, generally "chanced by" on the days she cleaned the halls and followed her about, making comments on everything she did. Ambrosia would not have minded that so much if he hadn't persisted in looking at her like a hungry wolf drooling over a fat chicken. That look, and the way he had managed to "accidentally" brush her breasts and buttocks far too often in the past month, made Ambrosia's flesh crawl at the mere thought of facing him again. If she hadn't needed the money so desperately, she would have doused him thoroughly with the bucket of strong lye soap and water, and told him what he could do with his filthy Yankee tenement house. But she couldn't afford the luxury of losing her temper just yet.

She fixed her eyes on the scrubbing brush and moved it vigorously over the planked wooden landing, trying not to think about the lecherous eyes that were probably on her already. The footfalls came nearer and stopped. Her fingers gripped the brush tightly and she clenched her jaw, scrubbing, scrubbing.

A pair of freshly polished black leather boots moved to block the next stroke of her brush. Her mouth dropped open in surprise. The boots were not Mr. Skinner's, whose feet were ridiculously small for a man of his girth and always spattered with mud or something worse. Slowly, hesitantly, her eyes drifted upward. Her breath caught and she stared at him for a long moment, feeling a joyous excitement at the sight of his dark face, his blue eyes. She started to smile, but quickly caught herself, realizing she had no reason to smile. She lowered her eyes. He was her enemy, and she had promised herself that she would never feel anything but hatred and shame if she saw him again. She certainly wanted no part of the temporary "arrangement" he had offered her. And there had been that pretty dark-haired girl at the market that day, clinging possessively to his arm. At the thought of that girl, Ambrosia suddenly realized that there was a good chance he no longer wanted her at all. He might have come here strictly by chance, she thought, feeling shame and self-loathing that she had ever thought otherwise.

Drayton heaved a sigh as he drew off his gloves and tucked them into his belt, torn between the desire to take her into his arms and an equal need to give her a piece of his mind. She ought not to be working in a place like this, especially not in her condition. Her skin was pale and she was so damned thin it almost hurt to look at her. Her cheeks were hollow, the squared line of her jaw much too prominent, and her eyes were too bright and enormous for her face. For a moment, she had almost seemed pleased to see him. But that moment had quickly passed. She was not happy to see him now.

He took off his hat and stooped down, his hand covering both of hers, effectively stopping the vigorous movement of the scrubbing brush. Ambrosia looked up, startled. His face was only inches from her own. She swallowed hard and lowered her eyes again, fixing them on the lean tanned fingers which covered hers. A hot blush crept into her cheeks and her voice came small and timorous. "What are you doing here?"

"I was just about to ask you the same question."

She heard the familiar cocky tone and felt a surge of anger. Her eyes flashed indignantly. "I work here."

"So I see." He glanced about, scowling at the peeling paint and chipped plaster, grimacing as he drew a deep breath of the tainted air. He wrenched the scrubbing brush from her hands and shook his head, pretending to study it intently. "Not the most pleasant of working conditions . . . and it couldn't pay as well as Maggie's. . . ."

She wrestled the brush away and dunked it in the pail, sloshing a considerable wave of water on the floor. She was pleased when a bit of it dulled the brilliance of one of his shiny black boots. "What do you want?" She tossed him the question as she began to scrub fiercely at the floor.

"I wanted to see you." His voice was gentle and Ambrosia felt her heart begin to pound. "I was very concerned about you."

A part of her actually wanted to fling herself into his arms like a helpless woman, to allow herself to feel his strength, to allow herself to cry. But she could never do that. "And now you've seen me," she returned with a flippant shrug. She took the scrubbing brush to the corner and worked industriously at the buildup of dirt there. "You have nothing more to be concerned about."

There was a moment of silence. Drayton's cheeks flexed with irritation. "We need to talk, Ambrosia." His voice had changed again. He was giving her an order.

"We have nothing to talk about."

He grasped her shoulders hard and brought her abruptly to her feet. His eyes were hard and bright as they met hers. "Do you realize that you left me that morning without a single word of explanation?"

Her eyes were narrowed and every bit as bright as his. "I owed you no explanation."

"Are you trying to tell me," he said slowly, "that what happened between us meant nothing to you?"

For what seemed like an eternity, she could not answer. It had meant far too much to her, and she had spent many nights trying to rationalize away the feelings she could not explain. But then the flames of Heritage flared in her mind, and the softness left her expression. She had lived with that memory too, these past weeks, and she wanted no part of Drayton Rambert.

"It meant I drank too much brandy," she said finally, "and made a very bad mistake."

His disbelieving eyes questioned her statement for a long moment. Slowly he released his grip on her shoulders and turned his back to her, letting out a weary sigh. He leaned forward against the curved banister, his fingers turning white as they dug into the wood, his eyes becoming distant as they pondered the steps that wound below.

"I am bound by honor to marry you," he announced after a long silence.

For an instant Ambrosia was stunned. He had offered her marriage! But something in the way he had offered it was very wrong. Bound by honor, he had said. Not by love or by choice. It was as if he was simply doing his duty, carrying out an order that resulted from his taking her virginity. Insulted, Ambrosia gave a derisive snort. "What do Yankees know of honor?"

He whirled to face her, his jaw taunt, his eyes piercing. "I will not see my child born a bastard, Ambrosia."

A startled gasp burst from her lips and she felt herself trembling inside. Her bravado crumbled. "H-How did you know about that?" she whispered, her hand instinctively covering her stomach.

"It's true then?"

She turned away and blinked back a tear. His proposal had little or nothing to do with her. He knew about the child. His pride would not allow a part of himself to be born in shame. No wonder he had seen fit to offer marriage. "Are you so certain the child is yours, Major?" she flung back at him, feeling hurt and angry and not daring to ask herself why she felt those things. "How do you know I haven't had other men?"

He straightened abruptly, a muscle in his jaw twitching. He grasped her arm and turned her about to face him squarely, meeting the familiar intransigent gleam in her green eyes, and beyond that, something else . . . fear? uncertainty? hurt? Whatever it was, it lessened his anger. He lifted his hand to touch her cheek and bent close to her, his eyes pleading. She swallowed hard and tried to pull away. "Is the thought of marrying me so repulsive, Ambrosia?" he breathed. He paused, allowing his lips to play warmly over hers. "Do you feel nothing when I touch you?"

She turned away, wishing she could hide the shudders that echoed through her with every touch of his mouth. It frightened her, to know he had such power over her senses.

"I am not so naive as to place value on any such feelings," she managed to say.

He raised his head and gave a small smile. "It's a beginning."

Her jaw tightened defiantly and her eyes were hard. She knew all too well where such "beginnings" led. She would be expected to serve him like a slave, to obey his every command, to give up what little freedom she had as a woman and what little pride she had regained these past months. She looked at the floor. "You're a Yankee. You don't really expect me to marry a Yankee, do you?"

"I didn't expect you to come to me that night, Ambrosia." He saw her stiffen and clench her fists at that, her face twisting with sadness and regret. A distant look came into her eyes then, the look of a lost child waking from a nightmare. He knew that look, knew she was thinking of the man she loved, the man who had held them apart, even that night. The knowledge filled him with jealousy and despair . . . and pity.

"I do not expect you to forget him," he said in a brittle tone.

She started, staring at him in bewilderment. He had read her mind.

"But I give you no choice as to the marriage," he went on coldly. "I would pray, Ambrosia, that you care enough about the child you bear to see that he has a name."

His words stung her and filled her with guilt. It had been her greatest fear these past weeks, that the baby would suffer from her mistake, that an innocent child would be made an outcast because of the circumstances of his birth. She would have lied to protect the baby, of course, but such lies had a way of being discovered. And even if she could keep the secret, Ambrosia had cried more than once over the kind of life she knew her child would have, a life of poverty, of dirty tenement houses, like this one, a life of hiding from the truth.

Drayton was right. The child deserved a name. Even if it was a Yankee name. Even if it meant she would have to endure the hell of a loveless marriage and the humiliation of an unfaithful husband.

"The child might be a girl," she snapped. She scowled at the grin that lit his eyes, as if that possibility actually pleased him. Before she could think of something else to say, he pulled her rather roughly into his arms and kissed her long and hard, until every shred of her resistance had melted away. Her hands slid shyly about his neck, her lips quivered, then parted at the gentle insistence of his tongue. She swayed against him, her body suddenly remembering everything about a night that seemed an eternity ago. It was only when a loud, scandalized gasp echoed in the hallway that the passionate moment came to an abrupt halt. ''Miss Lanford!''

Ambrosia's head twisted about to meet the wide, rounded eyes of her employer, who stared aghast at the scene before him.

Drayton was actually smiling when he picked up the scrubbing brush and pail and deposited them into Skinner's pudgy hands. Without a word, he then scooped up a somewhat startled Ambrosia and carried her down the stairs. His grin widened when her arms flew instinctively about his neck.

Ambrosia began to laugh when Mr. Skinner finally found his tongue and ran after them, waving the scrubbing brush threateningly and shouting that she was fired. Drayton had never heard her laugh before, and he resolved this would not be the last time.

When they reached the street, he set her on her feet, clucking his tongue and shaking his head. ''Your shameless behavior will probably send that old man to an early grave.''

''The world should only be so fortunate!''

''You mean you didn't like him much?'' he teased.

''Like him! That filthy, disgusting, conniving—'' Her voice cut off abruptly. The words were very similar to the ones she'd used to describe Drayton not so very long ago. ''I hope he gets what's coming to him,'' she mumbled.

Drayton's grin faded at the sudden hardness in her eyes. It was going to be difficult for a while. It would take time for the bitterness to heal and an even longer time for her to learn trust. But there was a bond between them now, perhaps the strongest bond of all. A child. A new life fashioned of a man's love and a woman's desperation. It was a beginning. For now, it was enough.

Chapter 23

They were wed in a brief, private ceremony three days later, with only the ladies from the Vermont Christian School and Colonel Beam, one of Drayton's closest friends, in attendance. During those three days, Drayton managed to rent a house and see to its cleaning and arranged for a short leave from his duties. Ambrosia proceeded somewhat numbly through the vows, accepting the good wishes afterward with an acute awareness that she was the lone Confederate among Yankees. Susannah, Mary, and Colonel Beam, who had witnessed the ceremony for Drayton, seemed in joyous spirits as they toasted the happy union, while Rebecca stood by with a brittle smile and enviously eyed the small group of Drayton's friends who came by, uninvited, after the ceremony to meet his bride. Ambrosia stared at them blankly as they smiled at her and made lighthearted remarks to Drayton. There was no one here from her past life, no one here who even recognized the name Lanford or knew what it stood for. To them she was the woman who had worked for Maggie, the woman Drayton had taken as a wife, and nothing more. She felt empty and humiliated, as if yet another part of her pride had been destroyed when she relinquished her name.

Ambrosia was uneasy about the possessive arm Drayton always seemed to have about her, and uncomfortable whenever she met his eyes. There could be no question about the warmth in those eyes or the promise in his handsome smile. Surely the others must have seen it too. She felt the color flooding her cheeks at the thought.

Sometime after the ceremony and numerous bottles of champagne, Drayton finally managed to whisk Ambrosia outside into a waiting buggy. She settled into the seat and did her best to relax, but the truth of what she had just done refused to allow her peace. Married. To a Yankee. The thought of being owned, of belonging to him for the remainder of her life, made her feel ill. She tried to conjure up all the bitterness and hatred that was in her to combat the panic that was taking hold, but her face was white, her eyes bright with fear and dread as the buggy stopped and Drayton alighted. Drawing heavily on her reserve of courage, she braced herself against the feel of his hands, the closeness of him as she slid into his arms. He frowned down at her in concern. "Are you feeling well?"

She nodded mutely and turned away from his questioning gaze, only then noticing that they had stopped before a row of shops, not houses. She lifted her eyes in confusion and he immediately propelled her toward one of the shops. There was no large painted sign on the small building, only a few discreet lines of lettering on the door: "Madame Loreau's Fashion Apparel." Ambrosia's eyes widened when she read the name, which she readily recognized from the women customers' idle talk at Maggie's. According to what she'd heard, Madame Loreau, who had arrived only a few months before, was the only woman of "true fashion" in the South, except perhaps in New Orleans. Any Yankee woman who could afford to frequent her shop did so, but no self-respecting Southern woman would dream of stepping inside such a place. Ambrosia drew back as Drayton opened the door, but his firm grip on her arm prevented her from scrambling back into the buggy. A moment later she stumbled reluctantly in the direction of the arm Drayton had already pulled inside.

A small bell tinkled pleasantly as he shut the door, and a graceful, middle-aged woman immediately responded to the summons. The corners of her mouth lifted upward as she offered Drayton her hand, which he touched gallantly to his lips. He did not protest when she rose on tip-toe to briefly press a second kiss to his cheek. "It is always a pleasure, Drayton." She spoke English with a dramatic intonation and a distinct accent, softening and smoothing each consonant that was foreign to her native French. She smiled at him a moment longer than what Ambrosia considered proper, then perked up her brows in curiosity as she stared over his broad shoulder at the woman he had brought with him. She wore a perfectly awful dress that had obviously had the sleeves turned and seams mended repeatedly. There was even a patch on the skirt near the hem! She wore not a single ornament or decoration, not even a brooch, nothing but a small gold band on the third finger of her left hand. Moreover, she had not come forward, demanding an introduction, but stood rather stiffly just inside the door, as if she did not want to be here at all.

"Ah!" Madame purred as she hurried toward the strange girl, anxious to put her at ease. "What have we here?"

"Madame Loreau, may I present my wife, Ambrosia. Ambrosia, Madame Janette Loreau."

Ambrosia nodded with cold politeness while Madame Loreau tried to hide her astonishment. His wife! And he had accompanied Carolyn Craig here just last week to give his opinion on a gown she had ordered especially to please him. Of course, that visit would have been entirely Carolyn's idea, a sort of statement to everyone who found out about it that Drayton Rambert was "taken." Madame wondered for an instant if Carolyn knew. She certainly hadn't said anything yesterday when she'd come in for a final fitting. Heaven help this tiny slip of a girl Drayton had married when she did find out! *Mon dieu!*

"Ah, Drayton! You are so clever! Such a lovely lady! Small, *petit,* like ze *papillon, non?*" And younger than Carolyn by a good five years, Madame determined quickly, though she could not bear the sight of the girl's calloused, reddened hands. She smiled at Ambrosia and turned quickly to Drayton again. "And you wish for me to dress zis *papillon, n'est-ce pas?* To make her ze loveliest"— she frowned as she struggled to remember the English word—"er . . . butterfly in all of Sharleston!"

Ambrosia shook her head at the same time Drayton was nodding with hearty approval.

"Oui! It shall be done. It will take time, *naturellement,* but we will begin *tout de suite."* She began chattering in rapid French as she whirled and scurried off into the back room, returning a moment later and beckoning Ambrosia to join her.

Ambrosia turned a reluctant pair of green eyes on her husband. He meant to dress her like one of those Yankee women who frequented Maggie's. He knew perfectly well that Southern women wore their tattered gowns of homespun and black proudly, a banner to all that the Confederacy had not been forgotten, would never be forgotten. The rags Ambrosia wore now were almost sacred to her. They represented the only part of her that was still tied to the past, and she could not give up that part of herself without a fight. "Drayton, please. I don't—"

To her humiliation, he cut off her protests with a brief kiss. "Did you imagine that I would allow my wife to dress like a beggar?" he said with a smile. He kissed her again, expecting a smile in return. He did not receive one. He lifted her chin and searched her face. "Are you certain you feel well, Ambrosia?"

Her eyes were cold and indifferent. "Yes."

He sighed and pressed a kiss to her hand. "I shall be back for you in an hour or so. Take good care of her, Ja-

nette,'' he called cheerily as he made to leave the shop.
There was the light tinkling of the bell on the door again,
and then the two women were alone.

Madame's sharp eyes flashed over Ambrosia a bit
more appraisingly once he had left, assessing every as-
pect of her coloring, every curve of her figure. She grimaced at the gown the woman wore, which did much to
disguise what might just be a lovely body. Still Madame
knew immediately that Ambrosia would prove an interesting subject. There was something about her, a latent
fire in the smoky green eyes, a grace, a pride to her
movements, that the proper gown and hairstyle would
bring to the fore. And as Madame studied her face, she
became intrigued with what she saw there, and intent on
enhancing the enigmatic beauty of the woman Drayton
had married. The potential was certainly here . . . the
strength in the lines of nose and chin, the sensuous fullness of the mouth, the long, slender column of the throat
. . . Madame smiled at the challenge before her and at
the thought of the very generous fee she would collect for
her work.

Madame continued her intent study as Ambrosia stood
in a much-repaired, worn cotton chemise, enduring the
endless measurements that were being taken by a young
black girl and recorded by Madame. The dressmaker
brought out a large pile of fabric swatches, pointing out
several fabrics she considered appropriate for day
dresses, evening dresses, traveling attire, and of course,
lingerie. She gave adamant advice about choosing colors
to flatter her skin and eyes. Only bright, dramatic colors
would do, greens and reds and sapphires, and certainly
no pastels.

Ambrosia looked without interest at the swatches and
politely waited for Madame to finish, though she already
despised the dressmaker's false smile and felt very much
like one of the strumpets that had so often visited the emporium.

"And now, Madame Rambert, we shall begin ze list of ze gowns you will need."

"I will require four gowns, Madame Loreau," she said with quiet authority, as if she were accustomed to giving such orders. "Three of this fabric"—she indicated a swatch of plain black muslin—"and one of this." She touched her finger to another swatch of black silk. "Each must be simple, and easily altered to allow for—to allow for a child." She met the Frenchwoman's incredulous dark eyes and added pointedly, "I will need nothing more."

"But—but—your husband! He would insist zat you have ze best!" she protested vehemently. "And you cannot wear black, Mademoiselle! It is all wrong for you!"

"It's *Madame,*" Ambrosia corrected frigidly. "And I will wear black. I am in mourning."

"But—but you will not be in mourning forever!"

"I just might," she muttered.

"Pardon?"

"Nothing. I will need the four gowns, Madame, and nothing more," she repeated.

Madame bowed her head and swallowed an angry retort. *"Oui,* Madame Rambert. Four gowns. All simple, all in black." The smile had finally gone. "But—but surely you will also need ze *cotillon,* and ozer . . . personal items? To allow for ze child to grow?"

Ambrosia's eyes regarded her sorry chemise and pantalets and became uneasy. It was true. She hadn't a single decent petticoat anymore and only one shimmy that had been mended in too many places to fit properly. Her cheeks colored and she bit her lip. Madame must have noticed that as well. As to a proper nightgown, she had "borrowed" one from Susannah these past few months, the hem of which dragged on the floor a good four inches, the sleeves of which fell below her fingertips. She let out a reluctant sigh, realizing that she had little choice. "A few things," she relented finally.

Drayton was surprised to find Ambrosia at the door of

the shop awaiting him when he returned. He had never known a woman to be prompt before, particularly when shopping for clothing. Once inside the buggy, he took a seat beside her and took up the reins, tossing her a speculative glance. He had hoped that the visit to Madame's would cheer her, and he had to hide his disappointment at her continued somber mood. "How did it go?" he asked lightly as he slapped the reins on the mare's dappled back and the buggy lurched foward.

She fixed her eyes on the passing buildings, feeling tired and drained at the thought of what lay ahead. "Well enough, I suppose," she said sullenly.

He forced a smile as he took the reins in a single hand and reached for her hand with the other. "I have a surprise for you."

She glanced up, her eyes mildly inquiring.

"I think you might like this one," he said slowly.

"What is it?"

His blue eyes lit with amusement and he pursed his lips like a small boy with a big secret. Ambrosia scowled and returned her gaze to the passing buildings. She did not really care what surprise he had in mind. If it were anything like the visit to the dress shop, she would just as soon he never revealed it. She tried to tug away her hand, but he held it fast, and drew it to his thigh. Ambrosia bit her lip and found herself wondering how long it would be before he tired of her, before he left her in peace, as Jackson Lanford had left Lucille in peace, as Ledger had left Melissa. She wondered briefly if she would even retain her sanity until then.

He stopped the buggy before a house she had never seen before. She allowed him to assist her in alighting, though she felt as if she were walking to her death. She stoically preceded him through a large iron gate and lovely little garden toward the house. He stopped her at the door and lifted her into his arms to cross the threshold. Once inside, he watched her face intently as she glanced about the foyer. "There's not much in the way of furniture," he apologized, "but I thought you might want to choose some things yourself, so—"

"Everything is lovely. Please put me down."

He regarded her for a long moment, then slowly allowed her feet to touch the floor. His arms remained about her. She attempted to break free of the embrace, but he held her fast. "You might at least smile, Ambrosia. I could not possibly have made you so miserable in so short a time."

Her expression did not soften and she did not answer him. Reluctantly he released her and went into the parlor to fix himself a drink. She followed. "I'd like one of those, please."

"This is straight whiskey, Ambrosia," he began.

"I know."

He scowled at her, but filled the bottom of a small glass with Kentucky bourbon. She took a defiant gulp of it and he watched her struggle to keep from choking as it burned a path down her throat. The fire subsided after a time and she quickly drained the glass.

"Are you hungry?"

She placed the glass on the table. "No."

"That's too bad. The cook will be disappointed, after she went to so much trouble."

"What cook?"

"Didn't I mention that I'd hired a cook?" he returned innocently. "Oh . . . Well, I was extremely fortunate to find her, a woman so experienced and totally trustworthy. I know she'll take good care of you."

She eyed him warily. "I'll have another drink."

He handed her a second glass with hardly a single swallow of bourbon in the bottom. She downed it quickly, hoping that it would affect her soon. The thought of being coddled by a strange servant who answered to her husband was not a very pleasant one. She needed no one to take good care of her; she was perfectly able to take care of herself. She wished that Drayton's mood were less pleasant, that he would lose his temper so that she could release the tension that was coiling ever more tightly inside her. But there was no anger in his eyes, only a warm expectancy that was swiftly wearing her nerves to a frazzle.

He pulled a bell cord in the corner of the room, then leisurely unbuttoned his tunic and removed it, withdrawing a thin cigar from the pocket before he laid the coat over the back of the chair. He ran the cigar under his nose. "Do you object to my smoking?"

When she shook her head, he struck a match to the heel of his boot and lit his cigar, turning away to draw on it long and pensively. Ambrosia watched him while his eyes were averted, until she saw his gaze slide toward the parlor door. Following his stare, her eyes widened in disbelief. The empty glass fell from her hand.

"Dinnah's ready." The large, wrinkled black woman smiled broadly at Ambrosia, who rose slowly from her chair, her mouth struggling to form the name.

"Sheba!" In the next moment Ambrosia was running to greet her, her fingers clasping about Sheba's wide, dark-skinned hand and pressing it fondly to her cheek. "It really is you!"

The black woman blinked back a tear as she gave a short nod. "Yes'm, Miz Ambrosia. It sho' is. An' ah'm in charge o' de kitchen, jus' like de ol' days. Yes'm. Jus' like de ol' days."

"But—" Ambrosia slowly released Sheba's hand and turned toward Drayton. Her eyes were confused, bewildered as she met his gaze. She could not bring herself to ask how this had all come about, to ask him why he had gone to so much trouble. The warm light in his eyes, the hint of a smile, fully answered those questions.

Grinning knowingly at the look on Ambrosia's face, Sheba left the room and discreetly closed the door behind herself. Ambrosia stepped slowly, hesitantly toward Drayton, her wide, troubled eyes never leaving his. "I—I am deeply grateful," she managed to whisper.

He tossed the cigar into the empty fireplace grate and

took her gently by the shoulders. "I've told you before, I don't want your gratitude."

Her eyes darkened. She searched his face. "What then?"

He sighed and touched his lips to hers. "I am your husband now," he said almost lightly, though his eyes were dark and intent. "I want what husbands generally seek from their wives."

She was disappointed by his answer, though she wasn't really sure what she had wanted him to say. One of his hands moved to encircle her waist, to pull her close. Her heart quickened, her cheeks burned. "I have already vowed to be your wife," she breathed unevenly. "What you seek is no longer a matter of choice."

His fingers slid upward toward her breast, until the pounding of her heart thudded against his palm. "And if it were?"

She closed her eyes as his mouth began to play with soft yearning upon hers. And she realized that she had longed for this moment, dreamed of this moment, for months now, ever since that night.

"If it were your choice?" he murmured again. "Would you willingly yield to me?" He withdrew a bit and awaited her response.

Her green eyes met his with the answer her lips refused to give. She quickly closed them and turned her face away. "No."

"Damn you!" he muttered harshly, jerking her hard against his chest. His lips were at once insistent and demanding as they slanted roughly against hers, at once arousing the response he sought. With a tiny cry of defeat she slipped her arms about his neck and welcomed the thrust of his tongue.

Chapter 24

The room was dark and shadowy when Ambrosia woke, the shutters drawn tightly against the morning sunlight. Her eyes blinked open and searched the strange room. She remembered then. She was not alone.

She stared at her husband for a long time. He slept soundly at her side. She rose on one elbow and reached to brush a stray lock of his shiny black hair from his brow. But just as she was about to touch him, she froze. She withdrew her hand, wondering what had possessed her to even think of doing such a thing. She had never really imagined that it would be like this, not even when she had dreamed of marrying Ledger. . . .

A frown flitted across her brow. She had not thought of him once last night. Drayton's lovemaking had banished everything and everyone else from her mind. Her frowned deepened and she felt a pang of guilt. She had enjoyed it. She had responded to him without reservation, had surrendered a vital part of herself in return for a few fleeting moments of pleasure with a man who was her enemy. How easy it was to fall into such a trap! To become no better than Maggie or the woman who had so brazenly paraded Drayton through the market that day. Ambrosia understood now what those women had wanted. She rolled onto her back and stared at the ceiling, feeling a surge of self-loathing.

"Good morning, Mrs. Rambert."

Ambrosia started at the sound of his voice. She pulled the comforter modestly above the curves of her breasts before she returned her eyes to the ceiling. She was suddenly very uncomfortable lying beside him, very self-conscious about the way his eyes lingered on her bare shoulders.

His finger traced the line of her collarbone. "Hungry?"

She shook her head, then bit her lip hard. Last evening she had been hungry when she and Drayton finally emerged from the parlor. She had eaten a very hearty dinner hours after Sheba had first announced it served. She had never seen Sheba wearing a grin quite like that before, and she was probably wearing it again this morning. Ambrosia didn't look forward to facing that. Or to facing Drayton, after she had responded so shamelessly to him.

Drayton stared at her, wondering at the seriousness of her expression. "Are you feeling well?"

"I wish you'd stop asking me that!" she snapped. She turned her back toward him and pulled the comforter up to her chin.

Drayton frowned, then vented a reluctant sigh as he rose from the bed and began to dress. "I'm going down to breakfast," he announced as he fastened his uniform trousers and reached for a freshly starched blouse. "Shall I have Sheba bring you something?"

She shook her head.

"Shall I bring you something up?" He grinned.

Her mouth tightened. She refused to look at him.

He let out a long breath as he laid the shirt aside and strode toward the bed. "Ambrosia."

The eyes which lifted were bright and mutinous, and they made his eyes light with impatience. "What is it?" he demanded.

She looked away.

In a single fluid movement, he sat on the bed and jerked her to a like position, ignoring her gasp of outrage as the comforter slipped to her waist. "What is wrong with you?" he growled. "Or do you simply make a habit of waking up in such a foul mood?"

She crossed her arms protectively over her breasts and narrowed a pair of furious green eyes. "I make it a habit to wake up alone," she articulated with icy brittleness. "You'll have to pardon me if finding a Yankee in my bed turns my stomach."

"You didn't seem to mind it last night," he reminded her with an amused arch of his brow.

"I must have been drunk last night," she retorted. "Otherwise I would never have been able to endure it."

Ambrosia shocked herself by telling such a blatant lie. She was even more stunned by the momentary hurt that shone in Drayton's face. It was gone so swiftly that she wondered if she had imagined it. And then he was angry. Furiously angry.

"You are not drunk now," he said softly, prying her hands away from her breasts and forcing her back against the pillows. "Shall we see if you can endure it this morning?"

Ambrosia struggled violently against him, even as his lips pressed insistently to the smooth line of her throat, even as his tongue sought out the dark, velvet peaks of her breasts. She twisted and lurched in panic, crying out against the ease with which he held her immobile, gasping in mortification as he thrust a knee between her thighs. He freed his hardened shaft without bothering to remove his trousers. Ambrosia froze in horror at the thought of being taken in anger, in violence. He seemed to hesitate for a moment, as if he sensed her rigidness, but he knew far too much about her body to allow her to retreat. He kissed her deeply, an experienced kiss that feigned gentleness, probing, urging as he caressed her breasts lightly, as he moved his hands in a knowing, calculated manipulation of her most sensitive areas. In spite of her panic, or perhaps because of it, the blood of passion raced through her veins. A desire born of her own anger and frustration and fear surged inside her, a dangerous, volatile desire that demanded immediate release. She arched against him with a cry of need, aching to be satisfied, hungering for the burst of physical satisfaction that would end this frenzied, mindless battle. He satisfied her then, roughly, almost ruthlessly, as he himself was satisfied. But for both satisfaction faded almost instantly in an aftermath of guilt and emptiness.

Ambrosia moved quickly away from him, curling up like a frightened kitten. She did not want him to see her cry. But she felt used, soiled, little better than a bitch in heat. She let out a choked sob as his hand touched her shoulder. She was rigid when he lifted her by the shoulders and forced her to face him. She could not. She braced herself, fully expecting to be taunted for her response. He had proven his dominance, had stripped away the last remnant of her pride by catching her in a lie. Yet his voice was low and apologetic, and it held nothing of a taunt.

"Forgive me, Ambrosia," he whispered. She felt him pulling the comforter gently over her trembling body. "I never meant to take you that way."

She felt a tear slip quickly over her cheek from beneath her closed lid. He pulled her into his arms. She would never have admitted it, but she was actually comforted to feel those hard, muscular arms about her. She opened her eyes and slowly raised them to meet his. He laced his fingers tightly through hers and touched them to his lips. "I would not begin this way with you," he murmured.

She swallowed hard and looked away. The fault had been hers. He had merely reacted in anger, as any man might have done.

"You should not have lied," he reproved in a low voice, as if reading her thoughts.

She lifted her eyes again and he gave her a little smile.

"You're much too good a liar. Remind me never to teach you how to play poker."

"I learned to play when I was seven."

He grimaced and let out a moan. "God help me."

He sighed as he let his hand slip behind her head, testing the softness of her hair, moving beneath it to knead the downy skin at the nape of her neck. "Why did you lie?"

Ambrosia's eyes fixed on the small gold band that seemed so out of place on her finger. "I—I don't want to like it," she admitted after a long silence, her cheeks flaring with color.

He watched her fidget nervously with the ring, half-amused by her answer, half-angry. "I am your husband, Ambrosia. Things might be simpler if you took pleasure in pleasing me, as I take pleasure in pleasing you."

Her eyes narrowed. "You're a Yankee. I'll never take pleasure in pleasing a Yankee."

He bent her head back and touched his mouth to hers, but his voice was sterner than before, not quite so gentle. "Someday you'll realize that I am not your enemy, Ambrosia."

She pulled away from him again, afraid that he might make her forget that he was a Yankee, that he might make her want all the things he offered her. Reluctantly he rose and finished dressing, forcing away the doubts that were suddenly clouding his mind, telling himself that it would only take time. . . .

Ambrosia was kept busy during the next few days, visiting many shops in the northern section of Charleston she hadn't even known were there, buying the furnishings necessary to make the house Drayton had rented comfortable. All the while she kept a watchful eye on the cost of every item she purchased. The want of the war years made her feel uneasy about spending so much money at one time, in spite of the fact that her husband seemed far more concerned with pleasing her than he was with money. Ambrosia also felt guilty about buying fine things when so many formerly wealthy families still suffered in their proud poverty. She thought of the Bowmans, existing on so little, relying so heavily on the salary she had contributed just a few months before. At the first opportunity, she asked Sheba privately how the Bowmans were "getting along." The black woman told her that she was not to worry, that there was money from another source now that "Massah Ledgah done sol' some o' his writin', an' lookin' t' sell mo'."

Ambrosia quickly lowered her eyes, trying to hide the fact that she felt empty and sad rather than pleased with the news. He had turned to writing, as she had dreamed he would. He had never even told her that he was going to try. She did not notice that Sheba was gnawing nervously at her bottom lip, wondering whether or not to mention the fact that Melissa had run off with a flashy, white-trash scalawag several weeks before, that Ledger and his mother were alone now. Sheba had overheard enough of the ugly accusations Melissa had flung at her sister that night to know why Ambrosia ran away. And though Sheba's loyalty to Ambrosia was strong, she could not deny the feelings she saw in Ambrosia's eyes, and had seen for years. Even though Melissa had run off with another man and had no intentions of ever coming back, Ledger was still married to her. And now Ambrosia was married to someone else as well. No, she could not say anything about Melissa or Ledger. . . .

Ambrosia's eyes lifted again and she asked in a shaky voice, "Does he—does he know I'm married?" she asked reluctantly. "To a Yankee?"

The black woman nodded slowly. "He know. De majah talk t' him when he come t' ask me t' work." She saw Ambrosia's face fall and quickly added, "He wish you all de best, you an' de majah."

Ambrosia did not meet her eyes again, but Sheba saw her lips tremble as she forced a nod. "Yes . . . I'm sure he does. . . ."

* * *

On the third day after their marriage, Ambrosia and Drayton were finishing breakfast when Sheba offered Drayton a plain white envelope that had been delivered earlier that same morning. Ambrosia peered curiously over her coffee cup, watching Drayton's face expectantly.

"We've received a personal invitation to attend a reception tomorrow evening," he said as he handed her the formal printed card and flashed her a brief smile. "A reception given by General and Mrs. Sickles."

Her eyes scanned the announcement, then studied the personal note at the bottom, penned and signed by the general's wife. "Must we go?"

"Have we other plans?"

She reluctantly shook her head.

"Then we certainly must." He smiled and covered her hand with his own. "I should enjoy showing you off a bit, Ambrosia." He felt her stiffen and she abruptly withdrew her hand to fidget with her spoon.

"I haven't anything to wear."

"Janette can remedy that, I'm sure. We'll pay her a visit this morning and explain our dilemma. She's had ample time to come up with something."

Ambrosia lowered her eyes and said nothing more, but her feelings were clear and Drayton understood them. It would not be pleasant to face a horde of curious, gossipy strangers who would make her the center of attention. And Drayton's hasty marriage to a Southern woman, after weeks of keeping constant company with Carolyn, would naturally stir speculation and gossip, gossip which had no doubt already reached Mrs. Sickles's ears and prompted this invitation.

Carolyn was another matter entirely. Drayton had little doubt that she was seething and anxious to confront him with her anger. He hadn't meant to humiliate her. He had never expected Ambrosia to enter his life again and had certainly not expected her pregnancy. He had involved himself with Carolyn for all the wrong reasons, and now he would have to be careful that Ambrosia was not caught in the cross fire when Carolyn vented her anger. Still, he was not about to turn down the invitation from the general and his wife. Facing gossip squarely was the only way to silence it. Ambrosia's pregnancy was not yet evident, and by the time it was, Drayton hoped to be far from Charleston. He'd formally requested a new assignment even before making final arrangements for the wedding and had spoken with General Sickles personally about being assigned to Atlanta or New Orleans. But he would not be hiding from the world until those new orders came through. Like it or not, Ambrosia would have to reconcile herself to her new role as his wife.

Ambrosia rose and left the table without protesting Drayton's decision, but the thought of socializing with Yankee soldiers and their women filled her with dread. And Drayton's own words only reinforced her worst fears. He wanted to show her off. They would all believe she had seen the light of salvation and obtained protection and security by marrying a handsome Union officer. There was just enough truth in the notion to make her feel sick with guilt. She had, after all, surrendered her freedom and her dignity in return for a name for her child. But she was not one of them. She would never be one of them!

Madame Loreau listened sympathetically as Drayton explained his wife's situation, then shrugged her slender shoulders and gave him a sly smile. "But of course! I have been working on ze gowns so much already! Ze first is nearly finished, ze silk," she went on happily, relieved that Drayton had returned to the shop with his wife. She felt certain that he would see that his wife ordered a few more gowns at least, and in appropriate colors. Major Rambert was a generous man, and he wouldn't want his wife to look like a widow! "Wait here," she said, sliding a palm up his chest. She flashed him a smile and crooked a finger at Ambrosia. "Come in ze back an we will do ze final fit."

In the tiny back room, Ambrosia donned the sheerest chemise she could imagine and added several lovely starched petticoats that felt wonderfully new and luxurious. Madame Loreau's forehead puckered as she inserted a thousand pins to hold the various pieces of black silk and lace in place. Sometime later, Ambrosia gingerly turned to have a look in the glass. Her hand flew instinctively to her breast, and she could hardly restrain a gasp of surprise. The dress was elegantly simple, subtly designed to draw attention to Ambrosia's womanly assets. Four braces of delicate black lace stretched from shoulder to tightly cinched waist, and a touch of the same lace edged the throat. Yards of black silk fell in loose folds from a stylish fourreau skirt. The French woman raised a self-satisfied brow. Even in black, Ambrosia's skin carried a youthful glow, her eyes were luminous as a cat's, and her figure was alluring and graceful. "Madame Rambert is pleased?"

Ambrosia gave a small nod. She had not had a new gown in years, not since she was a thin, shapeless girl, and she was amazed at the changes now as she looked in the mirror. It was like seeing herself for the very first time. She touched her cheek and then the soft folds of the skirt, trying to convince herself that this was all real. Madame began working with her hair, pulling it back and fastening it with an ornamental net of gossamer black and silver. A thin black velvet ribbon at the throat and a pair of black satin slippers completed the ensemble. Ambrosia felt all but transformed.

She held her breath as she stepped out of the back room, feeling giddy and excited as a girl at her first ball.

"Your bride—she is so—so—"

Drayton's blue eyes locked with Ambrosia's and he gave her a slow, deliberate smile. "Lovely, Janette," he supplied huskily. Ambrosia's cheeks flooded with color. But he abruptly turned away from her to face the French woman again. "But I'm disappointed with the black. I had thought of green, or blue, something bright and—"

"Ah! *Oui!* But Drayton"—Madame gave an exaggerated shrug of helplessness—"your bride, she orders only ze four gowns. And all of zem in black. Such a pity! It is not her color, black."

Drayton's disbelieving eyes flew to Ambrosia's and the animation in her expression vanished. She had forgotten for a moment, in a flurry of excitement over her new dress, who and what she was. For a moment she had actually wanted to see the pleasure in his eyes. How had she forgotten that he was a Yankee, and that she was a Lanford? She bowed her head, vowing that she would not forget again. "I am in mourning for my father, Drayton," she said quietly.

"Your father died over a year ago," he returned with a growl.

She lifted her chin and her eyes were bright and cold. "I still grieve for him. And for my home."

Her home. Drayton's eyes grew every bit as cold as hers at the reminder. She would not forget. And she had not forgiven him for his part and probably never would forgive him. She would wear her bitterness like a banner, announcing her hatred to his friends before she even gave them a chance.

"Janette, would it be possible to finish another gown by tomorrow night?" His eyes remained locked with Ambrosia's as he spoke, and he felt a certain satisfaction at the anger that flared in them at his request. "Something bright and fashionable, like the other women are wearing?" Ambrosia actually winced at that.

"I—I do not know—" Janette responded, tapping a forefinger to her pouting lips. "Even if I were to work very hard . . . if I were to drop everyzing else . . ."

"I will not wear it, Drayton." Ambrosia's tone was so sharp that Madame's eyes widened in shock. .

"You are my wife," Drayton returned slowly, his voice edged in steel. "You will wear what I tell you to wear. If I have to bind you hand and foot and dress you myself.''

To Madame's astonishment, Ambrosia squared her shoulders. "That is exactly what you will have to do."

Madame held her breath. Drayton's frown went black, and for several moments the room was so fraught with the clash of their emotions that the French woman stepped backward and cringed. She was certain that Drayton would strike his wife, and he would be perfectly justified in doing so. Madame had never seen a woman display such blatant disrespect for her husband's authority before.

To Madame's total bewilderment, Drayton suddenly turned away from his wife. "Finish the black dress for tomorrow, Janette," he ordered softly.

She tried to conceal her shock as she gave him an uncertain nod. His eyes were on his wife again, and his voice sounded calm, though the strain of keeping it so showed clearly on his face. "I yield to you in this, Ambrosia, but only because it is too late for Janette to begin another gown. I warn you now that in the future I will not be so likely to make concessions." He paused, his eyes holding hers as if to emphasize what he had said.

"I will send Sheba for you in an hour or so," he went on curtly. "I suddenly recall some unfinished business I must attend to."

Without another word he left the shop, leaving Ambrosia and the stunned Frenchwoman staring after him.

Chapter 25

The house was vaguely familiar to Ambrosia, though she did not really remember the last time she had been there, attending a party for Ledger and Melissa five years before. The odd feeling of familiarity coupled with Drayton's stiff restraint made her feel uneasy from the moment she stepped inside. She did her best to ignore the scores of curious eyes which suddenly riveted on her, the hushed comments that buzzed behind the fancy fans as the ladies noticed her gown. She met the onlookers with a look of defiant courage as she stood beside her husband. It was a look Drayton had come to know well. She nodded a cool greeting to Colonel Beam, who came forward to take her hand. "I had a feeling you'd be facing the vultures tonight," she heard him say to Drayton. "You've caused quite a sensation, you know."

Drayton had no chance to respond, for Mrs. Sickles, a rather plain Italian woman dressed in a hideous yellow gown, came forward. Ambrosia nodded but did not return the woman's smile. In the hours that followed Drayton introduced her to a hundred officers and their wives, to treasury officials, to men who worked for the Freedman's Bureau. Many of the faces were familiar from her work at Maggie's; a few of the women were openly hostile, curiously eyeing her gown and asking themselves

279

what on earth Drayton Rambert saw in her. But none seemed so threatening as Carolyn Craig, the pretty brunette who had obviously been Drayton's favorite these past months, the same girl Ambrosia had seen with him at the market. Ambrosia attempted a dignified posture of indifference when Carolyn leaned forward to finger Drayton's collar, exposing a generous view of her breasts. Ambrosia pretended not to notice the way Carolyn smiled up at him, giggling and chatting. She told herself she did not really care, but relief flooded her when her husband made an excuse and led her off toward another group of soldiers. At least he had spared her the ultimate humiliation by offering the woman no encouragement.

For a time it appeared that Ambrosia would survive the evening without incident. Though she scarcely said a word to the ladies who attempted to draw her into conversation and coldly refused all invitations to dance, Drayton adeptly managed to steer her away from Carolyn all but once, and to avoid anyone who might broach a topic any more controversial than the weather. But when Mrs. Sickles accosted him and insisted he bring his bride to the private parlor to meet a few of her husband's closest friends, Drayton had no ready excuse and reluctantly complied. Mrs. Sickles chatted happily as she led them into the room, introduced them to her husband and the others, and saw them seated comfortably near the general. They were there only moments when the conversation took an ominous turn toward politics, but Drayton could think of no graceful way to make a quick exit.

It began with talk about the "courageous leadership" of Thaddeus Stevens, the man who had effectively crushed South Carolina's hopes of quick reentry into the Union. In accordance with President Johnson's plan for Reconstruction, ten Southern states under their provisional governors had held elections and framed new state constitutions repudiating secession and affirming the abolition of slavery. Though many Southerners then naively supposed that Reconstruction was complete, the nightmare was only beginning. The radical Congress which met in Washington in December of 1865 refused to seat claimants sent by any of the new Southern governments, and worked diligently to replace the President's plan with a much stiffer, much more demanding method of Reconstruction aimed at breaking the strength of the Southern Democrats. Included in the Congressional plan was the mandatory ratification of the Fourteenth amendment, which conferred citizenship on Negroes and disqualified from public life any person who had ever taken an oath to support the Constitution and subsequently supported secession.

Drayton was relieved when Ambrosia clamped her mouth shut and lowered her eyes. In the face of such a heated debate, no one seemed to notice her tightly clenched fists or the slight flare to her nostrils that clearly showed her agitation.

"It is ridiculous to place power in the hands of the same men who caused the war! Any man who held public office before the rebellion ought to have been loyal to his country and rejected the idea of secession. Any who supported it are traitors and they will always be traitors." The man's face was a familiar one to Ambrosia, as well as his fancy clothes and blustery manner. He was a carpetbagger, like thousands of others who had come here in the past year, anxious to rape the prostrate South as she lay helpless from the ravages of war.

"Why, in heaven's name, did we fight for four years if not to liberate the Negro and to insure his rights as a citizen?" asked a balding Sergeant Lane.

"Come, come! You can't mean to give an ignorant fieldhand the right to vote!" This comment from one of the wives.

"Not ignorant for long," the carpetbagger corrected. "The bureau's working hard to educate them."

"Yes." Colonel Beam nodded wryly. "They're being taught—to vote Republican."

"As well they should," the carpetbagger retorted, ignoring the laughter Beam's remark had generated. "They ought to know which side their bread's buttered on. We're trying to help the colored get what they've got coming to them, after all the years of bondage. And we won't let these highfalutin white folks off the hook for their crimes just because they took an oath. Anyone who would fight a war to keep an entire race in chains is totally without conscience."

"But if you disqualify those men who held office before the war, and take into account the number of men who died, who is left? Who will pick up the pieces of this sorry, battle-scarred land and rebuild it? Who will rule?" demanded Beam.

"The freedmen will rule," returned the carpetbagger, "and they'll do a damned good job of it too."

There were several outraged gasps at that, resulting both from the man's coarse choice of words in the presence of ladies and the radical viewpoint he had expressed.

"Gentlemen, gentlemen," cooed a sweet, indulgent voice. Ambrosia's eyes lifted at the sound, and she faced the pretty, smiling face of Carolyn Craig. She had entered the room just moments before and she was intent on becoming the center of attention. "None of us really knows all that much about the Negroes," she said softly, meeting each pair of gentleman's eyes with a sweet, captivating gaze. "Who knows if they are able and competent, as some tell us, or shiftless and ignorant, as others say? I mean, none of us has ever actually lived with any of them"—her eyes hardened, though her smile and tone remained innocent—"except perhaps Drayton's bride." She turned to Ambrosia and gave an expectant lift of her brow. "Do tell us, Ambrosia, did you actually own slaves?"

Ambrosia cringed inwardly at the woman's use of her familiar name, but her face was perfectly calm. "Yes."

Carolyn feigned shock and a murmur of disapproval

went up from the crowd. Then suddenly all was very quiet.

"Well, tell us! Were you forced to beat them often?" Carolyn smiled at her own cleverness. "Do you think them competent enough to hold public office?"

Ambrosia laced her fingers primly at her waist and seemed at ease. "The Negroes I have known have been at least as intelligent as the Northerners who are so anxious to put them in office," she responded coolly. "If there is one thing I've learned from you Yankees, Mrs. Craig, it's that ignorance is not limited to any one race."

The murmurs of indignation stirred the otherwise silent room. "And what of those who supported the rebellion?" Carolyn pressed, sensing that this woman would easily condemn herself with a few more rash statements.

"Yes," interjected the carpetbagger. "What of those who aided in the slaughter of thousands of loyal Union men? Men like your husband? Do you think it fair to let them off scot-free, demanding nothing more than the taking of a simple oath of loyalty?"

Ambrosia's eyes burned with indignation. "I know of not a single man who has been let off scot-free," she returned sharply. "Most have suffered far worse than anyone here could even imagine. If you think otherwise, then you know nothing of the destruction of those four years, of the burning and looting and—"

"Are you saying that the Rebels have suffered enough?" the carpetbagger cut in incredulously. "That you believe an oath erases all their crimes?"

Ambrosia lifted her chin and purposely ignored the hand which suddenly gripped her arm. "I believe," she began, avoiding the warning in Drayton's eyes, "that the taking of such an oath is the greatest crime of all, sir. To swear allegiance to one's enemy is an unforgivable crime of betrayal—a betrayal of conscience, a betrayal of loyalty to one's self."

"Do you mean that you have not taken the oath?" Carolyn burst out in a shrill voice. Her eyes flashed with excitement.

Ambrosia met Drayton's eyes and saw them narrow with barely restrained temper. But she never even considered sidestepping the question for his sake. She was glad of the opportunity to remind him what she was. "I am proud to say that I have not," she announced succinctly.

Several women in the room blanched and waved their fans or lacy handkerchiefs furiously before their noses. The men stood aghast. A Rebel in their midst! A woman who refused to take the oath! Who actually referred to them as the enemy! General Sickles rose with a dark scowl and met Drayton's eyes with a look that spelled trouble. Carolyn saw that look and could not hold back a triumphant smile. Drayton's bride could not have done a better job of hanging herself, of ruining her husband's position with the army in Charleston.

Nothing more was said as Mrs. Sickles graciously directed her guests to the music room, where the daughter of a colonel on the general's staff was persuaded to show off her skill as an accomplished pianist. Drayton took the opportunity to mouth regrets to the host and hostess and effect a hasty departure. He did not receive any argument.

Drayton's eyes were hard and impassive as he stared straight ahead. His lean, gloved hands gripped the reins tightly as he guided the buggy through the streets. A brief, sidelong glance told Ambrosia that he was still terribly angry. A tiny muscle near his temple twitched erratically as he struggled to restrain himself, and his teeth were clamped hard on a long, unlit cigar. Let him be angry, she told herself. She had been a reluctant intruder at that party anyway, forced to play out a pointless, nerve-wracking charade. She had not deliberately sought a forum to publicize her beliefs. But she had not backed away from a confrontation, and she had not been willing to lie, just to win the approval of Drayton's friends. If he had expected her to do that, then he fully deserved to be disappointed.

He pulled back hard on the reins and brought the buggy to a too-quick stop before the house. Ambrosia braced herself and stole another glance at him, wondering if he would behave tonight as he had the evening before, after the altercation at the dressmaker's shop. What little conversation they had shared at dinner and afterward had been polite, yet stilted and false. Neither had spoken of the incident that weighed so heavily on their minds. When they retired he had turned away, leaving her to stare at the broad, sinewy muscles of his back until she fell asleep.

Ambrosia averted her eyes when Drayton lithely slipped from the buggy and turned to assist her, but she could not keep a frown from tugging at her brow when she felt his hands encircle her waist. She reminded herself that she ought to be relieved, even grateful for his anger, his coldness. There was security to be found in keeping him at arm's length. She was already frightened enough by the power he held over her.

She lifted her chin and strode haughtily toward the house, aware that he followed close behind her. He nodded brusquely to Sheba but did not pause, did not even say a word until they were safely in the confines of their own room. Ambrosia took a seat at her vanity and gazed absently at her reflection. She removed the ornamental net from her hair and ran her fingers nervously through the long, black strands that fell about her shoulders. Drayton stood beside her, staring at her for a long moment as he removed his gloves. All at once he slapped them hard against the vanity. Ambrosia winced. His voice rang sharply in the otherwise silent room. "You can't forget for a single moment, can you?"

Without turning to face him, Ambrosia met his eyes in the mirror. They were threatening, accusing, like chips of polished sapphire. She swallowed hard and looked away.

"You don't even want to forget, do you?" he flung at her. "You enjoyed humiliating me tonight, enjoyed flaunting your arrogant Southern heritage in front of their noses!" He let out a short, frustrated sigh and turned away, running a hand roughly through his hair "I've tried to understand you, to understand what you've lost, to be patient with you. But you've built a wall around yourself that doesn't let patience and understanding inside. You despise me for breaking through that wall once, don't you? You hate me because I know that you were in love with him, because I saw how much he hurt you."

Ambrosia's face tensed, her lips trembling violently. He met her eyes in the mirror again, his nostrils flaring. "Sometimes I think you actually feed on the memories of what's happened to you. You don't want anyone to pity you or even to care for you. You just want to be left alone so you can draw some perverse pleasure from your bitterness and your hate, don't you?" He gripped her shoulders hard and spun her about roughly to face the accusation. "Don't you?"

"Yes!" she screamed at him, her eyes every bit as hard as his. "Yes!" she screamed again. "Did you really expect me to forget? Did you really think I would ever forgive you for what you did to my home? I despise you even more than the rest of them—you and your little acts of charity. I hate you more every time you touch me!"

Suddenly there was a desperation in his eyes, the look of a man grasping, groping, fighting for something to hold on to. "My God . . ." he whispered.

He released her slowly, his eyes still searching, still not wanting to believe what he saw. And then his face hardened, and he turned away and was gone.

Chapter 26

Drayton's hand poised uncertainly above the letter he'd just written for a long moment before his mouth set with determination and he hurriedly affixed his signature to the document. He tossed the pen aside and leaned back in the chair, pressing the heels of his hands to his eyes. It had taken him all night and half a bottle of whiskey, but the decision was finally made. He was going home.

Home . . . the word still held too many memories for him, ghosts of a past he had run from for six long years. But there would be no more running. There was a child to consider now, a child he would not see born in the midst of hate and destruction, a child whose future must be secure. And there was no security in his present situation. If anything were to happen to him here, Ambrosia and the child would be alone, with no one to turn to. Besides, Ambrosia would rather starve than turn to anyone for help.

Drayton vented a sigh as he rose to cup his hand over the chimney of the desk lamp, extinguishing the light with a quick breath. He gathered up his things and left his office, placing the letter of resignation in the center of the corporal's cluttered desk on his way out of the building. The cool moist air of morning might have felt pleasant on his face as he mounted his impatient stallion and reined in the direction of the house, had he not felt so defeated. He had been so sure that he could reach her, so certain that it was only a matter of time and patience and love. In desperation and need, he had used his superior strength and his knowledge of physical love in a pathetic attempt to reach her, to make her care. But the brief, physical release he felt after imposing his will, or after seducing her, only ate away at his pride and degraded him as a man in his own eyes. He had been a fool to believe that she would ever care for him. The truth had been in her eyes last night, and what he had seen there had forced him to face reality. There would be no reaching her; and he was no longer sure he wanted to.

But there was still the child. His child. A seed of love that grew within her in spite of her hatred. For the sake of that child, he would return to the home he'd left years before, to the aunt who had cared for him as a boy, to the memories. . . .

The streets were all but empty just before dawn. A few peddlers could be heard in the distance, shuffling about as they loaded their carts for the day's vending. The birds were just beginning to rouse one another with their noisy chatter. Drayton slowed the stallion's pace as he neared the house, wondering what she would say when he informed her of his plans. She would not want to leave the South, he knew. But she was his wife and legally she had no choice. He intended to give her no choice.

He took his time stabling the stallion before he entered the house. He was tired and anxious to have the thing over and done with. He steeled himself as he strode resolutely up the steps. The sooner he confronted her with the news, the sooner he would be able to sleep.

The eastern sky was softly etched with silver gray when Ambrosia opened her eyes and turned her head to stare out the bedroom window. She propped her weight on a single elbow and punched hard at the pillow before she settled her cheek against it again. The night had been long, and morning refused to come. She closed her eyes again and waited, forcing herself to think about trivial, boring things . . . the draperies she would choose for the parlor, the furniture pieces she would need to finish the spare bedroom. . . .

"Swimp! Ro, ro, Swimp!"

The vibrant, melodious cries of Negro venders broke the silence of the early morning. A new day had finally begun. Ambrosia rose and went to the window, breathing a sigh as she leaned forward against the sill. He had left her alone hours ago. She had watched him leave with a feeling of relief and triumph. It was what she had wanted. And yet she had seen something in his eyes that had made it all wrong.

"Porgy! Porgie-e-e-e!"

The familiar Gullah chants rang out across the streets. She listened for a time. And then there was another sound. The sound of heavy footfalls on the stairs, the click of the door latch. She spun about.

She eyed him uneasily for a long moment. She was embarrassed at being found awake and about at such an early hour. It was far too obvious that she had not slept well. But if Drayton was surprised at finding her awake he gave no sign. His face told her nothing.

He shed his tunic as he crossed to the opposite side of the room. He loosened his collar and rolled back the sleeves of his blouse to splash his face with cool water. Ambrosia perched a hip tentatively on the sill and watched him in silence. She wondered, in spite of herself, where he had spent the night. He dried his face and hands on a clean linen towel which he tossed back on the washstand before he turned to face her. The lovely, butterscotch rays of the sun stretched across the room and bronzed his dark, chiseled features. He was incredibly handsome even now, when fatigue and tension were etched clearly in his face.

"I came to a decision tonight," he said as he impatiently rolled down the sleeves of his blouse. "A decision that affects you as much as me."

Ambrosia's eyes were wary. "What decision is that?"

"I turned in a letter of resignation to General Sickles this morning. I'm going home."

Her jaw dropped for an instant. "Home?" she repeated in a small voice.

He nodded. "That's right. Home. To New York."

She stared at him dumbly for a long time, struggling to find her voice. "You—you're joking."

He gave a tight smile. "I can assure you I'm quite serious." He searched his tunic pocket for his last cigar.

She took a step toward him, still certain she must have misunderstood. She had expected him to be angry, but he did not seem angry at all. He seemed indifferent. "B-but you don't really expect me to go there!"

He said nothing but eyed her significantly as he bit off the end of the cigar and reached for a match. Ambrosia felt a cold knot tightening in her stomach. "You actually expect me to live there?" she whispered in horror. "To raise my child a Yankee!"

His eyes narrowed and brightened as he slowly expelled a cloud of aromatic smoke from his first draw on the cigar. "You're forgetting that the child is already a Yankee."

She straightened abruptly, almost as if he'd slapped her. "I won't go."

"Yes, you will."

She clenched her fists, her breath coming hard. "No, I won't."

"You are my wife, Ambrosia," he said softly. He took a seat in a nearby chair and stretched his long legs out comfortably before him, his eyes never leaving hers.

She clenched her teeth, all the more angered by his surface nonchalance. "You'd have to put me in chains and drive me with a whip every step of the way!" she ground out.

He flicked an ash to the floor, and something in his

eyes made the tiny hairs at the nape of her neck stand on end. "At the moment, I can think of nothing that would give me more pleasure."

Her eyes were wide and stunned; he seemed not to notice. "I have finished playing the part of doting husband, my dear. It was a role that never really suited me in the first place. From now on, you will do exactly what I tell you to do. And if you choose to be difficult . . ." He paused to take a long draw on his cigar. "I'll force you. It's that simple." He drew one last time on the cigar before he tossed it into a brass spittoon that stood in a corner some distance away. "Once the baby is born, you will be free to leave me. I won't stop you."

"You expect me to leave my own child!" she gasped.

He shrugged noncommittally. "The decision will be yours at that point."

Her eyes narrowed. "I could leave you now if I wanted to. You'd never find me."

"Don't bet on it. The law is on my side now that you are my wife. If I have to, I'll use it. And do not doubt, Ambrosia, that I have both the will and the means to use it effectively."

"Are you threatening me?"

"No. Just stating a fact. If you choose to test me— well . . ." He shrugged and a challenging smile played about his mouth. "That is your choice. But I warn you, Ambrosia. There will be no more games."

She stared at him for a long time, wondering if there was any chance he was bluffing. He was so dangerously calm, almost as he had been that day at Heritage when he'd held a gun on that Yankee colonel and dared him to call his bluff. She had known then that he would not hesitate to pull the trigger. And she knew now that he meant every word he said. She frowned in confusion and gnawed pensively at her lower lip, realizing just how vulnerable she had become. There was no denying his right to the child. Nor could she truly hope to escape him now, with nowhere to run, no one to whom she could turn for help. It hurt to admit it, but the truth was obvious. He held the upper hand.

"What of Sheba?" she asked suddenly, her voice much smaller and almost childlike.

"She'll come along, if she wants to."

Ambrosia swallowed hard and turned away to face the open window, to gaze at the blazing sun rising over the familiar roofs of Charleston. She was afraid of leaving the South, afraid of being lost in a strange place filled with strange people she already despised.

She closed her eyes and let out an anguished breath as her hand pressed instinctively to the curve of her stomach that was a new life. A bitterness welled inside her. The Yankees had taken everything from her. And now this . . .

She opened her eyes and lifted her chin, blinking back the tears. This child was hers, far more her flesh and blood than his, she was certain of it. And somehow, even if she was forced to leave here, to live among Yankees, she would raise that child to be strong and courageous, and to love the South as much as she loved it. And she would never let Drayton know that she was afraid, or think for a moment that he had broken her. She would never be broken by anything he or any Yankee did to her. Never.

Part Three
New York
May 1866

Chapter 27

On the second day of May, Ambrosia and Drayton departed the city of Charleston. Susannah and Mary were there to see them off, as were Colonel Beam and a pair of soldiers whose names Ambrosia did not trouble herself to remember. With Sheba beside her, she stared absently at the trunk which held all her worldly possessions as it was carried onto the ship that would take them to New York. She felt hopelessly trapped and very much afraid. At times she felt as if she were caught in a tidal wave, being thrown and tossed about with nothing to latch on to.

The cabin she shared with Drayton was clean but small and cramped for two people on less than friendly terms. Ambrosia avoided it almost entirely that first day, spending hours alone on deck, feeling the moist, salty air on her face as she watched the last remnants of familiarity slip away. The first hours seemed to pass with agonizing slowness. After that the miles of water and coastline seemed nothing more than a monotonous blur, and she endured the hours of traveling, of meals, of dressing and undressing, with little conscious thought given to where she was or how much longer it would be before they reached their destination. She was glad that Drayton left her alone for the most part, glad that Sheba said very little. She needed to be alone, needed time to sort out her feelings. She was so confused, so terribly afraid of losing control of her emotions. She willed herself to be strong, just as she had always done. But a part of her was succumbing to the loneliness, to the grief of past losses she had never come to terms with. It was becoming more and more difficult to hold herself together, but she could not afford to forget that she was a Lanford, that she was strong. She had plenty of hatred inside her to make her strong.

In his starched white shirt and black broadcloth suit, Drayton was a polite but distant stranger, just as he had been in the weeks before their departure. He saw to her comfort but avoided conversing with her, even avoided meeting her eyes. Though they continued to share a bed, he never touched her. He never retired before midnight, long after she had gone to sleep, and he rose early and was generally gone before she woke, though he always returned to the cabin to accompany her to breakfast, luncheon, and dinner. His days were spent socializing with the sailors and other passengers. The strain of keeping up appearances began to show on his face, but Ambrosia did not notice. After only two days of confinement, she was restless, irritable, and angry. She blamed Drayton for everything, since he had made her a virtual prisoner. She hated him for that as well as for his cold indifference to her, especially since he was all charm in the company of others. He was a popular gentleman on the ship, attentive and polite to everyone but her and obviously very attractive to the ladies. Ambrosia felt curious eyes upon her whenever she was at his side, measuring her, dissecting her piece by piece, wondering how in the world her handsome, dashing husband had made such a terrible mistake. Day after day she would return their stares with her head held high, enduring the false smiles and the insults in their eyes with less and less patience and restraint. Her wall of defiant control was beginning to fail her and that frightened her. She was not accustomed to being afraid of what she felt inside. She could not live like this; she must somehow escape.

The idea took firm root in her mind during the endless days she spent in the cabin. She thought of taking a small portion of his money, just enough to get a good distance away, and of returning to the South before the baby was born. She could support herself; she had already proven that. She did not dwell on the fact that her pregnancy would make things much more difficult, or what her decision would mean to the child. She only knew that she had to escape or go completely mad. She must plan her escape, though she had never been outside of South Carolina and did not really know what to expect in New York. She had heard that it was a much bigger city than Charleston, and that would make it much easier for her to get away. But she would need to be very, very careful. Once she left Drayton, he must never find her again.

After seven days of quiet sailing with only a hint of a coastline visible from the deck, the voyage ended in a scene of unimaginable confusion in New York's busy harbor. Ambrosia's eyes were dazed as she glanced about at the frenzy that surrounded her. The idea of escape was momentarily pushed to the back of her mind. The place was beyond anything she'd ever imagined. Every inch of space was packed with people or ships or barrels or bales or carts. Sailors and longshoremen shouted loudly at one another as they worked in an effort to be heard above the mad cacophony of animals and people.

Somehow Drayton managed to hire a wagon into which a strange-looking man with a thick foreign accent loaded their possessions. Drayton helped her to a seat, then aided Sheba as she climbed into the back of the wagon. The funny little man squeezed himself into the seat beside Drayton and Ambrosia and sang out a long string of unintelligible orders to his horse. The wagon was promptly submersed in a tangle of traffic the likes of which Ambrosia had never seen before. Her eyes darted everywhere as the driver somehow managed to inch his conveyance through a snarl of public busses, private broughams, wagons, buggies, carts, equestrians, and pedestrians. So many buildings towered overhead that Ambrosia instinctively huddled lower in her seat. The streets were crammed with huge, imposing structures of granite, marble, and brownstone, and rows of horrible cramped tenements with waste-strewn walks. Dirty-faced children scattered to avoid the traffic. How easy it would be in a place such as this! she thought suddenly. Her eyes began to survey the passing buildings with a purpose now, trying to imagine what she would do when she finally escaped.

Drayton was in a world of his own as he contemplated the city he had left almost seven years before. So many things had changed in his absence. Once-fashionable homes had been sold and left to the poor and the aged. Poverty and its accompanying filth and disease had crept like a cancer northward. Everywhere he looked his eyes met a strange blend of things old and new, of the same crowded streets he remembered shadowed by taller, newer buildings, or cluttered with garbage and decrepit structures badly in need of repair.

The wagon took them across the island to the west side, where they boarded a train at the Hudson River Station. The train proceeded northward, up the western side of the island into open land, woods and farm country with sudden clusters of shanties and taverns and an occasional small farm or wealthy gentleman's country estate. The high land overlooking the Hudson boasted several lovely residences, but many of these had been converted into inns or pubs.

The train's last stop was a small village, a haphazard collection of shops, houses, and taverns that seemed to have been generated spontaneously by the train's turnabout. Drayton was acquainted with several people in the village, including the man who ran the livery. He was able to quickly secure a horse and wagon, and they were soon traveling along an unpaved, narrow lane which the stableman had called Bloomingdale Road. Trees were thick all along the road, forming a green canopy that filtered out most of the sun's brightness. All was quiet. The air was much crisper and cleaner here than in the city, almost like the air at Heritage. Ambrosia drew a deep breath and sighed as her eyes scanned a meadow with walls of fieldstone and old rail fencing. For a moment it reminded her of home. And yet she knew each mile they traveled took her that much farther from home and made escape that much less likely. She would have to get into the city somehow. Once she was there, Drayton would have no hope of ever finding her.

Drayton said nothing as he turned the wagon off the road onto an even smaller lane which wound about and upward until a huge, two-and-a-half-story red brick house came into view. Six imposing white columns spanned the front of the house, and several great elm trees seemed to embrace it from the side and back. There was a graceful line to the soft grass and trimmed shrubs, and even in the small curl of smoke that rose from one of the chimneys. Ambrosia tossed a questioning glance at Drayton as he pulled the wagon to a halt and shifted the reins to a single hand, securing them about the seat. She stared at the house again, hearing the quiet rustle of the wind through the trees, the rush of a nearby creek. This was his home. This was the life he had left behind to go to war years before. And in all that time, this place had remained untouched and beautiful, as Heritage had once been. She hated the sight of it.

Without a word Drayton jumped down and turned to assist his wife. There was a tenseness to his manner when he touched her, and he quickly turned away to help Sheba from the back of the wagon. He came to take Ambrosia's arm, to lead her to the door. He knocked. He waited barely a moment before he knocked again, more impatiently this time. He raised his fist a third time. The door flew open and a short, round-faced maid with a lacy white cap perched crookedly atop a mass of brown corkscrew curls gazed at them breathlessly. She opened her mouth, then closed it again, her eyes wide with the shock of recognition. "My heavens! It's you! You've come home!"

Drayton grinned at her as he gave a polite nod. "Good afternoon, Bessie. Is Aunt Lily at home?"

"Home? Of course she's home!"

Bessie stepped forward, and in a flurry of emotion stretched her arms to take hold of both his shoulders. She gave him a thorough perusal. "You really have come home!" she exclaimed again. "Miss Lily will be so happy she'll—" Her smile faded as her gaze slid toward the young woman in black who stood beside Drayton in serious silence. Behind her stood a large black woman with warmer eyes but a similar unsmiling face. Self-consciously Bess released her motherly hold on Drayton and straightened her cap. She cleared her throat. "You brought along guests, sir?" she inquired in a tone of perfect respect.

Drayton tossed a glance at Ambrosia. "Not exactly, Bessie. This is my wife."

"Your wife!" she squeaked, her eyes all but popping. A moment later she managed a smile. "Yes, sir. Your wife," she said in a much calmer tone. "Well, come in, come in. . . ." She swiftly stepped aside and held the door open. "Miss Lily's in the library, sir."

As they were ushered toward the library, Ambrosia's eyes scanned a foyer papered in gold leaf on ivory; a long, curving staircase of ornately carved dark wood which wound to a great picture window on the second-floor landing.

The library door stood slightly ajar. Bessie paused at the doorway, her eyes darting uncertainly from Drayton's to Ambrosia's and back again. "She'll be wanting to see you right away, I'm sure, sir. Just ring if you need anything." She gave a swift curtsy and left Drayton and Ambrosia to announce themselves.

"Bessie! Is that you?" A soft, melodic voice rose from

the library as Drayton opened the door. The woman sat behind a huge mahogany desk, her glowing white head bent in deep concentration over a letter she was writing.

"It's not Bessie, Aunt Lily."

At the sound of his voice, her head shot up and the pen dropped from her hand. "Good Lord!"

Ambrosia remained at the door as Drayton rounded the desk and bent to embrace his aunt warmly. She was a strikingly beautiful woman, younger than Ambrosia had pictured her to be. Her features were delicate and fine. Her hair was snowy white, but a pair of piercing blue eyes edged with tiny laugh lines at the corners reminded Ambrosia very much of Drayton. She watched as the woman's eyes filled with tears as she drew back to gaze at him with obvious devotion. "You—you look well," Ambrosia heard her say in a tight voice. Lily wiped away a tear. "Handsome as ever . . ." The woman's fingers trembled as she brushed tenderly at his hair. "Thank God you've finally come home!" she whispered.

Drayton's arms went around her a second time, holding her tightly against himself, his face twisting with emotion. Ambrosia unconsciously straightened her stance. She did not belong here, watching this Yankee come home from the war. She couldn't help but remember the day Ledger had come home, the way she had wanted to hold him as Drayton now held his aunt.

It seemed an eternity before he released her, and the two stared at one another with ever-deepening smiles. "You might have given me some warning, Drayton, after all this time." Her eyes caught sight of Ambrosia then and were suddenly full of questions.

"Aunt Lily, I'd like you to meet my wife, Ambrosia. Ambrosia, my aunt, Lily Collinsworth."

Ambrosia gave a cold nod and made no move to step forward. Lily smiled at her from her seat, then reached to take hold of a cane which had been propped against her chair. She rose to a pair of shaky feet. With slow, halting movements, she came toward Ambrosia and paused to

extend a hand which shook all the more as she attempted
to hold it steady. "I am so very happy to meet you, my
dear," she smiled.

Ambrosia took hold of the hand briefly, trying to hide
her surprise at the woman's crippled legs and trembling
arms. "Thank you, Mrs. Collinsworth."

"It's Lily to you, my dear." She flashed Drayton a
suspicious glare. "Drayton did not tell me that he had
married, but I could not be happier. Of course, you will
stay here—"

"For a little while," Drayton cut in. "Until we can
move into a place of our own."

Lily was smiling again. "Are you hungry? Of course
you are. But more exhausted than hungry, I'm sure.
Come along to the parlor. I'll have Sarah serve an early
tea and tell Bessie to see to your rooms. But once you're
rested, I'll want to find out everything about you, my
dear. Everything! You are such a pleasant surprise to me!
I cannot imagine why Drayton didn't write. . . ."

As her chatter continued, Ambrosia watched her struggle laboriously, painfully through the hallway toward the
parlor. Though her face contorted with concentration,
her pleasant conversation never ceased. Until she noticed
Sheba. "My word!" she exclaimed. "Who's this?"

She pivoted to glance at Ambrosia, then turned back to
Sheba. "Did you come with Ambrosia, my dear?" she
questioned the old black woman.

Sheba gave a solemn nod.

"Then we shall have to make you comfortable as well.
Come into the parlor so that I can demand a proper introduction."

The parlor was a pleasant room with light blue walls
and walnut rococo furniture upholstered in soft green velvet, a color echoed in the floral motif of the thick Persian
carpet and again in the silver-green draperies. True to her
word, Lily demanded an introduction to Sheba the moment she had settled herself in a high-backed parlor
chair.

"Sheba was the head cook for my family for nearly thirty years," Ambrosia told her. The black woman's eyes glowed with pride.

"A cook, you say?" Lily asked in some surprise. She had taken for granted that Sheba was the girl's personal maid.

Sheba gave a nod, and Ambrosia added, "One of the finest cooks in all the South."

"I am honored to welcome you to our household, Sheba. My cook is a woman named Sarah who complains constantly about the amount of work she's forced to do, and even more about the girl I hired to help her do it. Perhaps you would consider sharing duties with her for a little while . . . ?"

Sheba glanced at Ambrosia, requesting permission to agree, then gave a happy nod. She had missed her kitchen and would be pleased to be a cook again, even if it meant working with another woman.

"Ah! Here is Bessie now. Bessie, I want you to settle Sheba in a room near the kitchen. When she is comfortable, prepare the master suite for Drayton and his bride. Oh, and have Sarah bring in tea as soon as possible."

Bessie dropped a curtsy. "Yes, Miss Lily."

Ambrosia rose abruptly from the seat she had taken as Sheba made to leave the room. "I shall go along, if you don't mind. To see that Sheba is properly settled."

Lily had difficulty hiding her shock at Ambrosia's tactless insinuation. "I can assure you, my dear, that Bessie will see to her needs."

"All the same, I believe I will—"

"You will sit down, Ambrosia." Drayton's voice was low and cold in the sudden silence of the parlor. Her eyes clashed with his for a long, tense moment before she reluctantly stared at the floor and resumed her seat. Neither said another word.

Lily cleared her throat, troubled by the tension that was all too apparent between them. "I'm sure you must be starving," she began.

"Actually, I'm not hungry at all," Ambrosia said coldly. "We had breakfast on the ship."

"Breakfast!" Lily gasped. "What of lunch?"

Only the threatening look in Drayton's eyes made Ambrosia bite back a reply that, thanks to the Yankees, she and all Southerners had grown accustomed to doing without regular meals.

"I suppose tea and cakes will hold you both until dinner," Lily inserted in the uneasy silence. She cleared her throat again, aware that Ambrosia wanted no part of frivolous conversation. A few moments later an old, pinched woman with thin, silver hair pulled back severely in a small net at the nape of her neck entered the parlor with a tray of tea and sweets, which she gracefully placed on the serving table near Lily. "Shall I pour, Miss Lily?"

Lily met Ambrosia's cool green eyes for a moment, then shook her head. "Thank you, Sarah, no. I'm sure Ambrosia wouldn't mind pouring."

Ambrosia hid the irritation she felt at being tested so obviously by Drayton's aunt. For a moment she toyed with the idea of spilling the entire pot. Something in Drayton's eyes made her decide against that. Lily studied her openly as she accepted a cup of tea in her shaking hands with a half-nod of approval, then sipped at it daintily. The girl was no street urchin, surely. And her face was striking, beautiful in a way, even though she wore black and did not arrange her hair in a flattering style. Still, there was something in her eyes that troubled Lily. An anger . . . no. Something that went beyond anger, that was rooted deep in the girl's soul. Lily noticed that Drayton took a cup of tea from her without meeting her eyes and sipped at it without interest. Neither spoke or touched the platter of cakes that sat on the serving tray. After some space of time, Drayton set his cup aside and strode to the large parlor window to stare out on the familiar grounds. Lily's eyes softened as she considered him, forgetting his bride, remembering that long years ago, as a boy, he had stood at this window and gazed out on snow or rain. . . .

"It is good to have you home, Drayton," she said softly. "So very, very good!"

He turned to face her, a hint of a smile in his deep blue eyes. "It's good to be home, Lily. I've missed you," he sighed. He turned his eyes toward the window again. "Missed this place."

"The people hereabouts will be forming a line at the door when you hang out your shingle again. I don't know who will be first in that line—Mr. Brent with his gout or Bea Hanover with her headaches." She shook her head and gave a smile. "I've been listening to their complaints since the day you left. It will be a relief to let you handle them the way you used to. I remember once when Bea showed up at your door in the middle of the—"

"There won't be anyone coming to my door late at night, Lily," he broke in, his voice low. "I told you that a long time ago."

A tiny frown tugged at Ambrosia's brow at the comment, and she suddenly remembered the night at Heritage, the skillful way Drayton had wielded a knife and saved the lives of two men who otherwise would surely have died. She had known then that he was a doctor. Yet he had pointedly denied it. Now, though she told herself firmly that she didn't care, she wondered why, and she listened more closely.

Lily met her nephew's eyes with a challenging lift of her brow. "You are a doctor, Drayton. A very good one. You can't erase all the years of study and practice and turn your back on—"

"I'm not a little boy, Lily," he interrupted stiffly. "I know perfectly well what I can and cannot do."

She flinched at that, as if he'd insulted her. She flashed a sidelong glance at Ambrosia and noticed the hint of a puzzled frown on the younger woman's face, even as she stared at the floor. She let out a breath and shakily set her cup on a nearby table, wondering just how much Ambrosia knew about her husband's past. There was trouble between the two of them, that much was very apparent. Perhaps a part of Drayton's cold attitude had to do with his wife's presence. She forced a small smile. "Well, you are more than welcome to stay here with me, regardless of what you decide to do. I have missed you, Drayton."

The next quarter hour passed slowly, in a tedious test of Lily's patience as she alternately tried to draw the strange girl Drayton had married into polite conversation and attempted a similar feat with her nephew. Each proved totally impossible. She was relieved when Bessie entered and announced that their rooms had been prepared, and sought the solace of her garden the moment they left the parlor.

It was a wide, open garden that spanned the entire length of the house with a low, ivy-clad wall marking its boundaries. A maze of flagstone paths wound around the trees and flowerbeds, all tended by a slight old man named Jake, whose intimacy with growing things was obvious to everyone though he hardly ever spoke beyond a simple "good day." The flowers and plants he cultivated grew fuller and more colorful every spring, and Lily, who had taken so little time in her youth to notice the beauty in living things, now knew a devotion for her garden and often found comfort within the shelter of its low walls. This day, however, there was little peace to be found in the beauty she saw.

Drayton had come home. After all these years, he had come home, safe and sound. He had even brought a wife along, who was obviously with child. A wife! Lily had never expected him to marry again. But none of that erased the fact that something was very wrong between Drayton and the woman he had wed. Lily took a seat on a stone bench and stared at the willow tree, whose branches stirred like long tendrils of hair in the soft breeze. All of her hopes had been dashed by what she had seen in that young girl's eyes. And she could not rid herself of the fear that Drayton's dreams had been destroyed a second time by the very same thing.

Bess flounced her rounded body proudly up the staircase, anxious to show off the luxurious master suite that Lily had ordered prepared for Drayton and his bride. It had seen so little use since Lily's illness confined her to the first floor years before. Bess flung open the massive double doors and stood aside, eagerly awaiting the young woman's exclamations of delight. But instead Ambrosia strode silently into the sitting room and glanced about. If she was impressed by the richness of the carved mahogany furniture, by the lovely blend of royal blue carpets and draperies with cream-colored walls, she gave no sign.

Beyond the sitting room was a spacious bedroom of the same color scheme, and on one wall was a pair of French doors which opened onto a small terrace above the garden. Frowning a bit at her indifference, Bess stepped past Ambrosia and flung open a second, smaller door.

"Your private bath, ma'am," she announced with a lift of her chin. She was happy to see Ambrosia's eyes widen at that. She watched the younger woman enter the room, run her hand across the enameled tub, and curiously twist the brass knob from which water immediately flowed. Drayton stood at the doorway. "I trust everything is to your satisfaction?" he inquired with a slight smile.

Ambrosia withdrew her hand and straightened abruptly, angered by his mildly chiding tone. "All the trappings of a comfortable prison," she retorted.

Bess let out a startled gasp. "You may go, thank you, Bessie," Drayton said softly, though his eyes remained on his wife.

The stout woman bobbed a nervous curtsy. "Yes, sir. Emily will be up to help the missus dress for dinner, sir." She whirled about and hurried from the room, anxious to be away from the harsh words that were surely forthcoming, though she remained just outside with her ear pressed hard against the thick double doors.

For a long time there was only silence. Drayton stood motionless, eyeing his wife, his blue eyes aflame.

"Lily Collinsworth is a generous, loving woman," he articulated slowly, softly, "and I will not have you insulting her or any of her people ever again. Do you understand me?"

Ambrosia's eyes narrowed and she raised her chin a notch. Stubborn defiance was written all over her face. He took hold of her arm. "Do you understand me?" he repeated in an even softer voice.

She noticed that his teeth were clenched, that a tiny muscle in his jaw twitched with restraint. She did not care. The resentment that had churned during the endless days in that tiny ship's cabin had surfaced. She tried to twist free of his hold. He grasped both her arms then, hard. "I want your word that you will not insult anyone in this household again."

"Or what?" she flung back at him. "What will you do if I refuse to give it?"

For a long moment his fingers dug painfully into the flesh of her arms. "Don't tempt me, Ambrosia. It would be too easy for me to lock you away in a real prison."

Her eyes reflected enough fear at the threat to make him loosen his hold somewhat. "You are a guest in my aunt's home. As long as you are here, you will behave in a civil manner."

Her eyes were lowered. "You give me no choice," she said bitterly.

"No, I don't," he admitted freely. "But cheer up. A few months from now you'll be free to go as you please. As long as you leave the child to me."

Her eyes lifted, shooting daggers of outrage and frustration. He abruptly released her and stepped away. "You'll want to rest before you bathe and dress for dinner. Emily will be up to help you."

"I don't want any help."

"She'll be here all the same. And you will accept her help if you don't want any trouble." He paused at the door and gave her a cold smile. "Until dinner . . ."

Dinner that evening proved a trial of nerves to match that of the afternoon tea. Drayton drank far more than Lily would have liked, said little, and ignored his wife as a polite host ignores a guest with poor table manners. Ambrosia said even less than he, ate little, and never once even attempted a smile. Lily stared at her coffee, relieved that the meal was nearly over, wondering if she ought to have had Bess prepare separate rooms for the two of them. Neither had said anything, but it was quite obvious that . . . She took a long sip of coffee and decided not to broach that delicate subject.

Lily stole yet another glance at Ambrosia and tried to piece together what little information she had gleaned from the stilted conversation of the past hour. The girl's table manners were impeccable; she was educated, intelligent. Yet she was purposely frigid, decidedly hostile to every overture of friendliness and even to conversation. Most troubling of all was the way she looked at Drayton—warily, with distrust and even fear. Almost the way a puppy looks at a master who's whipped him once too often. Lily wondered if it were possible that Drayton deserved such a look.

Ambrosia excused herself from the table before dessert was served and retired immediately to her room. She was exhausted, frustrated, and nervous, and the confrontation with Drayton that afternoon had drained her completely. She needed to be alone. She needed to think, to plan. As Drayton had recently reminded her, she had only two months to find a way out before she was trapped forever. She knew well enough that he would never allow her a chance to escape with his child. She dismissed Emily after she had readied herself for bed and silently paced the floor, trying in vain to still the panic that was taking hold of her. She must be patient. She must not make any

wrong moves. She must choose the best possible moment
and use it to her full advantage if she hoped to get away.
She must remain alert and healthy so that when the right
moment did come, she would be ready. Drayton was no
fool, and escape would be all the more difficult in her
condition, since the added weight of the child made her
tire so easily. With a sigh of resignation, she slipped beneath the light blanket in the four-poster bed and willed
herself to sleep.

The house quieted quickly after dinner. Drayton and
his aunt lingered over one last cup of coffee before moving to the parlor. Neither had much to say, though both
were obviously troubled by the young woman who had
left them so abruptly after dinner. Once in the parlor,
Lily settled herself in her favorite chair and propped her
cane on the chair's arm.

"Do you mind if I smoke?" Drayton asked her.

Instead of the brief shake of her head Drayton expected, Lily bent forward and opened the drawer of the
small table next to her chair. Drayton watched in amazement as she retrieved a tobacco pouch and dainty silver
pipe, then flashed him an almost impish grin. "Don't
mind at all . . . if you'll give me a light."

One side of his mouth pulled down with disapproval,
but he struck a match and obliged her, possibly because
he was so anxious to have a smoke himself. She drew on
her pipe long and gratefully, eyeing him as he made himself comfortable in the chair nearest her and puffed on his
cigar. His face had changed in the past years; how very
little it told her of what he was thinking.

"A little brandy would be nice," she hinted. "There's
a tray in the dining room."

Drayton dutifully rose and went off in search of the
brandy, returning a few moments later with the tray. He
sat it on the table near the lamp and bent to pour her a
small glass. "Anything else?" he inquired as he offered
it to her.

"A little more brandy," she prodded. "I think I've earned it tonight."

"Yes, I suppose you have." He smiled wryly as he filled it a little more than halfway, then placed it in her slightly trembling fingers. Then smashing out his cigar, which had not given him the comfort he sought, he turned to pour himself a glass a bit more generous than hers.

"Welcome home, Drayton," she toasted solemnly as she lifted her glass.

"Thank you, Lily."

There was a long silence as the two studied one another quite frankly, each noting the passage of time on the other's face, remembering the years before. "You ought to have written me about her, Drayton," Lily said at length.

"We were only married two months ago, Lily," he responded lightly. "There wasn't much to say."

"Still," she reproved, "you might have given me some warning, told me something about her. . . ."

"And what should I have told you?" he challenged.

"That she is very different from Kathryn, for one," Lily blurted out. "Pretty, I suppose, beneath all that black. But—" She searched about for a tactful way of saying "rude." "But quiet and distant," she said after a moment. She smiled. "I suppose if you had suddenly written me that you were bringing home a bride, I would have expected a flashy, giggly sort of woman no matter what you said about her, the kind of woman that can quite sweep a man off his feet. Ambrosia is hardly that! Though perhaps, if she smiled . . ." Lily frowned thoughtfully. "Tell me, Drayton, why doesn't she smile? What troubles her so?"

Drayton shifted uneasily in his chair and took a sip of brandy. "She was tired today, Lily. It was a long trip."

Lily finished the last of her own brandy, pondering his unwillingness to speak. Something in his eyes told her not to push him. At least not now. She decided to set off on another course. "You haven't quite convinced me that you're really finished with medicine."

"I've been away from it for seven years, Lily," he returned casually. "What could be more convincing than that?"

"You were running away from something then, Drayton." She waited until he met her eyes. "The people here need a good doctor. And besides, you have a responsibility to yourself, to the years you devoted to studying . . . and to me."

He cocked his head and his smile was doubtful. "You?"

"A minor consideration, to be sure. But I was the person who encouraged you to follow your heart, rather than go into business like your friends were doing, or studying law as Henry would have liked. I was the one who loaned you the money you needed to study, to buy all of those fancy books. I was the one who paid for your apprenticeship under Dr. Mott. And I was the one who believed in you, Drayton. As I still believe in you."

He stared at his brandy, his fingers nervously rotating the glass. "And if my heart now tells me to leave all that behind, to make a new life for myself?"

"Then I would encourage you to do so. But I don't believe that's what your heart is telling you at all."

Drayton rose and went to stare at the empty hearth, sighing wearily as he propped an elbow on the carved mantel. "I can't go back to it, Lily."

"You're afraid to go back, you mean."

She watched his broad shoulders sag with the weight of his burden. "Yes."

Her brow furrowed deeply. She had never expected him to admit to that, not after all this time. It was several moments before she could find her voice. "You must know, deep in your heart, that what happened that night was not your fault. If you had been home with Kathryn that night, you might have—"

"I don't want to talk about that night," he broke in sharply. "It does no good to talk about it."

Lily bit her lip hard, wondering what she could say to comfort him. For a time she was silent. She took a lengthy draw on her pipe, and a memory of Kathryn, blurred after long years passing, sharpened in her mind. She had been a lovely girl with a warm, promising smile, and Drayton had loved her from the first moment he saw her. The fire that had taken Kathryn's life had all but destroyed him. It was almost as if a part of his soul had perished in the flames along with his wife and unborn child. He had not been strong enough to live with the memory, so he had run away from the reminders of all he had ever loved. Lily had prayed that time and distance would heal his heart. But in all the years he had been away, he had not forgotten. The past was still an open, festering wound.

Lily's face softened with compassion and her eyes glazed with tears. In some ways he was so much like Henry had been, loving with his whole being, leaving himself completely vulnerable. She blinked tersely at her tears as he turned to face her. He would not want pity; he was too proud for that. She saw that the sadness had eased from his features, that a cool mask of nonchalance had slipped neatly into place. Lily watched him drain the last of his brandy from the glass, a strange thought striking her like lightning in a summer's storm. The expression he wore was so similar to the girl's—cool, distant, uncaring . . . but not quite convincing to someone who knew better. How a girl like Ambrosia managed to catch Drayton's eye had been a mystery to Lily, until this moment. She puffed on her pipe and rearranged the puzzle pieces in her mind, knowing instinctively how very much alike the two of them were, and chiding herself for having dismissed the girl too quickly.

"Widow's weeds don't become your bride, Drayton," she said suddenly. "Perhaps if she were to dress in something bright and—"

"Ambrosia prefers black." He paused in refilling his glass to flash her a cynical smile. "It reminds her of the part of her life the Yankees destroyed."

"What on earth are you talking about?"

"I'm talking about my wife, Lily. The war isn't over for her. I doubt if it ever will be." He took a seat and sipped at his brandy.

In spite of his efforts to appear indifferent, Lily could see that the admission hurt him. "She's your wife, Drayton. She would hardly have married you if what you are saying is true."

"She didn't marry me because she wanted to," he blurted out. "If circumstances hadn't forced her into it—" He clamped his mouth shut then, realizing that he'd said far more than he'd wanted to say.

" 'Forced her'?" Lily gasped, unable to hide her shock. "Are you trying to say that the child she carries is not yours?"

His mouth set with grim tightness. "The baby is mine. I have no doubt of that."

Lily let out her breath. Drayton was too well versed in such matters to be tricked by a conniving woman. "Unless my eyes deceive me," she said slowly, "your wife was carrying that child for some time before your marriage." She paused, giving him ample time to deny it. He did not. "I cannot imagine that you forced yourself on her, so I must assume she was willing." Again she paused, but he carefully avoided her eyes. "Why does a woman willingly give herself to a man," Lily asked slowly, "unless she seeks marriage? Or unless . . . she is in love with that man?"

Drayton said nothing but drained his glass and rose quickly to refill it again. She had come to him that night alone and afraid and desperate, seeking something from him that he had not been able to give her. And yet, for a single moment, something he had said or done had somehow broken through the wall of hatred she had erected between them, and he had seen a part of Ambrosia Lanford that no one else had ever seen, a part she kept so closely guarded that he doubted she even saw it herself. He took another sip of brandy and closed his eyes, wishing he could erase that night from his mind forever.

Lily drew another puff on her pipe and looked away. Drayton had told her enough for now, perhaps too much. There was a lengthy silence as Lily made herself busy emptying her pipe into a small silver tray and replacing it in the drawer.

Drayton stared at his empty glass for a long time before he set it aside and rose to pace before an empty hearth. "I'm going into town tomorrow to speak with Warren Pierce. He wrote me several times while I was in Charleston, advising me to come home. Apparently there's been trouble with the business Father left me." He paused, reflecting for a moment on the father who, after a lifetime of neglect, had made him sole heir to his estate, his house, his business. . . . "I am seriously considering taking charge of Rambert Paints."

Lily straightened and struggled to contain a cry of protest. He had ignored his inheritance for two years. And he had never shown any interest at all in anything besides medicine. Taking charge of Rambert Paints was just about the last thing Drayton was cut out to do . . . with the possible exception of being a soldier. That last thought made Lily hold her tongue. He had left here without asking for her advice and had not even written her for months after he had left. She had understood that he was coping with his grief the best way he could. And though it was hard to accept after all the years he had been gone, she forced herself to understand that he was still trying to cope with that grief.

"I hope to move into father's house soon, since it's large enough for—"

"Move into your father's house?" Lily broke in, unable to hold back any longer. "But you know this house will be yours someday! You belong here!"

"I'll need a house in town if I'm to work there."

"Town is no more than an hour away on a decent horse," she argued. "Besides, you always hated that house of your father's. You can't think to move into it now, with a baby coming. Your wife will need help when the time comes, help that only a family can give." She paused, quite out of breath. "And beyond all that," she went on more calmly, "I want you here for purely selfish reasons."

"Such as?"

"I happen to be a lonely old woman," she told him firmly. "And you happen to be my family."

He lifted an amused brow. "You? Lonely? From your letters I assumed that you were quite busy, Lily. Let's see . . . The Sprindle sisters come every Wednesday to play cards . . ."

"Weather permitting," she inserted.

"And you visit Bea Hanover and a half-dozen other needy souls each month with a basket of fresh-baked bread and fruit . . ."

"Those are hardly social occasions, Drayton," she insisted. "I am seeing to those people's needs."

"And the preacher comes every other Sunday to dinner, and stops by whenever he has the time . . ."

"Those are professional calls, Drayton," she corrected. "I finance many of his charity projects, you know." She met his blue eyes evenly, without a trace of levity in her own. "Oh, all right. So I have quite a few friends hereabouts. But friends are not the same as family," she said earnestly. "I never had a child of my own to comfort me in my old age. But I do have you, Drayton. You're like a son to me. You know that. And I need you—no, don't shrug that need off so easily. I want you to stay with me." She hesitated, and suddenly her voice was soft. "I—I'm asking you to stay."

He held her eyes for a long moment. "It's late, Lily. I'm going to bed."

He came forward to kiss her cheek. She stretched a trembling hand to touch his hair. "Drayton?" He met her eyes again. "I—I have missed you these past years," she whispered. "I have kept myself busy, but—"

He took her hand in his own and touched it to his lips. "I've missed you too, Lily. God knows, I've missed you too."

He smiled at her as he released her hand but made no promises as he turned away and left her alone in the parlor.

Chapter 28

The following morning when Drayton came down to breakfast, he was surprised to find Lily already at the table, looking fresh and lovely as she had the day before. She glanced up at him and smiled, daintily touching a linen napkin to her lips. "I apologize for starting breakfast without you," she said as he took a seat to the side of hers. "But I woke early this morning with a voracious appetite, and I wasn't sure when you'd be up and about. And Ambrosia—I completely forgot to ask if she would take an early breakfast, though I didn't expect she would after traveling half of yesterday. I read somewhere that Southern women have a habit of sleeping till noon," she added thoughtfully.

"Not this Southern woman," Drayton said wryly as he poured himself a cup of coffee. "She'll be down directly."

Lily watched him take a sip of coffee, all the while gnawing nervously at her lip. "Drayton . . . about last night. There's no reason to rush into anything—"

"And no reason to put off making decisions which must be made."

She sighed, fixing her eyes on her half-empty plate, no longer feeling an appetite for the hotcakes she had attacked so eagerly just a few moments before. "I'm only asking you to consider all the options," she said quietly. "You could stay here for just a little while. You've been gone so very long, after all. And I—I hardly feel as if I know you anymore. . . ."

He sighed and leaned forward to cover her hand with his own, touched by the emotion in her voice. "I haven't made any final decisions yet," he relented.

On the threshold of the dining room Ambrosia stopped short. She had rarely been witness to such open intimacy and would have been uncomfortable in its presence regardless. But the fact that she was a complete outsider, that she did not want to be here in the first place, made her much more so.

She waited in silence until Drayton's eyes lifted to meet hers. The warmth in his instantly died. He withdrew his hand from his aunt's and focused his attention on his coffee, while Lily, who just now noticed her standing there, welcomed her with a wide smile. "I hope you slept well, Ambrosia."

"Thank you for your concern," Ambrosia mouthed perfunctorily as she approached the table. She was rigid as Drayton rose to assist her with her chair and she carefully avoided his eyes. She shook out the linen napkin which lay to the side of her plate and placed it on her lap.

To her dismay, Lily found that she was actually holding her breath in an instinctive reaction to the tension which filled the now silent room. "Your woman," she blurted out, needing desperately to ease the silent uneasiness which had all but taken over the meal. "What is her name? I have such a time with names! Sheila? Stella?" Lily frowned and shook her head. "Sharon, is it?"

"Her name is Sheba," Ambrosia answered coldly. "And she is not *my* woman. I'm sure you must have heard that Mr. Lincoln freed the slaves."

Lily's smile froze on her face. "Yes . . . well . . . You must forgive an old woman's loss of memory," she attempted lightly. She paused, giving Ambrosia ample time to respond, but the younger woman said nothing.

"As I was going to say," Lily tried again, "Sheba is an absolutely marvelous cook. I've never tasted anything as light and delicate as these hotcakes of hers. I'm going to see to it that Sarah steals the recipe."

The glance Ambrosia tossed at her as she took a sip of coffee was enough to make Lily think twice about further conversation. From that moment on, the meal was a repeat of the dinner the evening before.

Drayton left the house within an hour after breakfast, leaving Ambrosia to explore the house and grounds on her own. She spent every moment of the time planning her escape. She took no note of the beauty surrounding her, concentrating instead on the various exits from the house, and taking a particular interest in the stable. A tall, muscular man with thick blond hair and an engaging, if bashful smile, paused in currying a fine dapple gray mare to introduce himself as Debbs, and show her all the horses. Debbs's devotion for the animals he tended was very apparent, and he eagerly lapsed into stories about each horse, mentioning Henry Collinsworth's name often, adding that Miss Lily was reluctant to sell any of her late husband's fine animals. Ambrosia asked a few pertinent questions as to which horses were most gentle, all the while eyeing the saddles and bridles kept in an orderly fashion on a pegged wall opposite the stalls. Taking a horse from here would not be so difficult as she had feared at first. She felt a twinge of guilt as she decided on a pretty white-faced mare and a spotted gray for Sheba, both of which she realized she would need to sell once they got into town, to get money for the journey south. She would have to locate one of the more questionable livery establishments in town, since she would have no proof of ownership. She bit her lip and tried to shake off the guilt. She had never stolen anything before, yet she could not imagine living out her life like this, in this strange place so full of Yankees, living with a man who owned her simply because she carried his child. She patted the mare's neck and nodded a thank-you to Debbs before she left the stable. There was no other way.

Ambrosia had already acquainted herself with the rooms of the house, including a ballroom of extravagant dimensions that obviously saw little use these days. When she returned to the house from the stable, she headed instinctively for the library. The room had intrigued her at first glance, probably because it was so very much like her father's study at Heritage. It was empty now, so she was free to explore the fine leather-bound volumes of every sort that filled floor-to-ceiling shelves on three of four walls. The fourth wall was paneled with a fireplace and carved mahogany mantel, and above that hung a portrait of Lily's late husband, a heavy-set man with a ridiculously small, almost feminine mouth that did nothing to compliment his broad features. There was something appealing in the man's expression, however, a gentle, jovial look to his dark, round eyes that belied an otherwise serious expression. Ambrosia studied that face for a moment, thinking how unlike her father the man must have been. She turned away to choose a book from the nearest shelf, removing a thick, slightly worn copy of Sir Walter Scott's *Ivanhoe*. She idly flipped through the pages, pausing at one beautifully drawn illustration of knights and fair ladies in their finest attire. Her eyes lingered on the young nobleman and the shy, lovely woman at his side, and she found herself thinking of Ledger, of the few, precious moments he had shared with her so long ago in Columbia. Every step she had ever walked with him, every word he had ever spoken to her, was etched forever on her heart. She remembered one party she had attended at age fourteen, wearing a flowing green gown that made her feel so grown up and pretty. She had danced with him that night—

A sudden sound from behind her made her memories scatter. She spun about and saw Lily, who smiled at her even as she turned away. "I'm happy to see you have an interest in books," Lily said as she made her way toward the younger woman. "I'm afraid I've never been one to sit still long enough to read much, though my husband tried many times to convert me." She glanced at the book which lay open on the desk. "Henry bought that book for me years ago, just after my illness. He even read the first chapter to me aloud, to arouse my interest in the story. A part of his plan worked too—I just *had* to know what was going to happen to those people!" She paused and met Ambrosia's eyes with a mischievous grin. "So I forced him to read me the rest of it!" She chuckled softly.

Ambrosia's gaze remained cold. After a moment, she returned her eyes to the picture, silently dismissing the older woman. In the face of such indifference, Lily's good humor faded quickly. Her blue eyes dropped to the brightly colored picture that Ambrosia was studying so closely. "Such lovely gowns they wore in those days!" she remarked with a wistful sigh. Her eyes flickered over Ambrosia's plain black gown. "Drayton told me," she began hesitantly, "that it is your choice to wear black. It seems a great sacrifice for one so young and lovely."

Ambrosia lifted her chin. "There are many things far more important to me than fashionable clothing, Mrs. Collinsworth."

"Obviously," Lily returned with a lift of her brow. Her tart response surprised Ambrosia a little. She closed the book and avoided Lily's eyes.

The older woman said nothing for a moment, then decided to speak her mind. "An injured heart seeks to grieve, Ambrosia, just as an injured body seeks to rest. Mourning is a part of the healing we must experience if we are to accept hurt and loss and get on with the business of living." Her words became more forceful. "But dwelling on our sorrows, or constantly reminding ourselves of the pain is very wrong and very destructive. Eventually we must learn to let go of what is past and focus our hearts and minds on what is here and now." She placed a hand on Ambrosia's arm. "Do you understand what I am trying to say, Ambrosia?"

The green eyes which met hers were bright with indignation. "You think I am wrong to wear black."

"That's part of it, yes. But there is more to it than that."

"You are telling me to forget the past," Ambrosia continued in a brittle tone. "To forget my father and my home and the war."

Lily's brow knitted as she let out a sigh of frustration. "You will never forget entirely, Ambrosia. That would be impossible for you, for anyone. But you must learn to forget some things—like the bitterness and hatred you hold against all Northerners. Feelings like that serve no useful purpose." She paused. "And I wonder if your widow's weeds aren't a part of those destructive feelings."

Ambrosia's mouth tightened into a thin, white line. She stepped haughtily around Lily and strode toward the mantel portrait of Henry Collinsworth. "Do you know how fortunate you are to have this painting of your husband, Mrs. Collinsworth?" she inquired with sarcastic politeness. "To be able to come here, to this room filled with his things, and gaze upon his likeness, remembering the wonderful moments you shared with him? Do you know how envious I am, Mrs. Collinsworth?"

Ambrosia's eyes narrowed, her tone became accusing. "The Yankee soldiers who came to my home destroyed a library much like this one. They carted away some of my father's things, but most of them they simply left to burn. I was not permitted to take anything of value from the house . . . not a single book or picture"—she gave a short laugh—"not even a proper change of clothing."

Her eyes lowered suddenly, and she stared down at her fingers as her voice became soft. "It—it was raining that morning . . . I watched as they ran about the house, screaming and laughing as they set it aflame. I thought perhaps the rain would keep the fire from spreading. I prayed to God that somehow, somehow—" Her voice broke painfully and her fingers laced tightly together.

She shook her head and lifted her chin. "The Yankees left me nothing, Mrs. Collinsworth. Nothing but my life and my hatred. And now you are telling me that I must forget that too."

Lily swallowed hard. "I—I did not know about your home," she said quietly.

"No?" Ambrosia feigned surprise. "Well, I suppose Drayton forgot to mention it to you. Or perhaps he thought it an unimportant detail. . . . He must have watched his men burn so many."

The shock that registered on Lily's face gave Ambrosia a small measure of satisfaction. "I believe I will retire to my room now," she informed the older woman. "I find I have completely lost my appetite for luncheon." With a lift of her chin, Ambrosia strode arrogantly from the library.

Warren Pierce looked perfectly at home in his spacious William Street office, behind his massive oaken desk. He rose from his worn leather chair to stretch a thick, welcoming hand across the desk's surface toward Drayton, all the while measuring James Rambert's son. He'd been only a boy the last time Warren had seen him, and there were definite changes in his face, his manner. Drayton was a man now, but Warren saw far more than just maturity in his eyes. There was a hardness that could not have come with time alone, something only war or tragedy could do to a man. Drayton had seen both.

Drayton settled himself comfortably into a chair opposite Warren and eyed the older man with admiration. Though he was all of seventy years of age, the clever, sharp intelligence that had made Warren's fifty-odd years of practicing law so successful was still apparent in his glittering dark brown eyes.

"You certainly took your time about getting home," Warren began with a wry smile. He closed the flap of an envelope which lay on the polished oak surface of his desk and placed folded hands atop it. "I was beginning to think your inheritance would be gone by the time you returned.''

"You wrote me that the paint business wasn't doing well,'' Drayton returned nonchalantly, removing a cigar from his coat pocket and offering it to the older man. When Warren declined with a shake of his head, Drayton lit it for himself.

"That's not what I wrote you at all,'' Warren denied impatiently. "I said that the business was in real trouble and would be as long as your stepbrother had charge of things. I advised you to come home immediately. That was well over a year ago.'' When Drayton said nothing, Warren's eyes narrowed. "I was named executor of your father's will, but there was very little I could do to protect your interests since you ignored my advice, and since your stepbrother was already managing the business when your father died. Oh, I could have dragged him into court, but I wasn't about to do that without you here to back me up. Aaron is your stepbrother, after all. I wasn't absolutely sure how far you'd want me to go.''

Warren lifted the top file from a stack of similar folders at the edge of his desk. "The paint business is in serious trouble. I haven't had access to the books, but it's no secret that there've been layoffs at the factories, or that very important clients have been lost in the past year. Your father had planned to expand production, had even invested in new machinery just before he died. From what I've heard, that new machinery has never even been used.''

"Why is that?''

"Management!'' Warren growled irritably. "Or rather the lack of it. The business has been hurt by poor management for nearly two years. And it's nearly gone bankrupt because of it. You're home now, so there's no reason why you can't sell what's left of it and use the money from the sale to invest in stocks. That kind of investment will give you a comfortable income for life. But

I wouldn't wait, Drayton. Every day that passes, the business is worth that much less."

Drayton sat quietly for a few moments, puffing indifferently on his cigar. "I'm not sure I want to sell the business, Warren."

Warren could hardly have been more astonished at the announcement. He forced a tight smile. "Would you care to tell me what you do intend to do with it?"

"I was thinking of taking it over myself."

Warren held his temper, assuming an indulgent smile. "Perhaps you didn't hear me, Drayton. The business is on the verge of bankruptcy—"

"And all because of the way it's been managed," Drayton finished for him. "You see, I was listening, Warren. And what I heard you say is that the problem isn't with the carriage paint business at all. It's with my stepbrother."

"I'll concede that point. But even if you remove Aaron from the picture now, you'll still have a failing business on your hands."

"A business that could be turned around."

"Not without a miracle," Warren shot back at him, "and one hell of a lot of work." He shook his balding head, the flush in his cheeks making the patches of hair above his ears appear silver-white. "You don't have any idea what it cost your father to build that business, do you? You don't realize how much of his sweat and blood went into making it thrive."

An oddly distant look touched Drayton's eyes. He knew all too well. The only thing James Rambert had ever cared about was his business. His only pride had been in selling the "purest and finest carriage paints in America." After all these years it was strange to feel a twinge of pain at the memory. Henry Collinsworth had more than filled the void in Drayton's life, had made him forget his real father's neglect. But suddenly he was remembering, and he felt a burning desire to prove to Pierce, and perhaps to himself, that he could do what his father had done, that he could make this business succeed.

"You could never hire anyone to manage the business the way he did," Warren went on. "And that's what it will take."

Drayton said nothing for a moment, drawing one final puff on his cigar before he leaned forward to smash it out in a small onyx tray. "How do I go about getting rid of Aaron?"

Warren eyed him narrowly for a long space of time before responding. "You could simply tell him to get out. He has no legal hold on the company that I'm aware of. But I'd be careful about how you go about it. Aaron's a strange one; you never know how a man like that is going to react."

Drayton lifted an inquiring brow. "What do you mean, 'a man like that'?" The Aaron he remembered had been a spoiled, demanding child. Drayton had seen him steal and lie and even feign illness to get his way, but that had been a long time ago. Aaron was no longer a boy.

Warren frowned uneasily. "When the will was read and he found that James had written both him and his mother off in favor of you, he went into a rage. He screamed that James Rambert owed everything to his mother." Warren shook his head. "Threw things around this office just like a child having a tantrum, even threatened to burn it down. I honestly think he might have done it if his mother hadn't been there to stop him." He paused. "I wrote you about her death a few months back, Drayton, since the will allowed her to live out her days in your father's house before you were given full possession. Aaron's living in that house now, so you might want to discuss some sort of arrangement with him as to paying rent or purchasing it from you."

A slight smile played about Drayton's lips at the irony of the situation. Years before, Aaron had cleverly seen to it that Drayton was forced out of his father's house, out of his father's life. But now everything had been turned

around. The house was his now, and Aaron could be
forced to leave. He let out a sigh and said nothing, considering. Perhaps Warren was right about making some
kind of arrangement with Aaron. He had lived there since
his childhood, after all, and surely felt some attachment
for the place.

"You're within your rights to force Aaron to vacate
the premises, of course," Warren said, not understanding Drayton's silence or the smile. "But I would be careful, Drayton. A desperate man makes for a dangerous
enemy. Aaron's recently lost his mother, and if he loses
his home and income so suddenly, it—"

"I'm not afraid of him," Drayton said quietly.

"I never imagined that you were." The lines in Warren's brow deepened. "But I do hope you will reconsider
selling the business, at least. You're going to need quite a
bit of money to get it back on its feet. And I think it's a
mistake to gamble like that when you could sell and have
your future security handed to you on a silver platter."

Drayton rose and stretched his hand across the desk for
a farewell handshake. "Thank you for your advice, Warren. I'll be sure to keep it in mind."

Ambrosia remained in her room until dinner time,
pacing the floor and staring out the window for the long
hours in between. When Drayton returned from the city
just an hour before dinner, she sat in the sitting room in
silence, all but daring him to order her to change for the
evening meal. But he said nothing to her, did not even ac-
knowledge her beyond a brief, impersonal glance when
he entered the room. The wall between them was growing thicker and more impenetrable.

At the table, Ambrosia carefully avoided Lily's eyes
as well as her husband's as she placed her napkin on her
lap and sipped at her wine in an attempt to ease the tension. Lily watched her for a time, searching about for
some remark to break the uneasy silence. But the confrontation in the library had left her at a loss. The meal

progressed without conversation, each soft clank of silver on china plates echoing unpleasantly throughout the room.

"I saw Matt Desmond today," Drayton said finally as they were being served coffee at meal's end.

"Matt Desmond!" Lily repeated ·in some surprise. "Why, I haven't seen him in years. How is he? How is Leanne?"

"Doing very well." He took a sip of coffee and let the steamy warmth flow down his throat. "I spoke with him about the possibility of taking out a loan, since that's what it will take to put Rambert Paints back on its feet."

Lily's eyes widened. "Is that what Warren advised you to do?"

"No," Drayton admitted, running his finger pensively about the smooth edge of the china cup. "As a matter of fact, he advised me to sell."

"And you're going to do the exact opposite? You're going to take out a loan and try to salvage it?" He said nothing, but evenly met her eyes. "You know nothing about making paint, Drayton!"

"I can learn."

She gave a snort.

"Do you doubt my ability?" he challenged, suddenly feeling the need for a drink.

"Certainly not," she returned brusquely. "But I doubt your sanity if you're serious about this."

"I'm quite serious." He sipped at his coffee again, but his eyes never left hers. He let out a sigh. "I intend to study the books before I make a firm decision either way. But my instincts tell me it would be foolish to sell now. And I've grown rather accustomed to trusting my instincts."

"I see." Lily's voice was soft, her eyes greatly troubled. He was like a stranger to her, with that cold, steely quality in his voice and his expression so closed, so challenging. "You could borrow the money from me," she offered slowly.

"I wouldn't even consider it."

Ambrosia, who had sat silently fingering her half-filled cup of coffee, suddenly rose. "Since I have nothing to add to this conversation, I'm sure you won't mind if I excuse myself. I've had a long and tiring day."

Lily's gaze followed Ambrosia as she left the room, then turned back to her nephew and saw that he was doing the same. For an instant she caught the look in his blue eyes, a look she had seen before. A long time ago, when the father he worshiped first brought him here to live, the small boy had watched James Rambert ride away, his lips pressed tightly together, his eyes blinking in a valiant attempt to hold back the tears. And again, years later, the gifted young doctor had looked much the same way as he stood beside the grave that held his wife and unborn child. He was a different man now, older, harder. But as he watched Ambrosia turn her back on him and coldly walk away, the look in his eyes was that of a child, silently hurting, anguishing within.

Without thinking, Lily leaned toward him and placed her trembling hand on his hard-muscled arm. He immediately tensed, and the eyes which met hers were guarded, as cool as she had ever seen them. "I have papers to go over tonight. And I plan to go into the city again tomorrow morning, so I know you'll understand if I forgo brandy and parlor talk tonight."

"Yes, of course," she murmured, forcing a small smile as he placed his dinner napkin on the table and rose. She said nothing more as he quickly left the room.

Chapter 29

It was just an hour after dawn when Drayton maneuvered his fine bay stallion through a vaguely familiar alley, around to the loading dock of the Rambert Paints warehouse. The place was all but deserted. Two men moved sluggishly as they loaded a single wagon, while a third man was propped casually against a wall, a bottle in his hand as he observed the other two. No one hurried, no one was there to urge them to do so. There were a few laughing comments from the third man, a grumbling remark from one of the workers. Otherwise all was strangely quiet. Drayton's eyes lingered on the men, amazed to find things so altered from the bustle of years before. Mornings had always been the busiest time of day for the warehouse, as the workers rushed to fill orders for the day. Pierce's warnings had not really prepared him for this.

He watched a moment longer before he clucked his tongue and guided his horse around to the front entrance of the building. As he tethered his mount to the hitching post, his eyes flicked up and down the red brick building, huge and imposing, though not quite the frightening structure he remembered. It was a small boy's memories which clutched at him now, memories of tagging breathlessly along in his father's shadow, feeling small and unimportant and afraid, though he had never allowed those feelings to show. Tears had always made his father so angry. Drayton remembered his father's brisk, independent strides, which had been almost impossible for his short, child's legs to match. And he remembered the terse, authoritative voice which never once softened the way Uncle Henry's often did, which had never once offered praise or encouragement or affection to a child who needed all. His father had seemed so wonderfully strong in a world that was confusing and rushed and frightening. But there had been no room for a child in James Rambert's life. There had been no room for anything but the business he had built from nothing.

Three years after his first wife's death, James Rambert had married Roselyn Van Ryt, a woman from one of the city's finest and oldest families. For James, Roselyn Van Ryt was the perfect overt symbol of his success. She was an expensive possession, just as his fine horses, his tailored clothing, and his fashionable brownstone residence in Gramercy Park were. Roselyn knew all the right people, gave the most elegant parties in New York, and had terribly expensive tastes which James happily indulged to prove to everyone that he had achieved wealth beyond measure. The child she brought to the marriage had made no difference to James. One child was the same as the next, a problem to be dealt with until years brought adulthood and usefulness. James had never anticipated the problems that arose between his own son and Roselyn's.

But the rivalry between the boys had been immediate and intense. Fiercely protected and spoiled by his mother, Aaron was determined to keep her entirely to himself. He learned very quickly that he could do nothing about the man who was now his stepfather, but that man's son was another matter entirely. For weeks he plotted and lied and played on his mother's sympathies until James agreed to send his son away, to be raised by an aunt and uncle the boy hardly even knew.

In the years that lay between, Drayton's feelings for the man who had been too busy for him had faded away. But as his eyes fixed on the faded brick building, the memories came back to life.

He entered the warehouse with a pensive, measured step, the lingering scents of oils and pigments and turpentine filling his nostrils, the intermittent sounds of the men on the loading dock filtering in muted echoes through the huge, open spaces. He traced a path up a narrow flight of steps to the office that had been his father's. The smaller, outer room was empty except for a thin young man dressed in a stained blue shirt and patched brown trousers. The youth lounged carelessly in a chair reading a newspaper. He glanced up when Drayton entered the office, but said nothing and went on reading his paper.

"Is Tom Landon expected here this morning?" Drayton asked him.

The younger man looked up in annoyance. "Don't know any Tom Landon."

"He is—was the factory foreman." For thirty years, Drayton almost added.

"Tom Landon . . ." the younger man repeated thoughtfully. "Oh, yes. I remember now. The old man with the white hair. He was fired a few months back. Got a job on the docks, I think. Doesn't work here anymore, at any rate." He unfolded his newspaper and began to scan a new section in a gesture of dismissal.

"I'll speak with Aaron, then." The ring of authority in his voice made the boy look up again.

"He's not in."

"When will he be in?" Drayton inquired in a slightly too polite tone.

The younger man lowered his paper to consider Drayton a bit more closely. "Might not come in today at all," he said unconvincingly. "Do you have an appointment with him?"

"A long-overdue appointment, as a matter of fact," Drayton said with an unreadable look in his eye. Without another word he crossed the room and opened the door to the inner office.

"Wait a minute!" The youth scampered after him in an attempt to stop him. But he was too late and watched in wide-eyed horror as Drayton took a seat in Aaron's chair and began examining the papers on his desk. "What do you think you're doing?"

Drayton's eyes lifted, and the younger man took a step backward, wondering why he hadn't seen the cold, dangerous anger there sooner. "I'm cleaning off this desk," Drayton told him slowly, his eyes daring him to challenge the move. "When Aaron arrives, be sure and send him right in."

The office clerk struggled to swallow as he forced a shaky nod. "Who shall I say is—er, waiting for him . . . . sir?" he stammered. He watched as Drayton lifted a stack of papers and began to sort through them.

"Just tell him his stepbrother is here."

"Ye-yes, sir." He turned quickly away and gingerly closed the door behind himself as he left the room.

It was just after ten when Aaron Rambert finally arrived at the Fulton Street warehouse on his burnished stallion. He cut a fine figure on horseback with his sleek gray broadcloth suit and bright green brocade vest. He spent a great deal of money on clothing and horses, having acquired his mother's expensive tastes during his formative years. But since his mother's death, he had lost interest in so many things and turned again and again to gambling just to feel alive. It was almost like a sickness, a complusion that made him forget everything else and play hand after hand of poker, all the while believing that he would win the next, or the next, or the next. Winning had been so easy at first. He could not understand why his luck had so suddenly run out. But he'd lost a fortune in the past few months, more than he would have dreamed he could lose. And now he could not afford to give up the game, since he had gambled away too much of the company's money even to meet the payroll this week. Besides, he was certain he would win again soon. Perhaps tonight. Tomorrow night at the latest . . .

He tied his horse to the post and paused to eye the black stallion tethered alongside his horse. Someone was waiting to see him, in spite of the orders he'd given to the clerk to tell any visitor that he wasn't expected. He hesitated, considering remounting and leaving rather than facing another disgruntled customer or a supplier demanding to be paid.

He muttered a curse and turned toward the building, deciding there was no sense in putting off a confrontation that was inevitable. He would handle it the way he usually did, smoothly proclaiming his innocence and promising whatever would make the visitor happy, just to get rid of him. If only he had clear title to the business or the land, he would have sold or mortgaged either in order to raise money. But such a move would be totally illegal, and the lawyer handling his stepfather's estate was probably just waiting for him to try something like that.

He stepped into the building, scowling darkly at the smell of paint, at the sight of the place he abhorred. He'd all but kowtowed to the old man in the years before he died, working harder and longer than he'd ever worked in his life. He'd been so sure that the old man would change his will, giving Aaron the inheritance he deserved. But when James Rambert breathed his last, every penny went from the old bastard to his blood son. The only reprieve had been that Drayton was away at war. There was no one to stand in Aaron's way if he worked quickly and cleverly to claim a part of what he felt was owed him. His mother had urged caution and restraint, and had seen to it that most of the money was invested in railroad stocks that would secure his future after his stepbrother came home to claim his inheritance. But when his mother died, Aaron began to gamble using company money, to sell warehouse inventory and pocket the money without even bothering to alter the books. To keep the factories going a bit longer, he contracted to buy cheaper materials, less expensive "extenders" to take the place of the costlier pigments. Several of the business's largest accounts had been terminated as a result of inferior products manufactured by Rambert Paints.

Aaron mounted the steps to his office, his mind going over and over the business's assets and liabilities. He frowned as Timothy Huber, the office clerk who usually bowed and scraped and brought him his coffee, instead rushed forward in a fluster. "Someone's here, Mr. Rambert! In your private office! He—he forced his way in—I swear it! I tried to stop him, but—"

"Someone forced his way into my office?" Aaron repeated furiously.

The younger man gave a breathless nod. "I tried to stop him, truly I did. But he—" He scurried after Aaron, who was already swinging open the door.

Aaron stopped short, frozen to the spot. Lounging in the high-backed leather desk chair, a cigar poised near his mouth, was his stepbrother. Drayton continued to scan a paper as if he were totally unaware of Aaron's interruption. A moment later, his eyes met Aaron's without the slightest change of expression. He tossed the papers on the desk and casually drew on his cigar, expelling a curl of gray smoke which rose to the ceiling. "Close the door, Aaron. I have a few things I want to discuss with you."

For what seemed an eternity Aaron could not move. The hatred he'd always felt for Drayton Rambert was overpowered now by fear. For a terrifying instant he thought Drayton knew about Kathryn, about what had happened that night. Something had changed him, that was frighteningly apparent. The Drayton who sat at James Rambert's desk was a hardened, dangerous man whose total control unnerved Aaron completely. When his mind finally began to function, Aaron assured himself that Drayton knew nothing about that night. No one knew. No one would ever know. He calmed himself and began to wonder just how long Drayton had been in this office. Minutes? Hours? What had he found out in that time?

Aaron forced himself to smile. It was possible that Drayton knew nothing at all. He stepped forward to offer his stepbrother a hand in greeting. "I—I hope Tim didn't keep you waiting long. He ought to have sent for me the moment you arrived."

Drayton's eyes lingered pointedly on Aaron's extended hand. "Sit down, Aaron," he said, making no move to take it.

Aaron attempted to disguise the shudder that ran through him as he withdrew his hand and moved to take a seat. He forced a second nervous smile, all the while feeling Drayton's eyes saw right through him. "I—I was beginning to wonder if you would ever come home," he stammered nervously. "You were gone for such a long time—"

"Almost long enough for you to ruin everything," Drayton finished for him in an oddly silken tone that made Aaron cringe inwardly.

He felt the flesh on the back of his neck rise with apprehension. "That's not true, Drayton. I've worked hard these past two years. I've done my best."

"I know exactly what you've done, Aaron," Drayton went on quietly. "I know about the money you've embezzled, the ridiculous salary you've collected, the cheap paints you sold to men who trusted the Rambert name."

"That's a lie!" Aaron shot back at him. "You know as well as I do that things can go wrong after the paint is sold. The men who claim the fault is mine were all friends of the old man. They liked doing business with him, and now that he's gone, nothing can please them."

Aaron held his breath and watched Drayton puff calmly on his cigar. The silence was tense and it seemed those icy blue eyes remained on him an eternity. Finally Drayton leaned forward and ground out his cigar in a small brass bowl. His eyes were narrowed on Aaron's face. "There's only one thing in this world I hate more than a coward," he said softly, almost pleasantly. "And that's a liar." Aaron's jaw slackened visibly as Drayton lifted the papers he had been reading a few moments before and tossed the pile across the desk. "I'm calling you both."

Aaron didn't have to do more than glance at the papers to know that he was caught. The office had been littered with past-due bills, lists of factory materials he'd contracted for, the company ledgers . . . Small beads of sweat broke across Aaron's brow as he lifted his eyes slowly to the cool, impassive face.

"I want you out of here, Aaron. And I don't want you to ever set foot in this warehouse again. Or any of the factories. And I want you to vacate the house in Gramercy Park. You have until tomorrow to remove all of your personal belongings, or I'll see that it's done for you."

Aaron sprang from his chair, his fists tightly clenched. "That was my mother's house! I've lived there since I was a child! I can't possibly be out by tomorrow!"

"You belong to several clubs, Aaron. And there are hotels in town. I prefer the Saint Nicholas, myself."

Aaron's breath was coming in short, labored bursts. His nostrils flared with indignation. "I can't be out by tomorrow. I've already made plans. I've invited guests—"

"Then you'd better inform them of your new address," Drayton broke in quietly. "Or I'll have them thrown out along with you and your things." He paused. "I'm being very generous, under the circumstances." He withdrew another cigar from the breast pocket of his coat and studied it intently. "But touch one stick of furniture or remove one painting from that house, and I'll have you thrown in jail, so help me. I'd take you to task now for embezzling if I thought you were worth the time and effort." He glanced up. "But I don't. You might consider my leniency a . . . courtesy . . . between brothers."

Aaron wanted more than anything to smash his fist into Drayton's face, but he dared not make any move in that direction. Something told him his stepbrother would like nothing more than an excuse to fight him. "Don't you ever call me brother, you bastard," he hissed. "You and your father are two of a kind. But neither of you can hurt me now. I've invested enough money in stocks to last me for the rest of my life," he boasted. "No matter what you do, you can't hurt me."

Drayton leaned back in his chair and casually lit a cigar. He was more than a little tempted to drag Aaron into court, to make him pay for what he had done. But a long-drawn-out legal battle would only cost them both, and Drayton had better things to do with his time and his money. "I'm happy to hear that, Aaron," Drayton said finally. "Because you've collected the last dime you're going to get from me." He took a long draw on his cigar as Aaron turned his back and made a furious exit from the office.

Chapter 30

Every day for the following week, Drayton worked at the warehouse office trying to untangle the mess Aaron had left behind. The work was long and tedious, and the tallies of losses and past-due invoices owed by the business proved far higher than Drayton had expected. He visited the Brooklyn factories as well and authorized a final payroll for the employees from his personal savings, since the company could not cover the amount owed them. Then he temporarily suspended all operations until he could make a decision as to the company's fate.

There were so many things to be considered, so many possibilities to be turned over in his mind. The sale of the business at this time would never bring the security Warren Pierce had thought. The company owed too many thousands of dollars to suppliers, not to mention back payments on the machinery his father had purchased shortly before he died. But Aaron had done something far more serious to the firm than ruining it financially. He had destroyed the company's reputation for quality. Regaining the trust of the businessmen Aaron had taken advantage of would be a difficult task at best. It would mean taking on a staggering debt that would have to be repaid, regardless of whether the business succeeded or failed. Quality raw materials would have to be purchased. Competent workers would have to be hired and trained on the new machinery. But the greatest cost of all would be the cost of waiting, of holding on while the slow rebuilding of trust came about. It would be a gamble. It would also be a challenge. And more than anything else at this moment, Drayton needed a challenge, needed a means of proving himself.

Only the child Ambrosia carried forced him to hesitate, to consider more fully the consequences of failure. He painstakingly went over the books, time and again, from five years before to the present, calculating costs as closely as he could, projecting profits if all went well, losses if all did not. And he pored over page after page of books from his father's library in the Gramercy Park house, studying the chemical makeup of paints, the various components of a fine, durable product as opposed to a poor one. Finally, after three long weeks of pondering, he took his favorite stallion from the stables on a hot summer morning and rode hard over the land he had traveled as a boy, driving all physical tension from his body, leaving his mind open and clear. It was a freedom he had not allowed himself in a long time. When he returned to Elmwood late that afternoon, he had made his decision. If he could secure an adequate loan from the bank, he would fight to rebuild Rambert Paints.

The days seemed endless for Ambrosia, hours upon hours of mounting anxiety, and nothing to occupy her time but going over and over her plans for escape. Every morning she watched with jealousy as Drayton went about his business. She envied him his work, though she didn't know or care where he went each day or what he was doing. She felt hopelessly trapped here. How many times had she dreamed of riding away and never coming back! She had even lost her patience once and asked Debbs to saddle a gentle mare for her so that she could ride about the grounds. But he had only stared at her queerly and offered gallantly to hitch up the brougham if she wished to take a ride. He was visibly shocked that she had even considered riding in her present condition, and she didn't dare suggest it again for fear he would tell Drayton. It had been foolish of her to consider leaving in broad daylight anyway. She planned to take Sheba along with her and could think of no plausible excuse for the black woman to come along on a pleasure ride about the grounds. And she would need a fair amount of time to get away before anyone realized that she had gone. She had thought it over a thousand times and always the answer was the same. She would need to slip away silently, under cover of darkness. She had only to wait until Drayton spent the night elsewhere.

Escape was an obsession now, the only thing she could hope for. There was nothing else to fill her hours, no challenge, no work, no responsibility, nothing of the life she had known before. She had to get away! She did not allow herself to dwell on the fact that she had no set destination in mind, that she would need money for food and shelter if she were to travel south. She had survived on her own before, and she desperately needed the challenge of survival after all these weeks of being a coddled prisoner. She was too strong to be doted upon and treated like a hopeless, brainless creature. And she was determined to prove her strength by escaping, by making her own way and surviving on her own.

Nearly three weeks had passed when Ambrosia finally saw the chance she had been waiting for. It happened at the dinner table one night, just after Drayton told his aunt that he had come to a decision, that he intended to seek a loan for the painting business. He mentioned his plans to meet with a man who had worked for his father for years, and then meet with a banker friend of his afterward. Ambrosia paid little attention to that as she mechanically ate her dinner.

''Do you think you'll be home in time for dinner tomorrow evening?'' Lily asked him softly, trying to sound casual, though she was worried about the hours he'd kept of late and by the constant tension etched on his brow. She didn't understand what he hoped to prove by taking on this impossible task, but she guessed it had something to do with pride and something more to do with his relationship with Ambrosia.

In response to her question, Drayton shook his head. "I doubt it. In fact, I was thinking of spending the night in town, since I plan on meeting with Matt over dinner."

Ambrosia's eyes flew to his face and met his gaze for the barest moment before darting nervously away. Her heart was suddenly pounding. Tomorrow night! She kept her eyes carefully lowered and tried to keep her breath steady and calm. Tomorrow night she would flee. And long before anyone even knew that she was gone, she would be in the city, hidden safely by the crazy, frenzied traffic, until she could find a way south.

The following day passed with such agonizing slowness that Ambrosia thought she would surely go mad before nightfall. She chose a book from the library and tried to concentrate on it to pass the time, but again and again she set it aside and paced her bedroom, going over her plans. At lunch and dinner she could hardly force down a single bite, even though she had also eaten a sparse breakfast.

"Are you feeling well, Ambrosia?" Lily questioned her anxiously, noting that she seemed preoccupied and hadn't eaten anything to speak of the entire day.

"Quite well," she responded evenly. "I'm just not hungry." She paused. "I think I shall retire early. I feel tired all of a sudden."

Lily forced a smile, but her eyes remained anxious. "Of course, dear. If you should feel hungry later or if you need anything, please don't hesitate to ask," she added. Her smile faded quickly as she watched Ambrosia leave the dining room.

* * *

It had already been a long day for Drayton when he met Matt Desmond for dinner at the private gentlemen's club on Fifth Avenue. He'd spent most of the morning combing the docks on the East River searching out Tom Landon, convincing him to come back to Rambert Paints.

After a leisurely dinner with Matt in the club's smoky but elegant dining room, talking about the carriage paint business and the economic outlook in general now that the war was over, Drayton turned the talk to serious business, asking Matt point-blank if he intended to make him the necessary loan.

"To be honest," Matt began with a little smile, "I'm surprised you really want to go through with this. When you mentioned taking over that business a few weeks back, I didn't really take you seriously." He paused to offer a cigar to Drayton and to light one for himself. "What makes you want to take over your father's business now? After two years of letting it fend for itself? All this might have made more sense if you'd come home sooner, if you'd shown interest before the company was ready for bankruptcy."

There was a long space of silence. "I made a mistake," Drayton admitted softly, studying his cigar as he considered what might have been if he had come home sooner, if he hadn't married Ambrosia, hadn't fathered a child. "But I intend to rectify that mistake," he went on, his blue eyes determined as they lifted to meet Matt's, "if I can borrow the money I need to do it."

Matt let out a lengthy breath as he flicked an ash into a small brass tray. "What do you know about carriage paint, Drayton?"

"I've gone over the books more times than I can count. The demand is there. It's a matter of producing a good-quality product again and winning back the confidence that was lost. I don't pretend to know every facet of the business yet, but I know someone who does. Tom Landon was father's right-hand man, and he knows the business inside and out. I offered him a partnership if he'd come back, and he's accepted.''

Matt's mouth curved into a slow smile of admiration. Drayton was a persuasive talker. He made everything sound perfectly logical and sound. "It's still one hell of a gamble, Drayton. You know that, don't you?"

"Probably better than you do," he responded evenly. "But I'm willing to take it."

A hint of a smile touched Matt's eyes. "Then I suppose I'm willing to convince the bank to go along with you."

As if on cue, a waiter appeared at the table and asked if either gentleman would be wanting brandy. Drayton gave a nod, and was surprised when Matt declined.

"I hope you'll excuse me if I run along. I have an appointment with someone who vehemently objects to my indulging in alcoholic beverages. I'll have a devil of a time as it is explaining away the bourbon I had before dinner." He rolled his eyes and gave a wry smile. "I know, I know. I could easily find a mistress with less fastidious tastes. But she's really a darling otherwise, pretty as a picture and lively as a sprite." He withdrew his pocket watch and glanced at it. "And she'll be mad as a wet hen if I keep her waiting much longer." He replaced his watch in the pocket of his silver brocade vest and rose, tossing his napkin on the table. "Audrey has several lovely friends, if you happen to be free for the rest of the evening," he suggested discreetly. "There was one little blonde—"

"Another time, perhaps," Drayton broke in, taking a long sip of the brandy that had been set before him.

"Another time," Matt repeated. "Well . . . I'll state your case at the directors' meeting Thursday and get a message to you sometime Friday." With a smile and a brief handshake, Matt left Drayton alone.

For a long time after he had gone, Drayton sat at the table rolling the stem of his glass thoughtfully through his long fingers. He wondered why he had been so quick to refuse another woman's comfort when the one he desired offered him none. He felt a sudden stab of self-reproach for being such a fool, but more sharply, more acutely, he was aware of his loneliness, of the cold emptiness that filled his soul. He sipped at his brandy slowly, trying to shake off the feelings, knowing that he ought to go to the house in Gramercy Park, the house that had been his father's . . . and Aaron's. But the huge brownstone held nothing for him but memories of an unhappy childhood, of a loneliness too much like what he was feeling now. He wasn't sure he could face any of that tonight.

He drained his glass and rose from the table. Foolish as it was at this late hour, he was going back to Elmwood.

Chapter 31

As soon as the house was quiet, Ambrosia slipped from her bed and dressed, then groped her way downstairs to Sheba's small room near the kitchen. She sat on the narrow bed and shook the older woman for several moments before she finally managed to rouse her from a deep sleep. Then a pair of huge brown eyes stared at Ambrosia in disbelief. "You's gonna what?"

"I am going to leave here. You are a free woman now, and I cannot force you to come along, but—"

Sheba's face reflected her hurt. "You ain' nevah had t' do no forcin' in de past," she reminded her. "An' I stayed wi' you den." Her broad forehead creased with concern as she fidgeted with the sleeve of her nightdress. "But, Miz Ambrosia, why you wanna leave heah? Yoah time a-comin' soon and dis seem like a good place t' hab a chile. Dez fine folks heah, deh is. An' de majah, he ain' nevah done nothin' t' hurt you, hab he?"

Ambrosia stood abruptly. "He forced me to come here," she said, her eyes as hard as her tone. "But he cannot force me to stay. I won't raise my child a Yankee. I am leaving this place tonight, Sheba. If you're going with me, then you'd better hurry and dress."

Sheba bit her lip hard as she scurried from the comfort of her bed. She knew enough not to argue with Ambrosia

347

when her mind was made up. And she could hardly consider remaining behind all alone.

Reluctantly Sheba followed Ambrosia to the stables in the darkness of the night. The ground was damp, and the moon, though full and bright, was hidden now and again by clouds. Holding a warning finger to her lips, Ambrosia left Sheba outside the stable and felt her way to the wall hooks, from which she removed a saddle. She carried it outside and threw it over the upper slat of a split-rail fence. She repeated her movements until she had two saddles, two bridles, and blankets, then led each of the two mares she had chosen weeks before into the warm, humid air of the night. It took her more time than she had planned to saddle both horses. Hefting the saddles proved a real struggle of will, even with Sheba's help, which was clumsy and hesitant at best.

When the horses were ready, they walked them a good distance from the stable before Ambrosia turned to Sheba and gave a nod. Then she looked about for a large rock or line of fencing that would aid them in mounting. She quickly found a flat-topped boulder that was perfect. Sheba had little trouble climbing atop her horse's back while Ambrosia steadied the animal. She promptly handed the older woman the reins, climbing the rock herself. She flung her small bundle over the pommel and hitched up her skirt to mount. She chose to ride astride, as she had done as a child, simply because of the control the position allowed her, control she might well need. Once in the saddle she turned back to Sheba, who stared dumbly at her hands and nervously twisted the reins. "Ready?"

Sheba gulped. "Uh . . . uh . . . Miz Ambrosia?"

"What is it, Sheba?" Ambrosia asked impatiently.

"Ah—ah ain' nevah rid no horse afore."

Ambrosia let out a breath through clenched teeth. "There's nothing to worry about, Sheba. You get on the horse's back and the horse does everything else. Just get a firm hold on the reins. My horse will be leading."

Sheba nodded, her thick lower lip trembling in the moonlight. "Yes'm. A firm hol' on de reins. A firm hol' on de reins."

Ambrosia coaxed her horse to a trot, then glanced over her shoulder to see that Sheba's horse still stood grazing leisurely. Ambrosia retraced what little ground she had covered and brought her horse around to face the older woman.

". . . firm hol' on de reins," Sheba was muttering, her eyes squeezed tightly shut. "I gots t' keep a firm hol' on de reins. . . ."

With a sigh of frustration, Ambrosia turned her horse again so that they both faced in the same direction. "Sheba."

The black woman winced and hesitantly opened her eyes. "Ah's got 'em tight, Miz Ambrosia."

"Give me the reins."

Sheba happily complied. "Yes'm."

"Now hold on to the pommel."

Her face went blank. "De what?"

"This!" Ambrosia indicated the pommel and Sheba nodded vigorously as her plump fingers took firm hold. She felt much better about holding something that was secure, instead of a few flimsy strips of leather.

"Hold on tight."

Sheba nodded and held on for all she was worth when the beast beneath her began to move. Ambrosia led the horse slowly at first, knowing that Sheba was frightened out of her skin. But after a time at an easy trot, Ambrosia's patience waned. And then she was galloping at full speed, the air cool and moist on her cheeks, her mouth breaking into a triumphant smile. She was free!

For a time movement was free and easy, in spite of the darkness. The horses almost seemed as eager to reach the city as Ambrosia herself. But her mare slowed a bit as the road wound through a thick growth of trees and shadows overlapped in a dense curtain of black, cutting visibility to nothing. The mare's strides became uncertain and hesitant until she was picking her way gingerly over the rutted roadway. Ambrosia's breath quickened and her hands tensed on the reins as she became aware of the danger of traveling unfamiliar ground in such darkness. But she did not for a moment consider turning back. Escape was the only thing that she had thought about these past weeks, and this was her only hope of succeeding.

The light broke through the branches overhead and her mare once again took up an eager canter which Sheba protested with a loud grunt. But the reprieve was short-lived. Again and again the darkness surrounded them, the thick foliage that arched over the roadway making their journey a treacherous game of chance. Time slipped quickly by. The slow, nerve-racking pace continued. Ambrosia began to feel the stress in her muscles as the heavy burden of the child she carried made controlling the horse all the more difficult. Her confinement of the past weeks had robbed her of so much of her stamina! Her arms ached, her body demanded rest. She steadfastly refused to give it. Her only safety lay in reaching New York before she was discovered missing. There was far too much at stake to risk stopping now. She clicked her tongue and urged the mare to proceed a little faster, stopping only when the road forked to consider two markers before choosing the way. She felt the weariness taking hold of her as she forced herself onward. Her eyes began to play tricks on her, to imagine grotesque shapes in the darkness that made her start from a half-relaxed posture and twist about to be certain that she hadn't dropped Sheba's reins. Her heart beat frantically, her stomach was a tight knot. She could not free herself from a mounting dread of passing the village, or the groups of shanties or huts that had lined the road for a good mile just outside the city.

The road opened up again, the moonlight flooded her path. Ambrosia prodded her mare to take advantage of the length of road ahead, her confidence returning as she squared her shoulders and lifted her chin. It was then that she became aware of a faint thudding of a rider in the distance. She smiled. It could not be much further to the village now, she was sure of it. The approach of another horse made her all the more certain.

The horseman was still at a fair distance when Ambrosia felt an eerie prickling at the nape of her neck. She slowed her pace a bit to consider the all-too-familiar form, not wanting to believe what her instincts were screaming at her. But as he drew nearer and nearer, she could not deny what she saw.

She let out a small cry of frustration and fear as she jerked back hard on the reins. The mare reared and whinnied, pawing the air in confusion as Ambrosia struggled to maintain her seat. "It's Drayton!" she cried, tossing a bewildered Sheba the reins. "Run! Run!"

Ambrosia twisted her horse about and headed in the opposite direction. But the maneuver cost her precious time. Drayton had drawn close enough to hear her cries and to recognize Sheba. Now he was urging his stallion to full speed in pursuit.

Ambrosia dug her heels repeatedly into the mare's belly, wanting to scream as the thundering hooves behind her drew closer and closer. In a last effort to lose him, she turned her horse abruptly off the road toward an open field, but the rhythm of a second horse's thudding hooves still echoed in her ears. She felt more than saw him beside her. She urged the mare all the more frantically. A hand shot out to grasp her horse's bridle, and strength far superior to hers pulled it back, slowing the confused animal to a rough stop.

Ambrosia slid from the saddle and ran as fast as her legs would carry her through the thick meadow grass, hoping to reach the woods where she might hide. She stumbled to her knees, got up, and began running again, her chest aching with the exertion, her leg muscles twitching and shaking as she forced them on. She had to escape him! She had to! This was her only chance!

Drayton caught hold of her before she covered even

half the distance to the woods. Restrained by his grasp, she whirled and fought him savagely, kicking and biting and scratching, wanting desperately to hurt him. Drayton might have subdued her easily had he not been so concerned about her pregnancy. As it was, it was all he could do to hold her.

"I hate you!" she screamed as he wrestled her slowly to the ground. "I'll never go back there with you!"

"And just where do you intend to go?" he demanded, his breath coming just as hard as hers.

"I hate you!"

"Answer me! Where?"

She spit at him and suddenly his face was a frightening mask of rage. He had never really imagined that she would try to run away. The anger that took hold of him was so strong it made him shake as he stared at her face, as the last of his hopes for any kind of a life with her were wrenched from his heart. And in that moment he hated her as passionately as he had ever loved her. If it had not been for the child, he might have killed her with his bare hands.

"I won't go back with you!" she sobbed hysterically. "I won't!"

"Oh, yes you will." He took brutal hold of her arms and pinned them behind her back. Then he removed his belt and roughly turned her sideways, so that he could bind her hands securely. A fresh flow of tears splashed over her face. He grasped her shoulders and yanked her to her feet. "Yankee bastard," she muttered.

He gave her a none-too-delicate shove toward the horses. "Move."

Somehow Sheba managed to get her horse going in the same direction as Drayton's and followed them back to the house without making a single sound. Ambrosia rode half the distance with her hands bound, her mare's reins in Drayton's hands. Only when her body sagged forward in exhaustion and threatened to slip from the saddle did Drayton loosen her hands and place her on his own horse, where his arms encircled her limp body and give her support the remainder of the ride.

The three reached the house in the darkest hours of the night. Sheba hurried away without ever daring to look Drayton in the eye, but she saw him pull Ambrosia from the saddle and heard him carry her up the stairs. She mouthed a silent prayer for her mistress's safety, then huddled in her own narrow bed and tried to get some sleep.

Once upstairs in their room, Drayton removed Ambrosia's shoes and stockings and most of her clothing before he left her to tend to the horses. She was almost grateful for his help, since she was too tired and weak to undress herself. She was asleep long before he returned to the room, her mind unable to focus on the fact that she had failed to escape and what that failure meant.

Chapter 32

Ambrosia woke when the painful brightness of the sun fell across her face. She turned away from it, groaning as her sore muscles and bruised skin protested the movement. She let out a long breath as she forced herself to relax again, but her mind was alert now, and the memory of what had happened the night before quickly jarred the sleep from her body. She struggled to sit upright, leaning heavily on one arm while the other groped for the bedpost.

"I didn't expect you to wake so soon. Not after last night."

She jerked to attention at the sound of his voice, meeting his cool blue eyes with a sneer before turning away and pulling the bed linens up to her chin. She had to fight to keep from wincing with every move, so tired, so sore were her muscles.

He rose from the chair he had occupied throughout the night and strode toward the French doors which opened onto a small terrace. For a time he was silent. When he turned to face her, his face was a perfect calm. "You have tried me for the last time, Ambrosia. I never actually thought you would try to leave here in your condition, without a penny to your name, with no protection. You might have been thrown last night. Or worse. Did you ever stop to consider the dangers facing you?'' He paused, then gave a short laugh and shook his head. ''How little you must care for the life you carry to act so selfishly, without giving a thought to the consequences.''

She stared at the opposite wall, feeling a terrible stab of guilt. What he said was true. Until this moment she had not really considered the baby's safety. She had only known that she must get away from here at any cost. Escape had been the only thing she had thought of since coming here. And now she had failed.

''I told you before that I could easily make this a prison for you. You have seen fit to challenge my words. So this morning,'' he went on indifferently, ''you will move to new quarters, to a room in which you will remain until the birth of our child. I will see that meals are brought up to you, that you are made as comfortable as possible. But you will be locked in the room at all times.'' There was no anger in his voice, no emotion at all.

Ambrosia's lip trembled at the thought of being locked away. There would be no hope of escape. There would be no hope for anything. She stared down at her hands, vaguely wondering how she would survive the confinement.

''To my knowledge, no one but Sheba knows what went on last night. And I have no intention of telling anyone, except Lily, the truth . . . unless your behavior forces me to do so. I prefer to say that you have contracted a fever which might be contagious, that you will remain in your room until you have fully recovered.'' He paused. ''I would advise you to consider the future complications should you choose to cross me again, Ambrosia. I could easily have you placed in an asylum once the child is born.''

''No!'' Her cry was full of panic, her eyes wide and frightened. He meant it! Dear God, he meant every word of it! She stared helplessly at the hard set of his mouth, at the icy blue eyes, and she realized just how much he hated her now. A terrible fear gripped her at the realization and she felt herself tremble in dread. "Please," she whispered, "please don't do that."

He let out his breath and faced away, feeling revulsion at the thought of doing what he had threatened to do. He had seen the horror of asylums, but he would do it if she tried him. The anger in him was that strong. He needed to prove to her, and perhaps to himself, that he was capable of hurting her in the same brutal way she had hurt him.

He turned to face her. "Don't test me, Ambrosia," he said tersely, ignoring the frightened, childish look in her eyes. "Get dressed now," he ordered gruffly. "I'm taking you to your room."

Lily nearly stumbled in her haste as she made her way to the parlor, where Bessie had told her her nephew would be waiting. "Drayton, is it true?" she demanded the moment she crossed the threshold. "Bessie says that Ambrosia is seriously ill. She didn't eat well yesterday—"

Her voice broke off in midsentence as he turned to face her. A half-filled glass of whiskey was in his hand and his eyes were hard and cold. "Sit down, Lily."

She stared at him for a long moment. "What is it, Drayton? Did she lose the baby?"

He sighed and glanced away a moment. "No," he answered in a much gentler tone. "It's nothing like that." He set his glass on the mantel and strode past her favorite chair, pausing to give its upholstered high back a pat. "Sit down, Lily. Please."

Lily eyed him anxiously but did as he requested without further protest. He moved to close the parlor doors and returned, momentarily contemplating the chair nearest Lily's. He drew a deep breath and began to pace the room, obviously in far too much turmoil to take a seat at all. "Ambrosia is not ill," he began finally, stopping at the mantel to retrieve his glass. "She tried to leave here last night, Lily."

Lily let out a startled gasp. "Tried to leave? But how?"

He met her eyes and seemed almost amused. But there was something else in his eyes that was nothing like amusement. It was hard and ugly. "As a matter of fact, she stole two of your best mares. She took Sheba with her, though I don't blame Sheba for any of this. It wasn't her idea, I'm sure."

"But—how did you know that she meant to leave?"

"Quite by accident. I decided to return here last night, after I finished my meeting with Matt. Unfortunately for her, we met on Bloomingdale Road."

Lily stared at him, her eyes still wide. A moment later she shook her head vigorously. "No. I cannot believe any of this," she said firmly. "Why, in her condition she could hardly saddle a horse herself, much less ride properly. And Sheba—"

He slammed his fist hard on the mantel. "Dammit, don't you understand? She wasn't thinking of her condition; she can't think of anything but the war, and the hate it filled her with. She'd do anything to be free of her Yankee husband." He lifted his glass of whiskey and drained it in a single swallow while Lily watched in silence, agonizing over what she saw in his eyes and heard in his voice. She was shocked and angered, and she could think of nothing to say to comfort him.

There was a long silence. Drayton stared stonily at his empty glass, then let out a lengthy breath and shook his head. "She has nothing, no money, no land, no family to speak of, yet she would have left here, would have given birth to our child God-knows-where and worked herself to death to keep him fed and clothed rather than accept the home I offered her." His voice became like steel as he went on. "She wants no part of me. And now I want no part of her." He straightened abruptly and went to pour himself another glass of whiskey. He took a long swallow, and spoke in a low, harsh tone. "I will not allow her to ruin a child's future just to satisfy her hate.

The baby is mine too, and it will be born here, where I can protect it.''

''But how can you—?''

''I have locked Ambrosia in the attic room.''

''But you can't mean to keep her there! There must be some other way!''

''There is no other way. She will remain there until the child is born.'' He finished off his drink and went to refill it again. ''I shall tend to her needs for the next few days myself, until I can find a woman to—''

''A woman! I have plenty of help here, Drayton,'' Lily protested. ''Surely Emily is trustworthy enough to be given the task. I insist on it.''

''It's too late for coddling, Lily. I've already made up my mind. I've told Bess and the others about Ambrosia's illness, and none of them will be allowed on the second floor until she recovers. I shall be going to town tomorrow morning to hire someone to care for her.''

''You are acting in haste, Drayton,'' Lily said softly. ''Please reconsider before you do something you will regret. Ambrosia is not an animal. If you reason with her—''

''Reason with her!'' he flung back. He let out a short laugh. ''I am doing what I have to do, Lily, and nothing more.'' He finished off his bourbon and once again made to refill his glass.

''Getting drunk won't solve anything,'' she reproved.

He half drained the glass he had just poured. ''I know.''

She watched him for a moment, then let out a breath through clenched teeth and rose, leaning heavily on her cane. He had drunk quite a bit in the days following Kathryn's death, and Lily had learned not to argue with him when he was in a mood like this. Better to give him a free rein until he settled down a bit on his own and was ready to listen to reason. She bit her lip hard then, recalling that he had never gotten over Kathryn's death, that he had never spoken of it to her, to anyone. . . . She looked one last time at his face, so hard and cold and closed. There was no hope of reaching him now. With a sigh of reluctance, she left him to himself.

Chapter 33

The room was large, the walls simple rows of rough, exposed beams, the ceiling dipping low to follow the slope of the roof. Three small, four-paned windows, one on each of three walls, were without curtains, and a long row of neatly stacked boxes and crates lined the remaining wall.

Ambrosia's furnishings consisted of an old but comfortable trundle bed, a plain wooden chair, a washstand with pitcher and basin, and a small table on which stood a brightly painted oil lamp and hand bell, which she was instructed to ring if she wished to summon help.

During the first days of her confinement Drayton brought her meals on a tray, paced the room in silence while she ate, then collected the tray and cutlery and left her alone again. He spoke to her only once, when she questioned him about Sheba, saying that since she had only acted out of loyalty, he had no intentions of punishing her for her actions. Ambrosia lowered her eyes and bit her lip as she slowly gave a nod. She asked him nothing more.

She was a far more docile prisoner than Drayton had expected, sleeping much of the time, idly sketching with the paper and charcoals that had been left in the table drawer by someone long forgotten, silently accepting and eating the meals he brought without comment. Still, whenever he entered the room, a tangible air of tension hung between them.

Ambrosia felt an odd sort of numbness during those first days, a feeling almost like an involuntary complacency . . . until Drayton entered the room. She was always tense when he was with her, and the threats he had made about placing her in an asylum after the baby's birth always echoed in her mind. She did not allow herself to dwell on those threats otherwise, choosing instead to sketch pictures of the places and people she remembered from years past. It was a pastime she had been too busy to pursue since her days at Barhamville, and she found some solace in it now, a comfort in allowing her mind to relive a past that was no more. When she was not sketching, she would lie on the bed and study the odd distortion of her stomach as the baby wrestled and squirmed in her womb. She would try to picture the infant— sometimes she imagined a boy, other times a girl—but always the baby was in her arms, always smiling up at her. The child was the only part of her present reality she could bear to consider.

The woman Drayton hired to care for Ambrosia was a tall, thin Englishwoman whose lips were naturally pursed dourly and whose left brow was perpetually raised in an expression of arrogant inquiry. She spoke very little, answered questions with a simple yes or no, and in general avoided conversation. She began bringing Ambrosia her meals in Drayton's stead, regarding the younger woman with her left brow raised even higher than usual in a gesture of disapproval. She eyed Ambrosia warily all the while she changed the bed linens or swept the floor or cleared away the dinner tray, as if she honestly thought the girl would pounce on her from behind like a lunatic. When Ambrosia questioned her about who she was, Miss Wilcox explained brusquely that she was a nurse hired to see to Mrs. Rambert's needs until the baby came, then added pointedly that *Mr.* Rambert paid her salary, and that she was prepared to take orders only from him.

As soon as Drayton had hired Miss Wilcox, he threw himself into his work, spending long days and even some nights in the city, arranging for the sale or disposal of an entire warehouse of paints of questionable quality, visiting each of three Brooklyn factories with Tom Landon, who went over and over each facet of production with him until he knew almost as much about the process as Tom himself.

Drayton's teacher was a burly, ruddy-faced man with a raspy voice and gruff manner that had frightened Drayton as a boy. Tom personally saw to the dismantling and cleaning of the machinery at the factories, explaining the intricate workings of each piece to Drayton as he went along. Tom was a man whose life had always centered around his work, and in that respect, he and James Rambert had been two of a kind. And Drayton was beginning to live his life in much the same way.

The days grew longer, hotter, and unbearably boring. Ambrosia unpacked the various boxes and crates that lined the wall, found nothing that interested her, and so methodically repacked everything and put each item back in its proper place. Several times she asked Miss Wilcox if she might have a book or a newspaper, only to be informed that Mr. Rambert had said nothing about either of those items and until he did, she was not at liberty to supply them. As the days dragged on in dismal sameness, Ambrosia memorized the views from the windows and counted the wallboards and rough beams a hundred times over. She took to pacing the floor for hours at a time, to keeping track of her steps and the number of times she turned. She began to write down what she had eaten for breakfast, lunch, and dinner. Time ceased to have any real meaning to her. With each passing hour she grew more subdued, quieter, less able to think clearly. Often she would sit in silence, reliving the days before the war, remembering the sound of her father's voice, the smell of freshly turned ground after a spring rain, the way she had felt when Ledger laughed.

One morning, she sat on the edge of the bed, lost in her thoughts, staring vacantly at the opposite wall. She did not realize at first that Lily had opened the door and stood on the threshold of the room, trying to catch her breath. The struggle of climbing three flights of stairs had left the older woman totally exhausted. When Ambrosia finally started and turned toward her visitor, Lily made no attempt at a warm greeting. "May I sit down, please?" she requested, still breathless from her climb.

Ambrosia eyed her warily for a moment before offering her the only chair. She herself went to stand by a nearby window and fixed her eyes on the familiar grounds below.

"I apologize for not coming sooner. It is only that the stairs are so difficult for me these days . . . and Drayton . . . Drayton did not approve of my visiting you."

Ambrosia's eyes touched hers for a moment. She showed no expression. She stared out the window again.

"Sheba has been asking after you. She's very concerned."

"Please tell her not to be," Ambrosia returned evenly, without turning to meet her eyes. "I'm quite well."

Lily's jaw tightened. "Come here, Ambrosia." Her voice was firm. Ambrosia looked at her in surprise. "Please." The older woman patted the bed and nodded, urging Ambrosia to take a seat.

Ambrosia hesitated, then did as Lily requested.

"I was astonished when Drayton told me you had tried to leave here," Lily began somewhat haltingly. "I knew, of course, that you were unhappy. But I never imagined you were so desperate as to consider running away."

Ambrosia's green eyes were cool and distant. "My leaving here had nothing to do with you personally, Mrs. Collinsworth."

"I never imagined it did," Lily returned sharply. "Indeed, how could it? When you have never bothered yourself to deal with me or anyone in this household personally . . . even politely." Her face was indignant for a moment and she quickly looked away, struggling with her emotions. "I'm sorry," she said softly. "I ought not to have spoken in anger. I know that the war cost you dearly, and I understand what you must have felt, coming here." Her eyes met Ambrosia's again, this time with a direct, uncompromising look. "I understand, Ambrosia. But I cannot condone your behavior."

Ambrosia's chin lifted and she rose from the bed, returning to the window where she had stood a few moments before. Lily closed her eyes and sighed, then struggled to her feet and hobbled after her. She stood staring at Ambrosia's back for a long time before the words would come. "Whatever happened to you in the past is over now. It cannot be undone. And though it is quite obvious that you are unhappy here, the fact remains that you are Drayton's wife, that you are carrying his child. This is his home. And it will be yours and your child's as well."

Ambrosia turned, her eyes hard, a defiant spark of color at her cheeks. "This will never be my home."

"It won't unless you put an end to your childish tantrums and face the truth!"

Ambrosia stiffened and faced away. She was not a child!

Lily let out a difficult breath and touched her arm. "I do not pretend to know how you came to marry my nephew," she said softly. "Or why you choose to despise him, to blame him for what the war cost you. But the war is over, Ambrosia. And destroying him will never, never atone for the past. If only you could see that, if you could understand how deeply he cares for you—" With a sigh, Lily reluctantly withdrew her hand from Ambrosia's rigid arm. She wondered if the girl had even heard a word she'd said.

"It was not my intention to lecture you this way," she said softly, after taking a moment to compose herself. "But I want so much for you to see that what you are doing is wrong, to understand that all your hatred and bitterness will never bring back what the war has taken away from you." Lily stared at her back, trying to see anything that might indicate she was listening. But Ambrosia did not move, did not even turn to face her. Again Lily sighed, stretching a shaking hand to touch the coal-black hair that hung down the young girl's back. "The past is dead and gone, Ambrosia. You can never bring it back. We have only today, and we must be strong enough to face that."

Lily waited, but again there was no response. The hopeful gleam in her blue eyes slowly faded away. "I shall come again to visit you," Lily said as much to herself as to Ambrosia, not wanting to admit that she had failed to reach the girl. She sighed, and her shoulders were slumped in defeat as she left the room.

. . . *your hatred will never bring back what the war has taken from you . . . the past is dead and gone . . .* Again and again the words echoed in Ambrosia's head. She forced them aside as she took a deep breath of summer-scented air and closed her eyes. The past was not gone! Her memories kept that world alive and real and beautiful. Home—the lush summer-green plants against the dark brown soil; the endless fields, neatly plowed and planted; the house so imposing and elegant in the shadows of the huge oaks. She was a small child again, watching her father gallop down the long, shady drive, waiting for him, silently adoring him. She was a girl at Barhamville Academy, watching Ledger, young and dashing, as his shiny bay vaulted fearlessly over the stone wall. The ghosts of the past were all very real to her. And rooted in them was a vital part of who and what she was.

But then the war had come . . . and the Yankees. . . . Her eyes flew open, but the terrible pictures in her mind refused to disappear. Heritage was in flames, hissing and crackling as tongues of fire devoured it to the very last timber. She covered her ears in panic as she heard the sounds of gunfire and saw her father being torn apart by a thousand enemy bullets. She saw Ledger running, running to help him, running madly amid the deafening explosions of mortar shells, running until . . .

"No-o-o!" She let out a terrified scream as she crumpled slowly to the floor, sobbing hysterically with the realization of what it all meant. Everything, everyone she had ever cared about was past. And she was no longer strong enough to push the reality from her mind as she had always done before. The magnitude of it all struck her too suddenly, too sharply, like a rock hurled at her from behind. Her entire being shook with the impact and a pathetic sob of agony tore from her breast. A sob that held a lifetime of hurt, a sob that revealed all the secret pain she had never admitted was there, in her heart. There had been no time for grieving amid the past years' struggle for survival. Whenever her emotions had threatened to take hold, Ambrosia had worked herself into numbing exhaustion, or lashed out at her enemies, keeping the truth at arm's length. But the buffers were gone now. There was nothing left to fight against. In the quiet solitude of a sun-filled attic room, Ambrosia was finally confronting the truth of defeat, the truth she had never admitted, even to herself.

The tears came in a silent, burning flow as they had not come since her early childhood. So many hidden hurts locked so deeply within her soul, left to fester for so long. She curled up in a small heap and fought with all her strength against the sobs that wracked her body. But it was like trying to call back the waters of a flood. A part of her was dying, the part that had stood so strong, so brave, so unyielding in the face of defeat. For the first time in her life, there was nothing left of courage inside her. She was suddenly so cold, so aching with emptiness, so terribly weakened, and so terribly alone.

Miss Wilcox appeared as usual just after noon with a generous tray of food. She lifted her brow a bit higher as she set the tray on the table and routinely began to tidy the room. A few moments later, she paused in her labors. Her eyes fixed on Ambrosia, who sat unmoving on the edge of her bed, her eyes lowered, staring at the floor. Miss Wilcox's left brow lifted again in curiosity. The girl was normally so eager to partake of her meals. "What's wrong?" she inquired tersely. No response.

She laid a bony hand on Ambrosia's shoulder and shook her brusquely. "I brought your dinner," she announced in a clipped tone. "It won't stay hot forever."

Ambrosia lifted oddly distant gray eyes and glanced briefly at Miss Wilcox, then at the tray. She looked away.

The Englishwoman cocked her head in mild surprise, which swiftly became annoyance. She was being paid very well to tend to this young woman, and her employer would not be pleased if she were to stop eating. She went to get the tray and placed it on Ambrosia's lap. She lifted the cover from a bowl of vegetable soup and a savory aroma touched her thin, pinched nostrils. "It's time for your dinner," she told Ambrosia firmly.

Ambrosia glanced down at the tray, then quickly turned her face away, her cheeks paling at the sight of food. Miss Wilcox's eyes widened and she swiftly removed the tray from Ambrosia's lap. The nurse knew enough not to make extra work for herself. If the girl didn't feel like eating this meal, then what was the harm? There was no sense in forcing her and having it come right back up again. With a shrug she left the room with the tray, her left brow lowered in irritation as she locked the door and descended the stairs.

Two days later, Miss Wilcox felt the first stirrings of panic about Ambrosia's refusal to eat. The girl's skin was pale now, her eyes heavily shadowed, her cheekbones predominant in her face. On the third morning, she left the breakfast tray on the table in the attic room and went to get her employer. She returned with him a few moments later, her left brow lifted haughtily as she gestured toward the breakfast tray. "I've done my best, sir. But she won't listen to anything I say. Just sits there and stares like an idiot. I haven't a notion what's wrong, but you can see for yourself she's not quite right."

Ambrosia sat near the window in a plain cotton nightdress, having stubbornly refused to dress, just as she had refused her meals for the past days. Her gray eyes flickered indifferently over Drayton and the Englishwoman before staring out the window again. She had no awareness of her surroundings now. She was only aware of the emptiness inside her.

"Thank you, Miss Wilcox. I'll speak with my wife alone, if you don't mind." With a firm grip on her bony arm, Drayton led her to the door and closed it firmly behind her.

If Ambrosia had noticed Miss Wilcox's departure or Drayton's presence, she gave no sign. Her eyes were glazed, unblinking as they stared at the summer sky. Drayton studied her for a long moment, seeing sadness in those eyes, and a vulnerability that went deep. He had only seen it once before and it frightened him a little. The anger he had felt at being summoned here was suddenly gone. Something was very wrong.

"Miss Wilcox tells me you haven't been eating."

She started, then looked at him, the rich timbre of his voice somehow piercing the numbness that had imprisoned her for three days. She had forgotten how blue his eyes were, how perfect his mouth . . .

"Ambrosia?" His tone demanded a response.

She stared at his face dumbly for a moment longer before her eyes drifted aimlessly away. She wished he would not speak with her like that. She remembered once when his voice had sounded so different, so soft and comforting, when his arms had gone around her. . . .

"Ambrosia, are you feeling well?"

She glanced up at him again, then stared down at her hands, her fingers twisting nervously.

"You must eat," he told her firmly. "For the baby's sake, if not for your own."

She frowned, her eyes unmoving, and her hands instinctively sought the life inside her. An awareness suddenly clutched at her. The baby. Yes. She must think of the child. This baby was her future, the one part of her that still offered a reason to go on. How could she possibly have forgotten that?

"Ambrosia, are you certain that nothing is wrong?"

She met his eyes, so blue, so hard. What had happened to the spark of warmth she had seen there so often? There was no trace of it now.

He glanced toward the table. "I expect you to eat your breakfast."

She frowned again, feeling terribly disoriented as she stared at him. He had given her an order. In the past she had always fought against doing what he wanted. But there was no fight left inside her now, nothing but pain . . . and loneliness.

She stood and stepped woodenly toward the chair he held for her. He lifted the cover from a platter of eggs and smoked meats. She swallowed hard and lifted her fork. She had no desire to eat. But Drayton was right. She must do it for the sake of the child.

He watched her take a few small mouthfuls of the fare, somewhat surprised at what little resistance she had offered. He had assumed that her refusal to eat was a tactic employed to gain a concession of some sort from him. He had come here braced for an ugly scene. But instead he found her totally docile, detached from everything. The flashing defiance that had always taunted him was gone from her eyes. Instead there was the sad, totally vulnerable look of a lost child. He studied her as she finished a portion of the meal with mechanical precision, and his stomach knotted with some emotion he had sworn he would never feel again. He clenched his fists tightly and turned away.

"I expect you to eat your meals, Ambrosia," he said with forced sternness. "It is very important for the baby's health."

"Yes," she said in a half-whisper. She pushed away the partially emptied tray and let her hands rest on her swollen stomach.

His eyes narrowed suspiciously. He did not want to trust her. But there was no trace of willful defiance in the small, downcast woman before him. He let out a sigh of uncertainty. If he allowed her even the slightest bit of freedom, he might be playing into her hands. But her eyes were so dark and gray, so full of sadness . . . "A bit of fresh air and sunshine might do you good. I shall speak with Miss Wilcox about taking you out in the garden for a short time in the afternoons." He watched for any sign that she had expected the offer or was even pleased with it. But her eyes remained dark and empty. Just as they had been that rainy night in Charleston, so long ago . . .

Without another word, Drayton spun about and left the room. The Brooklyn factories would be opening again in another week, and he could not afford to contend with such memories now.

Chapter 34

The visits to the garden became a daily ritual for Ambrosia. While Miss Wilcox deposited her posterior primly on a stone bench near the house and worked on her knitting, Ambrosia slowly traced the flagstone walks, pausing now and again to touch the flowers. It gave her comfort to be with living things. It made her feel less isolated, less sad, to be reminded of beauty, of earth's endless renewal. Afterward, in the stuffy confines of her attic room, she would feel the pain all the more sharply. For the first time in her life, she wanted very much to be with someone who would understand, though she wasn't at all sure anyone could understand what she was feeling, since she did not fully understand it herself. The confinement drained her. She felt so alone, so desolate. Several times she tried to pray, but she wasn't really sure there was a God at all, much less one who would listen to her, or care. As the days passed her depression only intensified, until she had to force herself to eat and she found it difficult to sleep. She barely had enough energy to make the stairs for her day's single outing.

One day Lily rose early from her customary afternoon nap and chanced to see Ambrosia in the garden. Drayton had informed her of his decision to allow his wife this small privilege, just as he had informed the servants that

371

she was still quite ill, that they were to avoid her. Lily watched from her window as Ambrosia fingered a flower near the walk. The gesture was gentle and childlike, but all the same it made Lily angry. This woman had caused her nephew so much pain. Drayton had been particularly troubled these past weeks, working until all hours, sometimes staying overnight in town. When he did come home, exhaustion showed clearly in his features, and his light talk and forced smile could not disguise the fact that he was hurting. It had all begun that night when Ambrosia tried to run away. Such a foolish, irrational thing to do, and such a blow to Drayton's pride.

As she watched Ambrosia trace a path through the garden, Lily wondered indignantly what the girl had said or done to win this small concession from her husband, this bit of freedom. Then she bit her lip and shook her head. She did not want to be angry; it went against her grain. And hadn't she seen how destructive an emotion anger could be in the past weeks? She sighed, recalling reluctantly that she had promised to visit Ambrosia in her attic room again, in spite of her first visit's miserable failure. She wondered if she were really up to trying, since she was almost certain the girl would ignore her again. But then she remembered something she hadn't thought of for some time. She remembered how like Drayton this young woman was, with her fierce independence and pride, and her cool indifference to everything. . . . She leaned heavily on her cane and struggled toward the garden.

"The roses are the loveliest of all, aren't they?"

Ambrosia started and whirled at the sound of Lily's voice, though the sound of her cane and halting steps on the flagstone walk ought to have given her ample warning of the woman's approach.

"I'm sorry. I didn't mean to startle you."

Ambrosia looked away. "No . . . I—I was . . . I didn't hear you."

Lily balanced her weight on her cane as she bent to

pluck a lovely pale pink rosebud. "Did your mother keep a rose garden?" she asked as she removed the thorns.

"My mother?" Ambrosia repeated blankly, staring at Lily's face. She was smiling, and there was warmth in her dark blue eyes that Ambrosia had never allowed herself to recognize before. Lily continued to smile, but her brow lifted, reminding Ambrosia that she was waiting for an answer. "No," she said belatedly, "my mother wasn't interested in gardens much." Her voice trailed off, but suddenly her eyes brightened. "But there was a wonderful garden at Heritage. I remember that the smell of roses used to reach my bedroom window when I was a child. And I remember—" She stopped, her face clearly reflecting the pain of remembering. A part of her wanted to go on, to tell Lily everything. But something inside her could not let go.

"Heritage," Lily repeated softly. She ran the velvet petals of the rose thoughtfully over her cheek. "Was that your home?"

Ambrosia forced a nod. There was a long silence.

"Isn't it odd how the scent of flowers can bring memories to life?" Lily smiled. "Roses will always remind me of my mother. She was a poor woman, so she never had a rose garden of her very own. But she always spoke of having one." Lily sighed. "I think of her every time I walk by these roses."

"How sad," Ambrosia said softly, wondering at the regret in Lily's voice even as she struggled to contain her own tears over her own memories of childhood. She bit her lip then and slowly turned away, starting along the path, just barely restraining her emotions.

Lily walked beside her, as amazed at Ambrosia's soft replies as she was by the sorrow that ran so deep in her green-gray eyes. There was nothing of the flippancy or rudeness Lily had come to expect. And she could not help but wonder why.

Ambrosia paused at a patch of fragrant white lilies, breathing deeply of the heavy, sweet perfume that filled the summer air. But her throat remained tight, her chest aching with the effort it took not to break down. She still couldn't allow herself to do that in the presence of a stranger. Not after so many years of being strong.

"Lilies remind me of Henry, my husband," Lily said with an affectionate smile. She plucked one of the silken trumpets and studied it wistfully as she placed it against the rosebud. "Henry used to bring me lilies and say that they'd been named for me because I was so lovely, rather than the other way around." She chuckled softly and shook her head. "How silly of me to remember such things!" she scolded herself lightly. "But then, women usually treasure the trivial moments, don't we? To us, those moments when a loved one gives us flowers are every bit as precious as the moments of earthshaking decision, aren't they?"

Ambrosia could not meet her eyes. "Yes," she whispered.

She walked on in silence with Lily at her side. She paused beneath the drooping boughs of a willow tree, staring at the neat carpet of heart-shaped leaves, all that remained of the violets that had bloomed early in the spring. Lily noticed then that tears were slipping quickly over her cheeks. "Ambrosia?" She stretched a comforting hand toward her, but it was too late. With a tiny muffled sob, Ambrosia whirled and ran into the house.

That very same evening, Drayton returned from the city in time for dinner for the first time in days. He had almost finished his meal and was bringing Lily up to date on the scheduled factory openings when he realized that she wasn't even listening.

". . . and we hired enough workers to operate the new grinders, and are training them for the remainder of the week to—" He stopped in midsentence and frowned with annoyance. Lily was toying with her food, her eyes glazed and distant. "Lily, are you listening to me?"

Her face was blank and she continued to play with her food.

"Lily!"

She started to attention. "Hm? What? What did you say?"

"I said, 'Lily!' " he repeated with a half-amused grin.

She gave him a weak smile. "I heard that much."

"But not a word more. You haven't eaten a bite of your food, either." Lily gnawed her lip and stared guiltily at her untouched plate. "What is it, Lily?" he demanded. "Out with it."

She sighed nervously and began to play with her fork. "You aren't going to like what I have to say."

"At least I'm listening."

"Yes, I suppose you are," she mumbled. She drew a deep breath and placed the fork to the side of her plate. "I don't approve of what you are doing to Ambrosia. It's cruel to lock her away as you've done, and I cannot bear to see it continue." She lifted a shaking hand to stop his protest and went on firmly. "I know that she tried to leave here, that you acted for the sake of her safety as much as out of anger. But I do not think she would attempt such a thing again. She must have come to realize the dangers to herself and the child. And there has been . . ." She frowned, searching for the right words. "There has been a change in her, Drayton. A change that goes very, very deep. I could see it today when I spoke with her. It—It frightened me."

Drayton's eyes were hard. "You don't know her, Lily."

"And neither do you, Drayton."

The accusation caused a startled pair of blue eyes to meet hers, telling her just how accurate her guess had been. He let out his breath and pressed a hand to his brow.

"I'm sorry, Drayton. Perhaps I ought not to have spoken so honestly. But today, when I saw her in the garden, she was so different, so much like . . . like a lost child.

She was crying, though she tried to keep me from seeing that. She is not a woman who cries easily." She shook her head. "I cannot get the picture out of my mind." Her blue eyes sought her nephew's. "And I am beginning to wonder if you keep her locked away still because you could not bear to face the change in her, either."

"That's unfair, Lily."

"Is it?" she shot back. "As I see it, there is no more justification for keeping her locked in that attic room than there is for chaining her to an iron post. You've hired a guard to keep constant watch over her. Isn't that enough?"

"She brought it upon herself, Lily! I gave her fair warning."

"And you have given her ample punishment."

He was furious for a moment. He rose from his seat and began pacing the floor with quick, angry strides. But his anger was swiftly overtaken by guilt and doubt. The changes in Ambrosia had haunted him too, these past weeks. In spite of everything, a part of him still cared enough to worry about what was happening to her. "Perhaps you're right, Lily," he admitted softly, turning to face her, almost wishing that he had remained in town that night and allowed her to escape, rather than face the fact that, after everything she'd done, he still loved her.

Lily stretched her hand toward him, and he came to take it in his own. "I know I am," she told him gently.

He sighed, squeezing her hand tightly, then letting it go and turning his back to pace again. "Could you speak with Bessie about preparing my old room?" he asked her a few moments later.

"Your room?"

He nodded. "I shall be moving my things there tonight. I spend much of my time in town these days anyway, so it won't matter to me. Ambrosia can move into the master suite, where there's ample space for a spare bed in the sitting room. That way, Miss Wilcox will be able to stay with her at all times."

Lily nodded, but was more than a little disappointed by his decision to move his wife into the room with the Englishwoman rather than remaining with her himself. And the reminder that he was gone so much of the time bothered her further.

"Won't you stay and have coffee with me?" Lily pleaded as he came to kiss her cheek.

He shook his head. "I have some papers I need to go over tonight. And I'll need to be up early, to speak with Ambrosia about changing rooms. . . ." He sighed, planting a brief kiss on her cheek and forcing a small smile before he left the room.

It was still very early when Drayton spoke with Miss Wilcox, showing her the room where Ambrosia would be staying from now on, explaining that she would be staying in the adjoining room. Miss Wilcox seemed indifferent to the new arrangement, raising her left brow and nodding as she handed Drayton his wife's breakfast tray. Without making a single comment, she went to move her own things from a small servant's room near the foot of the attic stairs. Drayton fixed a closed expression on his face as he mounted the steps to the attic. He settled the tray on a single arm and knocked at the door, then unlocked it and pocketed the key. On entering the room, he set the tray on the table and glanced about. Ambrosia appeared to be still asleep. He approached the bed and laid a hand on her shoulder. He was surprised to find it trembling and tense. Almost at once, he was aware of her labored, uneven breathing. He called her name, his voice shaking with concern.

She turned toward him, her cheeks pale, her lips almost white. Small beads of sweat covered her brow. She gave a little cry and her fists twisted tightly about the bed linens, her face reflecting the rising strength of a contraction. For what seemed an eternity, she lay there, holding her breath, clenching her teeth against the pain. And then it was easing, and she was gasping for air like a drowning man, drifting into a near-sleep that prepared her body for the next contraction. Drayton's hand smoothed the tiny wisps of hair from her moist brow. "How long have you had the pains?"

"Last night . . . I woke with them. . . ." she whispered weakly. "I don't know exactly wh—ah—" Her voice broke off as she clutched at his shirtfront, her mouth becoming a thin, colorless line. The cramping was intense, agonizing. It eased only when she was certain she could endure no more. Her head fell back in exhaustion, her hands dropped limply from his shirt.

He slipped an arm beneath her knees and another just above her waist and lifted her from the bed. "Miss Wilcox!" His voice thundered through the otherwise quiet house. "Miss Wilcox!"

He was nearly down the stairs when Ambrosia began to tense again, her face contorting with the pain, her hands groping in panic for something to hold on to. Drayton's face whitened as he all but ran to the master bedroom. "It won't be too much longer," he told her softly. He laid her on the bed and hurried to moisten a towel with cool water and press it to her brow. "You've gone through much of the worst of it," he said aloud, as much to himself as to her.

Miss Wilcox finally appeared, her thin face creased with obvious irritation. "I was doing exactly what you—"

"The baby is coming," he broke in.

The irritation abruptly left the woman's face, and she was swiftly at Drayton's side. "I shall take care of everything, sir," she told him firmly. "You send up one of the servant girls to help."

Without a single word of protest, Drayton left the room, sending Bessie to help Miss Wilcox before he closed himself in the parlor and went to work emptying a bottle of whiskey. The sight of Ambrosia struggling against the pain of giving birth had triggered something in him. An icy sweat broke over his brow as the ghosts of the past rose to haunt him. Kathryn . . . lying limp in his arms, her face burnt beyond recognition. The tiny whimpers of pain before she died. The child, still moving inside her, still alive. The last part of her that was alive . . . Oh, God, no! He couldn't remember that—he couldn't!

He filled a glass to the top with straight whiskey, desperately seeking the only relief he knew, desperately seeking to forget. He drank it quickly and was pouring a second when Lily burst in on him, her blue eyes ablaze with disbelief. "Is it true?" she cried breathlessly. "The baby's coming? It's early, isn't it?"

"Yes." He looked away and drained the glass. "But only a few weeks."

"Then what the devil do you think you're doing?"

He made an attempt at nonchalance. "I'm getting drunk." His hands trembled so violently as he filled his glass that Lily almost laughed at him.

"You'd allow that woman—a stranger—to bring your child into this world?"

"She's a qualified midwife, Lily." He hurriedly swallowed a good bit of the glass's contents as Lily stepped forward to confront him.

"And you are a doctor," she reminded him angrily.

"She won't need a doctor," he said with as much bravado as he could force. "She'll be fine."

Lily gave a derisive snort and in a gesture totally at odds with her nature, knocked the glass from her nephew's hand. He stared at her in stunned disbelief. "You are the worst kind of coward, Drayton Rambert! The kind that's afraid of himself!"

He straightened abruptly, his face fully reflecting the impact of her words. A tremor of realization went through her, and her lip began to tremble almost immediately with remorse. "I—I'm sorry, Drayton." She touched her fingers to his cheek. "I—I didn't mean—"

He pulled away from her, his eyes hard. For a long moment their gazes locked, and then he spun about and left the parlor. A few moments later, Lily watched helplessly through tear-filled eyes as he galloped off on his stallion in a mad escape from the house.

Chapter 35

The baby was born just after one o'clock in the afternoon, following six hours of difficult labor. For nearly four of those hours Lily sat at Ambrosia's bedside, ignoring Miss Wilcox's constant suggestions that she leave, holding Ambrosia's hand, speaking words of encouragement and comfort, mopping the moisture from her face with a cool compress. When the child was born it was Lily who squeezed Ambrosia's hand and tearfully told her how brave she had been, how proud she had a right to be. And Ambrosia, grasping tightly to the older woman's hand, knew that a bond of deep affection had been forged during those hours, a friendship that eased part of the loneliness she'd felt for so long.

The baby was bathed, the soiled linens replaced with fresh ones, and Ambrosia was helped into a clean nightdress. She accepted the tiny, screaming bundle from Miss Wilcox then and shyly allowed the baby to find her breast. At the first sight of her daughter, at the sound of her first cry, Ambrosia felt a mother's love that far surpassed anything she had ever thought she could feel. Her eyes filled with tears as her fingers played lightly over the feather-soft, thick black hair that covered her head; smoothed the down-covered shoulders; and traced the tiny, squared jaw. There was already so much of Drayton in the baby's face that it astonished her.

Lily peered at the baby over her shoulder, her blue eyes holding much the same look of wonder. "She resembles her father," she said, letting the baby's wee fist encircle her shaking finger.

Ambrosia's eyes met hers and they exchanged a smile. "Where is he?"

The smile faded from Lily's face, though she tried her best to keep it there. "He—he had to leave the house . . . on business," she lied.

Ambrosia's face fell. "Oh."

"He'll be back soon," Lily forced brightly. "And he will be so proud!"

Ambrosia nodded, wondering why she felt such a deep disappointment in his absence. She bent to touch her lips affectionately to the baby's head. A few moments later, exhaustion overcame her and both she and the baby were fast asleep.

Lily nodded quietly in a nearby chair until darkness fell, then left Ambrosia and sought out Debbs, the liveryman, who regretfully shook his head when she asked if her nephew had mentioned when he would be coming home. "He went out of here in a devil of a temper, though," Debbs added, stroking his chin. "And I've a strong inkling where he might have been headed."

"Barlow's tavern?" she asked with a distasteful frown.

He gave a small shrug. "Or one of the others nearby. He spent a lot of time in all of them after Miss Kathryn died."

Lily sighed. "Yes, I know." She lifted her chin. "I want you to bring him home, Debbs."

"He might not be of a mind to come, Miss Lily."

"Undoubtedly not. But do what you must. He's no match for you when he's in his cups."

Debbs threw back his shoulders and tucked his thumbs beneath his coarse suspenders. "He's still a whelp to me,

Miss Lily. But maybe I'd better hitch up the wagon, just in case," he added.

Lily's face showed a trace of uncertainty. "Try not to do too much damage, will you, Debbs?"

It was after midnight when they finally returned. Drayton had been loaded onto the back of the wagon, stone drunk, though he had sobered somewhat by the time he met Lily at the door. Still fully dressed, she shook her head ruefully and almost began to lecture him. But when she assessed his condition more closely, she decided to hold her tongue, forcing him instead to drink several cups of coffee, strong and black, before she would even give him the news.

"You have a daughter," she said finally, when his eyes had cleared a bit and he seemed half sober.

"A daughter . . ." he repeated softly, his eyes misting with emotion.

"A fine, perfect, healthy daughter who looks very much like her Aunt Lily," she teased. "And a little like her father."

He looked at Lily with sudden anxiety. "Ambrosia? Is she—?"

"She was wonderful," Lily sighed, pleased at Drayton's concern. "She has a lot of spunk, that girl. Nary a word of complaint, or a single tear . . ." Her smile faded a bit as she said that, and she noticed that Drayton had fixed a sullen stare on his empty cup. It was wrong that Ambrosia kept such a tight rein on her emotions, Lily thought. And it was wrong that Drayton had left her this morning, to face the pain of childbirth with a cold, uncaring stranger. It was all very wrong. And yet it seemed that neither could change the way they were, as if each was a helpless victim to something deep within, something Lily didn't really understand at all. She sighed and placed her hand on her nephew's. "Drayton, about this morning . . . I—I'm sorry. I should not have said what I did."

He pulled his hand away to knead at the tension at his brow. "I'm tired, Lily," he said with a weary sigh.

"I'm sure you are. But you've enough energy to come upstairs with me and see your daughter."

"It's after midnight. We'll wake her, and Ambrosia too."

Lily nodded happily. "I'd like to see the baby again."

"But Ambrosia must be exhausted."

"Yes, the poor dear. But I have the feeling that she won't mind the intrusion, considering. She's been asking for you."

His frown was skeptical. "Since when?"

"Since she saw that the child looks exactly like her father. Come along."

Drayton found it difficult to take the stairs one at a time, and almost torture to assist Lily in her slow, laborious ascent. Several times he was tempted to pick her up and carry her, or rush past her, but he knew very well she would never forgive him for doing either. For all his excitement, when they finally reached the doors, Drayton hesitated. Lily reached forward to open them. He stopped her. "Perhaps we ought to wait until morning."

She gave him a look of exasperation. "After you nearly dragged me up those stairs?" She pushed him aside and opened the doors.

Miss Wilcox, clad in a plain, white nightdress and cap, bolted upright from her bed and began an indignant string of protests aimed at Lily for interrupting her sleep. But the moment she noticed Drayton, she stopped short, straightening, gaping, then hurriedly defending her modesty with the disheveled bed linens. Drayton followed Lily through the sitting room to where a lamp had been left burning low near the cradle, just beside Ambrosia's bed. As he drew closer, the small, dark head of his daughter came into view. The baby's eyes were closed in slumber, but she sucked insistently at her tiny fist and kicked a single foot at the blanket that covered her. At first glance Drayton felt his heart stop. As a doctor he had seen more newborns than he could count, each one a wonderful part of the ongoing miracle of creation. But nothing in his past had prepared him for the feelings that filled him now, knowing that he had had a part in the creation of this child. She was whole and real and beautiful as she slept peacefully in the cradle. Joy and pride flooded Drayton's soul. Hardly daring to breathe, he slipped a hand beneath the baby and lifted her into his arms. She was incredibly tiny and soft and warm, so warm as she nestled close to his heart. She was his daughter, and the bond that began in the moment he touched her would last forever.

The baby began to squirm uncomfortably, rooting about for the fist she had sucked on so contentedly a few moments before. Unable to find it, she let out a lusty wail and Drayton smiled down at her with even greater awe.

Roused from slumber by the baby's cry, Ambrosia opened her eyes and saw them. A moment later, Drayton's eyes met hers. She looked away uneasily.

"I'm sorry I woke you," he apologized as he moved to place the baby in her outstretched arms. Her dark hair was tousled, her cheeks pale, but her eyes glowing as she took the child into her arms and comforted her. The gentleness she so rarely allowed anyone to see was there, and Drayton felt himself falling in love with that part of her all over again. He also felt, in spite of himself, a pang of jealousy. She looked hesitantly up for a moment before she unfastened her nightgown to allow the baby to suckle at her breast. Drayton glanced about for Lily but found that she had somehow managed to slip from the room unnoticed. They were alone. He watched Ambrosia feed the baby in silence, sensing her closeness to the child. He clenched his fists at his side to keep from reaching out to his wife, to keep from touching her cheek, or holding her hand. Pride could not allow him to do any of those things after the brutal lessons of the past. So he simply watched her, feeling isolated, like a stranger observing from a distance, his stomach knotting, his fists clenching ever more tightly.

"She's beautiful, isn't she?" Ambrosia said softly, running the tip of her finger over the small, dark head.

"More than that," Drayton told her, his throat painfully tight. "She's absolutely perfect."

Ambrosia searched his face for a moment before she smiled, pleased that he seemed satisfied with a daughter rather than a son. There was a short silence. "Her eyes are very blue, just like yours. I—I'm surprised how much she already resembles you." His eyes warmed considerably at the comment, and she began to smile again as well. But suddenly she was aware of the lingering scent of cheap liquor that clung to his clothing, which was rumpled and soiled. For the second time that day, she knew a deep stab of disappointment. He had chosen to spend his day in a tavern even though he knew the child was coming.

"Lily said that urgent business took you from the house this morning," she said, toying with the baby's hand.

Drayton ran a hand nervously through his hair, and when Ambrosia glanced up at him, he was staring at the child. He said nothing. She bit her lip. "My father left Heritage when I was born," she said softly, after a long moment. "He wanted a son. He was terribly disappointed." She frowned, finding that she was suddenly very near tears. She did not know why she had told Drayton any of this. She had never come close to telling anyone before . . . even Ledger. She felt him take a seat beside her on the bed, felt the warm strength of his fingers beneath her chin, forcing her to meet his eyes.

"Who told you that?"

"No one." Her voice was small and childlike. "But I knew. A child always knows if he isn't wanted." For the next few moments she refused to meet his eyes again. All the same, he knew her words had come from the heart.

They touched his own. "This child is wanted," he said finally in a quiet voice.

She nodded, then lifted eyes that were dark and gray and bright with tears. Somehow he had known they would be. A moment later she looked away from him, as she always seemed to look away. He did not know that she was suddenly recalling the threats he had made of taking this child away, of placing her in an asylum, threats which frightened her more now than ever before. He only knew that she was withdrawing from him again, that the single moment of intimacy was gone as swiftly as it had come.

"It's late," he said softly, rising and putting a more comfortable distance between them. "And you must be very tired."

Still carefully avoiding his eyes, she gave a nod. He bent to touch the baby's hair, fine and soft as down, lingering a moment longer before he reluctantly mouthed a good night and left them to their rest.

Chapter 36

Drayton and Ambrosia spent the better part of the next morning choosing a name for their daughter, finally deciding on Mary Amanda, Mary for Drayton's mother who had died when he was a child, and Amanda for Ambrosia's grandmother Amanda Grayson. But within an hour the name was shortened to Mandy, a label that seemed to suit the tiny baby much better.

During the next two days, it seemed that Mandy spent every moment in Drayton's arms that she did not spend in Ambrosia's. He held her and studied her every move and expression, watching her as she slept, walking the floor and speaking to her in low, calming tones when she cried, smiling with joy when her wee fist wrapped tightly about his forefinger. He was every inch the proud father, even as Ambrosia was the adoring mother. But the apprehension, the uneasiness between husband and wife only fed on the time they spent together with their child.

The color flared in Ambrosia's cheeks whenever he watched her breastfeed the baby, clearly betraying her self-consciousness. And there were moments when suddenly their eyes would lock, and their smiles would vanish, a tense expectancy growing almost unbearable until one of them looked away. They were all but strangers to one another, held apart by barriers that had been erected long before. And a shared attachment to this small new life was not strong enough to begin to remove those barriers. As the novelty wore thin, the silent friction between them grew, and Ambrosia fearfully pulled further and further away.

Just two days after Mandy's birth, Drayton knew he could not remain at Elmwood. The child he had shared in creating, the warm little baby who slept so contentedly in his arms, needed her mother far more than she needed him. Mandy belonged with Ambrosia, and he did not belong at all. On the morning of the third day, he quietly packed his things and made known his intentions to move permanently to the house in Gramercy Park.

"But you're taking all of your things," Lily protested in bewildered disappointment.

"The factories are due to open soon, Lily. I can't expect Tom to handle all the responsibility himself." He turned toward her slowly and met her eyes. "I'm planning to stay in town," he told her evenly. "I have a house there, and it's foolish to waste time traveling back and forth."

Lily searched his face, biting back the words that rushed to her lips. She knew very well he hated that house, that he was leaving here for a different reason. But to confront him with that knowledge now would only drive him further away. Perhaps he merely needed time by himself to think, she thought hopefully. And perhaps, if he left for just a little while, Ambrosia would think things through as well.

"We'll expect you home for Sunday supper," she said in what she hoped was a light tone.

"Not this week."

"Then next. Promise me, Drayton."

He sighed as he lifted his bags, giving her a small smile that did little to boost her hopes. "We'll see."

Ambrosia was relieved that Drayton spent so much of his time in the city during those first weeks, since his presence made her so uncomfortable. She was still so very afraid that he would lock her away forever, that she would be separated from her baby. Ambrosia knew that she would never survive that. But when Drayton paid only two brief visits to Elmwood during the months of August and September, that fear eased a bit, leaving her with only a feeling of tension and anxiety whenever she thought of him. He said very little to her during those visits, concentrating his attention almost entirely on his daughter. Drayton was awed by Mandy's growth each time he saw her and thrilled with the way she was already beginning to respond to his voice. He questioned Ambrosia about her progress, about her daily schedule, and showed an interest in everything she told him. Yet Ambrosia noticed that whenever they spoke or chanced to touch, there was a cold, studied indifference to him, a careful keeping at arm's length. She was quite hesitant, therefore, to speak with him about dismissing Miss Wilcox, even though the older woman had become overbearing and almost impossible for Ambrosia to live with.

Almost two months after Mandy's birth, Miss Wilcox still insisted on clothing and diapering and bathing the baby, refusing Ambrosia's help and discarding any comments she made as to the baby's care. The older woman was increasingly adamant in her suggestions that a wet nurse be hired for the baby, since "a proper woman wouldn't want to risk the disfigurement long-term suckling might cause."

It was only when Lily insisted that Ambrosia speak with Drayton that she managed to work up the courage to make the request just after Sunday supper. Ambrosia had eaten next to nothing, but the moment the meal was finished, she politely requested that Drayton have a word with her in the parlor. In private. She was shaking slightly as he closed the door, feeling the same tension she always felt when she was near him. She told herself that she must be calm so that she could state her case clearly, briefly. But it was very very hard to control the trembling in her voice, which sounded thin and shaky in spite of her best efforts. Her eyes only dared to meet his once, briefly, so she was unaware of the anger that flared in him when she related things Miss Wilcox had said and done.

"The situation has become . . . quite difficult in the past weeks," she concluded. She paused a moment and searched his face, not quite knowing what else to say. He was silent. "I—I know that you hired her to—"

Ambrosia stopped short, her eyes quickly avoiding his, her cheeks paling as she recalled exactly why he had hired the woman. For the first time since that night she felt more than just a brief pang of guilt for having tried to run away, for having endangered Mandy's life as well as her own. She felt terribly ashamed. How had she ever rationalized such a reckless scheme in her mind, knowing that she carried a life? And how had she justified hating him for protecting that life, first in Charleston, by forcing her into marriage so that the baby would have a name, and again by keeping her prisoner here? She closed her eyes tightly against the burning tears that filled her eyes as she pictured Mandy, beautiful, healthy Mandy, thin and sickly and dressed in rags, a child of the streets, a child of poverty. She felt Drayton's eyes upon her, waiting for her to continue. But she could not begin to lift her eyes to face the indictment she was certain was there in his face. She swallowed hard several times, the silence tearing at her control, the shame flooding her heart. "I—I have no intention of—of leaving here," she said so softly that he hardly heard the words. She squared her shoulders and finally met his cold blue eyes, wanting very much to cry that she was sorry, that she finally saw how wrong she had been. But there was no reason to think he expected or wanted an apology now. His eyes said clearly that he wanted nothing from her. Nothing. "I—I give you my word that I will not leave Elmwood," she forced herself to say.

Drayton stared at her for a long moment, remembering

another time when they had played out a similar scene. She had disobeyed his order then and had only given her promise to obey when he had forced her to do so. He had won that battle, but all the while she had mouthed the words the hatred inside her had burned. And in the end that hatred had been the victor, leaving nothing of victory or even pride in him. He turned away from her squared shoulders and tear-brightened eyes, wanting to laugh now at Lily's assurances that she had changed, that she was no longer hate-filled and full of vengeance. His wounds were too fresh and deep for him to begin to believe that, for him to risk feeling anything beyond anger or indifference. He had been a fool once too often to see anything in Ambrosia's face that he could trust.

"I shall leave the decision of Miss Wilcox's employment up to Lily," he said finally, turning again to face her, knowing full well that Lily would dismiss the woman. At least by leaving the decision to someone else, Drayton had not admitted trusting his wife. It was something Ambrosia was instantly aware of and hurt by. "Is there anything else?" he asked in a cool, impersonal tone.

She swallowed a large lump in her throat and shook her head. Without another word, he turned his back on her and left the room.

After Miss Wilcox's departure in late September, Ambrosia struggled to keep up with her baby's immediate needs, clumsily changing Mandy's clothing and bedding and worrying herself sick each and every time the baby cried. Even with Emily's help, Ambrosia found it difficult. She had never realized that the skills of child care were learned with a great deal of time and practice, but she was determined not to relinquish her responsibilities to anyone else. She loved Mandy too much for that. And eventually her determination to learn won her confidence and skill.

By the first week of October Mandy had settled into a

schedule of regular napping in the morning and after-noon, leaving Ambrosia free for several hours each day. She began to spend her free time walking about the grounds of Elmwood, where the vivid colors of autumn were splashed so dramatically across hill and sky. The pleasant crunch of dried leaves marked her every footstep and a nearby brook rushed and gurgled, but otherwise there was only peace and quiet. Overhead were the same trees she had studied from an attic window weeks before, though they were no longer lush and green. The green had yielded to gold and brown and crimson, and the air whispered of a harsher winter than she had ever known at Heritage. Everything was different here. Often when she thought of home she was keenly aware of the emptiness that still remained in her heart. For so much of her life she had lived only to be strong and brave. Even as a child Ledger had recognized that part of her, had admired her for her courage and strength. They were the only quali-ties anyone had ever admired in her, the only ones she had ever thought to accept in herself. But in spite of her mightiest efforts to be strong and brave as her father had been, to deny pain and grief and loss as he would have done, she had failed. Loss had broken her. There was nothing left of the courage and strength that had been her identity. The realization filled Ambrosia with fear and despair. Sometimes when she was far from the house, she would fall to her knees and cry, wondering why she had been left to face life after her soul had been de-stroyed, almost wishing that her body had died as well. But then she would think of Mandy, so soft and warm and perfect, lying in the crook of her arm, depending on her, drawing nourishment from her breast. She did not feel worthy of the love Mandy gave her. And Lily . . . The woman who had stayed beside her and cared for her the day Mandy was born. Ambrosia could not understand why Lily had been so kind, so warm to her, after all she had done. It frightened her. So many things frightened her now. More than anything she feared that she would never deserve the love that was given to her so freely here, at Elmwood. But she did know that she desperately needed that love now, that she could no longer face the thought of existing without it.

It seemed there were never enough hours in the day for Drayton to accomplish all he wanted to do after the factories commenced production in early September. In addition to managing the warehouse, taking full control of the books, and monitoring the factories themselves, he made personal calls on over fifty carriage manufacturers in and around the city seeking to market his products. Though the new grinding process turned out an obviously superior grade of color, a fine texture never before possible, selling those paints still proved the most difficult task of all. Too many businesses had been hurt in the past year by unreliable deliveries or were still giving refunds for the inferior paints Aaron had substituted without their knowledge. Any carriage painter willing to talk with Drayton was offered full compensation for damages suffered at the fault of Rambert Paints in the form of the new, top-quality paints. Though an expensive proposition, it did prod several reluctant painters to try the new products, and by the end of October sizable reorders were being processed, filled, and delivered to companies who had begrudgingly accepted compensation six weeks earlier. The factories were only operating at a fraction of their capacity, but the first glimmer of light was shining at the end of a long tunnel.

Chapter 37

The month of October flew swiftly past without Drayton's visiting Elmwood a single time. Though clearly disappointed at his absence, Lily regularly excused her nephew by talking about the tremendous amount of work he was doing to rebuild his father's business, the almost impossible task he had undertaken. Whenever Lily spoke of Drayton, Ambrosia would force herself to appear pleasantly attentive, but she actually felt uncomfortable. She could not forget the guilt she'd felt the night she'd asked for Miss Wilcox's dismissal, and she was always relieved when Lily steered her conversation in another direction.

The days became shorter, the air sharper as the month of November began. In spite of Lily's repeated invitations, Ambrosia kept away from the parlor whenever the Sprindle sisters came for their weekly card games and refused to go with Lily on her visits to friends who lived nearby. She even shied away from sharing an occasional dinner with Reverend Walsh, taking her dinner instead in her room to avoid confronting an outsider. In her fear, Ambrosia carefully sidestepped strangers, perceiving them as threats to her quiet, peaceful existence here at Elmwood. As the weather turned cold, Ambrosia was forced to spend more and more of her time in the house, and the confinement forced her to rely on her sketching and Lily's bright chatter to fill her empty hours. While Mandy was napping, Ambrosia would sit sketching in the library, listening to Lily read amusing letters from friends of years past, or speak wistfully about the daring things she had done as a young girl. Often Ambrosia would find herself smiling, even speaking a little of her own childhood. Lily was both pleased and encouraged to see that the ice was finally breaking. But it worried her that Ambrosia still remained so closed to outsiders, so closeted in her life here. It was almost as if she was afraid of the outside world. Nearly every part of her existence hinged on Mandy's care, and as the days passed, Lily saw clearly that Ambrosia needed more.

One dark and rainy afternoon Ambrosia sat quietly sketching before a warm fire in the library. Lily was silent for the moment as she struggled to pen a letter to a friend who had recently written to her. "Reverend Walsh! What a pleasant surprise!"

Ambrosia's head shot up in surprise when she heard Lily's greeting. Lily rose and hobbled toward the reverend.

He was a larger man than Ambrosia had expected, his face full and striking, his thick shock of unruly hair prematurely steel gray. A wide smile lit his light brown eyes as he shrugged off a rain-drenched cape and stepped eagerly forward to grasp Lily's hand. They exchanged a warm greeting before Lily turned a beaming face toward Ambrosia and made an introduction.

"I feel very fortunate to meet you, after all this time," the reverend said as he took Ambrosia's small hand in his warm, strong grasp. "Lily has told me so much about you."

Ambrosia managed a weak smile. His eyes, though warm and magnetic, had noticed her black gown. She was grateful he had said nothing about it. "Lily's told me a great many things about you too, Reverend. I'm pleased to make your acquaintance." It was a lie that tasted bitter in her mouth. In truth she had no desire to meet him or any of Lily's friends.

She lowered her eyes and turned her attention back to the sketch of Mandy she had been working on. She was relieved when she heard the reverend and Lily take a seat across the room. The reverend told Lily about a young woman newly widowed, in need of immediate assistance so that she and her five children might travel to Philadelphia where the woman's family lived. Ambrosia thought about excusing herself from the room but decided she would be less conspicuous if she remained where she was and said nothing. She went on with her sketch, catching bits and pieces of what was being said, enough to know that Lily immediately wrote a bank draft to the reverend for an amount sufficient to cover the woman's traveling expenses. Ambrosia winced as she heard Lily invite the reverend to dinner and held back a sigh a relief when he declined. She heard him rise and retrieve his cape. But suddenly he came toward her and stood beside her. She lowered her piece of charcoal and bit her lip nervously as he openly studied her sketch. "You are very talented, Mrs. Rambert."

"Thank you, Reverend." She was feeling more ill at ease with every passing moment.

"I am happy to see that you are recovered from your illness."

Ambrosia said nothing in response to that. There was very little she could say.

"I am looking forward to seeing you at Sunday services, as soon as you feel strong enough." She met his eyes and saw the hint of a challenge there, even as he extended his huge, warm hand again. Ambrosia hesitated for a moment before she allowed him to take hold of her hand, trying hard to think of an answer. Before she could think of anything, he was smiling widely. "Lily always tells me that my sermons are inspiring. You'll have to decide that for yourself, of course. But I think you would fit quite nicely into our congregation. I do hope you'll come.''

Church services the following Sunday proved an uncomfortable experience for Ambrosia, since the church in the village was quite small and the members of the congregation so well acquainted with one another that an outsider was immediately recognized. Ambrosia was painfully aware of the eyes that followed her from the moment she and Lily stepped into the small, unadorned clapboard-and-stone building. She kept her own eyes carefully lowered as she took a seat in the rough-hewn pew, holding Mandy tightly in her arms. The building reminded her a little of the country church she had attended as a child, but the people here were different. The overwhelming majority of them were poor, Ambrosia realized in one quick glance. Many were immigrants wearing strange kinds of clothing, some of it as worn and ragged as she'd ever seen. The few obviously wealthy members like Lily sat here and there in the church rather than in special seats reserved for the elite. There were no hymnals, no organ or musical accompaniment for the songs sung before and after the minister's sermon. And the sermon was different to Ambrosia as well. Reverend Walsh first read from the thirteenth chapter of John, then spoke of the command Jesus had given his disciples to love one another. The reverend made no threats of eternal damnation and never mentioned the wrath of the Almighty God. Instead he reassured the people of God's love and forgiveness, the same love and forgiveness, he said, that each man was meant to offer to his brother.

When the service ended, most of the congregation gathered outside the church to talk with the minister and other churchgoers before departing for home. There was discussion about sick members of the parish, as well as talk about the family of a young man who had recently died, and a young couple who had just announced their engagement. Everyone knew everyone here, and everyone was eager to meet the young woman who had come with Lily to services. There were countless introductions and so many brief, smiling nods of welcome that Ambrosia was sure she would remember no one. Several women seemed to stare at her black gown, but not a single person remarked on her clothing. Instead, there was much attention paid to her baby, and hundreds of questions about Drayton, followed by looks of disappointment when Lily said he was working in the city now, and no longer a doctor. Only one elderly woman greeted Lily as a friend and warmly touched the baby's hand, then froze and turned her back on Ambrosia the moment she heard her accent.

"Don't mind her," Lily whispered. "She lost both her boys in the war."

Ambrosia bit her lip, understanding the woman's rude behavior all too well. She managed a smile for the last person out of the church, an ancient, hunched-over old woman with sparse, corkscrew curls here and there about a deeply wrinkled face. Bea Hanover moved as slowly as a tortoise, and reminded Ambrosia very much of one in her huge green hoop skirt with mended lace trim. She grasped Ambrosia's small hand tightly in her thick, gnarled fingers and leaned forward on a large wooden cane. "So you're the one who married our Dr. Rambert," she announced so loudly that Ambrosia knew she was terribly hard of hearing. "Well, where is he?" she demanded. "I need to talk to him about my headaches."

"My husband is working in the city," Ambrosia mouthed in what she hoped was a voice loud enough for Bea to hear.

"Why are you making him do that?" Bea pressed shrilly. "He belongs here, you know."

"I told you Drayton had taken over his father's business in the city, Bea," Lily broke in, noticing the color in Ambrosia's cheeks.

"Yes, you told me," Bea admitted begrudgingly. "But what's she doing here if her husband's living there?"

"Ambrosia has been ill," Lily told her in a sharper tone.

"Indeed!" Bea was still holding fast to Ambrosia's hand, but now her eyes ran pointedly up and down the length of her, as if still questioning why she was here and her husband was elsewhere. "You tell him I said he ought to come back here," she half screamed at Ambrosia. "We need a good doctor. Haven't had one since he left." She paused, eyeing her up and down again. "If I married a man like Dr. Rambert, I certainly wouldn't want him living in the city," she said bluntly.

"We really must be going now, Bea," Lily insisted, disengaging the older woman's hand from Ambrosia's and turning the younger woman toward the carriage.

"You tell him what I said," Bea called even more loudly as Lily and Ambrosia walked away. "You be sure and tell him."

Debbs assisted Ambrosia into the brougham, and she sank into the thick leather seat with a sigh of exhaustion. She had expected the stares, the curiosity about her dress, the questions about her manner of speech which so clearly betrayed her Southern background. But she had not anticipated the interest in Drayton since he had been gone for so long, for months even before the start of the war. And yet she ought to have expected it. She was his wife, after all. His wife, she thought numbly, even though she had never really been a wife to him. She pushed the troubling thoughts from her mind, unable to deal with them now. She held Mandy a little closer and reminded herself that she would be back at Elmwood soon, that she would once again be safe and secure.

Lily was silent for a little while as the carriage began its journey home. She knew that Ambrosia was troubled, that this morning would have been difficult for anyone, but especially for a woman who had isolated herself for months. "I'm glad you came to services with me this morning," Lily said finally, breaking the silence. "It gives me such joy to introduce you to all of my friends."

Ambrosia's eyes were dark and skeptical as they met hers, then quickly looked away.

"You mustn't let Mrs. Reed upset you," Lily went on. "As I told you, she lost both her sons in the war and she hasn't gotten over that yet. That doesn't pardon her rudeness, but it does help to explain it. As for Bea Hanover, well, she's all of ninety-three years old and practically destitute. I suppose that gives her some excuse for indiscretion . . . though I must admit that she was the same way years ago."

Ambrosia's eyes fixed on Mandy and her fingers toyed with the edge of the baby's blanket. "Drayton must have been a fine doctor before the war for so many of them to remember," she said softly.

Lily let out a sigh as she untied the satin ribbon of her bonnet. She was relieved that Ambrosia had finally spoken of her husband, after carefully avoiding any mention of him for weeks. "He was far more than just a doctor to them," she said with heartfelt pride. "He was someone who came whenever anyone called on him, someone who brought children into the world with joy, someone who stayed with those in need, regardless of their ability to pay, someone who comforted those forced to deal with death . . ." She stopped for a moment, thinking how ironic it was that Drayton had never allowed anyone to comfort him when he was forced to deal with death, and how tragic. "He truly cared for them, you know. He's that kind of man. People don't forget that."

Ambrosia bit her lip, a deep frown touching her brow as she stared down at Mandy's face. She remembered the way Drayton had looked after the wounded soldiers at Heritage, not only his own men but the Rebel soldier as well. And she remembered the way he had cared for her after the men had attacked her in the stable. . . . She closed her eyes tightly and clenched her fingers about the blanket, fighting tears of shame and guilt at the hatred she had screamed at him. How viciously she had tried to destroy him, and all because he had seen her weaknesses, had tried to care for her. She forced away the hot, stinging tears of regret, knowing that she must not think about this. She must not.

"I always enjoy the minister's sermons," Lily said after a few moments, pretending to study the passing woods. "He is full of love, that man. And he never tires of preaching love and forgiveness. I suppose that's because we need to hear it again and again. We need so much to know that we are forgiven, no matter what we've done in the past."

Still unable to speak, Ambrosia gave a nod. But a part of her knew that no matter what Lily said, Drayton would never forgive her the damage her hatred had done.

Chapter 38

A sudden flurry of holiday preparations banished the lingering memories of summer and replaced them with visions of bright, festive days before a crackling fire. Ambrosia had never celebrated Thanksgiving Day before, since it was primarily a New England tradition. Lily, who normally followed a flexible meal plan worked out with Sheba or Sarah each morning, took a great deal of time going over the holiday menu with the cooks as well as with Ambrosia. Debbs was sent into town fully a half-dozen times in search of special ingredients Lily insisted upon for her special recipes. And beginning days before, Lily oversaw every step of the preparation herself, from the turkey and bread stuffing and cranberries to the pumpkin pies that were integral parts of the celebration.

Ambrosia listened attentively as Lily spoke of "family traditions," most of which had been passed down from Henry's family rather than her own. "I used to think it all very stuffy and pompous," Lily admitted with a wistful sigh as they sat breaking bread the evening before Thanksgiving. "But there is something comforting in carrying on such traditions from one generation to the next. Think of it, Ambrosia. Someday Mandy will be sitting in her own home, teaching her daughter the very things I'm teaching you.''

Ambrosia happily took part in the holiday preparations, since she was anxious to keep busy and thankful for the laughter and kinship Lily lent to every task. Finally, after weeks of feeling very little beyond fear and timidity, she was beginning to develop a sense of belonging here, a sense of being important to life at Elmwood. Finally her heart was beginning to heal.

Thanksgiving Day began with an early-morning service at the church in the village which Drayton did not attend since he arrived at Elmwood so late in the day, well after noon. More than once during the minister's sermon, Ambrosia was aware of Bea Hanover's eyes upon her, questioning her husband's absence on this special day. Fortunately a cold drizzle prevented the usual gathering outside of church, and the parishioners sought the shelter of their conveyances immediately after the services.

Though Lily was clearly piqued by Drayton's late arrival and unconvinced that work had forced him to remain in town a few hours longer than he'd planned, the traditional meal was a wonderful success. Drayton expended a great deal of effort in charming Lily out of her irritation, and he seemed to enjoy the meal more than anyone else. ''No one can serve up a Thanksgiving dinner the way you do, Lily Collinsworth,'' he told her with a contented smile. He took one last sip of coffee, then leaned back in his chair. ''The turkey was perfect, the stuffing superb, the pie by far the best I've ever eaten.''

''I quite agree,'' Lily returned promptly. ''Although I can't really take credit for the pies. Ambrosia and Sheba convinced me to try a recipe that's been in the Lanford family for years. And they insisted on making it all by themselves.''

Drayton's smile faded as he met Ambrosia's eyes. He had not expected the announcement, that much was obvious. ''Perhaps someone forgot to tell you that Thanksgiving is a Yankee holiday,'' he said softly.

The glow in Ambrosia's eyes vanished and she quickly lowered her eyes. She hadn't realized how much she had wanted his approval, how much she cared what he thought.

Lily stared at her nephew in stunned silence, hardly able to believe what she'd heard. A moment later Ambrosia excused herself from the table, and before Lily could say a word, Drayton also excused himself and retired to his room.

Thanksgiving Day was hardly over when Lily began her annual shopping visits to the city. She was more than a little disappointed when Ambrosia refused to accompany her into town, using the excuse that the baby should not be left with Emily for an entire day, and of course it was far too cold to take her along. Lily assured her that they would return quite early and that the baby could surely survive one feeding of cow's milk, but no amount of prodding could change Ambrosia's mind. One day Ambrosia did go with Lily to the small general store in the village to purchase gifts for Jake and Debbs and Emily and Bess, as well as Sheba and Sarah. On that occasion Lily sensed Ambrosia's embarrassment over her black clothing when she was introduced to an old friend of the family as Drayton's wife. Perhaps, Lily thought, her reluctance to go into the city was tied to the clothing she had defended so staunchly just a few months before. And perhaps the time had come to give her a chance to break with that part of her past.

The first deep snow of the season began to fall two days before Christmas. Ambrosia woke on Christmas Eve to find a deep, crystal white blanket of snow covering everything, while the huge wet flakes continued to fall. After staring in awe through a frosted windowpane the entire morning and most of the afternoon, Ambrosia bundled herself in the heavy woolens Lily insisted she wear and ran from the house to frolic in the deep snow. "Isn't it lovely?" she cried happily to Debbs as she dug her gloved hands into the thick carpet of white like a child and tossed the snow high in the air. "I've never seen so much snow!"

"You'll be weary of it soon enough," he returned with a wry grin as he went back to clearing a path from the stables to the house.

"Never!" she called back as she ran toward her favorite trail through the woods. She paused to shake the glistening flakes from the drooping branches of the first tree she encountered, then ran on, laughingly trying to catch snowflakes on her tongue.

Ambrosia had just disappeared down the trail when Debbs saw Drayton coaxing his stallion toward the stables. He rushed out to take hold of the horse's bridle, assuring Drayton he would see to the animal's needs. "Go along to the house," he told Drayton. "Miss Lily's expecting you, and I don't believe she's quite forgotten your late arrival Thanksgiving."

Lily was indeed waiting for him when he entered the house. "Well, well, what have we here? A visitor from the city? Or is it a snowman?"

"I feel like a little of both." Drayton smiled. He removed his hat and brushed the snow from his sleeves. "Where's Mandy?" he asked as he removed his gloves and handed them to Lily.

"Napping . . . as she always is this time of the afternoon. You'd know that if you spent more time here."

"I keep myself busy," Drayton responded lightly, refusing to allow the comment to affect his good mood. He began to unbutton his coat.

"I'm sure you do." Lily waited until he had folded his coat across his arm, then handed him back his gloves and hobbled into the parlor, going immediately to the front window. "Did you see Ambrosia on the way in?"

"No. Should I have?"

Lily frowned as her eyes searched the landscape. It was difficult to make out much of anything as the snow continued and shadows began to fall. "Oh, dear. I hope she hasn't slipped and fallen in the snow."

Drayton paused in arranging his coat and damp outerwear near the fire to dry. "What the devil is she doing out in weather like this?" he demanded as he left his things to join Lily at the front window.

Lily gave him a shrug and a weak smile. "She'd never seen a real snowfall before, Drayton." She returned her attention to the window. "I saw to it that she dressed warmly enough, but she's been out a little longer than I expected. Almost two hours now." She bit her lip and shook her head. "Perhaps you ought to go after her . . . to make certain she's all right."

"Send Bessie after her," he said tersely, turning away from the window and making his way to the fire again.

"Oh, come, Drayton. You have your coat and hat right there. The least you can do is go after her." She glared at him, the impatience flaring in her blue eyes until the stubborn set of his mouth yielded.

He let out his breath, scowling darkly as he drew on his coat again. "I'll go."

Ambrosia's footprints were barely visible in the snow now, since it was still falling so heavily and winds were blowing drifts in every direction. Drayton followed the almost indiscernible path into the woods, his scowl darkening as he moved ever further away from the house. He stopped for a moment when he first heard her voice. She was singing aloud a silly childish song, her voice mingling with the howling of the wind through the trees. His scowl faded as he headed toward the sound and came upon a clearing where she was working industriously, putting the finishing touches on a snowman that was nearly as tall as she. For a time he watched her, thinking how much like a young girl she still was, thinking how like her Mandy would be someday.

All at once Ambrosia whirled about, her face flushed with the cold, her eyes wide with fear. Her frightened expression faded as she recognized him, and her eyes softened as she studied his face, the weathered, darkened skin, the dark blue eyes. It had been a long time since she'd seen those eyes touched with gentleness, touched with anything besides cold indifference. And she suddenly realized just how much she wanted to see the warmth there.

"Welcome home," she whispered slowly. She took a step toward him and started to smile. But suddenly his eyes changed, growing hard and cold again, warning her to keep her distance. She stopped short and the smile in her eyes died. There was bitterness and anger between them. She had put them there long ago.

He said nothing to her, but his eyes flicked over the lopsided snowman she had built and her eyes did the same. "I—I never built a snowman before," she told him, feeling very childish to have done so now. She smiled a timid smile, dusting off her hands and facing Drayton, wishing with all her heart that he would return her smile. But his eyes only bore coolly into hers, causing her small smile to fade again, causing her to remember all the times in the past when he had smiled at her and she had turned away.

"Lily was worried about you. She sent me out to make certain you were all right."

Ambrosia lowered her eyes, struggling with all her might against the painful tears that burned her eyes. "I was very worried about you," he had told her once, a long time ago. She remembered that so clearly now, when the anger in his voice cut through her like a knife. Oh, God, why did she have to remember?

"You'd better go inside before you catch your death of cold."

Without a word Ambrosia hurried past him in the slippery, snow-covered path. She ran, shivering now, aware of the cold that stung her cheeks, aware that her fingers were numb as well as her toes. The deep snow caught her feet with every step as she struggled toward the house. She almost stumbled several times, but she forced herself to run faster, faster, trying to forget, trying very hard not to feel anything. Her lungs ached as she ran, her legs cramped as she pushed them on, her eyes blurred with tears. She was not aware of how closely he followed her until she fell. Then suddenly his arms were about her, drawing her to her feet in a single, sharp movement, against his chest. She let out a tiny cry as their eyes locked, as a hot awareness flooded her, as her blood began to pound. She had forgotten how strong he was, forgotten what it was like to be held in his arms. His eyes held hers for a long, poignant moment, reminding her of everything that had been between them, of the single passionate kiss they had shared at Heritage, of the fullness of their wedding night in Charleston. . . . And all at once she knew. She loved him. With all her being she loved him and wanted him. And more than anything else she longed for him to share her need. She searched his face, waiting for his kiss, waiting and knowing that for the first time, she would joyfully kiss him in return.

But instead his eyes went cold and hard and he released her so abruptly she nearly fell again. Ambrosia turned away quickly, her heart aching, tears of despair spilling over her cheeks. Without ever looking back, she ran the remainder of the distance to the house.

Christmas Day dawned bright and clear on the snow-shrouded land. Ambrosia rose, smiling, to Mandy's impatient cries and hurried to gather her into her arms. She sang to Mandy all the while she dressed her in a frilly red velvet and white lace gown, a totally impractical frock Lily had insisted on buying her for the occasion. Ambrosia even told Mandy the story of the first Christmas, though she knew the baby was far too small to understand. Before leaving the room, Ambrosia closed her eyes and held Mandy tightly, remembering all that had happened in a single year. Last Christmas she had been alone, seriously ill and penniless, in the care of three Christian ladies who had taken her off the streets. She

could not have imagined then that she carried a child, a
daughter she would love so deeply. She could not have
imagined this house or feeling at home here, in this place
so different from Heritage, so far away from Heritage.
She could not have imagined feeling a kinship for someone like Lily, or feeling anything but hatred for any Yankee. She had been so blind, so bent on vengeance and
destruction, and dear God, she had made so many mistakes! She blinked back a tear as Mandy squirmed in her
arms. Today was Christmas. Today she must put the past
behind her and believe in forgiveness. Just for today she
would force herself to believe.

Ambrosia's face broke into a wide smile as she carried
Mandy downstairs and into the parlor. The baby's huge
blue eyes were full of wonder, and her tiny finger pointed
excitedly at the perfect fir tree, bedecked with glittering
moons and stars, cut-paper snowflakes, tiny animals, and
fragile glass angels. It seemed to reign over the spacious
room. Ambrosia had helped Lily to decorate it the evening before, and Drayton had joined them, smiling as he
helped string popcorn and berries, laughing over tales
Lily told of Christmases past, of his excitement as a boy.
He had carefully avoided meeting Ambrosia's eyes, but
the frictions between them had been hidden well beneath
a glow of holiday good cheer. If only that spirit could
continue, thought Ambrosia. If only the peace would win
out over the tension that remained, and the past could be
forgotten from this moment on.

Christmas Day began with a late morning service at
the church in the village. It was the first service Drayton
had attended with his wife and aunt, and Ambrosia was
very aware of the eyes that fixed on them as they took
their seats. More than once during the service Ambrosia's eyes strayed to her husband and softened at the sight
of the baby who slept so peacefully against his broad
shoulder. Drayton belonged here, in this church, at her
side, with Mandy in his arms. If only he would come

home to stay! If only he would not avoid her eyes or keep such a distance between them!

Though it was far too cold and windy to do extended socializing outside the church that morning, it seemed that just about everyone made it a point to greet Drayton and welcome him home, to make certain he knew his services were sorely missed, even after all these years. When asked about the future, Drayton left no question in anyone's mind about his intention to remain in the city and pursue the business his father had left him. The matter was resolved; his medical practice was a thing of the past. Still, beneath his decisive words and manner, there was something of uncertainty, of regret in his eyes as he answered the questions over and over again. A part of him wanted more than anything to return to these people, to serve them as he had before. But the ghosts of the past would not allow him to do so, and so he carefully hid behind talk of his new business, his new responsibilities.

When they returned to Elmwood, everyone enjoyed a magnificent feast of stuffed goose and a wide assortment of out-of-season fruits and vegetables. The meal ended with a scrumptious rum-drenched cake drizzled with thin white frosting. The remainder of the afternoon and evening was spent in the parlor opening gifts, laughingly watching Mandy try to devour every one of her new toys, singing carols, and toasting the season with wassail punch. From Drayton, Lily received a terribly frivolous pink bonnet along with a lovely ermine-lined cape and matching muff. From Ambrosia, she received a hand-stitched pillow as well as a miniature pen-and-ink drawing of Henry Collinsworth, copied from the library portrait. Lily stared in amazement at the gift, recognizing at once the time and effort that had gone into its making. Her eyes misted with grateful affection as Ambrosia came to embrace her. They shared a second brief embrace, and Ambrosia was smiling as she returned to her chair. But that smile faded quickly, and she held her breath as Drayton chose the gift she had wrapped for him

and pulled at the shiny satin bow. The room fell silent as
he tore at the paper, unwrapping the charcoal drawing of
himself, holding a newborn Mandy in the crook of his
arm. It was a special gift, a personal one. Ambrosia had
worked on it for weeks, coming back to it again and again
until every detail of his face, his hands were exactly as
she remembered them that night.

For a long moment he stared at the picture, his face
showing clearly that he had expected a token gift purchased with the money he had sent her through Lily
weeks before. Instead he had received a gift that held
meaning. In spite of himself the gesture touched his
heart. And because it touched him, he was suddenly angry. She had destroyed far too much of his pride to make
up for it with a simple gift. His eyes lifted slowly to meet
hers, those green-gray eyes that pleaded with hopeful expectancy, the same eyes that taunted his dreams.

"Thank you," he said curtly, setting the gift aside
with a stack of many others. There was no warmth in his
eyes as he spoke the words or as he set it with the rest of
his gifts and quickly rose to get himself a cup of punch.
He was telling Ambrosia that he wanted no part of it.

She swallowed a large lump in her throat. Lily rose
and went to retrieve the picture and immediately let out a
cry of awe. "Ambrosia, it's lovely! Why, the likeness is
startling! It's—" Lily's smile of delight vanished when
she met Drayton's eyes, and then Ambrosia's.

Ambrosia left her chair and all but ran to the opposite
side of the room, where she stood at the window, staring
at the black night, blinking to hold back a flood of tears.
She could not allow herself to cry now, she thought in
panic. She could not! Even as she struggled to restrain
her emotions, Lily was hobbling after her, coming to
place an arm about her shoulders. The portrait of Drayton
and Mandy had revealed everything to Lily. She knew
now without a doubt that Ambrosia loved him and
wanted more than anything to be forgiven. And she knew
just as surely that Drayton's rejection of the gift had been

a refusal to forgive, a refusal born of pride. It would take time, Lily thought.

"You haven't opened the rest of your gifts," Lily prodded her quietly, hoping against hope that Drayton had purchased something lovely for Ambrosia, something that would at least give her hope enough to ease the pain. Ambrosia moved woodenly to do as Lily asked, though she could not bear to meet her eyes.

"Drayton," Lily said gently, "please come and sit down. We haven't finished with Christmas yet."

Everyone took a seat again, but the excitement and joy of Christmas had gone now. The room was quiet and somber and grew more so when Ambrosia opened Drayton's gift to her. She stared at the two leather-bound books in her hands, one on household management, the second on child rearing. The same books might have been purchased for Miss Wilcox or any servant as a token gift, a meaningless gift. In giving them to Ambrosia, Drayton's meaning had been all too clear. She meant nothing to him and held no more importance in his life than a servant. She could not even lift her eyes when she forced a thank-you. She was merely playing out the polite charade for Lily's sake, when she wanted more than anything to fling the books into the fire and run from the room.

All the gifts had been opened when Bessie flitted into the parlor bearing one last gift that she set on a surprised Ambrosia's lap. "From Miss Lily," she said with a grin and a curtsy. "She wanted to save it until last." Bessie made to leave, then dropped another curtsy, her eyes shining with delight. "And I thank you again for the marvelous box of chocolates, miss."

Ambrosia's eyes flew to Lily's, but the older woman only nodded and smiled. "Well, go on. Open it."

Ambrosia stared at it a moment longer, still struggling with the hurt she felt over Drayton's gift, still trying very hard not to cry. But suddenly she sensed that this was a very special gift, and she began to tear at the package with the excitement of a child. As the paper fell away and she opened the box, she gasped and drew back in surprise. ''Oh, Lily!'' Her hands flew to her cheeks. ''Oh!''

''Well, what is it?'' Drayton inquired, his curiosity duly aroused. He held Mandy on his lap and gestured with his cup of punch. ''The rest of us can't see if you leave it in the box.''

Ambrosia's fingers were trembling as she lifted the deep green, grenadine gown from the box as if it were a fragile china figure. The bodice was tailored with a wide, rounded neckline trimmed in delicate light blue ruching, the skirt cut in a fashionably smooth, straight line. She stood and held it to her breast, admiring the lovely detailed blue lace at the cuffs of long, full sleeves, and the same lace about the hem and waistline. ''Oh, Lily! It's—it's beautiful!''

''I hope it fits you, dear.''

''It will!'' She was still smiling widely and her fingers were still testing the softness of the expensive fabric when her eyes met Drayton's. The smile froze on her face. His mouth was drawn into a hard, thin line of resentment, his eyes hard and cold as ice. And suddenly she remembered that he had offered her a gift very similar to this one, a wedding gift. And she had thrown it back in his face. His eyes narrowed in indictment as he rose and lifted the baby to his shoulder, turning his back on her for a second time.

In despondent silence, Ambrosia bit her lip and carefully folded the dress away. Wearing such a gown would only put salt in his wounds, would only serve as a reminder to herself of everything she'd done to hurt him. She couldn't bear the thought of living with those memories, with the shame and the guilt that were already tearing her apart. It was too late to change anything between them now, far too late to even hope for forgiveness.

Chapter 39

With the holidays past, Ambrosia found herself with more time on her hands than ever and more need to fill those hours, since the despair lurked constantly in the back of her mind. She began to accept Lily's invitations to go visiting, and discovered that many of Lily's "social calls" were simply a matter of spending time with the sick or the bedridden who lived in and around the village. She took them baskets of fruits and fresh-baked breads, offered an understanding ear to their complaints, and assured them that someone cared. Though Ambrosia couldn't help her awkwardness at first and said little or nothing until she became comfortable visiting these people, she watched Lily carefully every moment, learning from her sensitivity, her encouraging words and manner, her patience with the loudest complainers. For the first time Ambrosia realized that Lily had made herself needed by seeking out needs in her community that were already there and quietly filling them. She never spoke of "doing charity," or "giving of her time," and yet it was far more that than "going visiting." And Ambrosia, who saw the light in so many people's eyes whenever Lily came to see them, was beginning to realize that she could be needed here too.

The Sprindle sisters arrived at Elmwood one afternoon

in early February, their first visit since the December snow. Isabel and Victoria Sprindle were unmarried ladies, both plump, homely, pleasant women with high-pitched voices and flighty mannerisms. With little else to occupy their time, the Sprindles made it their business to know everything that went on in the city and out, though they were the first to say that nothing of real importance ever happened outside of New York. Their visits to Lily's house were important to their social calendars for one reason. They had acquired from their dear departed father a taste for the most unfeminine card game of all—poker—and seldom had an opportunity to play. It was their one and only vice, Victoria always liked to say, discounting the brandy or sherry Lily always insisted they have to warm them (in the winter) or refresh them (in the summer) after their long ride from the city. Making the visits even more attractive was the fact that Lily had far more interest in conversation than in cardplaying and so habitually lost to one or the other of the sisters. The combination was irresistible to the girls, who seldom missed a Wednesday during decent weather and were anxious to resume their games once the roads were cleared of winter snow.

Ambrosia managed to appear calm and collected during her first meeting with the Sprindles, even as she fielded dozens of personal questions about her background and how she had met her husband. The two older women stared quite pointedly at Ambrosia's black dress as she poured them tea, memorizing every detail of her clothing, her speech, her manner. Lily noticed the Sprindles' preoccupation and wondered again why Ambrosia had never worn the green dress that had been her Christmas gift.

The afternoon progressed smoothly enough, with the Sprindles becoming quieter and less inquisitive as Ambrosia won hand after hand of cards. Isabel, who was definitely serious about her game now, even declined Lily's offer of another brandy, something she'd never done before. When the Sprindles took their leave, having lost every dime of their pocket change to the young woman in black, their farewells were stiff and begrudging. Lily could hardly hold back her grin until the two of them were out of sight. Ambrosia watched in amazement as she collapsed on the settee in a fit of laughter. "Oh, Ambrosia! You were wonderful!"

"Wonderful?" she repeated with a doubtful frown. "Pardon my saying so, Lily, but neither of those ladies will ever be a poker player." She didn't add that Lily would never be one either. She didn't have to.

"Where on earth did you learn how to play?" Lily asked, still grinning from ear to ear.

"I used to watch my father," she admitted slowly. She paused for a moment before she added, "He always won."

"Well, I've never seen Isabel lose so badly to anyone before, and I've *never* seen her concentrate so hard that she turned down a brandy to keep her mind on the game! It was wonderful fun for me, after all these years of losing." She did her utmost to assume a sober expression, but the smile continued to tug at her mouth. "Perhaps you might let her win a hand or two next time, Ambrosia. Otherwise, she may never come back at all."

She giggled again and Ambrosia laughed as well as she gave a nod.

It was a Monday morning in early February when someone knocked at the door of Drayton's warehouse office. Drayton was sitting at his desk, writing up orders for factory supplies, completely engrossed in his work. "Come in," he called tersely without raising his eyes.

Matt Desmond entered the office and closed the door behind him, waiting patiently to be recognized. After several moments he shifted his weight, fingered his hat, and finally cleared his throat loudly.

"Yes, what is it?" Drayton asked, again without looking up.

"I want to speak with Drayton Rambert," Matt returned archly, "if he isn't too busy."

Drayton's head shot up in surprise. "I'm sorry, Matt. I thought it was the new warehouse foreman. Sit down. What did you need to talk with me about?"

"Your favorite subject," Matt responded lightly, waiting until he saw the slightest bit of irritation in Drayton's eyes. "Business!" he said to the unspoken question. "What else?" He smiled as Drayton scowled. "I have to admit that I'm pleasantly surprised at your commitment to this place. I always thought you were a country medicine man through and through. But in the past few months, I've seen you tear down a malfunctioning piece of machinery with your bare hands, shovel coal into a steam engine at the factory, and operate one of those newfangled grinders of yours. I've even seen you drive a wagonload of paints to—"

"Get to the point, Matt. It's Monday morning, and I have a lot of work to do."

"That's what I like about you, Drayton. You're totally dedicated to what you do, no matter what it is. That's why you're going to succeed. And that's why I'm going to help you."

"Help me what?"

Still smiling that same, cunning smile, Matt paused to offer Drayton a cigar and to light one for himself. "What if I told you I've found a way for you to increase your sales potential ten times over in the coming year?"

Drayton sat back in his chair and eyed Matt narrowly as he took a long draw on his cigar. Matt knew as well as he did that sales were still slow and that it was crucial to the business that they double within the next few months. "What did you have in mind?"

"A national distributor, already established in Chicago, Philadelphia, Boston, San Francisco—"

"What distributor is this?" Drayton broke in, his curiosity aroused.

"Ken Galbraith."

Drayton frowned as he repeated the name. "He distributes artists' supplies, doesn't he?"

"In addition to the finest British carriage varnish," Matt returned. "When he told me he was thinking of expanding his business in the near future, I brought up the idea of handling your colors."

"And?"

Matt gave a shrug. "He seemed interested."

"Did he now?" Drayton returned, pleased.

"Especially when I told him about the new method of grinding pigments being used in your factories. He only handles the best, you know."

"Rambert Paint is the best," Drayton told him matter-of-factly.

Matt grinned. "I know. That's why I'd like to see the two of you get together."

"I'd like nothing better myself. And the moment you can set up a meeting, I'll—"

"You'll squeeze him into your schedule like you're doing me right now?" Matt shook his head. "That won't work with Ken Galbraith. He almost never does business with a casual acquaintance. He's accustomed to being . . . shall we say, 'courted.' If you want him to take you seriously, you're going to have to befriend him socially."

"I've never even met the man," Drayton protested.

"No, but you will. Friday Leanne is giving a little party. You're going to come to that party, Drayton, and you're going to charm your way into his tight little circle of friends. It shouldn't be too difficult for you. They spend half their time catering to their wives, and the other half talking business. You ought to feel right at home . . . at least with the business part," he added with a slightly taunting smile.

Drayton scowled and smashed out his cigar. Matt heaved a sigh. "I've known Ken Galbraith for almost ten years," he said seriously. "He has a habit of doing business with fine, upstanding family men. Convince him you're one of those—''

''I'm not that kind of businessman, Matt.''

''Then you're not a businessman at all,'' Matt shot back. ''I'm not asking you to compromise any of your high-and-mighty principals, Drayton. I'm merely reminding you that locally, there's been a lot of resistance to the new products you're trying to sell. And the fact that your stepbrother is still here in the city, making a reputation for himself as a drunk and a gambler, certainly doesn't help your image.''

Drayton scowled, knowing full well the reputation Aaron had earned in the past months.

''Fact is,'' Matt went on, ''you and your stepbrother carry the same name as the paints you're trying to sell. That's hurt you. And it just might force you to play another facet of the game. There's no reason why you shouldn't. It's a simple truth that men allow friendships to sway their business decisions. And with your natural charm,'' Matt went on, tongue-in-cheek, since Drayton had been anything but charming since he'd taken over this business, ''you could make a lot of important friendships.''

Matt paused, waiting for the unyielding set of Drayton's jaw to soften. It did not. He sighed in exasperation. ''Dammit, Drayton, do you think the bank loaned you the money you needed to get this business back on it's feet on the merits of your sterling reputation alone? Whether you like it or not, our friendship had something to do with it. None of that matters at this moment, though. What does matter is the future. And nationwide distribution is the brightest future I can imagine for Rambert Paints. I'm asking you to meet the man who could make that future possible.''

Drayton vented a lengthy sigh, realizing that it would be foolish to refuse an introduction that could mean so much to the future, yet still unwilling to befriend any man for the sake of profit. "I'll come to the party," Drayton agreed.

"Good. Then I'll expect you at the house at seven sharp."

Drayton turned his attention back to his papers in a gesture of dismissal, but Matt made no move to leave. His eyes narrowed thoughtfully. "It might be a good idea to bring along your wife. She's been the subject of much speculation lately, you know."

Drayton's head jerked up, his eyes bright and angry. He hadn't known that at all, though perhaps he could have guessed as much.

"I must admit I'm a little curious about her myself," Matt admitted. More than a little curious, actually. Talk was that Drayton's wife had given birth to a child a scant six months after a hasty marriage in Charleston.

"Ambrosia was seriously ill a few months back," Drayton said stiffly. "And she's still recovering from Mandy's birth."

"There's talk that she's perfectly well, Drayton," Matt told him frankly. "I've heard it said she attends church services in the village—"

"I don't care what you've heard," Drayton flung back sharply.

Drayton's outburst surprised Matt a little and revealed something to him as well. Drayton was very touchy about his wife. Perhaps Mrs. Craig, one of Leanne's closest friends, had told the truth. Perhaps his wife had caused a scandal that ruined Drayton's career in the army, that forced him to leave Charleston. Matt had taken the story with a grain of salt, since Carolyn Craig had a tendency to exaggerate things a bit. But she *had* been in Charleston at the time . . .

"All right," Matt agreed pleasantly. "We'll leave your wife out of this for the time being. But I still expect to see you at seven sharp."

"I'll be there." Drayton quickly turned his attention to the papers on his desk.

"Don't work too hard," Matt called over his shoulder as he took his leave.

The Desmonds lived in a three-story brownstone in Gramercy Park just a block from Drayton's residence. Drayton stepped into the spacious entrance hall and surrendered his coat and top hat to the butler. A moment later a painfully thin woman with sharp, narrow features and mousy blond hair came forward and offered her hand. "I didn't really believe it when Matt told me you were coming. It's been much too long, Drayton," Leanne Desmond gushed. She smiled, a smile so obviously false it made her thin features appear even more pinched and unattractive. Drayton returned her greeting with one slightly less cordial.

Leanne smiled at him again after her eyes had appraised him thoroughly. He had changed a bit in the time he'd been away, but if anything he was even more attractive. It was quite easy to imagine why Carolyn had been so obsessed with him in Charleston . . . and was still obsessed with him. Her smile widened a bit when she realized that Drayton had come this evening alone, just as Matt had said he would. Wouldn't Carolyn be pleased when Leanne told her!

"I heard you married again," Leanne said, clinging to his hand a moment longer. "I'm dying to meet her. You must promise to bring her along next time." She couldn't resist, even though Carolyn would murder her if she knew. Drayton had treated Carolyn shamefully in Charleston, after all. Leanne knew all about that, and about the little Rebel he'd married. . . .

"I'm sure I mentioned that Drayton's wife was ill, Leanne," Matt inserted, coming to meet Drayton as well. "And she is still recovering from the birth of their daughter."

Leanne unfolded her lacy fan and waved it in front of her face. "Oh, yes, I suppose you did mention that. . . ." She knew better than to ignore the warning in Matt's voice. Drayton was a friend of his, and though Leanne relished the thought of making him squirm a little inside, she dared not overstep her bounds. Too bad tonight had been a business party, too bad Matt had prepared the guest list. The next time . . .

"You're early, Drayton," Matt said to change the subject. "But a few of the guests are here already. Excuse us for a moment, will you, Leanne? I want to introduce Drayton around."

The parlor was thirty feet wide and half again as long with dark wood couches and settees upholstered in deep red velvet clustered about the room. Matt introduced Drayton to four men and their wives, including Ken and Muriel Galbraith.

Galbraith was a tall man in his late fifties, with friendly brown eyes and a congenial manner. "You remind me of someone. . . ." he said thoughtfully, stroking his chin as he considered Drayton's face for a long moment. "I hardly ever forget a face, and yours seems so familiar to me." It was several minutes later when Galbraith interrupted the light conversation by saying suddenly, "You look like the boy who used to tag about after Henry Collinsworth!"

Drayton's eyes reflected his surprise. "Henry was my uncle."

For the next few moments the two of them exchanged memories of a man they had both known and respected. "I remember when I had my first job at a little tobacco shop on Broadway. I was only a store clerk then, but Henry Collinsworth used to talk to me as if— Sit down, Mr. Rambert, sit down. . . ."

The conversation was the beginning of an easy camaraderie between the two men. Drayton felt uncomfortable only once after that, when Mrs. Galbraith questioned him about his wife's absence from the party. He quickly repeated the excuse he had given to Matt and Leanne, but he noticed that more than one of the women in the group seemed openly doubtful, as if they'd heard part of the gossip already and had good reason to wonder.

Still, by the end of the evening, Drayton had received several invitations to forthcoming parties and dinners, and everything had gone exactly as Matt had expected it would. What neither Matt nor Drayton expected was that Drayton would be the main topic of conversation at Leanne's tea the following Tuesday, a tea attended by Carolyn Craig.

Chapter 40

On the last day of February, Drayton arrived at the Galbraiths' four-story red brick Georgian mansion on the north side of Washington Square, one in a long row of elite private dwellings built there three decades before. The affair was a large one, celebrating the engagement of the Galbraiths' daughter. Drayton entered the pretentious, art-laden hall and greeted the Galbraiths, then turned toward the salon. But the sight of a young, attractive woman in a stylish gown of bright yellow silk made him stop. The woman was Carolyn Craig.

Drayton said nothing as his eyes moved slowly over the silk that clung suggestively to the outer curves of her shoulders and scooped low over her breasts. He remembered the last time he'd seen her, a year ago at a reception in Charleston. She'd been angry then, rightfully so. He'd never thought to see her again, after that episode, after she'd gotten her revenge. He had pointedly avoided her, even ignored the letters that had begged and pleaded for one last rendezvous, a proper farewell. Nothing would have been gained by another meeting, Drayton knew. It would only have been an ugly scene. And now . . .

"It's good to see you, Drayton."

He hesitated before he stepped forward to take the

425

gloved hand she extended and press it lightly to his lips. "Good evening, Carolyn."

She felt the butterflies taking flight in her stomach at the sound of his voice and the touch of his lips to her gloved hand—but he released that hand much too quickly. She perched her palm on his lapel. "Is that all you have to say? After all these months?" She leaned forward until she saw his eyes fall where she wanted them, her breath coming short and fast now, as a result of his nearness. He was so much more handsome than she remembered! So tall and strong and masculine that every other man seemed to fade into the woodwork. "Haven't you missed me?" she asked softly.

"I didn't expect to see you here," he returned dispassionately, sidestepping the question. He didn't want a scene here, now.

"Did you expect me to stay in Charleston?" she sniffed. "Even after you left?"

"I never really gave it a thought," he returned coolly. His eyes shifted slightly when he noticed several women who seemed to have come from out of nowhere to eavesdrop on their exchange. One of them was Leanne Desmond. Carolyn was every bit as aware of their audience and decided to take advantage of it.

"I believe you still owe me a dance," she said sweetly. "You remember. From Charleston . . ."

Drayton thought about refuting that remark, but thought again and escorted Carolyn to the ballroom. A dance would do no harm and would allow them a few moments of private conversation, if nothing else. He slipped an arm about her tightly corseted waist while his other hand grasped lightly at her gloved fingers. The music began. Carolyn was disappointed when his eyes remained cold, his touch indifferent. She began to stroke her thumb suggestively over his palm.

"What do you want, Carolyn?" he demanded bluntly, catching her fingers tightly in his own to stop the gesture.

"I think you already know," she responded softly.

Her eyes traveled swiftly over the length of him. She had never seen him in black formal attire before. But his perfectly tailored cutaway coat accentuated the breadth of his shoulders, the magnificence of his muscular chest. A crisp, pleated shirt of snowy white contrasted sharply with his bronzed skin and made his eyes appear an even deeper blue. She felt a delicious shiver of anticipation pass through her at the memory of what was beneath all that fine, tailored clothing, at the memory of those all-too-brief days in Charleston, days when she had been so certain of her hold on him. . . .

"I'm a married man, Carolyn."

Her smile vanished at that. She forced her eyes to leave his face, to pointedly search the crowd. "Where does the little Rebel keep herself these days, Drayton? I heard she had a baby, but surely she's recovered from that by now. Has she gotten herself another job? Like the one she had at Maggie's? She seemed very well suited to menial labor." She met his eyes again with a catty smile. "Or is it true you keep her locked away in the country, so that she won't ruin your life here the way she did in Charleston?"

He straightened abruptly, and the look in his eyes told her she had gone too far. She trembled a little, and not with pleasure. She felt her breath catch as his grasp on her hand tightened painfully. "I—I'm sorry, Drayton," she said quickly. "I shouldn't have said those things, I know. But—but you were so unfair to me in Charleston! So terribly unfair! You let me believe that you were—were considering marriage, and then you married her. Without a single word of explanation or apology. You didn't even have the courtesy to tell me about it yourself! I might have forgiven you if you'd come to me, if you'd have explained that you made a mistake. But you told me nothing. I heard it instead from everyone else. Do you think that was fair, Drayton?" She blinked back a tear. "Do you?" When he didn't answer her her voice came soft and pleading. "After all we meant to one another?"

Drayton heaved a reluctant sigh and looked away. What she said was true. He hadn't been fair to her. He had married Ambrosia without giving much thought to Carolyn's pride, without offering her any explanation. But the feelings he'd had for Carolyn had been nothing like the ones he'd felt for Ambrosia. Their affair had been a shallow one for him, a physical one. She had offered herself to him when he'd thought Ambrosia was gone forever from his life. She had flattered him and bolstered his masculine pride, and most of all, she had allowed him to forget. He had used her, in the same way he had used women ever since Kathryn's death. And he had taken her the same way he had taken the others, in a mindless way that had nothing to do with gentleness, nothing to do with honest intimacy. And afterward, he had only been more aware of the emptiness that was so deep inside him.

But she had not been like the others, women he had paid well for their services, women who had simply been plying their trade. Carolyn had given herself freely, had risked her good name to share his bed. And though he had given her pleasure in return, he knew that he owed her more.

"I apologize, Carolyn," he said finally. "I ought to have told you myself."

Her eyes warmed at his apology and again her thumb stroked his hand. "All is forgiven, darling," she whispered. The dance was ending as she spoke the words. She sighed as he released her, and her eyes reluctantly scanned the crowded dance floor. When he did not request another dance, she rationalized that there were too many prying eyes taking in their every move for him to do so. "I want to see you again, Drayton."

"I'm very busy these days, Carolyn."

"So I've heard. But you've already told the Powers you'd come to their dinner party week after next, so I'll at least see you there."

He started to make an excuse. He had no intention of

beginning things again, of risking scandal by picking up the pieces of a relationship that had never been what he wanted. And there was a much more important reason why he would not seek comfort in Carolyn's or any other woman's arms now. There was Mandy.

She smiled prettily up at him and tapped her fan playfully on his lapel. "And if you don't come to the party week after next," she added, almost as if she could read his thoughts, "then you can expect me to pay a visit to that business of yours. . . ."

Chapter 41

The April sun was shining bright and strong in a clear blue sky, melting away the last remnants of winter's snow. Ambrosia gazed wistfully out on the lovely spring day and thought again of going off by herself to enjoy the warmth, the beauty of nature. But Lily had been so excited about the prospect of seeing her play cards again with the Sprindles that Ambrosia could not refuse. A series of snowstorms in late February and early March had kept the sisters from a rematch for weeks, but the roads were in fair condition again, and the sisters would be coming here today, anxious for a rematch after the sound defeat they'd suffered before.

Isabel shocked Lily by refusing any beverage but tea, obviously preparing to play some very serious poker this afternoon. Victoria shyly accepted a brandy, but only one, and was also quite subdued as she began her game. Ambrosia played indifferently, but her cool, unreadable expression stymied their best efforts to outplay her, since it was impossible for them to tell when she was bluffing and when she was not. After winning several hands in a row, Ambrosia took in the cards and prepared to deal, deciding that she would purposely lose the next hand regardless. Isabel's disposition had soured with each round until she was tossing cutting remarks at everyone.

Isabel lifted her cards and slowly fanned them open. A scowl darkened her features, telling Ambrosia that she had not been dealt a good hand. Ambrosia's eyes moved to Victoria, who always took a bit longer to arrange her cards. Her mouth was slightly tight, telling Ambrosia that she probably would be drawing to a straight or a flush, taking a gamble with none too good odds. Both Isabel and Victoria had been taught all the hard and fast rules of playing poker. They knew when to wager, when to check, and when to fold. But neither woman knew anything about keeping a straight face. And neither woman knew how to read an opponent's eyes, unless that opponent was Lily. After a single round of hands, Ambrosia had been able to tell each player's cards with amazing accuracy. She played a very different game than the other women at the table—a man's game.

Just as Ambrosia had guessed, Victoria requested a single card. Lily requested two, and Isabel three. Isabel's eyes narrowed as Ambrosia dealt herself a pair of cards. The older woman lifted her own cards and slowly fanned them open. A worthless pair of deuces! She slammed her cards on the table and shot Ambrosia an arrogant scowl. "It isn't really proper for a lady to win every hand," she announced suddenly, her temper getting the best of her.

"I haven't won every hand," Ambrosia responded coolly.

"You've won almost every hand," Isabel shot back.

Ambrosia straightened a bit at that and a frown pulled at her brow. "What about all the times you won?" Lily inserted defensively. "Why, you've beaten me soundly for the past ten years!"

Isabel's brow darkened as she turned to Lily. "I am a *guest,*" she informed Lily haughtily. Her glare slid to Ambrosia's cool green-gray eyes. "She isn't." She smiled a little, a malicious smile. "Sometimes I wonder exactly what she is. . . ."

"Ambrosia is my nephew's wife," Lily returned frigidly. "And you'd best remember that she is family, or

you will no longer be welcome in this house." Ambrosia
had never heard Lily's voice sound so stern.

In response, Isabel assumed an innocent expression of
surprise. "Is Drayton still welcome here?" she questioned.

Lily's eyes narrowed. Isabel could be sharp-tongued
when she put her mind to it, and she was putting her mind
to it now. "What do you mean by that?" she demanded.

"Well," Isabel shrugged, *"he* certainly seems to have
forgotten that she's his wife. Everyone talks about the
way he lives like a bachelor and carries on with Carolyn
Craig."

At the mention of Carolyn's name, Ambrosia's cheeks
paled. She had not known that Carolyn was in New
York. She had not even thought of the woman for
months, since they'd left Charleston. But now she realized how foolish she had been to think that the woman
was a part of Drayton's past. Carolyn had been so possessive of Drayton, even after their marriage. And now gossip linked their names, and everyone thought that . . .
Ambrosia's eyes grew dazed and distant, though her face
gave little other indication of how the news had shocked
her, devastated her. She rose numbly from her chair and
excused herself, seeming yet in perfect control, though
her exit from the parlor was a hurried one.

In a sobering burst of remorse, Isabel half rose from
her chair and called the girl's name. But it was too late to
call back her words, too late to negate the damage. Isabel
sought some spark of understanding in Lily's eyes, but
the older woman's face was hard as she struggled to her
feet and followed after Ambrosia. The card game was
over, Isabel realized. And there might never be another
one.

By the time Lily reached the hallway, Ambrosia was
nearly up the stairs. "Ambrosia?"

Ambrosia stopped short, gripping the banister tightly.
Lily struggled up the first step, wanting very much to put

a comforting arm about Ambrosia's shoulder. "Ambrosia, please come down here."

Still facing away from her, Ambrosia shook her head.

"Ambrosia, I want to speak with you."

"No, I—" Her voice broke painfully and she rubbed the back of her hand across her cheeks.

"Please," Lily urged. "Please come with me. We can talk in the library without being disturbed."

Ambrosia swallowed hard. "I—I was just going to my room. . . ."

"Please?"

It was the softness of the plea that made Ambrosia turn and slowly descend the stairs. Her eyes were downcast, and her arms were wrapped nervously, protectively about herself. Lily laid a hand on her arm, and when the green-gray eyes lifted, she gave Ambrosia an encouraging smile. "Come along. We need to talk."

"You must forgive Isabel," Lily told her quietly after she had taken a seat before the fireplace. Ambrosia had declined the chair nearby and stood near the mantel, her arms still wrapped about herself as she stared at the empty hearth. "She is quite an obnoxious loser, and I'm afraid that's something I wasn't aware of until now. It's my fault, really, for allowing her to—"

"Your fault?" Ambrosia cut in sharply. "It isn't your fault or Isabel's either. It's mine." She shook her head in an effort to win control, but the tears shown bright in her eyes as she went on. "I should never have married him! I should never have had his child!"

"I won't listen to that kind of talk, Ambrosia," Lily returned firmly. "How can you think for a moment that Mandy was a mistake? And Drayton cares for you—"

"He despises me. He cannot even bear to look at me."

"Only because he is so very much in love with you, and you have hurt him so deeply."

"No!" Ambrosia shook her head again, tears rushing down her cheeks now. "He never loved me."

"Ambrosia," Lily said calmly. "Come here. Sit down."

After a long hesitation, Ambrosia moved slowly to take the chair near Lily. Her eyes fixed on her fingers, which were laced tightly in her lap. Lily was relieved to see the tears coming so quickly. The emotions that had been kept too private, too tightly reined, were finally being released. "You've been very unhappy these past weeks, since Christmas. I've seen it in your eyes. Tell me what is making you so unhappy."

Ambrosia's eyes squeezed tightly shut. She gave no answer.

"You are in love with him, aren't you?"

Ambrosia bit her lip hard and her fingers moved to grasp the arms of the chair. She wanted more than anything else to deny it. Yet she knew it was true.

"It's not so hopeless as you imagine, Ambrosia. Drayton is your husband, after all. And he still cares for you—"

Ambrosia sprang from her chair and began to pace the floor before the hearth. The gesture reminded Lily so very much of Drayton that she almost smiled. How alike the two of them were, denying their feelings, trying desperately to run away from what was deep inside.

Ambrosia stopped her pacing after a time, regaining some of her composure as she stared again at the empty hearth. "You don't understand, Lily. It's too late. I've hurt him too deeply to ever hope for forgiveness. I've destroyed everything."

"You're being childish, Ambrosia," Lily began.

Lily was shocked when Ambrosia spun about, her green eyes bright with sudden anger. "You accuse me of being childish? How dare you! You know nothing of what was between us! What could you know of bitterness? Of despair? What do you know about losing everything you care about?" Ambrosia's voice broke and she turned away.

It was a long moment before Lily responded, and then

her voice was soft, a whisper, with all trace of confidence lacking. "I know a great deal . . . a great deal. . . ."

At the sudden change in her voice, Ambrosia turned to face her. She watched as Lily pulled herself to her feet and hobbled slowly to the far bookshelf. She removed several thick volumes from an upper shelf before she located a half-filled decanter bottle of whiskey which had been cleverly concealed behind the shorter books. Ambrosia's face fully reflected her shock as Lily removed the stopper and took a swallow directly from the bottle. She let out a sigh of pain or relief as she set it down again.

"You will have to forgive me," Lily said in a voice that was hoarse from the effect of the strong whiskey. Her blue eyes remained fixed on the cut-glass bottle. "I don't normally have company when I drink here in the library. It's been rather my secret these past years. Drayton disapproves of women drinking strong spirits, you know."

Ambrosia shook her head, her eyes still wide and stunned. She hadn't really known that, though she might have guessed as much. There weren't many men or women, for that matter, who approved of women who drank strong liquor.

Lily lifted her eyes and leveled them frankly on Ambrosia. "I've shocked you, haven't I? Well, I'm afraid I shall shock you quite a bit more with what I'm about to tell you. You must understand, it's not the type of thing I tell everyone. But there is a need for me to tell you now, and so I will. Though I certainly don't enjoy remembering . . ." She took another deep gulp of the whiskey before replacing the stopper and concealing it in its former hiding place. Slowly, haltingly, she moved to take the chair behind the desk, placing a distance between herself and Ambrosia, meeting her eyes for a long moment before her eyes slid significantly to the portrait of her late husband. Ambrosia's eyes followed.

"He was not a handsome man," Lily began matter-of-factly. "He was shorter than I by several inches, and he loved to eat chocolates, so he was never trim and dashing like the men I admired. But he was a good man, very rich and very successful, and very much in love with me. And I was ambitious and wanted all the things that he could give me.

"I was young and beautiful then, the toast of many, many fine gentlemen, though I wasn't quite respectable enough for most of them to court openly. Many men had offered me . . . many things besides marriage, but I wanted the security and the respectability of a man's name. And so I married Henry."

Her eyes changed then and her voice hardened. "My brother James and I were two of a kind. We had both run away from a strict home life where there was never enough of anything to seek our fortunes. He somehow managed to marry a girl with a fairly good-size inheritance, and along with the money I convinced Henry to loan him, he built a profitable business making and selling carriage paints. Everything was simple to James and me. We knew what we wanted and we went after it. Henry offered me what I wanted, and so I became his wife. The fact that I was hopelessly in love with another man at the time had nothing to do with my decision. The other man was neither rich, nor free to marry me. But he was ambitious too, so he understood." She lifted a silver letter opener from the desk and studied it, her words coming more slowly, with more emotion than before. "It could not have been easy for Henry those first years. He must have known that I was unfaithful to him, that others were laughing at him behind his back and calling him a fool. But I never thought about what he was feeling." She paused. "He desperately wanted children," she said softly. "He would have made such a wonderful father. . . ." Her voice trailed off for a moment. "I made very certain that I would never have to bear any child of his." She gave a weak smile. "Perhaps that much of it was for the best. There would have been no guarantee that he was the father, anyway."

Ambrosia paled, so utterly shocked at what Lily was saying that she dropped woodenly into a chair. Lily sighed and laid aside the letter opener without looking up, never seeing Ambrosia's reaction. "When Drayton's mother passed away, he was only four years old. It was Henry's idea to take him in. I wanted nothing to do with him, though he was my nephew. I told Henry that the boy was James's problem and not mine. But Henry argued that James was too busy to be a proper father. And three years later, when James married a woman with a son of her own who had no intentions of sharing his mother, Henry insisted on giving Drayton a home. It was the first time Henry had ever refused to listen to me, and I was quite put out. I'd made up my mind at the very beginning that I wouldn't allow a child to interfere with *my* life, especially someone else's brat."

She let out a lengthy breath. "I had everything I wanted then," she said softly. "Everything I had ever dreamed of having . . ." Her voice was wistful. Her smile faded slowly. "And then I became ill." Her face paled slightly and clearly reflected her grief and pain. "It was a sudden illness. It came upon me with no warning at all. I simply fainted one day, and when I woke, I could no longer move my left arm and leg. Little by little the feeling came back to me, but the control did not. One of the doctors recommended a few weeks in the country, and Henry immediately brought me here. This was his parents' summer house, and he loved it here, but I abhorred it. It was much too quiet and too far from everything important. But he left his work and his friends in the city and brought me here, to care for me." Her mouth twitched in a timorous smile. "There were so many visitors at first. So many flowers and so many letters. I had many, many friends, you know." She shook her head and frowned. "But they all forgot so quickly! Or perhaps . . ." she said with a thoughtful inflection, "perhaps they realized right away what it took me a long time to know. That I would never be the same again."

She met Ambrosia's eyes and smiled, her voice small and full of wonder. "Only Henry stayed with me. The man I had made a fool of left everything and everyone else and stayed with me. He used to carry me into the garden like a child, and to the apple orchard for picnics like the ones we'd had before we were married. He used to say that he was grateful for the time we spent together. . ." She looked away, and her voice hardened. "But I wanted nothing from him. Nothing! I wanted to be whole again. It was the only thing I wanted. And the only thing," she went on quietly, "that I couldn't have."

She picked up the letter opener again and toyed with it nervously, her eyes far away. "At first I prayed to God for a miracle. But I didn't really believe in God, and I thought that even if He were real, He would sooner punish me for my sins than grant me a favor. I became a prisoner in my own body. I felt so terribly alone in my suffering! Everyone else could run and dance"—she grasped the letter opener tightly—"while I was a worthless cripple. Nothing anyone said or did made a difference to me. Nothing until—"

Her eyes flashed with amusement at the same time she blinked away a tear. "Until one day Drayton brought home a horrid-looking little dog who'd been badly wounded in a dogfight." She chuckled softly and shook her head. "He brought the filthy, half-dead thing right here, into this room, and announced that he was going to care for it—can you imagine? He was always bringing home lost animals in those days, raising the ones that were orphaned, nursing the sick ones back to health. He had the shed full of them, and I allowed it because it kept him occupied. To be perfectly honest, I was happy to see him spending his time elsewhere. I did not want to be bothered with a nine-year-old boy. After my illness, I resented his presence in my life more than ever.

"He was such a serious child, quiet and totally docile thanks to Henry's love and discipline. He seemed unaware of my resentment of him. When I forbade him to keep the dog in the house, it never occurred to me that he might disobey. But that is exactly what he did. A few weeks later, when Bessie discovered the dog in his room, she let out a scream that was heard for miles.''

She met Ambrosia's eyes. ''I wanted the creature destroyed immediately. And Henry almost let me have my way. I screamed that the boy had deliberately defied me, that the dog would never recover anyway, that he ought to be put out of his misery. He was a perfectly hideous little thing, hobbling about on three legs, dragging the other leg uselessly behind. I hated the sight of him. And do you know what Drayton said to me?''

Ambrosia shook her head, then watched Lily's eyes misting, heard her voice filling with tears. ''He said—that I was—jealous. Jealous because the dog wanted to live, and I had given up.'' She gave a little laugh. ''Can you imagine? Jealous of an ugly, crippled little dog! Only a child would dare to be so honest!'' She tried hard to smile, but the tears would not be held back. She shook her head and wiped at her cheeks with the back of her hand. ''I was so angry at hearing the truth that I slapped him as hard as I could.'' Her eyes filled with regret, as did her voice. ''I have never really forgiven myself for doing that, though I know Drayton forgave me. He even came and apologized for what he had said. But he had been right, and I knew it. And Henry knew it too.''

Her eyes slipped affectionately to the portrait again. ''It had almost been a year since I'd been able to use my leg and arm, and it seemed that I was losing more control of my body with each day I spent in bed. A dozen different doctors had told us that the damage was irrevocable. But Henry refused to accept that. He began to work with me, every day, rubbing at my useless muscles until my skin was red and raw, putting me in hot mineral baths and moving my legs and arms and fingers until I could no longer bear the pain. There were times when I cried and screamed and actually begged him to stop. But he never did. He wouldn't allow me to give up.''

She let out a sigh and her lips curved into a small smile of triumph. ''He gave me back my life, Ambrosia. Or rather, he gave me a new life, in many ways better than the last. I could never run or dance or ride, but I did learn to walk again. I still feel a pride in every single step I take. I learned something from my illness that I'd never known before. I learned what was important in my life. And I learned just how much Henry loved me. He came to be everything to me.'' There was a long space of silence as Lily's eyes fixed to the portrait, her face reflecting the love she had just spoken of, as well as the pain of remembering. At length she rose to her feet and rounded the desk clumsily until she stood before Ambrosia.

''Why have you told me all this?'' Ambrosia questioned quietly.

''Because you needed to hear it,'' Lily answered simply. ''You needed to know that we all do things we are sorry for, that we all have need of forgiveness.''

Ambrosia avoided her eyes. ''Drayton could never forgive me.''

''Not unless you forgive yourself, Ambrosia.''

Her green-gray eyes lifted, searching Lily's face. ''You must accept the fact that you made a mistake. You're a human being, Ambrosia, and all human beings make mistakes. We learn from them, if we're brave enough to face our own imperfections and strong enough to try to change.''

With a small cry Ambrosia embraced Lily, her eyes filling with tears. ''Oh, Lily, I don't even know where to begin.''

''You begin,'' Lily told her firmly, ''by breaking with the past. You begin by getting rid of your widow's weeds and becoming the beautiful woman you are meant to be. You begin,'' she added with a smile, ''by coming to town with me.''

Chapter 42

The following morning, Ambrosia wore her new green gown and accompanied Lily into the city for a day she would never forget. Her eyes grew ever wider as Lily led her into one after another of the chic dress shops just off Broadway in New York's most fashionable shopping district, where she quickly exchanged her plain woolen cloak and black bonnet for a fur-trimmed green cape and a frothy little hat that was hardly more than lace and bows. Lily ignored Ambrosia's protests as she purchased over two dozen gowns for the younger woman, along with wraps, capes, hats, and slippers to match each dress. It was all "a late wedding gift," Lily insisted, turning a deaf ear to any objections as she limped from one shop to the next. Long after Ambrosia had lost count of the number of items Debbs had patiently loaded into the brougham, Lily led her toward a huge white marble structure on the east side of Broadway, a place which seemed all the more imposing after the whirlwind of quaint little specialty shops they'd just visited. The building bore no sign to identify it, but Lily only laughed when she asked what it was. "Everyone's heard of Stewart's!" she returned with a grin, relenting a moment later when she saw no recognition on Ambrosia's face. Stewart's Dry Goods Palace had been such a sensation from

441

its opening two decades earlier that Lily assumed everyone would recognize it on sight.

Once inside the building, Ambrosia was caught up in the crowded confusion and amazed at the amount of merchandise displayed under a single roof. The rooms of the store were quite large and elegant, unlike anything she'd ever seen before. Corinthian columns, fancy archways, and decorative chandeliers were everywhere.

She had hardly become accustomed to the place before Lily was dragging her on to Lord and Taylor's at Broadway and Grand. It was another huge, white marble building that resembled an Italian palace even more than Stewart's. From there it was on to Delmonico's for luncheon, stops at a few more specialty shops, and then Lily insisted on making one final stop, though Ambrosia knew she must be feeling the effects of a hectic day.

The five-story building housed Tiffany & Company, the largest jeweler in the country. As Debbs slowed the brougham to a halt at the door, Ambrosia's eyes fixed curiously on an amazing statue of Atlas, his huge, muscular arms supporting a clock that stood above the main entrance. She could hardly restrain a gasp of awe as Lily pulled her firmly across the threshold into a single room one hundred feet long with countless arched mirrors, six gaslit chandeliers, and a seemingly endless row of jewelry display cases, all trimmed in polished silver. Lily was still grinning at Ambrosia's wide-eyed stare when a well-dressed gentleman, who had been studying a display of women's jewelry, caught sight of them and immediately came forward.

"Lily Collinsworth!" Matt Desmond exclaimed. "Why, you look like a breath of spring, Lily," he added, taking hold of her shaking hand. "Lovelier than the last time I saw you, if that's possible."

"And you're every bit the charmer I remember, Mr. Desmond."

"I try to be," he returned with a smile. His eyes were already straying from Lily's to the smaller, quite lovely creature beside her. His gaze met a fetching pair of eyes that, because of the green hat and clothing, appeared a deep vivid green. "I thought I'd been introduced to every beauty in town, but I can see that I was mistaken." Ambrosia's cheeks colored slightly, prettily, at the compliment, and Matt could hardly tear his eyes away.

"My apologies," Lily said promptly. "Ambrosia, this gallant gentleman is none other than Matt Desmond. Drayton and Matt practically grew up together at Elmwood. Matt, this is Ambrosia, Drayton's wife."

Matt's smile faltered a bit at the introduction as he struggled to hide his shock. Nothing he'd heard about Drayton's wife—and he'd heard quite a bit of gossip in the past months—had prepared him for this. He eagerly took possession of Ambrosia's small, gloved hand and raised it to his lips. "An honor, Mrs. Rambert."

"For me as well, Mr. Desmond," she returned politely.

He smiled at her a moment longer before he remembered himself and released her hand. His mind was working overtime, as the possibilities struck him. Why, Drayton was a fool to abandon such a lovely little thing to the country when she could be such an asset to him here! If Matt had only known about this earlier . . . "I feel quite fortunate to have met you two ladies here today, since I was just about to choose Leanne's anniversary gift. Now the two of you can offer expert opinions," he told them, leading them back to where he had stood a few moments before. Two black-velvet-lined cases lay open on the counter for his consideration there, one a stunning display of emeralds mounted in gold, the other necklace of brilliant diamonds set in whitegold. "I think Leanne would prefer the diamonds," Lily said immediately.

Matt frowned thoughtfully, lifting the diamond necklace into his hands. "What do you think, Mrs. Rambert?"

"They're both exquisite, Mr. Desmond. And not knowing Mrs. Desmond, I—"

"That's right," he said suddenly, turning his attention away from the jewelry again and missing the scowl of impatience that crossed the salesperson's brow. "You never have met Leanne, have you?" His eyes lingered on Ambrosia's face, searching for any sign of the lingering ill health Drayton had claimed these past months. But there was only youth and health in her smooth complexion, and Matt had never really believed that story anyway. But he had believed the other stories, that she was loud, coarse, and vulgar, a troublemaker completely lacking in social grace. Obviously he had been very wrong to believe such tales, unless Lily had worked some kind of miracle on the girl. Regardless, the woman before him now was a beauty who could charm anyone . . . including, Matt was sure, Ken Galbraith.

"I insist that you both attend the anniversary party, then," he told them. "Leanne's parents are giving it next Friday, and I know they will be thrilled if you'd come. Lily, you know Leanne's mother. Why, she talks of you all the time."

"Does she . . . ?" Lily lifted an eyebrow doubtfully. "You know I don't attend parties in town anymore, Matt," she told him, sensing that Ambrosia was totally against the idea.

"Why don't you?" he demanded. "You know everyone misses you. Why, you were the most celebrated—"

"All that was a long time ago," she interrupted. "I'm an old woman now, and I've grown accustomed to retiring at a sensible hour."

"But you could make an exception, just this once. And you wouldn't have to make it an all-night affair. Think how wonderful it would be to introduce Drayton's wife to all of your old friends. Everyone is dying to meet her." Matt caught Lily's eyes as he said that, and he saw her wavering with uncertainty. So she was aware of the gossip, he thought, and she was beginning to consider coming just to see it silenced.

Ambrosia also caught Lily's uncertainty and quickly

came to her own defense. "I'm afraid it will be impossible for me to attend, Mr. Desmond," she began.

"Surely you don't retire at such a sensible hour, Mrs. Rambert," he quipped with a grin, attempting to lightly dismiss her refusal.

"No, but—"

"Then I insist that the two of you come. I simply won't take no for an answer. This is a very special occasion, you know. Our tenth anniversary." He turned to the clerk as if he considered the subject closed. "I'll take the diamonds. And I'll want the piece engraved, just as we discussed." The salesman gave a short nod, and then Matt was checking his pocketwatch. "My word! Is it three o'clock already?"

"Mr. Desmond, I cannot possibly attend the party. I'm sorry, but—" She searched about in vain for a more plausible excuse, but found none except the most obvious one. "I—I've made other plans."

Matt met her green eyes evenly for a long moment. He was absolutely certain she had no other plans, though it was difficult to read that face of hers. "You husband will be there, Mrs. Rambert," he said finally, a single brow lifted in challenge. "I would think you ought to cancel any other plans to take your place by his side." Ambrosia had no immediate response to that, so Matt quickly took advantage of her hesitation. "A week from this Friday, I shall expect to see you both," he said simply. He smiled at them and gave each woman a slight bow before he turned and left the store.

Ambrosia met Lily's eyes with a troubled, pleading look but was silent as the two left Tiffany's a few moments later. Lily let out a sigh of weariness the moment they had been settled comfortably in the brougham. She tugged at the strings of her ruffly pink bonnet and let it fall into her lap. "It's been years since I've gone shopping like this," she said sleepily. "Oh, I've been to town to buy things, of course, but not like this."

Ambrosia said nothing, still too upset by what had

happened at Tiffany's to think of anything else. She had no intention of attending that party. Particularly since Matt had made it so very clear that Drayton would be there. Carolyn would probably be there too, she thought, and that was why there had been that smug, challenging look in Matt's eyes. She slowly peeled off her gloves, avoiding Lily's eyes.

Lily sighed again as she studied Ambrosia's face. She was nothing less than a vision in her fur-trimmed cape and a bonnet of lace and netting and bows. Her dark, dramatic features seemed to glow with an intriguing mixture of innocence and sensuality. Matt had noticed it, and he had not been the first. Since their arrival in the city this morning, gentlemen had rushed to open doors for her, smiling and tipping their hats, every bit as anxious as Matt had been to make her acquaintance. Such attention ought to have made the trip a total success. But it did not seem to matter at all to Ambrosia that dozens of men's eyes followed her movements, or that her smile caused hearts to flutter, or that several of the women in the shops they had visited gazed at her with envy. She seemed unaware of the attention that was paid her whenever she entered the room. She was so cool, so indifferent to any man who showed an interest in her. Yet something about that unaffected disinterest seemed to heighten a man's infatuation. If only she were aware of the power she held, Lily thought. If only she believed in her own femininity enough to use it in winning back the man she loved.

"I can't attend that party, Lily," she said finally, still not daring to meet Lily's eyes. "Drayton would be furious with me if I did."

Lily thought for a moment. Ambrosia was probably right. Drayton would be terribly angry . . . at first. But he would get over that anger once he saw her, once he realized just how much she had changed. And there was the matter of Mrs. Craig. Lily didn't know the woman, didn't know anything about her relationship with Drayton. But she was almost certain that he did not love her. Not in the way he loved Ambrosia. Lily had seen the depth of Drayton's feelings for his wife too many times for her to believe that he had simply found someone to take her place. And Lily was also very sure that he would never openly court a mistress, for Mandy's sake, if for no other reason. No, Lily reasoned, it was all malicious gossip, perhaps inspired by Mrs. Craig herself. And the best thing would probably be to face that gossip squarely. "I think you ought to go, Ambrosia."

"No." Her voice was very soft, but very firm. "I can't possibly."

"You can hardly refuse to go now."

"Of course I can." She met Lily's eyes finally. "I'll simply come down with something contagious the day before."

"That's the coward's way out. And besides, everyone would guess the truth."

"Yes," Ambrosia admitted in an even softer voice, "everyone would know the truth."

Lily sighed in exasperation. "I feel very strongly that you should attend this party, Ambrosia. I think that you should write Drayton a note and explain—"

"No."

"Then I shall write him myself and—"

Ambrosia's gaze was direct and unyielding. "I'll never forgive you if you do."

"But don't you see? He's building a life without you. You must somehow stop him from doing that. He will consider you an unwelcome intrusion at first, I know. But that's only because he is afraid of his feelings for you." She sighed, knowing that Ambrosia was unsure of Drayton's feelings for her, that she doubted he felt anything for her beyond anger. "You are going to have to confront his pride sooner or later, Ambrosia."

Ambrosia bit her lip but still said nothing. She fixed her eyes on the long row of shanties that had sprung up along the northern edge of Central Park. If only she hadn't come to town with Lily today. If only they hadn't run into Mr. Desmond. But no matter, she had no intention of attending that party, no matter what Lily said. She would excuse herself when the time came and not think about what everyone would say. She didn't know them anyway. They were all Drayton's friends, just as the Yankees in Charleston had been Drayton's friends. . . . She closed her eyes and pushed aside the memories, and the guilt.

Her expression was one of forced brightness as she faced Lily again, only to find that the older woman was frowning, something she very seldom did. Ambrosia stretched forward and laid a hand on Lily's arm, and immediately the frown disappeared. "Thank you for today," Ambrosia told her earnestly. "I know that you took me shopping to cheer me up."

"I did nothing of the sort!" Lily protested. "I was hardly a recluse before your arrival, Ambrosia. If you must know, I insisted on this shopping trip to cheer *me* up. It does my old heart good to see the gentlemen eyeing you, since I can take credit for part of the sensation you cause."

Ambrosia blushed. "I think a good many of the gentlemen are eyeing you, Lily."

Lily brushed away Ambrosia's compliment with a brief wave of her hand. "I'm not in my dotage yet, my dear . . . though I did get my share of attention when I was your age. . . ." Her smile faded as she spoke the words and her eyes drifted away to fix on the passing landscape. Her gaze was distant, sad, a haunting mixture of regret and longing that touched something in Ambrosia's heart. All thoughts of Matt Desmond and the party and even of Drayton suddenly disappeared from her mind as she realized what Lily was thinking, what she must be remembering. "Is he still alive?" Ambrosia asked softly.

Lily started, her eyes wary as they met Ambrosia's. "Who? Is who alive?"

Ambrosia's gaze was even. "The man you were in love with before you met your husband."

"And for a long time after I met my husband," Lily added with a slightly cynical smile. "Yes, he's still very much alive." She held Ambrosia's eyes for a moment, wondering at the girl's perception, wondering just how honest she dared to be. "I am still in love with him, Ambrosia," she admitted reluctantly. She had never admitted that to anyone before. It was something that still hurt so very deeply, even after so many years of living with the pain. And yet somehow she knew that Ambrosia would not sit in judgment of her for her feelings, that she would understand. And she needed someone to understand, to listen, after such a long and lonely period of silence. "I will always be in love with him, I think. Though I learned to see my love for him for what it is: childish, foolish, a damnably enduring part of growing up." She looked away. "He never once came to visit me after my illness. It still hurts me so much to remember that. Even while I thank God for it. If he had not abandoned me then, I would never have turned to Henry."

She met Ambrosia's eyes again, her blue ones bright with tears. "And I did come to love Henry so very, very deeply. A selfish love at first, I think. You see, even with my horrid, crippled body Henry made me feel beautiful." Her voice rose painfully as she mouthed the words. How important that had been to her then! How important it was to any woman, but particularly to one who had taken her beauty for granted. She drew a deep breath and forced a small smile. "It is a rare and precious thing, to be loved so unselfishly. It is a blessing that so many people are blind to . . . as I was blind." And I, Ambrosia thought silently.

Lily sighed and forced another smile. "I do not think of my first love very much anymore. My heart does not ache for him one-tenth as much as for Henry. But sometimes, particularly when I go to town and see a beautiful young woman commanding so much masculine attention, I remember when I was young and lovely, and quite naturally, I think of him." She hesitated, thoughtfully fingering the soft fur lining of her muff. "And you, Ambrosia?" she ventured on instinct. "What of your former lover?"

Ambrosia's breath caught in her throat. "I—I don't know what you mean."

"Don't you?"

Ambrosia stared at her hands, unable to answer at first. "I—I never . . . never . . ."

"You were never actually intimate with the man," Lily supplied. "Is that what you are trying to say?"

Ambrosia gave a small nod, still unable to meet Lily's eyes. Lily felt relieved. At times the memories of passion, romanticized by time and distance, were the most difficult of all memories to cope with. "But you were in love with someone?" It was more a statement than a question. "Was he killed in the war?"

It seemed a long time before she shook her head. "Perhaps . . . perhaps a part of him was," she whispered. Her eyes were still fixed on her tightly laced fingers, but they lifted slowly, hesitantly, and Lily saw them fill with tears. "He—he lost a leg, and his face . . . his face was . . ." Her voice broke and she turned away, struggling in vain to hold back the tears.

"Ambrosia, come here." In a moment, Ambrosia was on the seat beside Lily, and she gathered the younger woman into her arms. No wonder she had been filled with such hatred, such bitterness! "Ambrosia, I am so sorry," Lily comforted her, feeling very close to giving into tears of her own. She gently stroked the girl's hair. "How difficult that must have been for you . . . for both of you."

"He was so brave . . . so handsome before the war," she said brokenly. "And then . . . then the war was over. And we had lost everything. My father was dead. And Ledger was . . ." She closed her eyes, the hot tears flowing quickly down her cheeks. "He didn't even want to live anymore."

"And so he refused to marry you."

She felt Ambrosia tense, then reluctantly shake her head. "He—he was already married," she admitted softly, "to my sister."

Lily's frail arms tightened protectively about her once again, and her blue eyes were warm and understanding. The pieces of the puzzle were all beginning to fall into place now. Ambrosia had loved a man who was not free.

"He never really loved me in return," Ambrosia said after a time. She tried very hard to smile, but her eyes could not carry it off. "He always thought of me as a foolish child, even after he came home."

Lily sighed as she brushed the tears tenderly from Ambrosia's cheeks. "Well . . ." she said with a smile, "you certainly aren't a child anymore."

Ambrosia met her eyes and nodded. It still hurt to remember that Ledger had never loved her as a man loves a woman, that his life had gone on after she left him. But sharing all of her feelings with Lily had somehow put a great many unresolved emotions to rest. Another woman, a fine, loving woman, had felt the same things. Knowing that made Ambrosia feel stronger.

How very strange, she thought, to find strength in admitting to past weaknesses. Weakness was something her father had never admitted to, something she would never have admitted to just a year before. She had been too afraid then to look inside herself, to find out who and what she really was. She was only beginning to find the courage to do that now.

And a part of her was still very much afraid of what she felt for Drayton. She could not confront him yet, could not risk asking his forgiveness and being refused. Perhaps because, as Lily had said, she had not yet forgiven herself. She let her eyes fix on the window and let out a lengthy sigh. No. She couldn't bear the thought of a confrontation, couldn't consider intruding on Drayton's life now. And she couldn't possibly attend the party, even if it meant that everyone would know she was a coward.

Chapter 43

The April sun shone bright and golden in a cloudless blue sky, and a light breeze stirred the mild, fragrant air. Carolyn Craig stood before her mirror in a pretty yellow print dress, twirling a lacy parasol and scowling at her reflection. The past two months had been depressing ones for her. She had tried so very hard and made so very little progress in her pursuit of Drayton Rambert. She saw him regularly at parties and dinners, where he was always polite to her and willing to accommodate her requests to dance every now and again. But he was never any more than polite or accommodating, and he always seemed more interested in discussing politics or business or the economy with the men than in paying particular attention to her. That first night, when he'd apologized to her, she'd been so certain they would resume their affair, that he might even consider divorcing his wife in time. But any overtures she'd made in that direction had been met with evasive excuses. He was too busy to take her to luncheon or dinner or the theater, or at the mere suggestion of a more private rendezvous he would remind her that he was a married man, or more tactfully that he did not want to risk compromising her reputation.

In the past month Carolyn had spent a fortune on a new, enticing wardrobe, had her hair arranged in a dozen different ways, and even tried flirting with other men. Nothing had worked. But today would be different, she told herself as she stood before the mirror. Today she intended to seek out the lion in his den, to go to his place of business where he spent so much of his time. Too much, in her opinion. She adjusted the already daring neckline of her gown to expose all but the very tips of her breasts and cocked her head to smile at her reflection. Drayton Rambert needed a woman. She was certain of that. He had that look about him, that cool, watchful look of a hungry cat on the prowl, regardless of what he said. And she intended to fill his needs before anyone else did.

Carolyn had her liveryman stop before the Fulton Street warehouse and help her alight. "Shall I accompany you, Mrs. Craig?" he inquired, looking askance at the building she seemed intent on entering.

"No, just wait here."

She swept her skirt to the side and entered the building, wrinkling her nose at the strong smells of oils and pigments and thinners. She saw no one at first but heard voices from the loading dock on the far side of the building and immediately proceeded in that direction. As she approached, a dozen workmen turned their heads to stare.

A burly young man in stained workclothes scowled as he noticed that all work had suddenly ceased. He quickly stepped toward her, but before he could demand an explanation, she gave him a syrupy smile. "I'm here to see Mr. Rambert. Could you direct me to him, please?"

The workman slowly narrowed his eyes in appraisal. There was no doubt that this woman was dressed—or rather, half-undressed—with one particular purpose in mind. "You his wife?"

Color shot through Carolyn's cheeks. "Why, no . . . I'm not," she stammered. "But I—I have a message for him," she lied, recovering quickly. So his wife had never visited him here . . .

"Oh, you do, do you?" the workman said doubtfully.

"From my uncle," she went on, her manner becoming condescending when the man did not respond to her charm.

"Well, I'm Tim MacGregor, the warehouse foreman. If you've got a message for Mr. Rambert, you're gonna have to give it to me."

"That's quite impossible, Mr. MacGregor," she sniffed arrogantly, unconsciously primping at her shiny brown curls. "It's a—a personal message. And I'm obliged to deliver it personally. So if Dray—if Mr. Rambert isn't here, then I suppose I'll just have to wait for him."

Tim eyed her distastefully, a deep scowl blackening his brow. If she stayed here much longer, there wouldn't be a single order filled correctly, since the workmen couldn't take their eyes off a half-naked woman parading in front of them. "You can find Mr. Rambert in his office," he told her tersely after letting out a sigh of irritation. "That way. Up the short flight of steps." He waved an arm in the direction from which she had come and abruptly turned his back on her. "All right, boys. The wench is leavin' now, so you can all get back to work."

Carolyn stiffened visibly and her eyes shot murderous sparks at the man's back. The nerve of him! She whirled on a heel, crossed the warehouse, and glided up the steps, her nose high in the air, her skirts lifted carefully to one side to keep them from touching the floor.

Seated behind his desk, Drayton flipped through the stack of last month's orders and made a quick talley. He tossed the pen aside and heaved a lengthy sigh, running his fingers over his tense brow. His figures only confirmed what he had already known. With the factories operating at a fraction of their capacity, the cost per unit of paint produced was rising. But hiring more workers to step up production and efficiency was out of the question for now. It was simply too expensive to consider, since sales were not growing at a rate to justify the production.

There was no chance of breaking even this year, much less making a profit, unless Ken Galbraith took on Rambert Carriage Paints for national distribution. Drayton was certain that the arrangement would be a profitable one for both Galbraith and himself. But without it, it would take years to build enough demand to put the factories at full production. And with fixed costs driving the prices ever upward, Rambert Paints might not last long enough to see that happen. It was the first time Drayton had ever admitted the possibility of failure. It was not something he could afford to dwell on now. He lifted his pen again and systematically began a list of necessary supplies when there was a rap on the door. "Come in, Matt."

Carolyn recognized the voice at once, and a catlike smile curved her mouth. She entered the inner office and closed the door behind herself. He sat at his desk, working intently on a list of some sort, his coarse white shirt opened in a revealing V almost to his waist, his sleeves rolled above his elbows.

"I'll be finished here in just a moment," he said without raising his eyes. "Have a seat."

Carolyn grinned impishly as she approached the desk. "It's not Matt."

Drayton's eyes lifted instantly at the sound of her voice, his expression registering surprise, then annoyance. He took in her expensive, low-cut gown; matching slippers; and parasol. "So I see."

"You don't sound very pleased," she pouted, setting her parasol aside and leaning forward so that her palms rested on the surface of his desk.

He pulled his eyes away from her all but exposed breasts and stood, tossing his pen on the desk. "What do you want, Carolyn?"

She straightened and smiled slowly. Her eyes strayed to his opened shirt, then moved to the dark trousers that clung to the muscles of his hips and thighs. He knew exactly what she wanted. And from the way he had looked at her in that single moment when she'd caught him off guard, she knew he wanted it too. Her smile widened. "I wanted to see where you worked," she answered with a playful shrug. She swept her gown to one side and rounded the desk. When she was less than an arm's breadth away from him, she perched a single hip on that desk. "I wanted to see where you spend all your time," she went on. Her voice softened as she let a single gloved finger play through the crisp mat of hair at his chest. "I wanted to see what keeps you so busy that you haven't any time for me."

He caught her hand and held it, his expression hard. "Carolyn, I've told you before—"

"I know, I know. You're a married man," she broke in before he could voice the excuse.

He released her hand and vented a sigh. "That's part of it."

"And what's the rest of it, Drayton?" she inquired innocently, her fingers raking lightly over his chest once more. "And don't say you're protecting my reputation. We could be discreet about things . . . the way we were in Charleston."

"I am the father of a child, Carolyn. I won't expose my daughter to scandal. Mandy means everything to me."

His words were deliberate, his eyes cold. They cut through her like a knife. If only he had gotten *her* with child in Charleston, he would have married her, Carolyn was certain of it. If only she had thought to trap him that way before that snippy little Confederate got her hands on him. What a fool she had been to let him slip through her fingers! But it couldn't be too late; it just couldn't be! "I could give you children, Drayton," she offered softly, her voice catching slightly. "I would gladly give you a daughter . . . or a son. . . ." Her hand caressed his cheek and she saw his eyes softening. She moved closer quickly, until her breasts made contact with the firm hardness of his chest. She heard him draw a sharp breath and saw his eyes begin to smolder, as he finally made a move to take what she had offered so many times. His mouth lowered to meet hers. . . .

"Good morning, Drayton . . . Mrs. Craig . . ."

They had not even shared a kiss when the greeting made them spring apart. Both pairs of eyes flew to Matt Desmond's face and watched as his tipped his silk hat in salute. "I do hope I'm not interrupting anything," he said solicitously.

Drayton's loose hold on Carolyn ended so abruptly that she nearly toppled backward on the desk. "No. I was expecting you, Matt," he responded evenly, facing Matt's amused grin with something less than amusement. "And Carolyn was just leaving."

"Oh, I'm not in any great hurry." Carolyn smiled. She wasn't about to leave so easily as that, in spite of Drayton's obvious displeasure at her announcement. "I don't mind waiting until you two finish your little business meeting." She fluttered her lashes as she retrieved her parasol and took a seat in the far corner of the room. Her smile was coy as she toyed with her parasol and pretended not to listen to what was being said.

"Speaking of meetings," Matt began with a twinkle in his eye, "you'll never guess whom I saw at Tiffany's day before yesterday. Your Aunt Lily Collinsworth," Matt went on without waiting for an answer. "It's been years since I've seen her, but she hasn't changed. Fortunately for me, she arrived just in time to help me choose Leanne's anniversary gift. We'll be married ten years next week, you know. You've promised to come to the party at her parents' house."

"Yes, I know," Drayton returned impatiently, anxious to get down to more serious matters. If this was what Matt had wanted to see him about . . .

"I invited Lily to the party and she accepted," Matt continued before he could say a word. "And of course . . ." He paused to offer Drayton a cigar and to bite off the end of one for himself. Drayton frowned as he accepted the cigar, knowing now that Matt was up to something. "I extended the invitation to the lovely little thing Lily had brought along shopping with her." He lit his cigar and expelled his first draw in a lengthy sigh. "She was lovely as a breath of spring, Drayton. And I believe Lily introduced her as your wife."

The moment he uttered the words, Carolyn dropped her parasol and her syrupy smile froze on her face. Though Matt's back was facing toward her, he had no trouble gauging her reaction. "She's looking quite well, Drayton. Seems to have recovered completely from her illness."

The two men eyed each other for a long moment. Then suddenly Drayton rose from his chair and rounded his desk. "I'll walk you to your carriage, Carolyn."

It was nothing less than an order, and she complied, though she wasn't happy about the circumstances. His stride was determined as he led her from the office, and his touch was cool, indifferent, as his fingers encircled her arm.

"We can't let him do this to us," Carolyn told him as they descended the short flight of steps.

"It's none of your business, Carolyn."

"She ruined your life in Charleston. Are you going to let her do the same thing here?"

He said nothing. They were nearing her carriage now, so she stepped in front of him, her eyes pleading desperately. "You could lose everything, don't you see?"

His eyes fixed on her face. "I told you, it's none of your business."

She stared at him in disbelief. He couldn't mean that. He simply couldn't. "You would have done more than kiss me if he hadn't interrupted," she cried.

Drayton couldn't deny it. He had wanted her. It had been so long since he'd had a woman that he'd responded to her softness, her femininity. . . . He was angry with himself now for having given in to a purely physical urge without considering the consequences. "Matt kept me from making a very bad mistake,'' he told Carolyn bluntly.

''No! You don't mean that! Admit it, Drayton. You want me every bit as much as I want you.'' She flung her arms about his neck and sought his mouth, thinking that he would respond to her now as he had just a few moments before.

But he only grasped her shoulders and pushed her away. ''For heaven's sake, Carolyn, stop it. Haven't you any pride?''

Her struggles ceased abruptly at his words, and her tear-filled eyes riveted on his face. With a tiny sob she broke away from him and ran to her carriage, departing without a single backward glance.

Matt was leisurely puffing on his second cigar when Drayton returned. He leaned forward in the chair to flick an ash in the tray on Drayton's desk. ''Terribly sorry if I said something to upset her,'' he lied. He rose from his chair and walked to the single small window and glanced out. ''But I thought Carolyn knew you were married.'' He turned to Drayton and shrugged. ''Everyone seems to know all about your wife, Drayton. I thought I knew all about her too. But it turned out I was wrong. I didn't know she was one of the prettiest little magnolias ever to leave South Carolina,'' he drawled. ''Why, I do believe she's enough woman to have started that little ol' war all by herself.''

''Are you finished?'' Drayton inquired calmly.

''Not quite.'' Matt smashed the tip of his cigar into the tray. ''I think it's time you used a little more discretion in your dealings with Mrs. Craig. A warehouse in broad daylight is hardly the time or the place for—''

Without warning Drayton's temper snapped, and Matt instantly felt a rock hard fist smashing into his jaw, sending him flying backward over the desktop. Papers flew everywhere as he struggled to gain his balance. He came to his feet slowly, supporting himself on an elbow until the fuzziness in his head faded a bit. His brown eyes met Drayton's, and he winced at the thinly restrained anger he saw there still. He wasn't really surprised that Drayton had thrown that punch, not after he'd pushed the man like he had.

"My personal life is none of your business," Drayton ground out through clenched teeth.

"The hell it's not." Matt was still unsteady on his feet as he tossed back the retort. He paused to press his fingertips gingerly to his jaw. "Your business is backed by my bank. And until you're independent of all your financial obligations to that bank, you aren't free to turn your back on polite society or live a life of public sin. There are other paint manufacturers in town—upright family men who go to church and live good, clean lives . . . or at least they appear to. And each and every one of your customers is going to turn to them if you offend their delicate sensitivities. As for Ken Galbraith, he likes you, Drayton. But he's not quite sure about trusting you. He's heard too many rumors about your wife, and he knows all about Aaron. He can't help wondering if you and your stepbrother are two of a kind."

He let out a sigh and shook his head at the stubborn set of Drayton's mouth. He wasn't getting through. "Think, man," he said earnestly. "A woman like Carolyn Craig can't do anything but hurt your chances at this point. You can't afford to risk a public affair. There's already too much gossip, and you know it. Take a mistress if you need one. Take several. But for heaven's sake, don't flaunt them. Be discreet. Or you'll lose any chance you have of making a fortune." He paused, then added pointedly, "And you'll also lose a friend."

A bitter smile twisted Drayton's mouth. "Thank you for the advice . . . *friend.*"

Matt straightened and dusted off his lapels. "Don't mention it." He retrieved his hat from the desk and gave something that looked like a smile. "I will expect to see you and your lovely wife Friday next. . . ."

Chapter 44

The sun had long since disappeared from the sky when Mandy finally fell asleep in Ambrosia's arms and was carried off to her bed. Ambrosia smiled to herself as she pressed a light kiss to her baby's cheek and tiptoed from the nursery. It had been a long day for both of them, since Mandy had suddenly become an expert explorer, curiously inspecting everything within her reach and trying desperately to reach everything that wasn't. This afternoon, the moment Ambrosia's mind was elsewhere, Mandy had promptly left her toys and crawled from the parlor to the dining room. Within minutes she was pulling herself up on a chair and then onto the table by grasping fistfuls of the linen tablecloth. It seemed that she was forever climbing, reaching, scrambling into trouble ever since she'd learned how to crawl.

With a sigh that was a mixture of pride and exasperation, Ambrosia descended the stairs and entered the parlor. She collected her sketch pad and a few pieces of charcoal and took a seat in a chair. Lily was seated nearby, playing solitaire at a small table. She drummed her fingers in frustration against the tabletop. "Is Mandy asleep?"

"Finally." Ambrosia looked up from the sketch she

461

had just begun and grinned. ''I wonder where she gets all that energy.''

Lily smiled in response and slowly began to go through her stack of cards again. She'd been through them four times already without finding a single play. But perhaps she had missed something, she told herself. She scowled as she turned the cards face up, snapping the last several loudly on the table as she did so. With a sigh of annoyance she finished with the cards and straightened them into a neat stack. She might as well admit it. She'd lost another game. She made to gather in the cards, then stopped and reconsidered. She tossed a brief, sidelong glance at Ambrosia to assure herself that the younger woman was already deeply engrossed in her drawing. With a pensive nibble at her bottom lip, Lily hurriedly slipped a few cards from the thickest facedown stack and added them to her playing cards. A foxlike smile curved her mouth as she placed a red queen on a black king, a play which made possible at least five consecutive plays.

''It doesn't count, you know.''

Lily's eyes lifted in startled amazement. ''What, dear?'' she inquired innocently.

Ambrosia's eyes remained on her sketch. ''I said, it doesn't count as a win if you steal cards from underneath.''

Lily frowned as she stared at Ambrosia, then at her cards, then at Ambrosia again. ''How did you know? You weren't even watching!''

''I was listening.''

Lily lifted an indignant brow. ''What does that mean?''

Trying hard to hold back a grin, Ambrosia laid aside her sketch and met Lily's eyes. ''When you're winning, you talk to yourself. When you're losing, you make all sorts of irritating noises with those cards. And when you're cheating''—she could no longer hold back the smile—''you're as quiet as a mouse.''

Lily's eyes widened in dismay. She quickly gathered

up the cards and made to change the subject. "What are you sketching?"

Still chuckling to herself, Ambrosia retrieved her sketch and gave a shrug. "Nothing in particular," she answered lightly, carefully closing the pad and rising to pace before the fire. The April day had been wonderfully mild, but the nights were still brisk and a fire was a wonderful luxury. With her back to Lily, she idly began to warm her hands before it. Lily sighed as she watched Ambrosia stare at the flames, knowing full well what occupied her thoughts. She had caught a glimpse of Ambrosia's sketch and recognized it instantly as a portrait of Drayton.

For a long moment the room was silent. But suddenly both women started at the sound of Drayton's voice cutting like a blade through the room. "Ambrosia."

She whirled, her eyes riveting on the threshold where he stood clad in a white cotton shirt and dark, tight-fitting trousers. Workclothes, obviously, since both shirt and pants bore stains of many colors and oils. Ambrosia's face lit up when she saw him, but almost at once that light died. His eyes were raking over her with open hostility, moving slowly over her pink muslin gown, upward to the ribbons that drew her hair into an attractive cluster of curls. She felt her stomach knotting, felt the color draining from her face.

Lily rose, struggling from behind the table to make her way toward her nephew. He had come home only three times since the holidays, and all of his visits had been made on Sundays. Something was very different now, something was very wrong. "Drayton, what is it? What's happened?"

He made no move to enter the room, and suddenly Lily stopped, aware of the tension that flared between Drayton and Ambrosia, aware of the way he was staring at her as if he wanted very much to slap her face. "Drayton?"

"I need to speak with my wife, Lily," he said softly.

His blue eyes never wavered from Ambrosia's face even as he spoke the words. "Alone."

Lily's eyes flew helplessly from one to the other, but Drayton's expression was ruthlessly cold, and Ambrosia's was cool and distant, a strange look Lily had not seen since Mandy's birth. They were bracing for a fight that could only hurt them both. "Drayton—"

"I shall be waiting in the library," he said tersely, ignoring Lily's stammering attempts at pacification. He turned on a heel and left the room with a brisk, angry stride.

For a long moment Ambrosia did not move. It seemed an eternity before she could find the strength to square her shoulders and lift her chin. Then, without a word or even a glance at Lily, she followed after him.

The fireplace lay cold and empty in the library. A chill pervaded the room. Ambrosia stood in rigid silence as Drayton lit the desk lamp and a second lamp on a nearby table. A soft yellow glow dispelled the shadows, but the terrible chill remained. He turned to face her, his mouth set in a tight, angry line, his eyes icy as they once again flicked over her new clothing. It was so much softer, prettier than the black gowns she had worn, and her hair seemed to beckon the touch of his hand. She stood straight and silent, meeting his eyes without any show of emotion. Just like before, he thought, she was being coldly defiant. "I was informed by Matt Desmond today that you plan to make an appearance at their anniversary party next Friday." His eyes never left hers.

She said nothing. She had known he would be angry. For a time she met the fury in his eyes, but then her control faltered. She stared at the floor.

"Well? Is it true or isn't it?"

"Mr. Desmond invited Lily to the party," Ambrosia admitted softly. "And out of politeness, he extended the invitation to me as well. But you needn't worry, Drayton. I have no intention of going."

It was what he had come to hear. Yet the words in no

way eased his anger. Without knowing why he felt a surge of new resentment. "What excuse do you intend to give?" he demanded.

She stared at her hands, her fingers lacing tightly. "The same excuse you have used this past year, unless you can think of a better one." She paused, her throat so painfully tight that she could scarcely speak at all. "If that's all you wished to speak with me about . . ." She turned as if to leave.

He moved to block her path. "I can hardly claim that you're seriously ill now, after you came into town the picture of health and put yourself on display for all the world to see."

She met his eyes, her lip trembling, her eyes bright with unshed tears. "I'm terribly sorry I've ruined your little lie," she told him with heavy sarcasm. "I can assure you it wasn't intentional."

His eyes narrowed. "I think it was," he accused hotly. "I think you had it in your mind to attend that party just to humiliate me."

She stared at him, her face reflecting the hurt she was feeling at his accusation. Then her eyes became distant, uncaring, far away.

"Matt told me you accepted the invitation," he went on. "He expects you to be there. He's probably told a dozen people that you'll be there."

"Well then," she returned with a weak attempt at a smile, "he'll be disappointed, won't he?" She let out a shaky breath and struggled to calm herself, to detach herself from what was happening. "Don't worry, Drayton. I wouldn't dream of going and ruining your lie for the rest of your friends."

When she would have passed him, his hands shot out to take hold of her arms. He could not allow her so easy a retreat. He was too indignant for that. "You are going to that party, Ambrosia. Not behind my back, the way you planned it. You'll arrive on my arm as my devoted wife, finally recovered from a lingering illness." His fingers tightened painfully about the flesh of her arms. "And if you say one word or make one move that's out of line, I promise you, you'll never see Mandy again." He released her abruptly, his anger suddenly spent as he saw the tears coursing swiftly down her cheeks. He had hurt her deeply, just as he had wanted to do. He wondered fleetingly why he felt so little satisfaction, even a twinge of guilt. He turned away.

Humiliated at being reduced to tears by his threat, Ambrosia wiped her cheeks with the back of her hand and struggled to straighten her spine. How long had it been since she had played out this same scene with this same man, listening to his threats, her strength crumbling beneath the weight of them? She had hated him then, had done everything in her power to destroy him. Just as he was destroying her now. She rubbed briskly at the flesh of her arms as a chill made her tremble within. "Is that all?" she whispered.

"I will expect you at my house by seven o'clock Friday," he said with cool authority, not even turning back to face her. He let out a lengthy breath before he abruptly turned and left the room.

Lily hobbled clumsily from one end of the hallway to the other, leaning heavily on her cane and resisting the urge to listen at the library door. If only Drayton hadn't been so terribly angry. If only he would stop a moment and see the changes in her. Surely he must have noticed her dress, her hair. He wasn't a man if he hadn't noticed that. And surely he would listen to—

"Lily."

She whirled about, her eyes lifting in an unspoken plea. He was eyeing her with cold resolution as he buttoned his coat. He picked up his hat and gloves. "Since my wife wants so much to attend a party in the city, I'm going to oblige her. She tells me that you were invited as well."

Lily moved to close the distance between them.

"Drayton, listen to me. The party wasn't Ambrosia's idea. She didn't even want to go."

He pulled his wide-brimmed hat low on his brow, catching sight of Ambrosia as he glanced back at his aunt. "I will expect to see you at my house Friday at seven sharp. I hope I can trust you to see that she wears something appropriate," he added, knowing full well Ambrosia heard the remark. Before Lily could respond, he was gone.

Chapter 45

The air was warm as they began their early-evening ride to town, though as the sun began its descent, it cooled considerably. Lily made a conscious effort to keep quiet during the greater part of their trip, and her warning glances at Bessie instructed the maid to do the same. She had not really thought about this being the first overnight separation for mother and child until she watched the way Ambrosia held her baby, her eyes pressed tightly shut, her mouth quivering with emotion. Mandy gave her a brief hug, then playfully waved bye-bye, a trick she had recently learned from Debbs. Lily gnawed nervously at her bottom lip as she watched Ambrosia gaze sullenly at the passing landscape. At the very least tonight would be difficult for her. She would be stared at and whispered about and probably questioned unmercifully all evening long. They were all dying to see her, this mysterious woman Drayton had married and then "locked away" in the country all these months. They were all speculating on her illness, on the hasty marriage that had produced a child and then driven Drayton away to live a life of his own in the city, to take a mistress. . . . No, Lily told herself firmly. She didn't really believe that he'd done that, in spite of what Isabel said.

468

And tonight would put an end to the gossip. Everyone would finally see for himself.

Darkness was descending as the brougham rolled to a smooth stop before the Gramercy Park brownstone. Debbs quickly moved to assist Ambrosia and Lily from the carriage, then saw to their safe entrance to the house.

The entrance hall was long and dark, cluttered with paintings and sculptures that seemed eerie and uninviting in the flickering gaslight. Ambrosia disliked the house the moment she entered it, hated the gaudy scrollwork that gilded everything, the objets d'art that filled every nook and corner, cluttering every inch of open space. A painfully thin, bent old man dressed in crisp servant's attire bowed and introduced himself as Bryson. He was the only servant in the house since all but a few of the rooms were closed and Mr. Rambert lived alone. Bryson settled them in their rooms with surprising efficiency, announcing in his proper British accent that Mr. Rambert would join them in the parlor precisely at seven.

Alone in the room that had been assigned her, Ambrosia stared at her reflection in the mirror, trying hard to summon courage from what she saw there. Her fingers lifted shakily to touch her cheek, pale beneath the slight touch of color Lily had insisted she use. She had never worn face paint before, had never even considered it, since it was something a Southern woman of breeding simply would not do. But the women here in New York were different from the women Ambrosia had known throughout her childhood. This world was a different one. And if she hoped to survive here, if she hoped to endure this night, then she could not allow anyone to see that she was terribly afraid.

She bit her lip and closed her eyes, remembering the single Yankee party she had attended in Charleston, remembering how lovely Carolyn Craig had been in her daring evening gown, remembering how pretty her hair had been. Ambrosia felt small and unattractive compared to that memory. She opened her eyes again and considered her gown, feeling oddly detached from the woman in the looking glass. The dress was a blend of soft lavender and rose lace with a low, off-the-shoulder bodice made demure by a transparent, high-necked tucker of pink-tinged lace. The sleeves, which began just below the shoulder, fell loosely to a satin bow at the elbow and were fitted tightly from there to the wrist. A single wide flounce of delicate rose lace followed the low scoop of the actual neckline, dipping to a V at the center of the front to suggest the curves of her breasts. The skirt fell in an almost straight line from the tightly cinched waist, leaving little doubt as to the firm curves of her hips and slender legs. Her hair was a mass of soft black curls clustered at her crown with matching lace-trimmed ribbons of pink. The shiny coils spilled forward to her brow and tiny wisps of curl also softened the lines of her face, giving the effect of charming disarray. All was elegant, eye-catching, a captivating mixture of innocence and inherent sensuality. But as Ambrosia met her own somber green-gray eyes in the glass, she felt almost as if she were a child again, playing a silly game. She remembered the way Ledger had never noticed the gowns she had worn, the way he had always noticed Melissa's every move. And then she remembered that Drayton had once looked at her with a hungry fire in his eyes, making her so very aware of her own femininity. But perhaps he looked at Carolyn that way now, she thought, and perhaps he would ignore her as all the young men had always ignored the sharp-featured, shapeless young girl so long ago.

She lifted her chin and turned away from the glass. No matter what he said or did, she would somehow endure it quietly and then return to Elmwood and Mandy and try to forget. It was all she really wanted now. She couldn't allow herself to hope for anything more.

Just a few minutes before the mantel clock chimed the hour of seven, Ambrosia entered the parlor and forced a smile for Lily, who was perched comfortably on a dark red velvet settee. She glanced about nervously for Drayton, but he had not yet arrived. She began to pace the parlor like a caged animal, back and forth, back and forth, until Lily could bear no more. "Ambrosia," she said softly, "do have a seat, won't you?"

Ambrosia stopped short and met Lily's eyes. "I don't feel much like sitting down, thank you."

"You look lovely tonight," Lily told her. "Everyone will be impressed."

Ambrosia eyed Lily's frothy pink-and-white gown of ruffles and bows, a combination that made her look almost girlish in spite of her years. "Thank you, Lily," she returned quietly. "I'm afraid no one will notice me after they've seen you."

The clock began to chime, and as if on cue Drayton appeared on the threshold, cutting a striking figure in his black swallowtail coat and pressed trousers, complemented by a pleated white shirt. His eyes lingered critically for several moments on Ambrosia, as if seeking some flaw in her attire. He scowled, pulling his eyes away without a single word or gesture of approval. Ambrosia had not really expected any. She felt her stomach knotting as he moved to assist Lily to her feet, pointedly ignoring her. Bryson, the manservant who had earlier shown her to her room, stood waiting in the hallway with the ladies' wraps. Drayton took Lily's wrap and draped it over her shoulders, motioning Bryson to assist his wife. "You look radiant this evening, Lily. Pink becomes you, you know."

"Thank you," Lily returned with a tight smile, infuriated that Drayton was using her to slight Ambrosia. She would have liked very much to give him a good verbal thrashing, or at the very least a sharp jab with her elbow, but she was afraid Ambrosia would notice and feel that much worse. So she simply glared at him whenever she noticed that Ambrosia's eyes were elsewhere and resolved that the thrashing would have to come later. His

behavior was unforgivable and she intended to tell him
so.

The carriage ride proceeded in an uncomfortable silence though Lily tried to fill the void with her lighthearted chatter about who would be there and how long it
had been since she'd seen this person or that. Both Ambrosia and Drayton seemed intent on staring at the passing houses and avoiding each other's eyes.

Finally the coach rolled to a stop. Drayton moved to
help Lily alight, then his wife. Ambrosia held her breath
as he assisted her from the brougham, feeling herself
tremble inside at the mere touch of his hands. His fingers
did not loosen for a long moment after her feet had
touched the ground, until her eyes lifted in a silent inquiry. "I trust you will not feel compelled to discuss politics tonight." His voice was low, his eyes challenging,
almost taunting.

Ambrosia turned away from him quickly, not wanting
him to know how much the remark had hurt. To him, she
was the same woman who had humiliated him in Charleston. He could not see that that woman had died, could not
know how painful that death had been, how terribly vulnerable that death had left her.

Drayton moved again to take Lily's arm rather than
Ambrosia's as they moved up the steps to a grand front
entrance, following a thick red carpet that had been un-
rolled to welcome guests. Just inside the elegant foyer,
he took the ladies' wraps and handed them to a man in
starched black attire who greeted him by name, then
nodded politely to the ladies. Drayton offered Ambrosia
his arm with a cold smile. "The charade begins," he said
just loud enough for her to hear.

The guests of honor stood with Leanne's parents just
beyond the foyer, receiving guests as they arrived.
Leanne stepped forward, smiling, to embrace Lily, as did
her mother. When they had finished with their gushy
welcome, Leanne made to extend her hand to Drayton,
then stopped mid-motion when she saw the woman at his

side. Matt had told her that Drayton's wife would be making an appearance tonight, and she had been looking forward to meeting her as much as anything else, certain it would give her an opportunity to gloat over Drayton's "mistake." But she hadn't been prepared for this—a woman of striking beauty, a woman who bore herself proudly, gracefully as she stepped forward for an introduction. For a moment Leanne couldn't find her voice.

"And I believe you've already met Ambrosia," Drayton said to Matt with a stiff smile.

Matt smiled at her, his eyes warm with appreciative regard. "At Tiffany's last week," he affirmed, bowing over her hand.

"Oh, yes," Leanne managed finally, "I remember you mentioning that, darling. But you didn't tell me how young and pretty Drayton's wife was," she went on, flashing Matt a brittle smile.

"You're very kind, I'm sure, Mrs. Desmond," Ambrosia returned, her cool green eyes seeing through Leanne's polite façade.

"Not at all," she shot back. "It's just that I'm . . . surprised to see you looking so—so healthy after so long and serious an illness. Why, you're all the picture of health! You must tell us later all about your remarkable recovery, my dear."

The foyer was filling with new arrivals, cutting short any further conversation, much to Ambrosia's relief. With Drayton's hand at her back, she passed a spectacular dining room that had been set for an elegant formal dinner, then several grand parlors to arrive finally at a huge ballroom where Lily insisted they remain for several minutes while she observed the dancers and listened to the music. It had been so very long!

Ambrosia felt like a girl again as she watched the lovely colors swirling about the golden marble floor. Everything seemed to have a soft, yellow glow in the flickering gaslights, all reflected in the scores of mirrors that lined the ceilings.

Ambrosia was introduced to many of Drayton's
friends and several of Lily's as well, all of whom seemed
quite surprised as they took in her appearance. The gossip had led them to expect something so very different.
And the reality gave them so very little to say. She was
neither ugly nor crude and uneducated; indeed, her every
move suggested refinement and breeding. So after several moments of staring and conversing with her, most of
them retreated.

After some time had passed, Lily grew weary of observing the dancers and suggested they move to a nearby
parlor. Ambrosia turned to leave the room, then stopped
short as she encountered an all-too-familiar face. Carolyn
Craig was standing just a short distance from where they
stood. She was dressed in a scandalously cut gown of
bright red silk that bared her shoulders and nearly all of
her ample bosom, and her face was heavily painted. Ambrosia was taken aback for a moment, shocked that the
woman who had appeared so lovely and fresh in Charleston now looked so garish and brazen. Carolyn was talking with a gentleman who was obviously quite taken with
her, and she ran her fingers slowly over his lapel as she
fluttered her lashes prettily. As if feeling Ambrosia's
eyes upon her, she glanced in that direction. A slow, deliberate smile curved her painted mouth as her eyes
moved pointedly from Ambrosia to Drayton and back
again. Though Ambrosia did not have the courage to look
at Drayton, she felt certain that he had returned the smile
because suddenly Carolyn's smile widened.

"Are you coming, Ambrosia? Drayton?" Lily asked
quietly, having noticed the exchange and guessed exactly
who the woman in red was.

"Yes." Ambrosia turned quickly away from Carolyn's smile to follow Lily into the parlor.

Drayton saw Lily seated comfortably on an elegant
settee of rose-gray velvet in one corner of the room,
where she was quickly surrounded by friends and ac-
quaintances from years past. Everyone, it seemed, was

anxious to talk with her, to reminisce over old times. Ambrosia followed Drayton to a chair a fair distance away and took a seat, trying hard to regain the composure that had slipped the moment she saw Carolyn Craig. Drayton remained by her side but said nothing to her, like a guard, Ambrosia thought miserably, on duty for a single night. She could not know that he had hoped that Carolyn would not be present tonight, that he was trying to prepare himself for the scene she would almost surely try to make. Ambrosia only knew that her husband hardly looked at her while he threw countless glances in Carolyn's direction. She swallowed hard against the tightness in her throat as she eyed the people who had gathered about Lily. Friends, some of them, from the warm smiles in their eyes. A few male admirers hovering close by. But there were also a few who had come to pat her hand sympathetically, as if they pitied her, even while Ambrosia saw clearly the jealousy in their eyes. Lily might be nearly sixty and partially paralyzed, but she was undeniably one of the loveliest ladies in the room, and hands down the liveliest conversationalist.

Drayton took two glasses of champagne from a servant's tray, offering one to Ambrosia and sipping at the other as he listened to Lily's delightful ripostes.

"I can't really believe you enjoy life so far from the city!" remarked one homely woman with a pinched face. "Why, it must be terribly boring for a woman like you."

"It's not quite that bad, darling," Lily interrupted before she could go on. "After all, life is what you make of it." Lily smiled then and winked at the gentleman who bent to offer her a glass of champagne. Ambrosia noticed that a tiny flicker of a smile touched Drayton's mouth as he caught Lily's eyes and lifted his own glass in a silent toast. But he made no move to include Ambrosia in the exchange. Indeed, when Lily's eyes drifted to hers and gave an encouraging smile, Drayton promptly looked away.

A few moments later, Ambrosia saw Drayton straighten slightly and fix his attention on a tall, gray-haired gentleman who was entering the room. Drayton moved to greet the man and his wife, his face breaking into a warm smile as he took the man's hand, then pressed a light kiss to the woman's hand. After a brief exchange Drayton retraced his steps to Ambrosia's side and introduced the couple as Kenneth and Muriel Galbraith. All the while he spoke his fingers rested on Ambrosia's shoulder, tightening when it was proper for her to respond, as if in silent warning. But the warning was unnecessary. Ambrosia had no intention of causing Drayton any embarrassment on this night. She forced a smile that seemed genuine as she made all the right responses and even laughed softly as she fielded Mrs. Galbraith's blunt queries about her background.

"I even heard that you owned slaves, is that true?" Muriel wanted to know.

"Why, it was all such a long time ago, I hardly even remember," Ambrosia told her. "But I can assure you, Mrs. Galbraith, that I don't own any now."

Irritated by the chuckles Ambrosia's remark had generated, Mrs. Galbraith's eyes narrowed. "Did you actually beat the poor, helpless things?"

"Why, I never struck anyone I can recall," Ambrosia returned innocently. "I was taught that a lady never behaves that way."

The questions continued, though both Drayton and Mr. Galbraith tried their best to turn the conversation to other matters. Mrs. Galbraith stubbornly reverted to Ambrosia's past life.

Ambrosia felt more than a little relieved when dinner was announced, until she found that the seating arrangement could hardly have been worse. Not only were Mr. and Mrs. Galbraith placed directly across the table from Drayton and herself, but beside Mr. Galbraith Carolyn Craig eagerly took her seat. To Ambrosia's other side sat an obnoxious, middle-aged man who reeked of liquor and constantly leaned close to speak in a loud, grating voice. Lily was seated somewhere at the far end of the table, completely out of sight.

The meal proceeded with agonizing slowness. The man beside Ambrosia became more and more obnoxious, bending ever closer to Ambrosia's ear and speaking louder than before, placing his hand on hers at every opportunity. Each time she hurriedly pulled away from him and turned her attention back to her dinner, though she could hardly bear the thought of eating with her stomach so twisted in knots. She made a valiant attempt to converse with Mrs. Galbraith again, but that proved a very bad mistake. Once again the woman began to question her about the South, then brought up a subject meant to back Ambrosia into a corner—Jefferson Davis. Carolyn joined the conversation, scolding Muriel for making Drayton's "war bride" uncomfortable with her talk about such things.

"My only brother was killed at Gettysburg," Muriel returned sharply, her eyes bright with hostility. Ken Galbraith quickly seized his wife's hand. "Muriel, please."

She snatched her hand away and went on. "I'd like to see every one of those no-good Confederates hung to pay for that. Hanging's just punishment for treason. But instead, they're left to live. Pardoned for their crimes. While my brother lies in his grave."

For a moment the entire section of the table quieted, and all eyes riveted expectantly on Ambrosia's face. "I am sorry about your brother," Ambrosia said softly, her eyes showing sadness and regret. She was remembering that she had once judged all Yankees as this woman was now judging her. And though she had felt a surge of indignation when Mrs. Galbraith suggested that all Confederates ought to die, she kept it hidden. Nothing would ever be gained by an ugly exchange of words, and rekindling her own bitterness would never bring back what was gone. Admitting that to herself did not heal the wounds in her heart, a heart that had loved the South, and

Heritage, and her father, and Ledger. Yet, as she felt
Drayton's eyes upon her and turned to find him regarding
her steadily, she realized that that very same heart now
loved her husband and child more than she had ever
loved anything in her past. For a moment their eyes
locked. Then Ambrosia looked away.

Deeply disappointed that Ambrosia had not jumped at
the bait, Carolyn promptly sought to change the subject
to an amusing incident that had occurred at a party a few
weeks before. She hoped that, since Ambrosia was the
only person who had not been present then, she would
feel a particular alienation now. But neither Drayton nor
Ambrosia seemed interested in what she was saying.
Both of them had turned their attention to their dinners.

Directly after dinner, Drayton located Lily and escorted her back to the parlor with Ambrosia. They had
only been there a short while when Matt Desmond approached them. "Ah! Here you are." He smiled warmly.
"I am about to impose on you, Drayton."

Drayton lifted a mildly curious brow. "How so?"

"I'm going to ask your permission to dance with the
loveliest woman at the party."

Ambrosia's eyes widened in surprise, then flew to
Drayton's face, hoping desperately that he would refuse.
The only man she remembered ever having danced with
was Ledger, and that was so very long ago. She wasn't
even certain she remembered how. But she was certain
about one thing. Matt Desmond's eyes held a spark of
something that made her uneasy, uncomfortable. Surely
Drayton saw that as well.

Drayton gave a disinterested shrug. "Be my guest."

Feeling the color flare in her cheeks at Drayton's dismissal, she rose and placed her hand into the one Matt
Desmond had extended. "My pleasure, Mr. Desmond,"
she forced herself to say graciously, giving him her most
attractive smile.

She followed him toward the dance floor, her smile
fading quickly as nervousness overtook her. He stopped,

his hand lifting hers, his arm encircling her waist. The music began and suddenly she was whirling about the floor in a quick, dizzying design of steps, remembering it all as she followed Matt's graceful lead, feeling giddy as a schoolgirl in spite of herself.

"Why, Mrs. Rambert! I do believe you're enjoying this!"

She met Matt's laughing brown eyes with a look of dismay. Had her reluctance been so obvious? she wondered. "I—It's been a long time since I've danced," she admitted carefully.

"Then your husband is even more of a fool than I thought," he returned promptly.

Ambrosia felt herself tensing at how intently he regarded her, at how closely he danced with her. She bit her lip and lowered her eyes.

"You must forgive me, Mrs. Rambert. But there's something about you that makes a man feel reckless and daring. And it's not just that you're beautiful, though you're certainly that." He grinned as the color flared in her cheeks again. "Do you know how fetching you look when you blush? No, of course you don't. That's part of your charm, you know. That you're so unaware of what you are."

He watched her for a few moments. She was silent and careful to avoid his eyes, but her breast rose and fell with her excitement . . . or discomfort. Unfortunately, Matt was fairly certain it was the latter. Not only was she lovely, she was innocent as a lamb. And beyond the innocence, he was sure, lay a smoldering fire. A passionate woman, in spite of her cool exterior. He had not been exaggerating when he told her she made him feel reckless and daring. Indeed, he felt just enough bravado to insist that she share a second dance with him, though he knew quite well that Drayton would not like it. Perhaps because Ambrosia knew it as well, she accepted.

Drayton watched as Ambrosia eagerly made for the ballroom with Matt, then went immediately to the smoking parlor to get himself a drink of something stronger than champagne. The evening had been a trying one from the moment he'd laid eyes on Ambrosia in that soft pink-and-lavender gown. It reminded him of a gown Kathryn had worn, with all the lace and softness, but he couldn't really remember Kathryn's face anymore. He could only remember Ambrosia's. Tonight, watching her so intently, listening closely for any sign of defiance in her cool responses only made Drayton aware of how desirable she was, of how much he still wanted her. His arms ached to hold her, his fingers to touch her skin, her hair . . . even as his soul cried out in anguish with the memories of each time he had.

And Carolyn . . . always there, smiling, taunting him with something he had taken once but never really wanted, offering to satisfy him without ever realizing that she never could. Drayton took a long swallow of straight bourbon and closed his eyes for a moment, allowing the drink to settle his nerves.

"I was hoping to find you alone."

He opened his eyes and forced a smile for Ken Galbraith, who ordered a drink of straight whiskey as well. Drayton frowned a little when he did that. Ken was not a drinking man.

"I—I must apologize for my wife," Ken said after he had tested his drink. "She took her brother's death quite hard, you see. But I didn't realize that she would blame your wife for—"

"It's all right, Ken. Ambrosia understands." Drayton said the words mechanically, but as he did so he remembered the look in her eyes, the sound of her voice when she said, "I am sorry about your brother." He shook off the uncertainty that assailed him at the thought and took another sip of his drink, berating himself for being a fool. She had acted out a part because he had threatened her, because she was afraid of losing Mandy. Nothing more.

"She's a very beautiful woman," Ken remarked thoughtfully. "I must admit I didn't expect her to be.

There's been a lot of talk about—not that I pay attention to that sort of thing," he inserted quickly. "But I've made it a habit to do business with upright family men. They just seem to be more reliable, more stable. And the gossip made me wonder if you'd come to town alone and taken on that business to escape a difficult woman. There were things said about a scandal in Charleston, and of course, Mrs. Craig has been very . . ." A flicker of something in Drayton's eyes made Ken stop before he finished that sentence. "Well," he went on with a forced smile, "anyone can see that the gossip was wrong. Your wife is a treasure. And her regard for you is just as obvious."

Ken finished off his drink and drew a lengthy breath. "What I'm trying to say is, I think it's time we talked a firm business deal between Galbraith Distribution and Rambert Carriage Paints. I leave for Philadelphia Monday morning, but when I return we'll work out the particulars. I think it will profit us both, Drayton." He smiled and gave the younger man a hearty pat on the back. "I think your Uncle Henry would have been pleased."

Drayton managed a smile in return, but something inside him twisted at the mention of Henry Collinsworth. Henry would never have approved of what he was doing. But James Rambert would have. How empty Drayton felt at the thought, a thought he quickly pushed aside. He had gotten what he wanted. Now he only had to work hard, to follow things through.

He drained his glass and excused himself, not wanting to leave Ambrosia alone once her dance with Matt was over. There was still a chance that she could ruin everything. But when he returned to the parlor, he found that she had not returned from the ballroom. Angry now, he made his way through the crowd and watched the last few rotations of the dance. Matt bent gallantly to kiss her hand as the music ended, and Ambrosia smiled at him, a small smile, a timid kind of smile. All the same it angered Drayton. He waited impatiently for her to leave the dance floor.

Ambrosia's smile vanished when she turned and saw him standing at the edge of the ballroom. So he had noticed that she danced more than a single dance with Matt, she thought. The brightness in his narrow eyes told her that he was angry. She was almost glad. She was also a little afraid. She lifted her chin and somehow managed to smile again as she made her way toward him.

"It's time we went home," he said curtly. "Lily's waiting."

He took hold of her hand and led her to the parlor with a stiff, arrogant stride. She followed without a word. It took every bit of her strength to hide her emotions, to smile and mouth all the proper farewells and thank-yous. Just a little longer, she told herself, just one more smile. . . .

Ambrosia's face tightened when Carolyn stepped in front of her, blocking her and Drayton's exit from the parlor. "You must come to tea tomorrow, Ambrosia," Carolyn insisted. "Both you and Mrs. Collinsworth, that is. Leanne will be there, and Muriel and—"

"I'm very sorry, Mrs. Craig, but Lily and I are leaving first thing in the morning."

Carolyn's eyes lit up immediately. "Are you really?" she pressed. Her eyes flew to Drayton's. "Drayton, is she really? You didn't tell me her visit would be so brief," she scolded him.

Lily cut off Drayton's reply by linking her arm in his. "You'll have to forgive us, Mrs. Criag, but we really must be going. I am so very tired."

Carolyn had no choice but to step aside and allow Drayton to escort his aunt and wife outside.

Ambrosia avoided Drayton's eyes when he lifted her into the brougham. She moved swiftly to the far corner, fixing her eyes carefully on her gloved hands, which lay tightly laced in her lap. She was grateful that Lily had come along, forcing her to hold back her tears of humiliation. She should never have attended this party, should never have come into town at all. She didn't belong here, acting the part of Drayton's wife when she had never been a wife to him.

Her fingers twisted as she remembered the days in Charleston when he had wanted her, when she had screamed her hatred at every turn. She closed her eyes tightly and forced that memory from her mind. That Drayton no longer existed. The hatred she had once felt for him had somehow changed hands, bringing them to this second battleground, leaving a part of her that had taken so long to heal lying weak and wounded once again. She felt almost as if she were dying inside a second time, as the hatred he felt for her cut and slashed her apart. She could not endure another battle like the one that had taken place tonight. She could not even face his eyes. Her head was filled with images of Carolyn in his arms, Carolyn whispering and giggling in his ear, Carolyn dancing with him . . . She bit her lip hard and shook her head to force back the tears. She couldn't cry now. Just a little longer, just a few minutes more.

Drayton studied Ambrosia's face now and again during the carriage ride, but only when he was sure Lily was not watching him. He was upset to think that Ken Galbraith had made a business decision tonight simply because Ambrosia had made the right impression. Months of backbreaking work and long weeks of talk had not been enough. What an irony it was to owe the success of Rambert Paints to her, when he had turned to it simply to forget her, to build something he could be proud of without anyone else's help. It riled him to know that now he was indebted to her. He didn't want to owe her anything.

He frowned as his eyes lingered on her face. She looked small and almost fragile huddled in her corner of the brougham, drawn up as far away from him as possible, her eyes fixed distantly on her hands. She had hardly met his eyes all evening and had done everything in her power to keep from touching him. Yet she had been eager to dance with Matt, had even remained on the dance floor, smiling up at him, after he pressed a kiss to her hand. *And her regard for you is just as obvious,* Ken had said earnestly. A bitter smile touched Drayton's lips as the words ran through his mind.

Ambrosia tensed inwardly as the brougham rolled to a stop before the pretentious brownstone. But she did not move until after Drayton had assisted Lily, using every moment to steel herself before she placed her hand in his, before her body slid briefly against him. She turned away without ever lifting her eyes, hurrying after Lily, barely mouthing a good night before she hurried off to her room. She felt Drayton's eyes upon her until she reached the shadows of the hallway. Then she abruptly abandoned her façade of calm and ran to her room. She closed the door behind herself and leaned heavily against it for a long time, biting her lip hard as she tried to keep from sobbing aloud. The tears rolled swiftly down her cheeks. It was over. Tomorrow she could go back to Elmwood, and she would never, never come back here again.

"I thought you were tired, Lily," Drayton said as she followed him into the parlor and asked him to pour her a brandy.

"I am. But there are things that need to be said tonight, and I intend to say them," she told him firmly, taking a seat on the settee. She eyed the dark, heavy furniture and the cluttered mantel, wondering how Drayton could bear to live in such a place.

He paused in pouring her a brandy and met her eyes with an inquiring lift of his brow. "Something tells me this won't be pleasant." She said nothing. He gave a slight shrug and finished pouring Lily's glass before he poured one for himself.

He offered Lily her glass, holding on to it a moment longer when she extended her hand, forcing her to meet his eyes. "What do you have to say?"

Lily's blue eyes met the question squarely. "She is your wife, Drayton."

He seemed almost amused as he turned away and sipped at his drink. "No one is more aware of that than I, Lily."

"She is trying very hard to be a good wife to you now."

"Is that what she's doing?" he tossed back doubtfully. "With all of her fancy clothing and constant primping with her hair? More likely she enjoys the way men look at her," he muttered under his breath, turning away again, remembering the way Matt had kissed her hand. "When she ought to be home with Mandy, she's out gallivanting in town, showing off her new gowns."

Lily's eyes lowered as she considered his reaction. So he had noticed that other men looked at her, and he was jealous. That was a start. "Ambrosia spends very little time away from Mandy," Lily told him, almost wishing the opposite were true. "And I practically had to force her to make that one trip into town. So if you want to blame someone, then blame me." She watched him pace the floor, his expression hard and distant. She heaved a sigh of frustration. "What exactly do you want from her, Drayton? Do you expect her to go about in sackcloth and ashes, repenting for the rest of her life?"

"I want nothing from her," he answered sharply. His eyes met hers with resolute hardness. "Nothing at all."

"You don't mean that."

"I most certainly do." He let out a long breath before he turned away again. "We had a child together, Lily. But Mandy is the only bond between us now."

"There ought to be much more between a man and his wife. Love and intimacy are—"

"Don't speak to me of love and intimacy, dammit!" he flung back at her. "I'm not the one who made a mockery of our vows!"

Lily waited a moment, allowing him to calm himself a bit. "Ambrosia has changed over the past months," she told him earnestly. "And she cares very deeply for you."

"That is unfortunate," he returned arrogantly, "because I could hardly care less about her."

"Drayton, I—"

"I won't discuss this any further, Lily," he told her firmly. He drained his glass and set in on the mantel. "Now if you will excuse me, I think it's time we both retired."

He was all but out of the parlor when Lily called to him. "Drayton?"

He turned back to face her, and she let out a sigh, her eyes pleading. "Promise me one thing, Drayton. Promise me that you will think about your marriage, that you will think about her. . . ."

He almost laughed aloud at that. As if he could possibly put her out of his mind. But he had what he wanted now. He had his contract with Galbraith, and he would reap a grand profit as a result. He would still have to work hard, but that was what he wanted, too. He would have his work and his financial success, and like his father, he wouldn't need anything or anyone else. If only it weren't for Mandy . . .

"Good night, Lily," was all Drayton said to her as he left the parlor and proceeded up the stairs.

Lily set aside her brandy and closed her eyes wearily. She wondered if time alone would ever heal the hurt in him. He was building a wall around himself, building a life Ambrosia could never hope to be a part of, and the longer he spent building that life, the more distant, the more unreachable he became. And Ambrosia . . . she was so lost, so hopelessly in love with him. And so afraid of swallowing her pride and reaching out for him, laying her heart bare, leaving herself open to the cruelest kind of hurt. Once, Lily would not have believed Drayton capable of that kind of cruelty. But there were so many things about Drayton now that she did not understand, so much that was hard and cold and angry. With a heavy sigh, she struggled from her chair and hobbled down the darkened hall to her room.

Chapter 46

The first day back at Elmwood Ambrosia spent with Mandy, hardly daring to let the child out of her sight. She spoke very little to anyone, and Lily did not press her since it was obvious she wanted time alone. After a few days of devoting herself entirely to Mandy, Ambrosia felt a restlessness, an impatience that she could not contain. One afternoon while Mandy was napping, she asked Debbs to saddle a horse for her. "A spirited one if you please," she requested, since she felt the need of a good, hard ride.

The physical exertion of riding proved a balm for her troubled mind, and she found that she had been craving such a release. With the wind pulling at her hair and the air cool against her cheeks, Ambrosia felt momentarily alive and free, just as she had felt as a child flying over the hills of Heritage on her father's stallion. She was unhappy and confused now, and her heart was alone and troubled, just as it had been then. She could hardly bear the thought of sitting quietly and sketching anymore, for she wanted no time to think, no time to feel, no time to consider the future. She came to dread the darkness, since she seldom slept well and found nighttime the hardest to endure. Often the wee hours of the morning found Ambrosia pacing the floor of her bedroom or prowling the library, leafing through book after book without really seeing the pages at all. The quiet of night made it so much more difficult to ignore that part of herself that felt so empty, so all alone. The loneliness tore at her, a silent, brutal torture. Again and again she would remember him, his deep blue eyes; his voice low and gentle; his touch soft, tender, offering her love as no man had ever done before. And then she would remember that she had destroyed that gentleness, that love.

It was impossible for her to forget, as she came to know each room of the house, as she came to know each meadow and hill, that this was Drayton's home. For the first time since Mandy's birth, she actually longed to run away from this place, from the constant reminders. But there would never be any escape, she knew. Every time she looked at Mandy's face and saw Drayton's deep blue eyes she would remember. Her child, her home, her dearest friend, all belonged to him as much as they did to her. They would always belong to him.

The first week of May, Lily caught a miserable cold that confined her to bed for several days. Since she stubbornly refused to see a doctor, Ambrosia busied herself finding plants and herbs for mixtures to ease the symptoms, glad to have something constructive to do. But as the time passed, she began to sit by Lily's bedside a good portion of every day, watching the older woman with concern. The potions seemed to help a bit, and after a while the fever and sniffles disappeared. Only a persistent, racking cough lingered on and on, weakening Lily far more than she would admit. She managed to attend church services, but did not stay afterward to socialize in spite of the agreeable spring weather. Instead she immediately sought the carriage and dozed nearly all the way home.

In the following weeks, she did little more than nap through the days, getting out of bed only to dress and come to the dining room for her meals. Just that small bit of activity seemed to drain her, and Ambrosia noticed that she was not eating well for all her insistence on coming to the table. Lily had already informed Isabel and Victoria that the card games were canceled indefinitely, so there was nothing pressing on Lily's calendar at first. But as the last few days of May drew nearer, Ambrosia fretted silently about what she ought to do. She knew full well that these were Lily's "visiting days," and that the visiting would be far too taxing for Lily in her present state. Finally, she convinced the older woman not to attempt the visiting because "someone just might pick up that terrible cough of yours, and then wouldn't you feel guilty?" Ambrosia would go in her stead, she promised, and yes, she would sit and listen to Mr. Gavin's complaints patiently, and yes, she would be sure and take Mrs. Cox an extra sweet roll or two. "And I'll report everything back to you, cross my heart," Ambrosia concluded solemnly.

"Tell them all I'm just fine," Lily insisted. "Just a touch of the croup is all. I'll be sure and visit them all in a few weeks."

"I'll tell them," Ambrosia nodded.

The items began appearing in the newspapers in late May. The *Herald,* the *World,* and the *Times* each carried a small article announcing the contract recently made between Galbraith Distribution Company and Rambert Carriage Paints. Mr. Galbraith was quoted as saying that the paints were of superior quality, with a finish as fine as porcelain. New management, the articles went on to say, was to be commended for taking Rambert Paints from "near bankruptcy" to "stability." "In the tradition of James Rambert, the company's founder," one paper remarked, "both quality and reliability have been restored."

Aaron gulped down a shot of whiskey, rubbed his eyes, and reread the article for the fifteenth time. With a snarl he crumpled the paper and threw it across the room. It was impossible, and yet there it was in black and white.

Like a cat his stepbrother had landed on his feet some-how, even after all the debts Aaron had left him, even af-ter all the carriage painters in town who would never con-sider using Rambert Carriage Paints again. Drayton didn't need any of them now, with the Galbraith contract. And there was little doubt that he would be successful, very successful, just as his father had been.

Aaron rose and paced his room nervously, refilling his glass and draining it again and again. He had a splitting headache; he'd had it for days. And he hadn't been able to sleep well since someone had mentioned the news about his stepbrother's company. Somehow Aaron knew that Drayton's good fortune was responsible for his own bad luck. Hadn't James Rambert always said that for one person to win, another had to lose?

He placed his empty glass on the table and dropped to the edge of his bed, his elbows resting on his knees, his head in his hands. The past months had been like a night-mare. He had moved into this modest room at a private gentleman's club after Drayton forced him to leave the house, and the gambling had gotten worse. At first he had won, making enough money to get by without touch-ing the stocks that were his security, his future. But sud-denly he had begun to lose, and he was unable to keep himself from losing more and more and more, from cashing in his stocks to finance his debts. Something in-side him would not let him stop, even when he knew he must. The next hand would see his luck change, or the next, or the next. But his luck had not changed. He had continued to lose. Thousands and thousands of dollars. He had cashed in nearly all of his railroad stocks, had even sold his mother's jewelry. He needed to win or he would soon be left with nothing. He could hardly believe that he had lost so much, that in less than a year's time he had come to this threshold of desperation. *I've put enough money in stocks to last me for the rest of my life,* he had boasted to Drayton. *Nothing you do can ever hurt me.* He glared at the newspaper, realizing now that he had been very wrong.

In order for one person to win, another must lose. . . . James Rambert's voice rang loud and taunting in Aaron's twisted mind. He glared at the crumpled paper that lay on the floor, knowing that his bad luck was Drayton's fault. From the very beginning their fates had been intertwined, Aaron thought, one dependent on the other. When one prospered, the other failed. Time and again it had happened and Aaron was sure it was happening again. Drayton had claimed the inheritance that ought to have been his, and now Aaron had nothing, and Drayton had everything. And it would remain that way unless . . .

Aaron's dark eyes clouded as they fixed on the paper. Unless he could destroy Drayton's luck. He would do it, he resolved. And like the fires he set years before, no one would ever guess that it had been Aaron Rambert.

Chapter 47

The June morning was clear and warm as the sun peeked over the horizon. All was quiet as Drayton slowed his horse to a halt at the warehouse and crisply dismounted. He tethered the animal at the post, since he would only be stopping here for a short time this morning to make a quick check of inventory and scheduled deliveries before he rode to the factories. It was important that everything proceed smoothly now that the initial order had been placed by Galbraith. Drayton wanted to be absolutely sure that the order was filled promptly and correctly. For a week now the factories had been running at full capacity, and the warehouse inventory was swelling accordingly.

Drayton grasped the padlock in his hand and inserted the key to unlock the warehouse door. But from the moment the lock fell free, he sensed that something was very wrong. He eased open the door, hesitating before he stepped inside. The smell of thinners and pigments was so much stronger than usual. It stung his nostrils as the air swept briskly by him. Someone had left a window open, or a door, he thought anxiously as he hurriedly entered the building. He stopped short. The warehouse was a shambles. Every one of the neat rows of carefully inventoried cans had been pushed over with such force that hideous puddles of color covered the floor.

Nausea twisted his stomach as he stepped slowly, carefully through the mess that was his warehouse. The paints were ruined. Thousands of dollars lost in a single night.

With deliberate calm he traced a path to the office, and again the sight there stopped him. Both inner and outer offices had been ransacked, files overturned, papers ripped and crumpled, strewn everywhere.

Methodically Drayton began to search about for clues. A window just to the side of the loading dock had offered a means of entry. It still stood open. It had been locked the night before, Drayton had checked it himself, and the small pane of glass had not been broken. Footprints, scores of them tracking paint throughout the warehouse, appeared to be from a single pair of boots. Drayton studied them for several moments. A single pair. He could think of only one person who would want this business to fail badly enough to do something like this. And something Warren Pierce had said months before made him that much more certain. *When the will was read, he went into a rage. Threw things around this office like a spoiled child having a tantrum.*

"Well, you don't have any proof," Matt repeated for the twentieth time. It was after midnight, but Drayton still sat at his desk sorting papers that had been strewn about the office the night before.

"There's proof enough for me."

"You can't know those footprints are your stepbrother's."

"No one else has a motive."

"Drayton, you heard the policeman. Vandalism isn't unheard of in this neighborhood, and vandals don't always have motives. Why, it was probably just an adolescent prankster, like he said." Drayton shot him an accusatory glare and he let out his breath in exasperation.

"Anyway, it doesn't matter who it was. It's over and done with. The insurance will cover the damages—"

"The insurance will cover the lost inventory, Matt," Drayton broke in shortly, "but it won't begin to cover the damages."

"Ken knows what happened," Matt told him. "I'm sure he'll agree to extend the contract until you can fill the order."

"I'm going to have it filled on schedule," Drayton told him matter-of-factly. "The end of July."

"The end of July?" Matt repeated in disbelief. "But it will take you more than six weeks to stockpile the inventory!"

"Not if I hire workers for additional shifts at the factories. And the regular workers will work overtime, I've already spoken with Tom Landon about it. We'll make it."

"Overtime? Extra shifts? Sounds like an expensive gamble, Drayton."

"I don't intend to lose."

Matt eyed him for a long moment. "What about Aaron?"

Drayton finished with a stack of papers and put them aside. "What about him?"

"You won't do anything foolish, will you?"

"I won't do anything at all until this contract is filled."

"And then?"

Without answering, Drayton sat back in his chair, withdrew a cigar from his pocket and thoughtfully ran it under his nose. He would do something, Matt thought, the moment the contract was filled.

Lily's health rebounded a little during the long, warm days of June and July. Only a deep, hacking cough continued to bother her, though a thick molasses-and-rum syrup Ambrosia concocted gave her some temporary relief. Still, there were other changes, subtle changes in Lily that worried Ambrosia even more than the cough.

She never regained an interest in eating and had to force down even her favorite foods. She was still so thin and pale, and her eyes were always so tired and lifeless. She stopped answering letters that arrived from friends, and instead spent each moment with Ambrosia or Bessie or Mandy, never wanting to be alone. Yet she steadfastly brushed aside Ambrosia's suggestions that she see a physician, saying that she couldn't be bothered, that she would be fine until Drayton came home, and then she would ask his opinion on the cough.

"Do you believe in heaven?" Lily asked Ambrosia one day as they sat on the stone bench in the garden.

Trying very hard to hide her surprise at the question, Ambrosia nodded. "Of course. Everyone believes in heaven."

"I'm not really sure I do," Lily returned softly. "Oh, I believe in God," she added quickly. "One has only to look at Mandy to know that He must exist. And I feel His presence sometimes, as if He's holding my hand, helping me along." She hesitated. "But I'm not really sure of heaven . . . or hell. And I want so to believe that I'll see Henry again. . . ." She broke off in a violent fit of coughing and it was several moments before she could speak again. "But—if life is all we have," she murmured, half to herself, "if there's nothing more, then it's been enough . . . quite enough."

It was one of many conversations that troubled Ambrosia deeply, that made her long to write Drayton and tell him of her fears. If only he would come home! But she knew he had written Lily to apologize for not coming, and that his note had mentioned a terrible incident of vandalism that had made it imperative he stay on in town, at least till the end of July. No, she thought reluctantly. She couldn't bother Drayton now, not when Lily insisted she was feeling so much better. She would wait another week or two.

Chapter 48

On the last day of July the warehouse and factories of Rambert Carriage Paints closed an hour early to celebrate the filling of Galbraith Distribution's initial order. In high spirits over the accomplishment, Drayton agreed to meet Matt for a celebratory dinner at the club. They had just finished with their meal and were about to order after-dinner drinks when Drayton saw his stepbrother making his way through the hall toward the adjacent gaming room. The sudden hardness in Drayton's expression made Matt turn and follow his eyes. Matt drew an uneasy breath and attempted to divert Drayton's attention with a light comment. "On his way to his nightly sport, I suppose . . . It's said he's lost a fortune in the past year, since you took over the business." He watched Drayton's face intently, hoping that the bright, animal-on-the-prowl look would fade away. It did not.

"How much cash have you?" Drayton asked him suddenly, his eyes still fixed on the hallway.

"Cash? A few hundred dollars . . . seven—"

"I'll need to borrow it." Still Drayton did not meet Matt's eyes. His gaze was fixed after Aaron.

Matt's eyes narrowed. "What for?"

Drayton's mouth curved into a slow smile that did not reach his eyes. "I feel lucky."

497

* * *

Aaron was so totally engrossed in playing his cards that he was unaware of his stepbrother's presence, unaware of the icy blue eyes that observed his every move. He was winning now, and winning was everything to Aaron Rambert. It was the only thing that made him feel alive.

The four men had been playing a high-stakes game for over an hour when a heavy-set man in a flashy checkered suit shook his head and threw in his cards. "You're too lucky for me tonight, Aaron. I'm out."

The man rose from his seat and left the table as Aaron gathered in his winnings, separating gold pieces from a stack of paper money. The man to the right of Aaron, an older gent with a thickly waxed handlebar mustache, retrieved the cards and shuffled them thoughtfully, eyeing the chair which had been vacated, then the man who slowly, deliberately came to take the seat. "May I join you, gentlemen?" the newcomer asked.

The man with the mustache paused a moment in his shuffling and shifted the position of the cigar that was clamped between his teeth before giving a nod.

"It's a friendly game," another man remarked, though there was something decidedly unfriendly about this new player, and he felt it immediately. So did Aaron.

Aaron glanced up briefly, his jaw slackening as he met those cold blue eyes. The man to the left of Aaron, a short, balding man whose sparse hair was slicked with Macassar oil, nervously fingered his money. "Well, what's everybody waiting for?" he snapped impatiently.

Aaron jumped slightly at the man's terse comment, but it was another moment before he realized that the next move was his. He tossed a hundred-dollar bill into the center of the table and forced himself to avoid Drayton's eyes. He had a streak going tonight, and Drayton's presence wouldn't change that. He'd seen to it that Drayton's luck ran out weeks before. "Ante up."

From the bar at the far side of the room, Matt observed

the game while he sipped at a scotch. Aaron won the first hand, the balding man to his left the second. But it was Drayton who won the third and fourth, with a full house and a diamond flush. Lucky indeed! After folding early on the next hand, Drayton won three in a row, the last two without showing a card. Matt's lips curled into a smile of amusement. There was no reading that face of his, no telling whether he held a royal flush or a pair of deuces.

Aaron's face was deeply creased with irritation when the man with the handlebar mustache collected the last of his money and left the game. Drayton had won nearly every hand since he'd joined them, while Aaron had hardly been dealt a passable hand. Something was very wrong here, he thought in panic. Suddenly his luck was gone while Drayton . . . He swallowed against the dryness in his mouth and opened his shirt collar, feeling tense and nervous. He could feel Drayton's eyes upon him, watching . . . watching . . . almost as if he knew. But he couldn't know; he couldn't! Aaron struggled to regain his calm, lifting his cards slowly, fanning the hand open a card at a time. His eyes narrowed in intense concentration as he took stock of his hand. Four spades and a heart. A chance at drawing to a flush. The balding man opened for a hundred; Drayton raised the bet to two. He must have a fair hand again, Aaron thought as he called the bet.

The balding man requested a pair of cards, Aaron one, and Drayton dealt himself two. Aaron placed his draw card atop the neat stack of cards he had been dealt originally, tapped them on the table, then lifted them and slowly fanned them open. His eyes glittered with excitement. All spades—he had made his flush and now sat with a strong hand.

His eyes lifted to Drayton's, those unwavering blue eyes so cold, so piercing, so completely unnerving. His hands trembled a little as he lowered his eyes again and reconsidered his hand.

The balding man began the second round of betting at five hundred dollars, a bet Aaron raised to a thousand, and Drayton called. The balding man then raised the bet two hundred more, and Aaron boldly made it fifteen hundred. He was somewhat surprised when Drayton called again, since he had expected him to fold with the stakes running so high. This was not a bluffing move; Drayton must have a very strong hand too. Aaron studied his cards again, his hands shaking a little more noticeably now, his mouth going dry again. He'd lost a lot of money in the past hour and needed to win this hand. Slowly, with a confidence he didn't quite feel, Aaron laid his hand face up on the table. "All spades, gentlemen."

The man with sparse, slicked-back hair tossed his hand to the table's center. "Beats my three ladies," he muttered.

Aaron's mouth curved into a confident smile as he made a move to take in the pot. Drayton placed a hand on his arm. "Are you forgetting that there are three players in this game . . . *brother?*"

Aaron straightened abruptly and jerked his arm away from Drayton's hold. He was furious at being called "brother" when he was nothing of the kind, and embarrassed at having appeared so anxious to collect his winnings. Barely restraining his temper, he watched as Drayton laid his cards on the table. A king of clubs, a six of hearts, a six of diamonds, a six of spades, and a six of clubs. Four of a kind.

A muscle in Aaron's jaw began to twitch and his face became mottled as he fought to hold his temper. The hand had been a costly one. The balding man was collecting what little money he had left and leaving the table. It was just the two of them now. One would lose and one would win, just as James Rambert had said. But the way Aaron's luck was running, he just might be the loser. He ought to leave the table now, before—but no. His luck was due to change now. Indeed, it was already changing. A flush was a good hand, his first good hand in hours. And only the first, he assured himself. While Drayton's luck was due to run out. He frowned slightly as he tried to figure out what had gone wrong in the past several hands. A fluke, that's what it had been. Only a fluke. He drew in the cards and began to shuffle them, his fingers clumsy with the deck because of their shaking. He muttered a curse as he dropped a few cards on the table, then hurriedly scooped them up again and proceeded with the deal. It was those eyes of his, those ruthless, unblinking blue eyes, he rationalized as Drayton lit a cigar and drew on it. It was those damn eyes that had him so flustered.

Still observing from across the room, Matt was keenly aware that Aaron was becoming unstrung. But then, Matt thought as he ordered another scotch, who wouldn't be anxious with Drayton sitting across the table, winning nearly every hand? And if Aaron was guilty of vandalizing the warehouse, as Drayton believed, then all the more reason for his odd behavior. Matt had to wonder why Aaron didn't simply leave the game, especially after he lost the next three hands in a row. His cards had obviously gone cold, and there was nothing forcing him to stay in the game . . . except perhaps the challenge in Drayton's eyes. Matt could see the sweat glistening on Aaron's brow, and when Aaron drained his glass, his hand was shaking violently. As he had done all evening, he quickly ordered another. He was drinking heavily and having trouble handling the cards when it was his deal. He ought to quit, Matt thought. Why in the hell didn't he simply quit?

Aaron was relieved when he finished shuffling and dealing out the cards. He let out a sigh as he set the deck aside and had a look at his hand. In the previous three hands, the best he'd been dealt had been a pair of jacks. His hands had gone cold. But that wouldn't continue much longer. He could feel his luck changing even as he picked up this hand. His eyes brightened as he fanned out his cards. King of hearts, two of hearts, king of spades,

ten of diamonds, king of clubs. Three of a kind. A strong
hand, even before the draw. He took a long swallow of
his drink and nodded to the bartender for another.
"Open?" Aaron prodded.

"A hundred." Drayton tossed the bill into the center
of the table.

Aaron eyed him narrowly, wishing his face gave some
clue to the cards he held. A half-dozen times tonight,
Aaron was almost certain he'd won on a bluff. Yet whenever Aaron called that bluff, he'd lost. But his luck was
changing now, he reminded himself. "Raise you two,"
he announced confidently.

Drayton drew on his cigar and lifted a single brow. His
own hand was mediocre, a pair of red threes, the four and
seven of hearts and a jack of spades. The look on Aaron's
face had already told Drayton his opponent held a good
hand. A very good hand, based on the bet he'd just made.
"Call."

"Cards?"

Drayton removed the three of diamonds and the jack of
spades from his hand and tossed them facedown on the
table. His luck was running well enough to chance splitting the pair and trying for a straight or a flush. "Two."

Aaron dealt him two cards, then dealt himself a pair as
well. He placed the deck on the table, then lifted his hand
and slowly fanned out his cards. He quickly reached for
his drink and downed a healthy swallow. A pair of nines!
He'd dealt himself a full house! His blood was pounding
with exhilaration and he was very, very sure he was
going to win this hand. "Two thousand dollars," Aaron
announced, opening the bidding.

Drayton cocked his head slightly, and for what seemed
like a long time he puffed on his cigar. "Two thousand
. . . and raise you two."

Aaron's jaw slackened as Drayton made the bet. New
beads of sweat broke across his brow and he motioned for
another drink as he finished off his last. He was bluffing,
Aaron thought. But whether he was or not, Aaron

couldn't allow him to walk away with this pot, not when he himself held a full house.

"Two thousand," he returned, counting out the bills, "and I'll raise you four." It was all the money he had on the table, everything but two thousand dollars he still had in his wallet. He smiled to himself as Drayton hesitated. It was too much money for a bluff. "Either drop or call," Aaron pressed curtly, anxious to collect his winnings and begin another hand.

"Neither . . . *brother.*" Drayton paused deliberately to take a draw on his cigar and lean comfortably back in his chair. "Instead," he went on slowly, "I'm going to raise you. The house in Gramercy Park."

Aaron's face was livid, his nostrils flaring. The house! Drayton was neatly backing him into a corner by bringing the house into this, and adding insult to injury as well. That had been his mother's house, ought to have been *his* house. The thought of Drayton living there, among the things his mother had loved, turned his stomach. Drayton had no right to be in that house. Yet it was worth more money than Aaron could hope to come up with, even if he sold every last thing he owned.

"The house and contents are worth a hundred thousand dollars at least. I—I can't match that kind of money."

Drayton casually flicked an ash to the floor. "I'm willing to accept your stocks."

Aaron was breathing heavily now, as if he'd run a mile. He took out his handkerchief to mop the sweat from his brow, then motioned for another drink. "I—I sold my stocks," he admitted.

Drayton's face showed none of his surprise. "All of them?"

Aaron's lips tightened, trembled with restraint. "Yes, all of them."

"Then I'll wager the house against what's left in your wallet."

Still struggling to control his shaking, Aaron again

wiped his brow. A cold sweat was running down the back of his neck as he slowly fanned apart his cards and contemplated them one last time. He let out an unsteady breath and removed his wallet from the pocket of his coat. Two thousand dollars, all that was left of his "security," his future. Drayton was offering to let him call with that small amount of money against the house in Gramercy Park, worth fifty times as much. Drayton must hold a strong hand, but how strong? That was the question. There was no hint of an answer in the cold mask of arrogance that was his face.

Aaron's hands shook violently as he added the contents of his wallet to the pot. He had no choice at this point, really. The stakes had already been carried too high to let Drayton win without calling his hand. "Call."

Drayton took one final draw on his cigar, then casually leaned forward to smash it out in a small tray. "Straight flush," he mouthed dispassionately as he laid the cards on the table.

Aaron's face contorted with rage and disbelief. "No!" he whispered. "No!" His voice became shrill and hysterical. "You—you cheated!"

"You dealt the cards, Aaron."

"You cheated!" he screamed again. He came to his feet abruptly, overturning the table and spilling its contents on the floor. Drayton moved quickly to avoid the table, but Aaron was already diving on top of him, knocking him to the floor. In a swift movement Aaron removed a derringer from his vest pocket and fired a single shot. Instantly a dozen men were rushing to grab hold of Aaron from behind, restraining him even as he continued to scream that Drayton had cheated him.

"Send for the authorities," Matt ordered as he bent to see the extent of Drayton's injuries.

The bullet had grazed his temple, causing a cut that bled quite a bit, but no serious injury. He was sitting up, staunching the flow of blood when Matt appeared beside him. "It's nothing," he assured Matt.

"Dammit, I knew there would be trouble," Matt muttered under his breath. He let out an impatient sigh as Drayton turned away from the hand he offered and struggled unsteadily to his feet on his own.

Across the room, Aaron continued to rant and rave, fighting the men who restrained him until authorities arrived.

Matt was relieved when Drayton agreed to press charges against his stepbrother, since Aaron appeared in need of an extended "cooling off" period. Matt watched as they all but dragged Aaron from the gaming room, realizing that Drayton was probably right about the vandalism at the warehouse. That vandalism had been a senseless act of destruction, the act of a deranged man. And as Aaron was dragged away, screaming promises of vengeance the entire time, Matt knew Aaron was precisely that. He could only hope that a few weeks of incarceration would make Aaron forget some of what he had threatened to do.

Chapter 49

The first days of August were hot and unbearably humid, and nearly every afternoon saw a heavy downpour that did nothing to alleviate the heat. Though Lily seemed to be growing stronger and recovering her strength during the last weeks of July, the extremely hot weather quickly sapped whatever strength she had and sent her to bed nursing a sore throat and aching head, along with the deep, raspy cough she'd had since the start of summer. "I'm going to send for a doctor," Ambrosia told Bessie firmly the moment she began to run a fever.

"But there aren't any doctors here. You'd have to go into the city," she told her. "And besides, Miss Lily has never been very cooperative with doctors since her illness. With the exception of her nephew, of course."

Ambrosia bit her lip hard and held back the cry of helpless frustration that was welling up inside her. Drayton ought to have been home last Sunday, the first Sunday of August. He had promised Lily that weeks ago. But Friday he'd written to say that he wouldn't be coming home for yet another week, something about a legal matter that needed to be taken care of or some such thing. Ambrosia turned away from Bessie and paced the floor, wondering what she ought to do. She dreaded taking all this to Drayton, but Lily hadn't been well for so long! And she was getting worse now, not better. He had to be told.

She squared her shoulders and turned back to face Bessie. "Run and get Debbs. Tell him I have a message I want him to take into town . . . today."

Ambrosia remained at Lily's bedside the remainder of the day, sponging her brow and cheeks with cool compresses, spooning broth and cool chamomile tea into her mouth. But the fever only grew worse as the hours passed. Her cheeks flushed unnaturally, her breathing became irregular and shallow as she slept, and her cough began to bring up blood. *Oh, Drayton, Lily needs you! Why don't you come to her?*

It was late that evening when he finally did come. Ambrosia was almost frantic when he entered Lily's room. She half ran to meet him, her eyes filling with tears of panic as she stepped an arm's length away. "Thank God you're here," she whispered.

Lily murmured something in her sleep, then writhed in agony as a fit of coughing tore at her weakened body. Drayton's eyes flew to his aunt, and he struggled to hide his shock. Slowly he walked toward her, bending low to take hold of her hand. "Lily? It's Drayton. Can you hear me?"

"Drayton?"

"Yes, Lily. I'm here." Still clinging to her hand, he moved to turn up the lamp, the tears burning his throat as he touched her feverish brow. He held her as yet another fit of coughing racked her weary flesh, then lay her gently back against the pillows, having seen enough to know. Pneumonia. He'd seen it before. And he knew at once Lily was too weak to survive it. "Lily? Are you in much pain?" he asked her softly, gently smoothing back a strand of snow-white hair.

"No," she whispered. "I'm fine. I—" She coughed again, a deep painful rasp that made Drayton's stomach knot. "I—I'm glad you're home, Drayton. It's so good to have you—'' Again she broke off in a fit of coughing, and Drayton shook his head.

''Don't try to talk anymore, Lily. Just rest. I'm going to fetch you something to make you sleep.''

He rose and turned down the lamp again, then motioned Ambrosia out of the room. ''How long has she been ill?'' he demanded the moment the door was closed behind them.

Ambrosia's lip quivered as she faced him. ''The cough has been with her for months. But—''

''Months! Then why wasn't I told? Why did you wait until it was too late for me to do anything?''

The tears Ambrosia had held back spilled over her cheeks. She shook her head, taking a step back, away from the accusation in his eyes. ''No! It can't be too late! It can't be! She was feeling better,'' she insisted brokenly. ''She was starting— Oh, no! She can't die! She can't!''

Without stopping to think, Drayton took her into his arms, his anger leaving him when he saw her fall apart. He held her tightly, longing to ease the fear he'd seen in her eyes, seeking a comfort for his own hurt and guilt. For a long time, they clung to one another, her tears spilling against his shirt, his against her hair, sharing their grief in a desperate embrace as if each was afraid to let go.

''What—what are we to do?'' she choked out finally.

''The only thing that's left for us to do,'' he told her softly, his own voice catching with emotion. ''We'll do our best to ease her pain.''

Lily died the following morning, breathing her last as the birds began their noisy welcome to the sun. In silence Drayton moved to draw a light blanket over her face, a face that was chalk white and marred by lines of pain and exhaustion. He swallowed hard against the nausea that twisted his stomach at the sight of her now. He'd seen death so many, many times before. But this was so sudden, so unexpected. And this corpse seemed such a pathetic shell when he thought of the woman who had embodied beauty and life and goodness. He squeezed his eyes tightly shut and wrestled with his emotions. Every harsh word he had ever spoken to her now echoed in his mind, driving a knife of cold regret into his heart.

He drew a long, calming breath and ran his sleeve slowly across his dampened cheeks. She was gone. Regret would not bring her back. Nothing would ever bring her back. He turned away from the bed, and his eyes settled on Ambrosia. She stood at the window, the first golden rays of the sun falling across her tear-streaked face. She was still and silent and her eyes were distant and glazed. He went to stand behind her, his arms slipping about her waist, his eyes closing as the scent of roses from the garden wafted in on the morning air. The world was alive with the riches of summer. Birds were singing, the brook was rushing just a few hundred feet from the house. The world, he realized, would go on just as it had before, as if Lily's passing mattered not at all in the scheme of things. And yet to him, and to Ambrosia, nothing would ever be the same again.

"The minister's here," Bessie called hesitantly from the threshold, her eyes red from weeping. "Shall I tell him—?"

Drayton turned to face her. "No, Bessie. I'm coming." He waited until she had left the room, then turned back to Ambrosia, his fingers touching her cheek until she met his eyes. For a long time their eyes held, touched with sorrow, then uncertainty, as if each questioned the validity of the closeness they felt at this moment, as if each doubted the bond that had formed in the past hours at Lily's bedside. "There are arrangements to be made," Drayton said at length. Without another word he turned away and went to meet the minister.

Ambrosia proceeded woodenly through the remainder of the day, eating nothing, speaking barely a word to anyone. She sat rigidly erect in a parlor chair as the min-

ister quietly discussed the necessary arrangements with
Drayton, who appeared calm and collected, as if he were
detached from all that was happening. When the minister
took his leave, Drayton wrote several brief notes to
Lily's closest friends in the city and sent Debbs into town
to deliver them, so that those who wished might attend
the simple burial rites scheduled for the following morning. Neither Drayton nor Ambrosia made any move to
touch one another again, nor did their eyes meet and hold
as they had that morning. The tenuous bond had slipped
away, leaving them worlds apart, separated by past hurts
and fears. And though the night before Lily's burial was
a sleepless one for both, neither had courage enough to
reach beyond those hurts and fears and seek the comfort
tasted so briefly the night before.

The following morning, Lily was laid to rest beside
her husband in a hilltop plot overlooking the Hudson and
the garden she had loved so dearly. The graves, marked
by two white marble crosses, were enclosed by a small
wrought-iron fence and a row of well-tended shrubs. In
accordance with Lily's written instructions, Reverend
Walsh opened his Bible to the eighth chapter of Luke,
reading aloud the word she had asked be read over her
grave. "Her sins, which are many, are forgiven: for she
loved much. . . ."

Ambrosia stood erect and outwardly composed during
the brief services that were conducted beneath a swelter-
ing August sun. Drayton stood at her side holding a
sleeping Mandy in his arms, his blue eyes distant, showing no emotion. Several of the other mourners were
weeping openly, including Carolyn Craig, who had arrived an hour before the service to offer condolences to
Drayton in his time of sorrow.

For Ambrosia, Carolyn's presence tore yet another
wound in her already aching heart. Dear God, what
would she do now? Lily was gone, and she was all alone
now, except for Mandy. Nothing would ever, ever be the
same again. She would never walk in the garden or enter

the parlor or even eat a meal without remembering, without feeling the loss.

The mourners began to depart just after noon. Ambrosia and Drayton stood side by side in the hall, politely accepting the condolences and offers of help or comfort from Lily's friends while Mandy toddled up and down the hallway, curiously eyeing the visitors, smiling at them, yet shyly keeping her distance. Only Carolyn made no move to leave. Ambrosia caught sight of her flouncing about the parlor, glancing out the window, running her hand impatiently over the upholstered furniture, waiting for Drayton to finish with the others and join her there. She had no intention of leaving until she saw him alone, Ambrosia knew.

When the last of the mourners had gone, Ambrosia squared her shoulders and tried to hide the awkwardness she felt at the situation, and the jealousy. She turned to Drayton, but he had stooped down to talk with Mandy and just as quickly had her on his knee. How swiftly she had warmed to him, Ambrosia thought. Just yesterday Mandy had shied away from him, had studied him intently only from a safe distance away, hugging her mother's skirts. Now she adored him just as he adored her. Ambrosia stood there for a moment, watching the two of them and feeling a painful tightness in her throat. If only Carolyn had not been here today, shattering what comfort Ambrosia might have found in Reverend Walsh's words, destroying the hope she might have salvaged in having Drayton stand at her side.

As if sensing her intent gaze upon him, Drayton looked up inquiringly. Before Ambrosia could say a word, Carolyn joined them in the hall and positioned herself deliberately between Ambrosia and Drayton as she bent low to speak with him. "Such a lovely little thing," she mewled sweetly, letting her lacy glove touch Mandy's cheek. "She's the picture of you, Drayton. You ought to bring her to town sometime and show her off to everyone."

Mandy shied away from her touch, her wide blue eyes distrustful.

"Would you like Aunt Carolyn to buy you a pretty new bonnet, precious?" she cooed. "Of course you would."

Mandy's arm went around Drayton's neck and she moved further away. Drayton came to his feet, holding her close, his palm pressing gently to her back in a gesture of fatherly comfort. "Thank you for coming today, Carolyn," he mouthed coolly, his tone one of dismissal.

"But you knew I'd come, Drayton," she answered, laying her hand on his sleeve. "You know how deeply I care." She smiled at him, then turned her attention back to Mandy, who was peeking at her warily even as she held tightly to her father. "Poor baby!" Carolyn crooned sympathetically, leaning closer. "You'll miss your Aunt Lily, won't you? But maybe your papa will bring you to town to visit me . . ."

Unable to hold back her tears, Ambrosia turned and hurried up the stairs.

In the hallway below, Carolyn smiled triumphantly, having finally gotten what she wanted. She was alone now with Drayton. She turned to him, her smile fading a bit when Mandy's quick fingers tugged curiously at her hat. "No, no, darling," Carolyn scolded sweetly, trying to smooth the strands of hair that had fallen free. "You mustn't touch Aunt Carolyn's hat."

" 'At," Mandy repeated, reaching again for the hat.

Carolyn took a swift step backward and her smile was false. "No, Mandy, dear."

"Shall I see you to your carriage?" Drayton offered.

Carolyn seemed surprised. "I'm in no hurry to go, Drayton."

"All the same, Carolyn, I think it would be appropriate for you to leave."

Her face reflected her deep disappointment. "I—I was hoping that you would join me for the ride back into town," she said softly. "We have so many things to talk about. I—I only met your aunt once, Drayton, but—"

"Thank you for the offer, but I've decided to stay here tonight." He surprised himself when he spoke the words, since he had not considered staying at Elmwood until the moment she offered him transportation to town. Suddenly he realized that he needed the time alone here, to think, to sort out his feelings, to come to terms with the loss. There was so much here he had turned his back on, so many things he had run away from. . . . And yesterday, when he had arrived, Mandy hadn't even known who he was.

Carolyn's mouth tightened at the thought of his spending the night here with his wife. He was particularly vulnerable now, after losing his aunt, and he had been quite attentive to Ambrosia today. Worse, his attachment to the child was painfully obvious. If only he would allow *her* to give him a child!

"I—I'll be waiting for you in town," she whispered, pressing a brief kiss to his cheek, scowling as she dodged Mandy's inquisitive fingers. "You know where you can reach me."

"I know."

She held on to her smile as she turned away and entered her carriage, blowing Drayton a kiss as her coachman slowly pulled away.

Ambrosia cried herself to sleep that afternoon and did not waken until nightfall, when Bessie knocked at her door with a tray of food. "Thank you, but I'm not hungry," Ambrosia told her quietly, not even looking at the food.

"But you must try to eat something," Bessie told her firmly. "Master Drayton made me promise I'd see to it."

Ambrosia walked to the pair of French doors and opened them, allowing the night air to flow into the room. She said nothing for a long moment, simply stared distantly at the star-filled sky. "Did—did Mrs. Craig stay to dinner?"

"Oh, no, miss. She left this afternoon, shortly after the others."

Ambrosia whirled, her eyes searching Bessie's face. "And did Drayton—did he leave with her?"

Bessie shook her head. "Oh, no, miss. But he's already eaten, I'm afraid. And retired to his room, just after Mandy went to bed. But he made me promise I'd see to your needs from now on, now that Miss Lily is—" Her voice broke off and she looked at the floor.

Without another word, Ambrosia ate some of the food Bessie had brought her, though she did not feel like eating at all. When she had forced down all she could, Bessie drew her bath and helped her into a nightgown before she left her alone. Ambrosia paced the room slowly, pausing now and again to gaze down at the garden, at the shadows that played across the walks in the silver moonlight. She inhaled deeply, savoring the fragrances of roses and lilies that filled the moist, cool air of night. She thought of the garden at Heritage, so long ago, of the roses she'd loved as a child. She thought of the tiny violet Ledger had given her in the garden at Barhamville Academy. And now this garden, Lily's garden. But Lily was gone now, as Heritage was gone, as Ledger was gone. None of them would ever be a part of her life again.

Ambrosia closed her eyes and swallowed hard against her tears. Emotions lashed forth like a tidal wave . . . grief, regret, helplessness, anger, they all tore at her. And today, there had been Carolyn, intruding on her sorrow, weedling her way into part of Drayton's life that ought to have been private, trying so hard to win Mandy's affections with the promise of a pretty new bonnet. Ambrosia wanted to scream aloud at the jealousy, the anger that festered inside her. Yet a part of her anger was not directed at Carolyn, but at herself. She couldn't forget that Drayton had tried to be a husband to her once, that he had swallowed his pride to offer her tenderness and understanding while she had only sought to hurt him. She could not despise him for seeking comfort elsewhere. She had left him little choice. Why should he turn his back on Carolyn, who offered him all the things his wife had denied him?

Ambrosia bit her lip hard to try to stop the tears that were rolling down her cheeks. She loved him. Oh, God, how she loved him and needed him! But it was all too late. There was nothing left of what he had once felt for her, nothing but pain and bitterness. She brushed her tears away with the back of her hand, remembering that yesterday he had held her, had clung to her in desperation, just as she had held to him. A shared grief had forced them to turn to one another then, to reach out in spite of the past. . . .

She drew a deep breath and stared at the moon, full and bright in the star-studded sky. How she longed to run away from everything, to be free of her guilt, of her regret, of her past. But there was nowhere to run; Drayton had told her that so long ago, on that first night in Charleston. She lifted her hand and ran her fingers lightly over her lips, remembering that night so very different from this one, remembering the cold and the rain, the terrible fight with Melissa, the look on Ledger's face. . . . She had run away from everything that night, and somehow, Drayton had known. She closed her eyes and sighed, remembering her fear and confusion, remembering the taste of brandy warm in her mouth, giving her the courage to offer herself to him. . . . She straightened and her eyes opened, staring with sudden realization at the garden swathed in moonlight below. He had kept his distance that night, even acted cold and indifferent until she made the first move. Then, only then, had he admitted to his own desire.

Ambrosia turned slowly away from the garden and went to stand before the glass, considering her own reflection. The flowing gauze gown she wore did little to conceal her womanly body, the loose neckline slipping over one shoulder, the darkened tips of her breasts visible beneath the thin fabric, the curves of her waist and slender legs outlined as the gown fell to the floor. Her black hair had been hastily pinned atop her head, but here and there a coil fell about her face, at her temples, at her neck. She met her eyes, dark, green-gray eyes heavy with black lashes. Somber eyes, cat's eyes. She was not as pretty as Carolyn or Melissa, she thought, and then she frowned, recalling that Matt Desmond had called her beautiful, that Drayton had once called her that as well. *You're everything a man could desire,* he had said. If only that were true.

She drew a deep breath, knowing that she must go to him now, before he left here, that she must tell him she was sorry, that she loved him so very much. Without giving herself a moment to reconsider, she turned away from the glass and left her room. A moment later she stood at the door to his room, her breath coming hard, her hands trembling. She hesitated for what seemed an eternity, wondering if he was asleep, wondering if he was dressed, wondering if she ought to knock. But if she did knock, and he told her to go away . . . She bit her lip and entered the room without knocking, without making a sound. She closed the door behind herself and leaned her back against it, her eyes searching the room. A lamp burned low on a table near the bed, but that bed was empty. It had not been slept in. She stifled the cry that rose in her throat when she saw him. He stood on the opposite side of the room, clad only in his trousers, gazing blankly out on the same garden she had stared at moments before. Lily's garden. He turned to face her, draining his glass and setting it aside as he came forward into the light. His eyes lingered on her face for a time, then drifted with slow deliberation over her thin gauze gown. Ambrosia saw a flicker of something warm in his eyes, but then it was gone, and he turned away.

Ambrosia stared at his back for a long moment, at his shoulders, broader than she remembered, at the muscles defined by his bronzed skin, at the scars . . . she had almost forgotten about the scars. She opened her mouth to say something, anything to break the silence. There was so much she had to tell him! But she did not know where to begin. What if he refused to listen? What if he laughed at her and called her a fool? What if he told her he intended to take Mandy with him into town?

"Drayton?" It was the only word she could force herself to say. He acted as if he hadn't heard her.

She took a step toward him, then another, then another, stopping only when she stood before him. She was trembling now, feeling weak and foolish and afraid. "Drayton?"

"What do you want?" His voice was cold, and he turned away from her again to pour himself another drink.

She watched him, blinking back her tears, unable to speak as he drained his glass and impatiently met her eyes.

"I—I need you, Drayton," she whispered finally, feeling a single defiant tear slip over her cheek. For a heart-wrenching moment she thought he would laugh at her. His eyes never left her face as he set his glass on the table and came toward her. His hand lifted, his thumb touching the dampness at her cheek, lingering at the softness of her skin, at the silken coils of hair that had fallen about her face. "I need you," she whispered again, her voice desperate, pleading.

She felt his arms go about her, felt the warmth of his hard chest against her cheek, felt his heart thudding strong and sure against her palms. "I need you, I need you," she whispered again and again as her lips pressed to his shoulder, his throat, to the mouth that lowered to find her own. His fingers touched to her cheeks again, his lips lingering to taste fully what she offered him, his tongue seeking, finding, seeking more. She moaned softly into his mouth and slipped her arms about his neck, tasting the strong, expensive whiskey on his tongue, her eyes closing in a sudden wave of weakness, of desire. She was aware of every inch of him, aware of the long, lean fingers, the slightly calloused fingertips that moved gently, so gently over her face, the muscles of his chest and torso, hard, tensing, the feel of his mouth. . . . She drew him closer and raised herself on tiptoe to meet his kiss, to feel the intimate molding of her flesh to his, to feel the evidence of his desire. His lips moved to graze her bared shoulder, to seek the swell of her breasts, to play at the darkened crests through the thin gauze of her nightgown. It was she who slipped the gown from her shoulders, wanting to feel his mouth on her bare skin, wanting to feel his body hard against hers. She grasped his hair and pulled him close again, whimpering as he took the lead, arousing her, wanting her, taking her. He lifted her easily and carried her to the bed, stripping off his trousers before taking a place beside her, his hands touching, exploring, his mouth tasting, questioning. With a cry of longing, she rolled to her back and pulled him with her, arching against him until they were forged into a single entity. He thrust insistently within her and she clung to him, moving with him and against him, straining, gasping, exploding with the sudden ecstasy of total surrender even as she felt his release deep within her, even as she heard him cry out her name. He buried his face in her hair and held her close against himself, tightly, tightly, as a man clings to life itself.

Not a single word was spoken after their lovemaking, though neither Drayton nor Ambrosia slept for a long time after it was over. They remained in each other's arms even as they slept, clinging to one another, unwilling, unable to let go.

Drayton woke long before the first rays of the sun peeked over the horizon. He stared down at Ambrosia's face, his eyes lingering on her dark, dramatic features, on the soft fullness of her mouth, the satiny skin of her cheeks. Strength was written in that face even now in the squared line of her jaw, the brief, definite arch of her dark brows. Strength and softness, the courage of a woman and the gentleness of a child; the wall of defiance and the vulnerability that lay beyond. The paradoxes had drawn him to her from the first, and they drew him to her just as firmly, just as inevitably now. His fingers moved to touch the flawless skin of her shoulder but abruptly pulled away again, as if they had been burned at the touch. It had been over between them. Past, dead. And then he had taken her into his arms. And somehow he had forgotten the past, forgotten everything but wanting her, loving her, needing her as he had needed her before.

He eased himself from the tangle of her arms and settled her head gently against the pillow, knowing now that he would always love her, that it would never really be over between them. He thought briefly of the gun she had leveled at his chest that night at Heritage, and a sad smile curved his mouth. Had he been a lone Yankee that night, she might well have used that gun. Perhaps things would have been better if she had. A clean, quick end in place of this slow erosion from within his soul. He let out an unsteady breath as he closed his eyes. It would not be easy to put away his feelings again, to leave her behind as he had left her for the past year. But too much lay unresolved between them for him to do anything else. The pain in him could never be healed by physical love alone. And that was all last night had been for her, a mindless respite from her grief. This morning when she woke, she would probably despise herself for admitting that she had wanted him and hate him just as she had before. And he was not strong enough to face that. That was why he had built another life for himself and taken on so many responsibilities away from here, away from her. He would go back to that life now, he would remember that there was no real place for him in Ambrosia's life, especially now that Lily was gone. He would think of his other responsibilities, of Tom Landon, of his obligations to the bank, to Ken Galbraith. . . .

Being very careful not to disturb Ambrosia, Drayton slipped from the bed and dressed. Without making a sound, without even looking back, he left her.

Chapter 50

The sky was ablaze with golden sunlight when Ambrosia woke from her sleep. She sighed contentedly and blinked her eyes open, staring at the strange ceiling, slowly remembering. A smile began in her eyes and spread to curve her mouth slightly, expectantly, as she turned her head. Her smile disappeared. He was gone.

She sat up abruptly, clutching the bed linens to her naked breasts, trying to convince herself that he had only gone downstairs to an early breakfast. But her heart knew better. He had gone back to the city. He had left her behind.

Her fingers touched the pillow where he had slept beside her just a few hours before. She closed her eyes tightly. She felt so empty as she remembered the way she had clung to him after making love, as she remembered the silence, a silence of withdrawal in spite of their physical closeness. And now he was gone.

She let out a ragged sigh as she lay back and stared again at the ceiling, knowing now what he had felt when she left him in Charleston without a word. She bit her lip and tried hard not to cry. Crying would serve no useful purpose, and she could not allow herself the luxury of self-pity. She drew a calming breath and forced herself to sit up again, to stare at the brightness of the August morn-

ing, to think of today, just today. She must think of
Mandy, of Bessie and Emily and Sheba and Debbs and
even Jake, all of whom would depend on her now that
Lily was gone. She must think of Mr. Gavin and Mrs.
Cox who would have no one to visit them now, no one to
listen to them if she was not here. Somehow she must go
on, if only for them.

The remainder of August passed by slowly, quietly, a
test of Ambrosia's strength and will. She counted the
days, twenty-six of them, since she had seen her husband, since she had lain in his arms. The memory comforted her even as it brought her anguish; it gave her hope
even as it filled her with despair. There were so many
things she had meant to say to him, so many words that
ought to have filled the silence. But instead there had
been no words. And she wondered if she would ever stop
counting the days.

Ambrosia had insisted on driving herself to Mr.
Gavin's house to go visiting that afternoon. She had
taken him a basket of breads and fruits and listened for
over an hour as he complained about his aches and pains,
then made dire predictions about the coming winter.
Winter, Ambrosia thought, allowing her mind to wander
a bit. Even with Lily winter had been long and cold and
lonely. She thought of the holidays, of Thanksgiving and
Christmas, and wondered if Drayton would be coming
home for them, or if he would merely send her money
and expect her to see to them alone. Alone. The word
rang in her mind as she forced a smile and left Mr. Gavin,
promising to come again soon. She was almost in tears as
she slapped the reins on the mare's back and urged the
animal to a reckless pace.

Dear God, what was she to do? She simply couldn't
forget, nor could she live with the memory. Perhaps if
Drayton had left her forever, if he had turned his back on
her to marry Carolyn, perhaps there would have been an
end to her feelings, a reconciliation with the future. But

instead she was left with just enough hope to eat away at her heart, to affect every part of the life she was trying so hard to build without him. He might be coming home to visit Mandy. Or perhaps he would not come home at all. Perhaps he would send a terse note, demanding that she bring Mandy to the city so that he could "show her off" to his friends there. Or perhaps he had forgotten all about Mandy and did not think about her at all.

She arrived at Elmwood just before dinner, but instead of going straight into the house, Ambrosia went for a walk along a path through the woods, allowing her mind to turn over the same possibilities she had considered a thousand times before. There were never any answers. Only conjectures, foolish suppositions, endless mazes of questions that gave her no peace. In utter defeat, she fell to her knees and cried, just as she had cried so many months before. "Oh, Lily, Lily, what am I going to do? I don't think I can go on like this! I just can't go on!"

For a long time she knelt there crying, unable to stop the tears. And then suddenly, as she rose to her feet and wiped the tears from her cheeks, she knew what she had to do. She would go to him.

Ambrosia hurriedly packed a single bag of clothing and informed Emily and Bessie that she would be going into the city for a few days. She ignored the inquisitive look they tossed at her when she added that she would be staying at Drayton's house in Gramercy Park, that they were to get in touch with her immediately if anything happened to Mandy. Even as she spoke the words, Ambrosia considered taking her along for the hundredth time, then decided against it. The house in Gramercy Park was dark and gloomy and cluttered with statues and paintings and figurines that seemed to scream, "Don't dare touch!" It was no fit place for an active, inquisitive child. And besides, Ambrosia had no idea what Drayton's reaction to her arrival might be. He might be anxious to get rid of her, to return to Carolyn. . . . She pushed the thought firmly from her mind. At least she would know. At least she would have said the things she needed to say.

"Mr. Rambert did not inform me that he was expecting guests," Drayton's manservant protested as Debbs carried Ambrosia's bag into the front hall.

"But I am not a guest, Mr. Bryson," Ambrosia returned softly. "I am Mr. Rambert's wife."

He eyed her uneasily, taking in the stylish cut of her lavender gown, the totally frivolous hat of net and bows that sat atop a mass of shiny black curls. He was a gentleman's servant and he had very little time for pretty young women. Invariably they proved more trouble than they were worth. And Mr. Rambert had been very annoyed when he arrived home a few weeks back and found Mrs. Craig waiting for him in the parlor. From what Bryson had overheard, he'd had quite a time convincing the young woman to leave. And now this one arrives totally unannounced and carrying a bag of her clothing! Wife or not, Bryson thought, Mr. Rambert did not expect her and would not appreciate such a surprise. "I beg your pardon, madame," he bowed. "But you are not a regular member of this household, and—"

"I *was* not," she interrupted him. "Until now."

"Mrs. Rambert, I must protest," he continued stiffly.

"Before you do so, Mr. Bryson," she broke in again, holding up her hand, *"I* must tell *you* that I intend to stay here unless my husband personally orders me to leave. Nothing you say or do will convince me to go until after I have spoken with him." She lowered her hand and her voice softened somewhat. "I understand that you are the only servant here, however, and I can assure you that my stay will not overburden you." She drew a deep breath and met his eyes evenly. They understood each other, and a temporary truce had been called . . . until Drayton came home.

"Shall I carry your things upstairs, Mrs. Rambert?" he offered with begrudging politeness.

Ambrosia ate very little of the dinner Bryson prepared and served to her. When she questioned him as to when Drayton would be returning home, he responded with a cool, "Mr. Rambert comes and goes at all hours, madame. There are nights when he doesn't come home at all." Ambrosia noticed that a single brow was lifted in a taunting challenge, so she asked him nothing more.

She remained in the parlor until after ten, pacing nervously, flying again and again to the window at the noises of passing carriages and street traffic. The mantel clock seemed to mock her expectancy, chiming relentlessly hour after hour as Bryson's voice echoed in her mind. *There are nights when he doesn't return home at all.* She tried hard not to speculate on where he might spend those nights.

The hours passed slowly, and Ambrosia dozed in a parlor chair, starting awake with each chime of the clock, at each strange sound that echoed from the street. Finally she left the parlor and slowly climbed the stairs to Drayton's room. She opened the door and closed it again behind her, staring at the travel bag she had insisted Bryson place in this room, studying the room's simple furnishings and realizing that Drayton must have cleared it of the clutter that filled every other before he moved into it. She noticed a half-filled bottle of whiskey on his night table and realized that he must have seen to that as well. She gnawed nervously at her bottom lip, then curled up in a high-backed chair and propped her chin on her knees. She would wait for him here.

It was after midnight when he entered the house and made his way up the stairs to his room. He extinguished two flickering gaslights that had been left to burn in the hall as well as a parlor lamp Bryson had forgotten to put out. He opened the door to his room and stopped short. At first he was certain his eyes deceived him. But no, she was there, curled up like a sleeping child in a high-backed chair, looking small and innocent and soft. . . . He closed the door behind him with force enough to startle her. She jumped to her feet. He stared at her and she felt every muscle in her body tense with apprehension as his eyes slowly turned hard and cold. "What the hell are you doing here?" he demanded.

She opened her mouth to answer, but no words came forth. She felt the blood draining from her cheeks. But she saw that he wore a stained white cotton shirt, opened to the waist and rolled at the sleeves, a similarly stained pair of dark trousers that clung to the muscles of his thighs like a second skin. He probably hadn't been with a woman, dressed like that. Relief flooded her at the realization.

"I asked you a question!" he growled impatiently.

She swallowed hard, the relief she had felt a moment before vanishing. She felt foolish standing here, and so very afraid of what he might do to her, of what he might say. It had been very bold of her to come here, but there would be no turning back now. It was too late to turn back. "I—I needed to—to talk with you," she stammered.

"What about?"

"About—about us."

He gave a short laugh. "We've never had anything to say to one another, Ambrosia." He turned away to pour himself a glass of whiskey. "There's never really been anything to say."

She watched as he took a long swallow of bourbon, biting her lip hard against an urge to cry. "You—you're wrong," she forced out, her voice small and inadequate. "Once . . . once, that first night . . . in Charleston . . ."

He turned to face her and their eyes met. But she quickly avoided the raw emotions she saw there, the anger, the resentment, the hurt. She wasn't strong enough to confront those things in his eyes.

He was remembering too. Remembering how much he had wanted her then, remembering the cool, velvet feel of her skin against his fingers, the taste of brandy on her lips, the haunting look of despair in her eyes, the sound of her voice as she cried out another man's name. He took another long sip of his drink, not wanting to remember any more. "Get out of here."

Her eyes filled with tears. "No," she whimpered, shaking her head with a resolve she didn't feel. "No. I—I'm your wife—"

"My wife?" he repeated bitterly. His eyes were hard. "No. You've never been my wife. And I don't believe you really want that now. I think you want to use me because Lily died and you need to forget your grief. You used me that night in Charleston, didn't you? Because you wanted to forget Ledger." He took a sip of his drink, his eyes still raking her. "Or are you just tired of Elmwood? Perhaps you enjoyed the Desmonds' party so much that you want to come live here in town, to play the part of Drayton Rambert's perfect little wife, to dress up and socialize—"

"I've never wanted that!"

"Haven't you? Then what have you wanted, Ambrosia? Certainly nothing I ever offered you."

She shook her head, the tears hot and stinging as they slid down her cheeks. "I—I cannot undo the past, but—"

"Neither of us can," he cut her off harshly. "Nothing will ever change what's already happened between us." He was breathing hard, his nostrils flaring, his tone as cold as his words. "Once I would have done almost anything to make you care for me. But everything I did only made you hate me more. And now it's over, Ambrosia. Over, do you understand? Anything I felt for you died a long time ago."

He saw the anguish in her eyes as he spoke, and he tried to tell himself he was glad. "Now get out of here. Leave me in peace." He turned away from her to pour himself another drink, suddenly needing it to still the trembling in his hands. How often he had played out this very scene in his mind, throwing her words back in her face, making her feel the same kind of hurt she had made him feel so many times in the past. But where was the sweetness, the soaring sense of triumph that ought to have come with her defeat? Why instead did he feel a bitter heaviness, as if he had lost more than ever before?

Ambrosia's tear-filled eyes followed him, staring after him in helpless silence. Silence. It always seemed to come between them. The angry words, and then the silence. She closed her eyes, feeling a part of herself dying, feeling the last remnants of childish hope slipping away. . . . *It's over, Ambrosia. Over, do you understand?* The harsh finality of his words smote her again and again. Over. Finally over. A clean break with the past. She tried to feel relief. An ending, she recalled Lily saying once, was only a chance at a new beginning. But deep in her heart she knew that she could never begin again, feeling what she felt for him. Perhaps, if it hadn't been for Mandy . . .

She stared at the floor, feeling numb and tired. "For me," she mouthed finally, in a whisper, "it will never be over." She swallowed hard and struggled for the composure to say the rest of what she had come to say. "I—I think I'll always love you," was all she could manage before she turned away, her hands brushing roughly at the dampness on her cheeks.

She moved slowly, leadenly toward the door, pathetically clinging to the hope that he might call her back, that he might take her into his arms. She lifted her hand to open the door, her eyes blinking fast against new tears as she glanced one last time over her shoulder. He was facing away.

The door swung open and she took a half-step toward the unlit hallway, then froze. The smoke there was so strong and thick that it struck her like a fist to her chest. She stood motionless, horrified, her senses reeling with disbelief.

The smell touched Drayton's nostrils a moment later. He whirled and pushed passed her, making his way halfway down the hall before he returned and pushed her back inside the room. "The stairs are impassable," he told her curtly, already pulling her by the arm toward the window. He threw open the sash, and at his order, Ambrosia obediently climbed outside and dropped onto the porch roof, just a few feet below. An eerie orange glow lit up the ground below and the hungry cackle of flames broke the stillness of the night. Ambrosia stared at the flames licking all along one side of the porch roof, remembering the horror and heartache of watching Heritage burn. She pushed the memory aside as Drayton took her arm again and guided her along the roof's edge furthest away from the flames. "We'll have to jump."

Her breath was coming hard and fast, but she obeyed without thinking, crouching at the roof's edge and dropping over the side as Drayton instructed her to do. Drayton lay flat on his stomach, holding fast to her arms, then her hands as she slipped lower and lower, as close as possible to the ground. When he released his hold on her, she fell freely, tumbling into the soft grass below.

The fall knocked the breath from her body with a painful thud, but her pain was forgotten as she felt Drayton drop beside her, felt him reach for her hand. "Ambrosia? Are you all right?"

Still struggling to catch her breath, she raised herself to her knees and gave him a nod. He lifted her into his arms and moved quickly away from the house, since the porch was surrounded by flames and the supporting columns about to give way. Ambrosia could not pull her eyes from the sight, even as Drayton carried her a safe distance away. He let her feet slip to the ground, and when her legs seemed unsteady, he took hold of her shoulders to shake her hard. "I don't see Bryson. I'm going back to make sure he's out. You stay back, away, understand? Don't go near the house."

Before she could answer he whirled about and darted

away. ''Drayton!'' She found her voice as she saw him shoulder open a side door and force his way inside. She started to run after him, then screamed and stumbled backward as one of the columns supporting the back porch splintered and collapsed. Flames swooped in a huge, hypnotic wave, bright and orange against the velvet black of night. Two windows burst in unison, like loud, grating bells that sent splinters of glass exploding across the lawn. The smoke rolled thick and black through the shattered remnants of the panes.

Ambrosia stifled another scream as she ran again toward the door, but before she could reach it, someone held her back. A pair of masculine arms restrained her easily though she twisted and thrashed like a demon trying to free herself. She was unaware at first of the great commotion all about her, of the people gathering about the lawn, of the horsedrawn fire wagon racing toward the house, of the men who jumped from the wagon and ran to fight the flames. A hiss of steam filled the air and a cloud of white smoke rose with the darker, billowing clouds of gray as water met flame.

''Ambrosia, are you all right?''

Still not comprehending what was happening, Ambrosia lifted her eyes and saw that the man who restrained her, and still held her tightly was Matt Desmond. ''He—he went back,'' she cried hysterically, tears streaming down her cheeks. ''He went back for Bryson!'' She pulled away from Matt as a huge flame shot from the door Drayton had entered moments before. But she was unsteady as she stumbled toward the house, and Matt quickly moved to restrain her again. With a cry of helplessness she gave up struggling and turned away from the sight. A moment later she was sobbing into his chest.

Drayton groped his way quickly down the hall toward Bryson's room, having little trouble until he reached the back stairs, which were entirely engulfed in flames. The house was an inferno beyond that point, the smoke like dark, murky swamp water, the fire like a thousand blistering suns. Coughing and gasping for breath, Drayton stumbled on past the back stairs, his nostrils stinging, his lungs almost bursting from the noxious fumes that filled them. He felt light-headed as he groped his way along, searching for the door to Bryson's room. He fumbled with the door latch, forcing the door open. The room was so thickly packed with smoke that Drayton had to feel his way to the bed. He shook the old man roughly, but there was no response.

Without waiting, Drayton snatched the unconscious man from his bed and dragged him across the floor toward the hallway. But the added burden of dead weight sapped his strength, and the need for oxygen clamped his lungs in a viselike grip. He gasped in the foul, acrid gas and half collapsed to his knees. The smoke was not quite so thick near the floor, and Drayton began to crawl, dragging Bryson along as he inched his way through the hall. Suddenly a loud snap rose above the hiss and crackle of the flames. Overhead a huge section of mahogany banister broke free and fell in a brilliant flash like a shooting star. Drayton lurched forward and rolled instinctively in an attempt to avoid the falling debris, but as the flaming banister crashed to the floor, a section caught his leg just below the knee.

A cry of anguish tore from his aching chest as his head began to swim, as his eyes lost their ability to make out shapes and shadows in the ever-thickening smoke. Only bright tongues of orange and yellow flashed before him now, hot and angry, as they had been that night so many years before.

Kathryn . . . Oh, God, no! No!

He felt his fingers loosening their hold on Bryson's lifeless body, but he was no longer aware of where he was. He only knew he had to get Kathryn out of here, that he had to save her, even while a part of him knew it was already too late. He struggled to his feet, gasping for air when there was nothing but smoke and ash and heat and pain. And then he fell again, his leg buckling beneath his weight, his hold on Kathryn loosening, his face striking the floor. In the next moment the flames shot wildly over him as a great current of air swept through the house.

Ambrosia stood still now, though Matt's hold on her did not loosen as she watched the firemen rushing into the house. She mouthed the same prayer over and over again, a monotonous recitation though her words were fervent. "Please, God, don't let him die . . . please, God, don't let him die. . . ."

Her breath caught as the building heaved a terrible, loud groan, as if anguishing in the flames, as if crying out its readiness to succumb to the inevitable. Men were suddenly scrambling out of windows, diving out of doors, hurrying to safety. In the final moments before the entire roof collapsed upon them, a pair of firemen appeared dragging two lifeless bodies out of the building. In that instant, Ambrosia broke free of Matt's hold and ran to them.

She was on her knees at Drayton's side a moment later, tears of panic flowing down her cheeks. He wasn't breathing! She grasped his broad shoulders and jerked him from the ground, shaking him with every ounce of her strength, screaming his name. "I won't let you die! I won't let you!"

He remained limp and lifeless, his head falling back as if his neck were a limp blade of grass. Sapped of her strength, she slowly let his torso slip to the ground, her eyes darkening as the defiant disbelief became an all-encompassing fear. With a sob she buried her face in his chest, whimpering helplessly. "I won't let you die," she repeated raggedly. "I won't let you die!"

Matt had bent to pull her away when suddenly Drayton's chest heaved in a short, rasping gasp. Everyone who stood about him froze, watching in fascination as he began to breathe again. For a time, he took only shallow, unsteady gulps of air, with long gaps in between. But he was breathing again. He was alive!

Ambrosia cradled his head in her lap, anguishing over each breath he drew, feeling her own lungs ache with the effort it took. His eyes fluttered open once and a moan parted his lips. Then he lapsed into unconsciousness once more.

It seemed forever before his breathing assumed a normal rhythm; even then it was broken by fits of coughing. Ambrosia glanced up when Matt placed a hand on her shoulder. "I've brought a doctor."

The man who knelt beside her and opened his satchel was old and wrinkled, his brow deeply lined. He lifted Drayton's eyelids and checked for his pulse, then listened to his chest. "He'll live," he told her simply. "But that leg of his will take some tending."

Still cradling his head in her arms, Ambrosia bit her lip hard as the doctor brusquely cut away the lower trouser leg, revealing a long, deep gash just below the knee. The flesh about the wound had been charred or blistered, and would need to be cleaned and bandaged properly. She watched as the doctor merely wrapped it in a piece of cloth, knowing that it demanded closer attention. She found Matt's eyes again. "I want to take him home," she told him firmly. "To Elmwood. I'll be able to care for him properly there."

With hardly a hesitation, Matt gave a nod. "I'll get the carriage."

Ambrosia's hand brushed tenderly over her husband's brow and down his cheek, silently mouthing his name. His hair was singed, his flesh scorched by the heat, his hands blistered, his shoulders . . .

She stopped the doctor as he began to rise. "The other man—Bryson," she questioned him, knowing that Drayton would ask about him the moment he came to his senses. The doctor glanced over his shoulder, then met Ambrosia's eyes again and shook his head. "I'm sorry."

Ambrosia bit her lip, her brow furrowing as she looked down again at Drayton's face. "It's all right, darling," she whispered, "I'm going to take you home."

Chapter 51

Drayton regained consciousness only briefly during the next three days. Ambrosia made certain that his leg wound was cleansed and properly bandaged, that his burns were treated with aloe after being sponged gently with cool water. He was feverish those first days, but his strength returned quickly as his wound began to heal. Still, he would need to stay off his injured leg for some time.

While still confined to his bed, he insisted on speaking with Matt, asking him to make inquiries as to whether or not Aaron had been released from prison, and telling him to inform the authorities that the fire had most likely not been an accident. He did not voice any of his suspicions to Ambrosia, however. Indeed, after he had talked with Matt, he said nothing to anyone about the fire.

Within a week he was out of bed and making his way clumsily about with the help of a pair of crutches. He spent a great deal of time with Mandy, who called constantly for her "papa." It was no wonder he was her new favorite. He acted very much like a child himself, playing games with her, building tall towers of brightly colored blocks that she gleefully knocked down. He asked her questions, listened solemnly to her garbled responses, repeated silly rhymes to make her laugh. The two of them shared secrets and conspired more than once to steal cookies from the kitchen the moment sour-faced Sarah was elsewhere. Sheba, though fully aware of their schemes, always looked the other way with a wide grin curving her generous mouth. Once when Ambrosia caught them sharing a still-warm oatmeal cookie just before dinner, Mandy's blue eyes met hers without remorse. She pressed her tiny forefinger to her mouth and warned, "Sh-sh!" while tossing a wary glance over her shoulder and looking so very much like her father that it was all Ambrosia could do to hold back a smile.

A week flew peacefully by, then another. They were the happiest days Ambrosia had ever known. Though Drayton insisted on sending Debbs to town every other day to keep close contact with Tom Landon and Tim MacGregor, and though he spent some time in the library each evening going over the paperwork, there was still a fullness to the days he spent at Elmwood that Ambrosia had never even dreamed of. Every night after dinner she dressed Mandy for bed, then took her to the library to say good night to Papa. More often than not, Drayton began a story about a beautiful princess and her handsome prince, who saved her from a fearsome giant and lived happily ever after. Ambrosia would listen to the story as well, smiling as Mandy yawned and nodded sleepily on her Papa's lap, as he bent to press a kiss to her dark hair. It was a side of Drayton she had only glimpsed before, the man who was meant to be a father. She was falling in love with him all over again, she realized one afternoon as he spoke to her about his childhood, as he spoke of Lily, as she watched him limp about the garden chasing butterflies with Mandy. It was as if all the harsh, ugly words and past mistakes had been forgotten, left behind in the fire. It was as if they had never tried to hurt one another, as if they had just begun.

If it hadn't been for the brief, unguarded moments when Drayton's brow furrowed with troubled thoughts, when his eyes showed a deep, secret pain, Ambrosia might have allowed herself to believe that their new beginning would last forever. She might have thought that he would remain at Elmwood with her and Mandy, leaving the business to his partner and the warehouse foreman, corresponding with them regularly, perhaps visiting them occasionally. If only there hadn't been that restlessness to him, that anxiety he was so quick to hide from her. If only there hadn't been the nightmare.

He had it nearly every night, sometimes several times in a single night. Ambrosia would waken when he began to gasp for breath, when his body went tense and rigid beside her. Even as she watched him, beads of sweat would break across his brow and he would shake, as if with a violent chill. His eyes would fly open then, ablaze with a terrible scene that played over and over in his mind. And he would scream a single word—"Kathryn!"—again and again, terror constricting his throat, tears splashing across his cheeks, eyes darting wildly about the room until he found his way back to the present, to reality. Afterward, though he held Ambrosia tightly, though he pressed his mouth to her hair and oftentimes made love to her, he said nothing about the dream and carefully avoided the unspoken questions he must have seen in her eyes.

Nearly four weeks had passed since the fire when Matt Desmond paid a brief visit to Elmwood to check on Drayton's recovery. Ambrosia bid him a cordial welcome, then left the men to discuss their business in the library. When she saw Matt leaving some time later, Ambrosia returned to the library and found Drayton staring distantly out the window, leaning on a single crutch. She closed the distance between them and slipped her arms about his waist, pressing her cheek to his broad back. He took hold of her arm and pulled her about to face him, pressing a brief kiss to her brow, smiling at her though the distant, troubled look remained in his eyes.

"What did Matt Desmond have to say?" she asked as

lightly as she could, wishing that his eyes were not so serious.

"Nothing much." He let out a sigh and released her, limping across the room, leaning only lightly on the crutch. His leg was healing quickly now, she thought as she watched him take a seat behind the desk. He lifted a few of the papers scattered here and there, as if he was looking for something in particular. Ambrosia ignored the gesture of dismissal. "He must have said something. He was here nearly two hours."

Drayton let out his breath and met her eyes with a touch of impatience. "He reminded me of my obligations to Rambert Paints, something I've forgotten lately, something I can't really afford to forget." He saw the mixture of fear, pain, and anger beginning in her eyes and faced it squarely. "Matt wanted to know when I plan to move back into the city," he went on more slowly. He paused. "I'm leaving tomorrow, Ambrosia."

Tomorrow! The words cut cleanly through her heart. Tomorrow. Her life was crumbling about her. She had to hold it together! "You can't leave tomorrow," she cried. "You—you're leg isn't healed yet."

He shrugged, unconcerned. "I'm getting around well enough. I have responsibilities, Ambrosia. Obligations . . ."

She was about to argue with him, but something in his eyes made her stop. There was a distance there, a holding back of the truth. And it had always been there, she realized, even when he made love to her. He had taken her gently, passionately, with tenderness, with fury. At times when he reached for her, she felt his need so strongly, felt his very soul reaching out for her. But never once had he told her that he loved her. Never once in all the times he held her and touched her and possessed her. Never once.

And now she was losing him. Perhaps she had never really held him at all. She looked away from his eyes, no longer able to face what she saw there. She heard him rise and make his way to her side. He lifted her chin and searched her face.

"You don't have to leave here," she said finally, her words brittle in spite of her efforts to soften them. "You could stay here and—"

"And travel back and forth every morning?" His fingers moved in a light caress over the squared line of her jaw. "Perhaps someday, when there isn't so much work to be done. But I've been away over a month, Ambrosia. There's simply too much waiting there for me to do. And with my leg the way it is . . ." He vented a sigh and turned away from the accusation in her eyes. He went again to contemplate the view from the window. "It won't be like before. I'll be coming to Elmwood regularly to visit."

To visit, she thought, feeling a terrible emptiness inside. It would not be the same. It would never be the same if he left. His work would be his life. He would never manage enough time with his "visits" to achieve any real intimacy. And this would never really be his home. "You could sell the business, Drayton," she said softly.

He whirled about to face her, his eyes angry and accusing. "And do what?" he demanded. "Stay here and while away the hours without any purpose? Live the useless life of a country gentleman while I squander my inheritance?" He shook his head. "I'm not that kind of man, Ambrosia."

Ambrosia hesitated, sensing that her next words would drive a deep wedge between them. Or perhaps, she thought briefly, it would only reflect the one that was already there. "You were a doctor once, Drayton. I think that a part of you will never be anything else."

He stiffened, almost as if she had struck him, but she went on, her eyes brightening with tears. "Your memories possess you, Drayton. You told me so yourself. You said that you ran away from your memories, from Kathryn. . . ." For an instant his face twisted with an emotion so strong, so overpowering that she almost stepped back. Instead she lifted her hand to touch his cheek. "Aren't you still running away?"

He turned away from her searching eyes and drew a long, calming breath. "What are you running away from, Drayton? What is it you're so afraid of facing?"

He said nothing for a time, then she saw him square his shoulders and turn back to face her. "I will never go back to medicine, Ambrosia. And I won't discuss this with you anymore." He slipped a finger beneath her chin and lifted her face to kiss her. The gesture held a gentleness his words had not, but when he withdrew and met her eyes again, the last traces of anger were gone. "I must go, Ambrosia. Please try to understand."

She bit her lip hard and forced a nod, then held tightly to him as his arms pulled her close. He kissed her deeply, intimately, a kiss meant to dispel any lingering uncertainties stirred by the harsh words of moments before. But as her arms slipped about his neck and she returned that kiss, she felt little of the reassurance he had meant to give. Tomorrow he would leave her to return to the life he had built without her. And she was very afraid that he would never be coming back.

Aaron Rambert tossed his last silver dollar to the aging barmaid and accepted the bottle of cheap whiskey without seeing the odd look she flashed him. He brushed a speck of lint from the soiled sleeve of his rumpled coat, failing to notice the deteriorated condition of his once fine clothing. He was in a world of his own, a world where nothing mattered but finishing what he had started years ago. Tonight, he thought as he sipped at his whiskey, Drayton Rambert would die as he ought to have died in the fire before the war, as he ought to have died in the house in Gramercy Park. Aaron started to check his watch, then recalled that it, like all his possessions, even the rest of his clothing, had been sold to buy whiskey

. . . and a gun. He would have to wait until nightfall anyway before he left this tavern and went to kill him.

His dark eyes were glazed and distant as he looked about the small, ill-lit tavern and remembered that night so long ago, the night he'd learned that his stepfather planned to write him out of his will and leave everything to his blood son, to Drayton. Aaron had stopped here that night, before going on to the white clapboard house, before setting it aflame . . .

He took another long swallow of his drink and grimaced at the taste of cheap whiskey. He had come full circle now. Again he was desperate, again he had come to destroy Drayton Rambert's life. But this time, he wouldn't fail. This time he wouldn't leave anything to chance. He'd been watching the house for over two weeks now, ever since he'd learned Drayton escaped the fire in Gramercy Park. His mouth quivered with unchecked emotion as he thought of that house, his mother's house, going up in flames. Aaron hadn't wanted to set that fire. But he'd been forced to do it. It had been the only way he could think of to kill his stepbrother.

He drained his glass and poured himself another, his jaw setting with grim resolve. Tonight Drayton wouldn't escape. Tonight Aaron would confront him with the gun he'd purchased especially for the purpose of seeing him dead. And then he would set the grandest fire of all, a fire that would see Drayton's body, and everything the man had ever cared about, turn to smoke and ash. Vengeance, Aaron thought with a slight smile playing about his mouth, would be sweet . . . and complete.

Dinner was a quiet affair that evening, and what little talk Drayton and Ambrosia shared seemed stilted and forced. Tomorrow, Ambrosia thought again and again as she picked at her food, he would leave her and Mandy to escape the troubling memories that haunted him. He was running away from something she didn't understand, from a part of him he didn't want her to understand, or even see.

Drayton declined dessert and rose from the table without touching his coffee. "I hope you'll forgive me if I excuse myself early tonight. I'm anxious to look over some of the papers Matt brought by this afternoon." He bent to kiss the side of her neck and smiled. "I'll be in the library. You will bring Mandy down to say good night before she goes to bed? If I plan to leave first thing in the morning, I'll need to say good-bye."

Ambrosia lowered her eyes, unable to face him as she gave a nod. She felt his fingers, warm and strong, take brief hold of her shoulders as he brushed his lips across her hair. And then he left the room.

Ambrosia blinked back a tear as she swallowed the bitter lump in her throat. He would expect to make love to her tonight. An ironic gesture of farewell to the life he had chosen to walk away from. How she longed to reveal her anger, her helpless frustration at the prospect of his leaving. She almost wanted to turn away from him, to deny him, to hurt him as he was hurting her. But she loved him too much to hurt him now. And tonight she knew she would give herself totally to him, holding back no part of heart or soul, even though she knew that he would leave her tomorrow with nothing but broken dreams. But perhaps he would remember what they shared tonight and someday, someday he would come back to her. She must cling to that hope now. It was all that was left to her.

Emily was just finishing Mandy's bath when Ambrosia dismissed her for the night. Ambrosia took her time getting Mandy ready for bed, trying to prepare herself for good-bye. Mandy yawned and rubbed a small fist over one eye. "Papa?" she mouthed with sleepy expectancy. Their good-nights had become a part of her bedtime ritual, but tomorrow—

"Yes," Ambrosia answered her softly, pushing the thought from her mind. "We're going to say good night to Papa."

Chapter 52

Drayton lit a lamp in the library after he had been there only a short time. The shadows were falling earlier now, and the nights were cool with the first stirrings of winter. He sat at his desk again and looked over the papers Matt had left him that afternoon, though his mind was elsewhere. He was thinking of the heartbreak he had seen in Ambrosia's eyes when he told her he was leaving. He vented a weary sigh, wanting more than anything to stay here. But the memories of his past, of the night that had cost him everything, suddenly had the upper hand again just as they had before the war. The pictures haunted him, infesting his dreams, filling him with guilt and despair. He could not stop them or push them aside. They confronted him no matter where he turned. Even when he looked at Mandy he found himself thinking of the child Kathryn had carried, the child who had died in her womb. It was almost as if the fire a few weeks ago had triggered something in his head, something he could not begin to control, something he had to escape somehow, somehow . . .

He left the desk and limped across the room to get himself a much-needed drink. He took a long swallow of the whiskey, his eyes closing against the thoughts that tormented him. He had to find some way to escape the memories. He would go insane if he did not escape, at least for a little while. Ambrosia had been so right when she had accused him of running away. He set the empty glass aside and pressed the heels of his hands to his eyes.

Suddenly a sound seemed to fill the silence of the room. It was a sound Drayton instantly recognized, the click of a gun being cocked. Every muscle in his body tensed as he turned to face that sound, as he stared at the barrel of a Colt revolver. His gaze lifted to meet his stepbrother's crazed, glittering brown eyes. He watched Aaron's mouth curve upward in a smile of triumph, an ugly, gloating kind of smile. "What do you want, Aaron?"

For an instant Aaron's smile faded. He had expected Drayton to tremble, to plead, to beg for his life. But instead he stood as cool as always, asking what he wanted. As if the gun that was leveled at his chest did not convey the message clearly enough. Aaron laughed aloud at the thought, a strange, maniacal laugh. And then his face was void of all laughter. "I want you dead," he said deliberately. "And this time, I will see you die. I won't let you get away this time."

"Is that why you set the fire at the house?" Drayton inquired calmly.

Aaron frowned at him, angry now and confused. "I—I didn't want to burn mother's house," he cried suddenly, his voice rising as his face twisted with emotion. "It was all I had left of her. Your father left her nothing, you know. He left everything to you." He straightened abruptly and his lip curled in disdain. "You ought to have died years ago, *brother,*" he spat. "I meant for you to burn years ago. But you were away, playing country doctor. She was all alone that night."

For a split second Drayton didn't understand. But suddenly it all fell together in his mind, all the pieces of the puzzle, after all these years. A lifetime of rage and helpless frustration exploded inside him. "You killed her!" His voice trembled with disbelief, with bitterness. "You killed her!" he screamed again, his eyes filling with tears.

He lurched blindly foward, deflecting Aaron's gun so

that the first bullet imbedded itself in the ceiling as they wrestled to the floor. Drayton's wounded leg twisted beneath him, causing him to falter, giving Aaron an advantage that almost cost him his life. As Drayton groaned and struggled to free his leg, Aaron broke free and rose to a single knee. He cocked the gun and aimed it, his finger poised at the trigger when he heard a woman's scream.

Instinctively, Aaron whirled about and fired in the direction of the sound. The wooden door frame splintered behind her, and he aimed his gun a second time. Ambrosia's knees gave way as she fell foward, clutching Mandy tightly to her breast as the gun fired again. The baby let out a startled cry and hid her face in Ambrosia's throat, her little fists tightening on the fabric of her mother's dress.

Even as Aaron made to fire the gun again, Drayton struggled to his feet and grasped Lily's letter opener from the desk. A flash of silver caught the lamplight as he lifted it, then plunged it deeply into the back of Aaron's neck. With a sickening scream of pain Aaron twisted grotesquely to face the man who had sent him to his death. Breathing hard, his blue eyes blazing, Drayton watched Aaron writhe about, then crumple to the floor, blood gushing in a thick stream from his mouth. With a cry of anguish Drayton fell to his knees and covered his face with his hands. All these years he had thought it an accident. All these years Aaron had gone free. After killing everything Drayton had loved, he had gone free. Even now, when his body lay hideously sprawled in a pool of blood, Drayton felt no sense of justice. He only felt hatred and a self-loathing for never having guessed the truth, for not having been there to protect his wife and child.

Ambrosia shivered with revulsion as she turned to face away from Aaron's mangled body. It was at that precise moment that she saw that Mandy's tiny fists no longer clutched tightly at her dress. Instead they lay open, limp, and a stream of bright red blood ran down her arm and dripped on the floor. "Mandy!"

Drayton's head jerked up at Ambrosia's scream, but

his eyes remained wide and dazed. He did not move. He watched Ambrosia lift the hem of her skirt and press it to Mandy's shoulder, heard her let out a cry of panic as it was instantly saturated with blood. But he was not really seeing her at all, could not really hear her cries. Something inside him refused to see.

Ambrosia looked up, her eyes tear-filled and pleading. But Drayton seemed in another world, apart from what was happening, indifferent to her need. One by one the servants rushed into the library, stopping short at what they saw. Ambrosia struggled to her feet and ran to Drayton, kneeling beside him. "Mandy's hurt! You've got to help her!"

A spark of comprehension lit in his eyes. His face broke into an icy sweat and he began to tremble violently. "No . . . no . . . I can't help her. I—I'll go for a doctor."

"There isn't time for that!" she cried back at him. "Don't you see?" She touched his cheek, her face streaming with tears. "Mandy's going to die if you don't help her! She's going to die!" She let out a heart-wrenching sob and shook her head as she tried to rein in her emotions. "You can't let her die, Drayton! You can't! I won't let you!" Her eyes locked with him, pleading, begging, praying. "Please," she whispered. "Please . . ."

It seemed a lifetime passed before he took hold of her hand. His fingers were cold and trembling, his eyes still touched with fear. But she saw him struggle to clench his jaw. And then he was pulling himself to his feet and limping his way to the dining room. It was a different Drayton who began to call orders to Sheba and Sarah and Emily and Bessie, an almost calm man who helped Ambrosia lay Mandy's inert body on the table. "I'll need you to hold her fast," he told her quietly. "I don't trust anyone else to do it."

Ambrosia gave a nod, thanking God for the strength she heard in his voice, for the courage she saw battling the fear in his eyes. She took firm hold of Mandy's arms as Drayton accepted the shears from Bessie and cut away Mandy's nightshirt. At the sight of the ugly wound marring her perfect little body, Ambrosia saw him falter. She bit her lip and squeezed her own eyes tightly shut, feeling weak and sick to her stomach. She had seen dozens of worse wounds, but only on soldiers' bodies, not a child's, not *her* child's. She forced her eyes open and watched as Drayton also regained his composure, reaching for a cloth to clean and closely examine the wound.

"A ricochet, I think," he said aloud. "It doesn't seem to be imbedded too deeply."

Ambrosia's eyes followed him as he moved to kindle a flame in a small brazier, to pass the knife in a strange ritual through the small yellow tongue of fire, just as he had done at Heritage. It took every ounce of her strength to hold Mandy fast as Drayton angled the knife and moved to cut her flesh. The small body jerked and twisted before it dropped into a fitful slumber with only a soft, weak little cry of pain. Ambrosia's eyes fixed on Drayton's hands, on the precise, agile movements he made cutting, probing, retrieving the small lump of lead. Twice he glanced up at her, as if seeking reassurance in what he was doing. But the looks were so brief that she hardly had time to respond.

It seemed to her that she held Mandy for an eternity, that Drayton worked on the torn flesh of her shoulder for hours and hours. She felt numb when he finished, and her eyes filled with tears as he drew his sleeve across his moist brow.

"She's going to be all right, isn't she?"

He sighed and his eyes warmed a little, a shadow of a smile. "Yes. She's going to be all right."

Chapter 53

For the next three days Drayton remained at Mandy's bedside, tending to her every need, watching her closely when she regained consciousness, when she slept, when she woke again, calling for "Papa." In all of that time he said very little to anyone, ate next to nothing, and refused to sleep. Only after his daughter's recovery was certain did Drayton yield to Ambrosia's urgings and seek his bed. But even his exhaustion could not allow him a peaceful sleep. His slumber was restless, fitful, and Ambrosia woke at dawn to find the bed beside her empty.

She expected to find him at Mandy's bedside, but Bessie shook her head, saying that she had been with the child all night and he had not been there. Ambrosia began to search the house, the stables, the garden, her anxiety rising when she found that his stallion was gone. He ought not to have ridden anywhere with his leg still paining him. She sent Debbs off to town to see if Drayton had returned to his work. But Debbs returned a few hours later and reported that Drayton had been neither to the warehouse nor the factories.

"And I—uh, already took the liberty of checking the taverns in the village," he added uneasily. Her eyes

547

lifted hopefully but he only shook his head. "No one's seen him, Miss Ambrosia."

"And there's nowhere else he might have gone?" she pressed. "Perhaps a place he went as a boy, to be alone?"

Debbs frowned thoughtfully and rubbed his chin. "He used to go lots of places with the Desmond boy, rounding up stray dogs and rabbits and such." His eyes narrowed thoughtfully. "But there was one place he only went by himself—"

"Where was that?"

"The pond. About a mile or so from here. He built a house there, years ago. It's gone now, though, burned to the ground before the war."

"Hitch up the buggy for me, Debbs," she instructed, "and tell me how to get there."

He gave her an odd look. "What makes you think you'll find him there?"

She met his eyes, then looked away. "I just know that I will," she said softly.

There was very little sign of the house that had once been: part of a stone chimney rose from the still-blackened ground, the crumbling foundation had filled with dirt and debris, and flagstones were covered with weeds and vines. Drayton's stallion was tethered to a tree nearby, and the animal whinnied and pranced restlessly as Ambrosia maneuvered the buggy toward him. She alighted from the buggy, looking about for the pond Debbs had told her was here, catching sight of it finally, just beyond the first hill. The early frosts had turned the dense growth to brown and withered weeds and brush, making the landscape seem old and lifeless beneath the bright, copper-red trees.

Ambrosia made her way along the narrow path, overgrown by years of neglect, toward the quiet pond that shimmered gray-blue beneath the autumn sky. She saw him while she was still some distance away, the stark white shirt, the jet black hair that lifted in the light wind. She stopped for a moment, studying his posture, knowing at once that it was the stance of a defeated man.

Slowly she closed the distance between them, expecting him to turn and face her, expecting him to give some sign that he had heard her approach. But he stood motionless, staring out on the pond, his eyes far away. "Drayton?"

He gave no response until she stretched a hesitant hand to his arm. Then he turned and slowly lifted his eyes, distant blue eyes filled with pain.

"I was worried about you," she told him softly. "I didn't know where you had gone."

His eyes showed no spark of comprehension as they slipped from her and fixed again on the shimmering surface of the water. She frowned, her hand trembling a little as she moved to touch his cheek. "Drayton?"

"I thought it was an accident," he said suddenly, his eyes still looking away. "All these years I thought the fire that killed her was an accident. And now, after all this time, I find that it was meant for me."

A silence fell, empty and hollow, a silence Ambrosia did not know how to fill. And then Drayton spoke again, his voice low and hoarse. "I should have died that night. Not her. Not Kathryn. Not our bab—" He closed his eyes against the memory, his voice breaking as he tried to speak the word.

"Drayton—"

"I was too late to save her," he went on after a moment. "She was already dead. Oh, dear God, she was already dead!"

She slipped her fingers into his hand, and he grasped at her tightly, holding her fingers almost desperately in his own. "There was nothing you could do, Drayton," she began quietly.

"Nothing I could do?" he flung back. She felt a shudder pass through him as his eyes met hers, as she saw again the pain that reached his soul. "I could have saved the baby. Our child—was—was alive," he choked out. "I—I saw it moving. I could have saved it. I could have saved that one precious part of her. I'd taken babies that way before. But I couldn't take my own child. I couldn't bring myself to take a knife to Kathryn's body. She was already burned so badly . . . her face was—oh, God!" he cried in agony. He covered his face with his hands and tried to hold back a sob, torn from the deepest part of him. And then he was in Ambrosia's arms.

"I—I couldn't hurt her any more," he said brokenly as she cradled his dark head to her breast and tenderly smoothed his hair. "So I held her . . . feeling the life inside her . . . knowing I had the power to save it . . . knowing I couldn't—I couldn't—"

She held him, whispering words of comfort, listening and blinking back tears of her own as his words revealed his pain and his guilt. But suddenly he turned away from her, brushing quickly at his face with his sleeve, his broad shoulders squaring bravely as he placed the distance between them.

"It's past, Drayton," she told him, her hand seeking his once more.

He brushed her away. "I can't forget it. I'll never forget."

"Then you must come to terms with it, accept it, so that you can go on."

"Come to terms with it?" he repeated bitterly. "Come to terms with the fact that I let my own child die? I was a doctor, Ambrosia."

"You *are* a doctor," she told him softly.

"No. I'm a coward. A coward, Ambrosia. Something you've never been."

She stared for a long moment at his broad back, and when she finally spoke, her voice was small and childlike. "You're wrong, Drayton. So very, very wrong. I was always afraid—don't you know that?" She swallowed hard as her composure slipped, her throat constricting painfully with so many things she had meant to say to him long before this, so many things she needed to say. "I was Jackson Lanford's daughter, you see. So I tried to be like him, strong and brave and sure of myself. I used to pride myself on being like my father was," she said with a little smile, a brief smile marred by the tears that filled her eyes. "I thought those were the only parts of me that had any value, and they were the only parts I wanted anyone to see, that I allowed myself to see.

"But you—" She drew a ragged breath and gazed out on the water, staring distantly at the play of sunbeams just as he had moments before. "From the first moment I saw you, that night in the rain, you made me see things in myself I didn't want to see. When you looked at me or—or touched me—I knew that I wasn't like my father at all, that I was a woman, that I wanted things from a Yankee, that I needed things. . . ."

Her eyes lifted and met his. She wondered briefly when he had turned to face her, when he had begun to listen, when the distance had faded from his eyes. She fought the tightness in her throat. "You—you cared about me. No one else had ever done that. I—I hated you for it. I hated you for seeing that I needed someone to care." She wiped tersely at her cheeks again and lifted her chin to meet his eyes once more. "I wasn't brave enough to face what I felt for you. So I blamed you for everything—my father's death, the war, even Ledger. . . . I lashed out at you with all of my strength and tried to hate you. How I tried! Only to find—" She bit her lip hard to stop its trembling, her voice catching with tears. "Only to find," she repeated in a whisper, "that I loved you more than I have ever loved anyone or anything else. . . ."

She stretched her hand to touch his cheek, and he slowly turned his head to place a lingering kiss to her palm. She gave a little cry, remembering the first time he had done that, the first time she had known without a doubt that she loved him. "We can't run away from what we are," she whispered brokenly. "You told me that once, and you were so right.'' She sighed softly as he drew her into his arms, as his mouth sought hers and gently awakened another memory. His fingertips played lightly beneath the coil of hair at the nape of her neck while another hand sought out softer flesh, prodding deliberately, touching, seeking, even as his mouth lifted and he met her eyes. He searched her face. The love in her eyes was everything he needed to see.

They made love slowly, tenderly, restraining passions until physical need overtook all else, feeling a wild fulfillment that swiftly culminated in a warm peace. For the first time each belonged to the other totally, weaknesses and strengths, successes and failures, hopes and fears.

The sun was dipping toward a pink-tinged horizon when they left the pond walking hand in hand. Drayton leaned heavily on her as they walked in silence, his leg cramped and aching though he wasn't aware of the pain. He was only aware of their newfound closeness, of the strength he had found in loving her. The pond was far behind when he suddenly stopped and took her into his arms once more. There was a serenity in his face that Ambrosia had never seen before, and no trace of the guilt or pain he had carried for so many long years. After all this time, she knew he had finally let go.

''I love you, Ambrosia,'' he whispered fervently against her hair.

It was the first time he had ever said the words. She smiled up at him, her eyes glistening with tears of joy as she slipped her arms about his neck. ''Then take me home.''

Epilogue
New York
Spring 1868

Ambrosia let out her breath wearily and opened her eyes as Drayton bent over her, pressing a cool compress to her sweat-moistened brow. Their eyes exchanged a brief smile, Ambrosia's disappearing as she felt the start of yet another contraction. She grasped tightly at his hand, her face contorting as she struggled to give birth. She distantly recalled the long hours of waiting for Mandy to be born, and tried to prepare herself for a similar ordeal. But the pains were so intense, so closely spaced! As she expelled her breath and dropped her head against the pillow, she wondered if she could endure much more. "Stay with me," she pleaded softly.

"I'm here, love. I won't leave you," Drayton assured her. "And it won't be much longer. I promise." He squeezed her hand and smiled again, and she drew much-needed courage from his words.

All at once she tensed again and gasped aloud. The pain took hold and blossomed sharply, forcing her to let out a deep, throaty groan. With all her strength she struggled, pushing, laboring, feeling the tension rise within her. And then, at the same instant the pain subsided, she heard Drayton's triumphant announcement ring throughout the room. "It's a boy! A boy!"

The lusty sound of a newborn's first cry filled Ambrosia's ears and she laughed as tears of joy slid over her cheeks. "A son," she whispered in awe, watching her husband's expert hands wrap the tiny infant in a blanket and place it in her waiting arms. She gazed down at the child with the same love she felt for Mandy, then met her husband's smile with a look no less tender. "I love you," Drayton whispered, his forefinger touching the baby's wee fist as he bent to kiss Ambrosia's moist brow.

"And I love you, Doctor Rambert," she returned softly, "more than you will ever know."